FANGS
FRANK BARVITCH

Cadmus Publishing
www.cadmuspublishing.com

Published by Cadmus Publishing
www.cadmuspublishing.com

ISBN: 978-0-9998590-4-9

This book is for my mother,
Who introduced me to the joy of books at a young age;
A pursuit which would form the core of all my years to come,
Professionally and personally.

CHAPTER ONE

Lawrence pulled the old minivan into a parking space and sighed as he shut off the motor. The engine hissed, mirroring his sigh: there was yet another radiator leak somewhere, it seemed. His angular, almost haughty face seemed passive, but it was not the passivity of contentment. This was a face too tired to be angry, too jaded to be disgusted. Some of the appearance may have been due to the lack of age lines, which also gave him the false look of youth, perhaps that of a 25 year old. His light brown eyes seemed to argue with his face about the age of their host: in them one saw a weary traveler, one who has seen far more than he wishes.

He closed his eyes and allowed his long, slim fingers to rest upon the smooth-worn faux-leather steering wheel. His shoulder-length black hair, in keeping with his harried state, was uncharacteristically tousled. Sitting back in his seat, the thought ran through his head: "You can't die, but you can still suffer." It was true, as he'd found out so often before. The bullet in his leg caused it to throb painfully. He could pinpoint the slug's location, right in the meatiest part of his thigh. At least it hadn't hit bone; that would have been far worse. He knew, all too well.

The wound in his chest was also a sensation he was not unfamiliar with, but the pain was much more penetrating. Not only had it hit bone, it had stopped its forward progress right in the center of his chest cavity. At least the bone fragments would be quickly re-absorbed. Those were like dozens of hot splinters throughout his torso, digging for more pain every time his upper body moved. All those shards of bone, however, still didn't equal the one bullet. As they say in real estate, location is everything. It was as though the body knew that a bullet through the heart should kill it. Never mind that the heart had not beat in hundreds of years; the body remembered, and this memory called for pain. He felt as though he was dying again. Unlike his death, this wasn't over in a mere ten minutes. No such luck this time. It wasn't shooting through his entire body like it had then, either, and he was still able to think and act rationally... but he may have just grown more accustomed to such agony over the years. Lawrence wasn't sure that was good.

He climbed out of his van and began limping awkwardly towards his apartment. It was not the greatest place he'd ever called home. In fact, it was probably the worst. His was a single unit in a structure (one could barely call such an architectural monstrosity a building) housing 23 other nearly identical apartments. This, in a tightly packed area containing nine other similar structures, with almost nothing for landscaping save a few acres of black asphalt for parking. The buildings themselves looked all of their 41 years of age, even with the paint job, which had been 'freshly' applied - eleven years ago. The surrounding neighborhood - not one of the better areas in Milwaukee - did nothing to add to the appeal.

To keep his gaze from the eyesore that was his home, he looked down. He looked no better than the buildings. Another shirt ruined, and the pants, too. He could patch them, as there was scarcely any blood, but that had never been one of his better skills. It would make the clothes look too ratty, anyway. Not that they were fine, custom-tailored threads to begin with, bought as they were from the discount store down the street, but the patches would render them conspicuously shoddy, and he simply wouldn't feel right wearing such garments. He hadn't fallen so far that he had to wear patches on his clothes, had he?

He cast a disparaging look back at his van as he approached his assigned parking spot. The minivan was about fourteen years old. Its once vivid green had faded to an unappealing shade, reminiscent of pea soup... at least in the places where it wasn't simply rusted through. He compared it to the sporty little red thing that had occupied his parking spot while he was out, forcing him to limp a block on a wounded leg. He let fly a kick at the offending vehicle in an attempt to vent his frustration. Wrong leg. The muscle's tensing and the jarring stop as his foot made contact with the car caused the bullet to worm its way in farther, which significantly added to what had previously been just a dull throbbing. An unpleasant way to contribute yet a little more spice to a decidedly wretched evening. He would try to ignore the pain.

He looked at the car, its finest details sharp to him even in the dim light cast by the poorly maintained fluorescent bulbs of the parking lot. Yeah, there was an obvious dent, but he felt no better. Perhaps another angry outburst was called for? Maybe cave in the entire front end? Forget it; he was too tired to put any force behind another kick with his good leg.

He made his way ponderously up the stairs leading to his apartment, advancing only with his uninjured left leg, his downcast eyes monitoring his progress. As he crested the top steps he looked up, eyeing the paper he saw taped to his door. That would not be good news, whatever it was. With a frown he walked up and pulled it off the door.

An eviction notice, just great. He should have seen it coming, though; he was three months behind.

He unlocked the door, wondering why he bothered with the lock in the first place, tossed his keys on the barren kitchen counter and dropped heavily into his chair. That was a mistake: the sudden movement jarred the wound in his chest, causing it to explode from a steady, sharp pain to excruciating agony with the sudden movement. Doing his best to ignore the throbbing, he sent his hand searching under the cushion for his remote. Finding it among the accumulated detritus of the years, he pulled it out and clicked on the TV. He should be okay for one more day. His wounds hurt too much to pack his stuff up, or even go out to feed some more. They should be healed by tomorrow; after all, they were just gunshot wounds. He put his feet up and tried to let his mind be numbed by the television.

His mind would not be numbed so easily tonight, though, and through no fault of the television. The television was the one item of quality he owned, his most prized possession. In that box he could allow his brain to stop working. He could allow what remained of his once agile mind to be pummeled into a vegetative state by the senseless drivel served up in the name of entertainment. No, the TV was performing its duties just as it had every night, so long as it was tuned to some sitcom or "reality" show. The fault lay in his wounds. He had been shot before, by crossbows, muskets, rifles, shotguns, once even by a cannon. Hey, it happened. But tonight...it was different. It wasn't his fault. That...mortal...had somehow managed to get the drop on him. He must have been careless not to even hear the cocking of the weapon. Not just a mistake: simple carelessness.

His mind wandered along those lines for a while longer; sometimes distracted by the television, but usually drifting back to his appalling failure tonight. Surprisingly, it was soon time to turn in. He could feel the sun approaching the horizon as it prepared to signal the beginning to a new day.

He switched off the TV and settled into his coffin to pass another day.

*   *   *

Lawrence awoke that evening with the knowledge that it was to be a busy night. Much to do, little time to do it in: it was only two weeks before the summer solstice, the shortest night of the year. He had a brief seven hours to pack, find a new place, unpack, and feed. He fumbled with the latch on the lid and pushed it open. The latch was something he'd installed himself. No coffin was made with latches on the inside, for obvious reasons.

Sitting up brought a resurgence of last night's pain. Had he still breathed he would have gasped. As it was, his hand flew to his chest as the pain struck him. Not as bad as last night, but a simple bullet wound, no matter the location, should be nearly gone by now. He reached under his shirt until his fingers found the injury. The hole was still there! In fact, the bullet had not even been ejected yet. The damage must have been far worse than he thought. Maybe one of those hollow-point bullets or something.

As he contemplated his ability to complete tonight's tasks he climbed out of his casket and appraised the contents of his small apartment. There was distressingly little to pack. His clothes; an old, worn chair; his TV; a cheap radio; a few second-hand books; odds and ends. The kitchen, of course, was empty.

It appeared as though everything would fit into his van, so he started to bring the stuff down for transport to whatever motel he could find tonight on the cheap. First to go: the TV. It was a fairly large RCA, but his enhanced strength allowed him to carry it downstairs with no problem. His wounds, however, cried out against even this minor - for him

- exertion. This was not going to be a good night.

As he'd unhappily suspected, it didn't take long to pack his things. He hadn't been sure the minivan's shocks could handle the load, light though it was, but the bald tires weren't quite rubbing against the wheel well. They still had about half an inch of clearance. Lawrence figured it would be good enough. He got in, frowning at the musty smell, and found the key on his key ring. The engine started just fine, only stalling once.

He drove aimlessly for about ninety minutes before finding a place just outside the worst part of town that might work. The neighborhood appeared just as one normally pictures low income: houses that appeared as though they should be condemned, yet with obvious signs of tenants; the windows of most of the local businesses boarded up, with gang graffiti painted on; the brick of those same buildings crumbling after years of neglect and decay. He could almost feel he was among his own kind here, for there were many who walked the night, preying on their own human brethren in some fashion or another.

The hotel he settled on was the "Biltmore", so proclaimed by a garish neon sign that also advertised "Free TV and Air". Given the surrounding area, Lawrence figured they were about as good amenities as he could expect. Not that he was looking for a hotel with a pool or anything; swimming wasn't his thing. His muscle mass was so dense, he tended to sink like a rock. Turning the squeaking and rattling minivan into the parking lot, Lawrence took a closer look at the faded sign stuck in the lobby window. Yes: if he paid the weekly rate, and not the daily or hourly rates they also listed; he'd be okay.

He turned off the van and removed the key. The engine coughed out a few more revolutions, refusing to die. With the engine still sputtering to a halt behind him in the parking lot, he limped into the lobby.

"Whaddya want?" the proprietor asked. He was a swarthy-looking man, his enormous gut seemingly wedged into the small area behind a counter that was rippled from water damage. Even when speaking, his eyes never left the cheap 13-inch TV he was avidly watching, where some woman was screaming at her boyfriend on a talk show. Lawrence knew the program. He swore he could feel his brain cells dying on the evenings he watched it.

"A room," Lawrence replied as he walked to the desk across the tile floor. He had to keep himself from high-stepping; he felt as though his shoes were going to stick permanently to the filthy gray tiles.

"For the hour, day, or week?" he asked, still riveted to the tube.

"A week, please." Inwardly he praised the man's brevity, as even this little bit of conversation was exceptionally painful. Usually, Lawrence's lungs were as still as his obsolete heart, though it was common practice among vampires to breathe when in the presence of mortals. While humans rarely noticed consciously that a vampire was not breathing, they were often visibly unsettled by it, even though they were usually unable to attribute their uneasiness to any solid reason. Subconsciously, they sensed the wrongness of someone not breathing. Lawrence wasn't going to bother breathing even for appearances, not for this oblivious fool of a man behind the counter. He was too glued to his TV to make it worth the trouble. Speaking, however, required the forceful passage of air past his vocal cords which necessitated that he breathe. Now, with every lungful of air he drew in, and every bit expelled as he spoke, he could feel the bullet and bone splinters rubbing at the various tissues in his chest. He was fairly certain his voice did not reveal his discomfort and was positive his face maintained its look of serenity.

The greasy man reached around behind himself and grabbed a key as Lawrence laid some money on the table. "If ya want fresh sheets while you're here, ask one o' the maids. I don't handle that shit." His eyes darted from the TV for a moment, quickly sizing up Lawrence. "I do handle a few other services, though." His voice took on a tone amusingly reminiscent of a street thug from some B-movie as he went on to list the services he offered. Lawrence managed to listen politely to the sordid illegal products and services the man claimed he could procure, "for a price."

"Thank you, sir, just the room will be fine," Lawrence said, taking the key. He noticed, but ignored, the lack of a receipt. How this man skimmed off the owner was none of his concern. The man was already re-immersed in the television, his mind regressing back to its nearly paralyzed state, as Lawrence walked back outside.

He started unloading the few items he'd need in the room from the minivan. First out, as always, was his coffin. For this, he had backed the vehicle as close to the Biltmore's rear entrance as he could, doing his best to avoid being spotted by any casual observers. The late hour helped some, and no one was visible nearby. Gritting his teeth against the pain this brought to his still open wounds, he trudged it over to the elevator, looked at the sliding doors, then turned towards the stairs. After all, there was only one sign that was ever taped to an elevator door: "Out of Order". He considered leaving the coffin in the van. After all, he could sleep for a few days anywhere there was no sunlight, but tradition, comfort and safety eliminated that option. The walk up the narrow stairs, toting 800 pounds of unwieldy dead weight was just as agonizing to his injuries as he'd expected.

He entered his room and let the coffin fall to the floor with a loud crash. Lawrence didn't care at this point if there was anyone in the room below to hear it. He dropped to the sagging bed, exhausted and in dire pain. Giving himself a moment to recover from his ordeal, he lifted his shirt and examined the hole in his chest. Just to the left of midline, the wound was pretty clean, but it was also pretty small. He made his decision. Up again, down the stairs, out to the van. He found the box he sought, and rather than make another unnecessary trip back down, grabbed a few other small necessities.

Once back up in his sparse room, he began rummaging through the box. Toothbrush, comb, hairdryer...Ah! There they were. Tweezers in hand, he sprawled out on the bed before realizing he still had his shirt on. A little bit of wriggling, and it was off. Now for the tough part. He didn't need a mirror, as he wouldn't be able to see what he was doing anyway, and not just because mirrors ignored him. Had they worked, it wouldn't have done him any good in this case for the same reason he didn't just reach in and use his fingers: the hole was too small.

Steeling himself for the coming pain, he reached up and slid the tweezers into the bullet-sized wound. He knew that the offending piece of lead had gone in at an angle, and so adjusted the tweezers' direction accordingly. He screamed. While he was able to slide the tweezers along the same path that the bullet had taken, there was not a simple, open tunnel through his chest for the tweezers to follow. Every millimeter of progress made towards the slug was done by forcibly pushing aside some of his body's tissues, be it muscle, lung, or something else. He discovered another reason a mirror would have been futile: his eyes were closed tightly against the pain, and there was no way he could have forced himself to open them. The bullet did nothing compared to the agony he was subjecting himself to. For a moment he considered giving up, letting nature, or what passed for nature in the undead, take its course. But for whatever reason, his body had not kicked out the foreign matter and healed itself as rapidly as it should have. Had the bullet been blessed by a priest? No, that was a stupid thought. Who would...

And there it was. He could feel the metal of the tweezers touch the lead of the slug. This was fortunate, as the four-inch tweezers could not have gone much deeper and still be manipulated properly. Slowly, his fingers let the implement expand. Forward, just a bit more...close them tightly, and pull back. Not too fast, don't want to squeeze it right out of his grip, but ohshitohshitohshit it hurts!

Out!

He lost his grip then, and both tweezers and bullet fell onto his bare chest, the bullet rolling off his left side; his hand, shaking, dropping back to his right side. After a few moments in which he thought he might have passed out, he felt around, picked up the projectile, and brought it before his eyes to examine it. He rolled it back and forth between his fingers a couple times and let it drop again. No matter how often he'd been shot, he was still no authority on ballistics. It could be a hollow point. But then again, it could be an explosive round for all he knew.

It didn't matter. What did matter was that he still had a hole in his chest and a bullet with its accompanying hole in his leg. No. There was simply no way he was doing that shit again. It wouldn't be nearly as bad, but no. As he hadn't fed well last night, he was half-starved, and almost certainly didn't have the energy to do any more primitive self-surgery. In fact, getting some nourishment had to be his next priority. He was already feeling horribly weak.

So, time to feed. Time to eke out another day of existence. Not life, for he had left that behind centuries ago. Even were the term used in a non-literal sense, he would not have claimed a life. Feed, watch TV, and sleep. What kind of life was that? Had it been possible, Lawrence was sure that at some points over the last centuries he could have literally been bored to death.

Unfortunately, or so it seemed, he still had enough desire to live that he didn't bring a true death upon himself, but what kind of life was this?

On occasion over the past few dozen years, and sporadically over the centuries, he had sought out companionship, but human women were not strictly creatures of the night as he was; they enjoyed strolls in the park on a summer day, a nice lunch out. Even a dinner, were it after sunset, was not a viable option for him: his body violently rejected - with swift regurgitation - anything but life giving, living blood. Definitely not a romantic date scene. No, most relationships he attempted to strike up with mortal women fizzled all too soon. Even those who claimed not to mind his "eccentricities" wound up ignoring his calls before long. One time, he had felt strongly enough about a woman that he'd tried to explain his situation, and gave her the whole truth of his story. Stephanie. She had taken him seriously, though - especially after he proved the matter - and he had been carefully optimistic for the chances of this one. She had asked him to make her into a vampire one night; he told her he could not.

He never saw her again.

He had tried calling, visiting her home. He'd even tried calling the office where she worked. After hours, of course. He was told she no longer worked there.

But that had been, what, 25 years ago? More? She would be well into middle age by now, almost certainly settled down and with a family, whereas Lawrence maintained his youthful appearance. Once, he'd thought that would be one of the greatest benefits of immortality; eternal youth. Now, in his years of enduring solitude he found that it mattered not at all. What solace was his eternally youthful, attractive looks, with none to appreciate them? He could not even appreciate them himself, if he chose to, for what would reflect them back to him if he cared to look?

Lawrence got up, pulled on his shirt, and went out the door to feed.

* * *

Lawrence woke two evenings later feeling very refreshed. While he still had an open wound on both his chest and his leg, the chest wound was beginning to close up and the slug had ejected from his thigh at some point during the day while he rested. He was still healing much slower than he should, but he could see some progress now.

That, and he felt almost back to his usual, vibrant self. He had desperately needed the feedings he'd taken the last couple nights. He had positively gorged himself, satiating himself on not just one, but two humans each evening.

His ebullient mood did not last long, though. With the bullet gone from his leg, he decided to walk as he searched for a suitable victim. Not that he was expecting a pleasant stroll; this was not a neighborhood particularly suited for such simple joys. But he had plenty of time to kill, a nice change from the last few busy evenings.

As he was walking past a theater, he decided to catch a show, whatever was starting soonest. The attendant handed him a ticket for theater four, and he went in and sat down. He walked out thirty minutes later.

It wasn't a bad movie. Quite the contrary, it had a fairly full audience to attest to the quality of the film. What he would have realized by the name on the marquee or the ticket stub, had he paid any attention to either, was that his ticket was for the summer's big romantic film. With all the happy couples around him, and the pair on the screen well on their way to an obvious romance, his isolation was again brought to the forefront of his awareness with crushing brutality. He left in a deep funk.

He walked. No longer was he walking with the upbeat, swift strides of a man with a purpose. Nor was it the leisurely pace of a man enjoying the evening. Now, it was just feet doing what they were made to do, acting without the command of a mind that was too focused on other matters to tell them what to do. So, his feet walked, the rest of him just along for the ride, now. His mind slowly contemplated the *life* teeming around him. Humans, even in these low-income environments, moving about with purpose. Many traveled with a companion, whether that companion was an old buddy or someone intimately closer. Of those who were alone, he could tell by the way they moved, the glow of life in their eyes, many were on their way to be with friends or lovers.

Companionship. That was what life was about. Everything else was a means to that end. Lawrence had no life; his was a hollow existence.

Where was Stephanie these days?

Bah. Put her out of the mind. How about Samantha? Or Kim? They, at least, were probably still close to his apparent age.

Not that that mattered. He just wanted companionship, not necessarily a lover. He'd be thrilled even to have Tomás, or Clive, some of his last original manservants, but they were dust long ago, dead for almost four hundred years. Such was the problem with using humans for companionship: so ephemeral. A mere flicker in his lifetime. No, that wasn't quite true. The sheer power of their life-force, their overpowering vivacity, made it more than a flicker; more of a flash. Still as brief, but so much more energy.

His feet stopped. Surprised, he realized the time. As a vampire, he had no need for timepieces He, like all others of his kind, could sense the movement of the sun, their truest enemy; they could feel its inexorable advance, limiting their time in the world of the living, and could accurately mark time by that method alone. He had been roving, lost in his thoughts for three hours. He knew what he intended, now. He looked up from his ruminations, and it seemed his feet had known his intention before he realized it himself. He'd given thought to dozens of solutions, from dropping in on a "Single's bar", taking up Fat Jack - the name he'd assigned to the disgusting desk manager at the Biltmore - on the services he'd offered of available women, or just languishing in front of his room's television, alone for yet another night.

He was no more than three blocks from his hotel. Good enough. Over the last couple nights he'd heard and observed the comings and goings of his two intended victims.

Victims? No, not really. He liked to think of it as a gift. That was the way the entire vampire community considered it, in fact. After all, who *wouldn't* want eternal life? Never mind that it's not really life. It was called Awakening, for it awakened so much that was beyond the mortal grasp, and who wouldn't crave all of the enhanced abilities, speed, power, senses? Never mind that Lawrence was miserable. He remembered when he had been first Awakened. Oh, how he'd desired it, coveted it, and how he had savored it once it was his. Now, he would again share it.

He found them easily. They both tended to stick to the same alley, at night anyway, which was a bit surprising given their natures. They probably spent their days begging on the street, hoping for any generosity from the passing pedestrians.

The first recipient of his gift, the first to be Awakened, was the black one. Sneaking up was no problem, as his quarry was asleep. Grabbing him by the scruff of the neck, Lawrence picked him up off the ground and bit him. This was not a bite for feeding, though no human could have told the difference. Initially, it still had its drug like effects, but that would be very temporary, as Lawrence poured his entire will into his task.

Even as the black one began to die, Lawrence set him down and with one leap crossed the five yards farther into the alley to where he knew the other one rested. Tossing aside the newspaper under which his second prey was sleeping, Lawrence dropped down and sank his fangs into his neck. Again he pushed his will out, taking only the necessary few drops of blood required for the process. He was already feeling rather fatigued from the first one he Awakened; it took the last of his flagging energy to push his will, this power, into the second. Finished, he staggered back against the alley wall, watched and waited.

It was often said that a body dies in the process of becoming a vampire. This is true, but only by half. After all, the body is still animated. The mind still functions. So to say the body is dead cannot be entirely true, and following that line of reasoning, how then could the body have died if it is not quite dead? In Lawrence's opinion this debate, which had gone on in the Council and among the lesser vampires for millennia, was pure semantics. He was a practical man, dead or not. The body felt like it was dying. Any normal doctor would proclaim a vampire dead were he to come across the creature lying in repose during the day. Perhaps a scan of the brain would claim otherwise, but Lawrence didn't know.

Dying hurt. A lot. And, when undergoing the change from mortal to undead, passing to the realm of the dead could take anywhere from five to fifteen minutes. Five to fifteen minutes of excruciating pain signaling the end of the life one had known.

Lawrence felt there was more to it than just the death of the body. After all, the mortal form held enough energy in just its blood to sustain a vampire. He felt that the living body, through some supernatural force, merely rearranged itself to another, more efficient system. So far as he knew, he was alone in this line of thinking. All the experts had told him he was a fool, and he hadn't argued. He knew it was probably nothing more than his own way of understanding something too complex for his mind to grasp, much in the way the Greeks had attributed much of the natural world to their pantheon of gods.

Lawrence stopped speculating and turned his attention back to the two bodies writhing on the ground in the alley before him. Even today, after five hundred years, he clearly remembered the agony of the mortal death and did not envy these two. The constant cries of agony, pitching all the way up and down the audible scale, were enough to make any possible witnesses hurry past with their heads down, their flesh pebbling out in goose bumps in a primal fear of whatever could cause such tortuous misery in a living creature. Just as bad was the sight of the contortions the body went through, the looks of unrelieved suffering on their faces, the sheer stink of fear pouring off them, overwhelming even the odor of the waste expelled by a body beyond conscious control in the throes of death.

And, finally, building in strength, rising to a crescendo as the move from life to undead neared its completion, the power. Raw energy, in the very air itself, radiating out from those undergoing the change. It was because of this that Lawrence held his theory of the rearranging of the body's energies once Awakened. He could feel the outflow of power, the tingling of his skin, almost like a light electrical charge. It was more than that, though. It wasn't just the body that felt the power. In fact, what was felt by the body was nothing compared to what his mind, or soul - if he had one - experienced. Pure, mystical power. It seemed to surround not his corporeal being, but his mind. Not the gray matter that was his brain, but that untenable essence which was Lawrence. His mind seemed to drown, yet exalt, in this rush of magical energies. And here he was, sitting now between two discharging storehouses of it. The power continued to grow, crashing into him like waves from both sides. Lawrence could taste it, the delicious force of life. He could weep, it was so overpowering. And then, when it seemed he could suffocate in bliss, it was gone; channeled back, sucked into the vessels in which it belonged. It almost felt as though he'd been in a storm, though there was little physical manifestation, and Lawrence reached up to smooth back his unruffled hair.

The first one to begin the change was also the first to finish recovering. It didn't always work that way, but it did tonight. As the twitching subsided and the eyelids fluttered open, Lawrence found himself looking down into a pair of deeply intelligent green eyes. The two vampires simply stared at each other for a moment before the owner of the green eyes got up on all fours. Still a little shaky, the cat looked over to the other new member of the undead world, who had also recovered now, and was getting unsteadily to his four paws as well.

The dog ignored the cat and looked at Lawrence. "You bastard," it told him.

CHAPTER TWO

They had been walking the three blocks back to the Biltmore after the dog and cat had recovered from the tribulations they had undergone. Lawrence had noticed over the centuries that animals seemed to recover from the change much more rapidly than humans. These two were no exception. Less than a minute after it was over, they were back on their furry feet and introducing themselves.

The dog, who said his name was Mac, didn't like him. Lawrence was used to that. There had been other animals he had Awakened who didn't like him. His first animal, a hunting dog from his own kennels named Iron, had hated him. He'd woken many nights to see Iron standing there, staring at him, telepathically feeding him a constant stream of vile, loathing thoughts.

Thoughts only, because that was how he communicated with the animals. The change did not affect their vocal cords, nor give them lips for forming sounds. They remained just as unable to speak as common animals. In at least ninety percent of the cases, however, the animals acquired a limited telepathic ability. This communication only seemed to work between Lawrence and his vampire animals, and the animals amongst each other. They remained incommunicado with the rest of the world.

Dozens of animals since Iron, including some others who had also disliked Lawrence, and now this dog. He hoped Mac wouldn't be as constant in his thoughts of animosity as Iron had been. Iron had been quite close to driving him insane toward the end.

Lawrence's conscience had always plagued him, though. Perhaps Iron's - and Mac's - spite was justified. After all, the animals he Awakened were never given a choice in the matter. How could they be? They were just simple animals prior to being Awakened. They didn't have the cognitive ability to consider such a choice even if he had been able to communicate it to them.

Oh, how he'd missed the companionship, though. Someone he could talk to, who could understand him and his ways. His euphoria at that thought was beaten down again almost instantly by reality. He had brought these two innocent creatures into a potentially dangerous existence. If they were discovered, especially by his own kind, they would certainly be destroyed; he had far too many experiences with this to deny it.

No. This time, he promised himself, they would live. He would make certain of it. He was responsible for their new existence; he was responsible for them.

Lawrence straightened a little from the slouch he didn't know he had. He had a purpose now. However rough the rest of his existence was, he again felt as though he had a life.

"My name was Pretty Boots," the cat was thinking at him. The reason for the name was evident; he was pitch black, except for his paws, each of which was white. "As I don't think any self-respecting vampire cat can walk in pride with a name like that, I wish to leave my name behind with my mortality. Any suggestions?"

The dog, Mac, was the first to respond. "How about 'Cute Shoes'?" He proceeded to howl with laughter. This ended abruptly with a yelp, and he turned to see Pretty Boots walking casually behind him, tail erect, nose high. His clawed swipe at Mac's back had been almost too swift for even Lawrence to observe.

"Watch your thoughts, mongrel. It'd be hard to kill you, but you can suffer all the more because of it," he said, almost echoing Lawrence's thought of four days ago. The cat seemed to possess a bit of a temper. Though Mac was obviously a mongrel, it was equally obvious that he did not like the term.

He was almost comically scruffy-looking, an uneven mix of gray and rust-colored wiry fur. His appearance was that of a two foot tall used and rusty steel wool pad with legs and a tail, all come to life.

"Let's get you two up to the room, and I'll try to think of a good name," Lawrence said.

The three blocks had been traversed rapidly as they talked. Lawrence headed up to his room, the quadruped vampires following at his feet. As he opened the door, both animals hesitated at the threshold, sniffing the room experimentally. Mac allowed a low growl to escape. Pretty Boots looked up at Lawrence. "This is it?" the cat asked, making no attempt to hide his disgust.

Lawrence avoided the cat's eyes, scanning the room. The phone was on the floor next to the bed. There was no stand for it. The linens appeared clean, but very stained and yellowed with age. This discoloration inadvertently matched the wallpaper, which was also a horrible shade of yellow, and peeling in many places. The final touch: a mirror on the ceiling above the bed. Lawrence's open coffin was against the wall opposite the window. "This is just temporary. We'll be in a better place soon. Much better." Mac's ears perked up and he drawled telepathically, "Oh, really?"

"Well, that's the plan," Lawrence replied uncertainly.

While Lawrence went back down to pay for another five days, the animals continued their perusal of their home for the week.

"What a loser. I can't believe he did this to me," Mac complained as he sniffed around the bathroom, occasionally sneezing in disgust.

"What is your problem? This is an awesome gig. I admit, this isn't the Hilton, but it's better than the streets. We've got it made now." Pretty Boots had already completed his quick examination and was curled up on the bed.

Mac came out of the bathroom, continuing his diligent investigations. "Do you realize our souls are now damned?"

"According to many religions, we don't have souls to begin with. So, what religion are you, and how often were you attending church? Which church was it? Our Lady of the Eternal Leg Humping? Or was it a synagogue? Really, though, I can't picture you in a yarmulke. The ears, ya know."

"Shut up! This is no laughing matter!" Pretty Boots apparently thought so, as the cat was making a strange, staccato purring sound that could only be a chuckle. Mac looked angrily up at the bed where Pretty Boots was lying with his tail wrapped around himself as he continued. "We have been taken advantage of! We have been stolen from our natural lives, and thrown into this evil existence, living only by feeding on the blood of those who had always cared for us! We're -"

"Oh, shut up already!" Pretty Boots pounced off the bed, landing square in front of Mac. The cat's hackles were raised, back arched threateningly. Mac hunkered down in response, growling, his eyes locked on the cat's in a reciprocal challenge.

Lawrence came back in at that moment, to see them facing off. "Would you two give up the hostility already? I swear, you fight like...oh, never mind. But cut it out, okay?" He looked around the room, searching for a distraction for the antagonistic pair. "Hey, maybe there's a dog show on TV. Lassie or something."

Mac looked over his shoulder at his vampire master. "Don't be stupid. I *hate* Lassie."

"Why is there nothing about cats?" Mac and Lawrence both looked over to Pretty Boots at his unexpected outburst. "Well, there were plenty of movies and TV shows about dogs, or with dogs as major characters. Where are the cat shows?"

Lawrence looked at the cat uncertainly. It had been a while since he'd had any company, and he was not sure how he should handle these two, with their open hostility towards each other. For now, he could only hope they would get along better as the shock of their new situation wore off.

Having no better ideas, and unsure how to reply to the cat's insight, he changed the subject. "Hey, I thought of a name!" he announced proudly. "How about Sir Bedivere?"

Pretty Boots' eyes settled on Lawrence as he sat, his tail flicking about in agitation. "I don't think I'd like it even if I *was* male." Lawrence tried to stammer out an apology; Mac jumped back as though Pretty Boots had announced she had the plague. Now that they reflected on it, however, her telepathic voice - the way it sounded in their heads - *did* have a feminine tone to it. Husky, but feminine. She continued, "I like your literary reference, however. How about a different era, different book. Lady de Winter."

"Lady de Winter? That's an... interesting choice."

"Yes, I know. I rather like its connotations; the attitude of the original. An amoral, soulless," she cast a glance at Mac, "evil woman who used those very traits, along with her stunning beauty, to get what she wanted. It's got style."

She purred, repeating the name. "Lady de Winter."

"You'll always be Pretty Boots to me," Mac chuckled.

"And you'll always be a scratching post to me." Lady de Winter held up a paw, extending and retracting her claws for him to see.

Brushing himself off for no apparent reason, Lawrence asked, "I haven't fed tonight. Do you guys want to come?"

The animals looked at each other. "Sure, why not?" Lady sent telepathically.

Given the neighborhood the Biltmore was in, it didn't take long to find an isolated location to wait for some prey to happen by. Lawrence had gotten a pretty good feel for the area in the last week, as well, so he knew about what they were looking for. The buildings around the hotel were largely vacant, often condemned, though even those sometimes held life. The street-lights worked only sporadically, perhaps one in three functioning properly, leaving most of the street in a flickering darkness. The trio found a small alley between two old, abandoned apartment buildings which looked as though they dated from the 50's.

"Why doesn't the idiot just go into one of the buildings? It's bound to be rife with bums taking shelter for the night. It's not like anyone would miss them, and our 'fearless leader' would fit right in with those vagrants."

"Alpo does horrible things to your brain, doesn't it?" Lady responded.

"Most, if not all of them, will be sleeping off the effects of alcohol."

"So?"

"So, you drooling fool, the alcohol in a bum's blood has the same effect on us when we drink it, only magnified. Same with most other drugs. Idiot." Lady moved off several feet farther into the alley, where she crouched down, perfectly still. The telepathic link shared by the animals and Lawrence involved no sound or movement, and Mac now found the experience of talking with her even more particularly eerie, coming from a rigidly frozen form. Even her fur seemed locked in time. "If he were to feed on them, he'd be positively blitzed."

Mac growled softly. "How do you know all this? I think you're making it up."

"My god, Mac, have you not given any thought at all as to our enhanced mental faculties, our ability to communicate telepathically in English, or any of this?"

"Well..."

"When Lawrence gave us immortality, and all the problems and benefits that go with being undead, we also received all his knowledge."

"Are you sure? I only remember being a dog."

"Not memories, bone-breath. Knowledge. Although the two of them are often closely intertwined. That's how I know of Lady de Winter, though I certainly don't remember ever reading any Dumas as a normal cat."

Mac's tail wagged a few short, hesitant strokes. "Now that you mention it, I do seem to know quite a bit of stuff that I wouldn't know normally."

"Not that one could tell by talking to you. But that's right. You should have all of whatever knowledge Lawrence had acquired up to the point of our transformation, our Awakening. That's not how it works with human vampires, just with us."

Her paw arced out with unnatural swiftness, giving Mac a start after her long period of statuesque immobility. He saw a large rat thud against the brick wall, and watched as Lady sat down contentedly in front of it, her sleek tail flicking in contentment behind her like a separate creature. Were a mortal pedestrian to pass by, they would have seen nothing out of the ordinary - just a stray cat eating its dinner of rat.

Lady de Winter picked up her thought where she'd left off. "Of course, knowledge and intelligence are two entirely different things as well. I'm afraid you got the short end of the stick on the latter, my canine companion."

"You're not going to eat that thing, are you?" Mac's disgust at the idea was evident in the voice Lady heard in her mind.

"No, you fool. I'm going to drink its blood. That's what we do now, remember?"

"Quiet, you two. Someone's coming," Lawrence whispered back at them. Mac lifted his head to the side: his version of a shrug. They *were* being quiet; even their conversation hadn't been sent out for Lawrence to receive.

"I get the feeling he's not terribly used to having company," Lady said, sinking her fangs into the stunned rat. She glanced over at Mac as she fed.

"You want me to catch you one of these?"

Mac looked at the rodent with distaste. "Yuck. No."

"What, are you going to have some of whatever Lawrence catches? Sheesh. Even undead, you're still begging scraps from the dinner table, eh?"

"No, I'm not. I won't be begging that fiend for anything, especially what he feeds on. Don't you get it? This is why we're damned! It's wrong for us to feed on humans! They were the ones who took care of me for years. They are the ones who fed me, and you, even as a stray."

"That's right, and they can *really* feed you now. Directly, even."

"Don't be crass."

"What? Besides, what do you owe people? You lived on the streets, same as me. Did your old masters kick you out? You owe them nothing."

"No, I wasn't kicked out. My past is none of your business."

Mac turned his furred back on Lady and padded lightly over to sit next to where Lawrence was standing in the shadows, waiting to spring on an unwary pedestrian. Mac sat down. Lawrence was quietly watching a young couple stagger past, apparently drunk from the local bar. Even when they looked directly at Lawrence, they seemed not to see him, though they did begin to stumble along at a quicker pace. A few quiet minutes later a lone figure, steady on his feet, rounded the corner thirty feet from their alley. Lawrence waited until the man was directly in front of the alley mouth before making his move.

The victim was a tall, skinny individual of about forty-five, and had only enough time to call out, "Who's -" before Lawrence was on him. Lawrence immediately grabbed hold of the unfortunate man, pierced his neck and began drinking the life-giving blood, stealing away the man's essence. This was done with a simple grace and economy of movement so natural it could only have come from long practice. No further sound was uttered by the human as the soporific effect of a feeding vampire acted on him like a highspeed narcotic. His arms hung limply at his sides, eyes open but unseeing, head tilted to the side to accommodate the feeding vampire.

After Lawrence had had his fill, he saw Mac sitting in the alley, watching him. "There's still enough for you to have some, Mac."

"You make me sick."

"Well, I guess that's a no. You couldn't get too much from this guy, anyway. Do you want me to find you a different one?"

"No. As I told the cat, I'm not going to lower myself to feeding on humans. And I certainly don't need your help." A low growl escaped from his throat, nearly inaudible. Lawrence was rifling through the man's pockets. "What are you doing? Are you robbing him?"

"Well, I have to pay the bills somehow," he shot back in irritation, not looking up from his pilfering. Had Mac not been at the wrong angle, he would have seen the deepening color of Lawrence's cheeks, though he would not have recognized the red flush of shame through his color-blind eyes.

After taking the $35.25 the unfortunate pedestrian had been carrying in cash, Lawrence began walking back to the hotel. The animals ranged all over, sometimes ahead of him, sometimes behind him. Every few seconds one or both of them would pause, head canted, as they listened to the city with their newly enhanced animal senses.

"I swear I can hear ants snoring," Mac commented after one pause. "And I can smell every individual within a mile!"

"Hmph." Lady had paused ahead of the other two, grooming her tail. "Not me. Your fetid odor overpowers all the other scents, and your incessant panting drowns out everything else below 20 decibels, you moronic mouthbreather. I can't detect anything but your annoying self. Why are you bothering to breathe, anyway?"

"You guys can sleep in my coffin, if you like," Lawrence informed the pair as they all walked up the stairs. He did his best to ignore their bickering. He slotted the key and opened the door.

"Do we really need to sleep in a coffin?" Mac asked. He trailed behind a few feet, apparently not over-eager to enter their dreary little room.

"Well, from my experience, animals don't, not really, but coffins are kind of a tradition."

"Actually," Lady de Winter put in as she did a brief survey of their small room, "there isn't much in the way of traditions for animal vampires."

"Well, no, but still, at the very least, it's good protection against accidental sunlight exposure. And besides, coffins can be quite comfortable." Mac snorted at this and looked pointedly at Lawrence's coffin, an obvious economy model, built with the belief that the corpse who would be laid to rest in it would not worry about comfort. "Well, okay, maybe not *this* one, but my *next* one..."

"Whatever." Lady leapt gracefully onto the coffin, balancing with ease on the open edge. "I think I'll take up your offer. I don't trust Mac, anyway."

Mac looked around. "I'll take the bed."

The arrangements made, Lawrence settled into the coffin, contending with the tickles engendered by Lady's tail brushing his nose. She had chosen to rest curled around the space between his head and the walls of the coffin, sending Lawrence into his daily slumber with the sound of her purring right at his ear.

Mac watched as the lid closed before he crawled under the bed.

* * *

The Council sat. As was tradition, they sat as one, with none elevated above the others, around the very table which had inspired the legends of King Arthur and his Knights of the Round Table. The truth behind the legend was far darker than the fairy tales which arose from this one aspect of it. This was the true origin of those tales, revealed by a mortal, a foreign apprentice storyteller who saw too much, but understood far too little. He had tragically died before relating all he had seen to his master, the storyteller; the master misinterpreted what little he had heard and spread heroic tales of the Knights of the Round Table, instead of what his foreign assistant truly spoke of, the nights at the round table.

The Council no longer held its meetings in a dingy castle of stone. These leaders met in what would seem near-total darkness to mortal eyes, around an ancient stone table whose age - had they known it - was measured in millennia. Their site was a modern edifice of glass and steel. The table itself had never been moved. Where it once sat in a small castle, that structure had been torn away, the new symbol of power built on its location. Through all of that the table remained, never moved while old symbols of station were torn down and a new one, this modern skyscraper, erected around it. This was a place of ancient power. The large stone table itself was a thing of power. Place and thing would be as nothing, however, without beings of power.

There are many in the human realm who blame great misfortune and prosperity alike on a few secret organizations that have survived for many years. Organizations filled with the unknown power players of that generation.

Skull and Bones. Freemasons. Knights Templar. Illuminati.

Pawns.

Such organizations were minor tools to the creatures gathered around this table.

Those in this room needed no such fancy names to proclaim their elite status, their power. They were simply the Council. They did not measure by generations, but by centuries or millennia. They changed with the times, yet remained timeless, as evidenced by their business suits and newly completed tower.

They dealt with issues of global significance. Minor issues and individuals were generally beneath their notice, with a few rare exceptions. Usually, such exceptions were because that one individual was used to influence issues of global significance.

One such example had occurred a short eighty years earlier, when a charismatic ex-con went about eliminating a large segment of the European population and instigated a costly war. Neither of these issues greatly upset the Council; indeed, they had profited greatly from the war, and felt the population at the time needed some culling. However, this leader began to delve too deeply into the occult for the Council's tastes, came too close to knowledge they had forbidden mortals, so they had him eliminated, an apparent suicide.

Another instance of their rare attention to individuals dated back two hundred years, when a unified Europe was something they felt was needed, if only temporarily. They were also of the opinion that a war was presently called for. This decided, they brought a particular French Revolutionary general to power. When he formed his own agenda and tried to expand into Russia, they pulled the plug on him, as well. They had other plans in mind for Russia, so they had the man exiled.

Humans were easy, though. Merely a business consideration. The Council's primary role was the governing of all vampire kind. Only vampires knew of the Council's existence as other than the leader of a large corporate conglomerate. For the undead, there was no other ultimate power, no other course of appeal. It was because of this that they were so aggrieved when, four hundred years ago, a young vampire with an affinity for Awakening animals escaped the death decreed for him. An individual had been exceptional enough to garner their attention; one of their own kind, over whom they openly wielded absolute power, and yet he had slipped through their long-reaching fingers.

Had their authority over the world's vampires not been so absolute, his deviance could have undermined their power. As it was, they'd had to eliminate a member of their own circle as punishment over such a magnificent failure.

Elimination from the Council was always... permanent. And they had yet to resolve the issue to their satisfaction, even after four centuries.

The Council was power, but to hold significant power is to be subject to tedious discussions and decisions at times. Today's meeting was called primarily to decide a question on vampire policies overseas. As there was no competing vampire government, the Council ruled throughout the world, and today's topic was the young American nations. The first item on tonight's agenda was a small takeover bid for a company specializing in medical research, located in Milwaukee. The cattle must be kept healthy.

A voice, aged not just with years but with power, came almost silently from somewhere around the table. There is always a first among equals. This voice commanded. It quite possibly knew no other tone.

"Buy it. Send that sycophant, Philip, to handle it. Next item."

CHAPTER THREE

"No!" The shout echoed through Lawrence's head, and Mac growled to emphasize it.

It was their fifth night together, but the first in which Mac had tried to interfere with his feeding. Mac was standing on the sidewalk between Lawrence and his intended victim for the evening, a well-to-do middle-aged lady who appeared to have been dining out tonight, based on the 'doggy bag' she carried. If she'd had a date for the evening, he was nowhere to be seen.

Lawrence and Lady de Winter had been hunting mostly in better neighborhoods. There was less chance of intoxicated blood, and more money on the victims. "What is your problem, Mac? I have to feed." Mac was crouched low, ready to spring. The woman stood frozen behind him, her bulging purse and doggy bag clutched together in both hands, pressed against her chest. She was looking from dog to man, wide eyes darting rapidly between them. She had barely seen them approach, they'd moved so swiftly.

"I'm not gonna let you feed on any more humans!"

"Bah! Fine. I'll let this one go. You've ruined it anyway, she's seen me. But don't you run off again. We need to talk about this." Ever since the first night, Mac had been wandering off on his own for the majority of each night. At first, Lawrence had been concerned, and the only explanation Mac gave was that he preferred to feed alone. He didn't seem to be getting into any trouble, and refused to say anything more about it, so Lawrence just had to take Mac at his word and let the subject drop.

For two nights, the dog had been waiting at the door when Lawrence and Lady had returned. The third night, he was scratching at the door not thirty minutes before sunrise. Lawrence had just about given up on him and had been climbing into his coffin - he seemed to be feeling the pull of dawn earlier than was common as of late. Mac never told either of them where he'd been or discussed his feedings.

Lawrence turned around and stalked off. His wounds weren't as bad as they'd been, but they were still there; his gait was still marred by a noticeable limp. He didn't need this right now on top of his other problems. "Meet me at the van. It's two blocks up and one to the right." Mac watched him as he limped around the corner, and then turned to look at the woman he'd protected.

"Hey, doggy," she called, coming out of her fear-induced daze. She crouched down to reach a hand out to him. Mac cast a quick glance around. Not seeing anyone, he advanced toward the kindly looking woman, his tail wagging quickly, nervously. "Yes, you're a good puppy," she murmured as she stroked his wiry coat. "Did you save me from some crazy ol' mugger? Yes, you did," she crooned. His tail was wagging in ecstasy now, his entire hindquarters moving in conjunction with his tail. She'd found the spot - right ear, one inch back - on her first try, and was scratching it vigorously Oh yeah, that was good. That was it. Just what he -

"Is the nice doggy getting his belly wubbed next?" The sardonic, heavily mocking voice could not be heard by the woman; it was sounding only in his head. His ears perked up uselessly as he looked around, trying to pinpoint the source. That stupid cat was obviously nearby somewhere. He growled without thinking, and the woman pulled back her hand. He didn't notice. That annoying feline was still nattering on. "Good god, dog, have a little dignity! We're vampires, for chrissake!"

There! A moving spot of white in the darkness. He bounded off, his barking echoing through the street.

The woman glanced around as she remembered she'd almost just been mugged and walked rapidly to her car.

* * *

Okay, he could admit it to himself. Not only was the cat sneakier than he was, she was faster. Lady had made it to the van a full block ahead of him. Lucky for her she did, too. Stupid cat.

"Damn right I'm faster and sneakier. I'm also smarter and smell better," she taunted him. Bah! He must have been sending his thoughts! Bloody cat!

"Not a chance, pussy cat: I smell far better than you. I'm part bloodhound." He trotted the last dozen feet to the minivan in pride, head held high. No cat could match his abilities in that arena.

"That's not what I meant."

He growled.

"Knock it off, you two." As he always did when alone with them, Lawrence verbalized his words to the pair, speaking aloud when mere thought would have sufficed. He started the old van and pulled out, heading back downtown. "Now, Mac, what is your problem?"

"I don't care what we are; I'm not going to tolerate you killing all these people!"

"What?" Lawrence's surprise nearly put the vehicle on the sidewalk as he spun to look back at where Mac was sitting.

"You heard me. I'm not gonna put up with it." He was sitting in the center of the middle row of seats of the minivan, looking at Lawrence with the sides of his muzzle pulled up in distaste.

There was a loud yowl, then a rapid-fire hissing. Mac and Lawrence were both surprised at this outburst until they realized the cause: Lady de Winter was laughing uproariously.

"What's so funny, cat?" Mac sent. The voice in Lady's head bore a deep, threatening growl.

"You. For all your sneaking around, doing whatever off on your own, you haven't bothered to take any time with Lawrence, to get to know who he is and how he operates."

"I know how he operates! He's a vampire! He kills others to keep himself alive! Just like we have to do now!"

Lady glanced over at Lawrence from where she was sitting on the worn, faded passenger seat. His eyes were locked straight ahead as he turned onto the highway. Only his white knuckles on the wheel gave any indication of his thoughts or feelings. He was apparently content to let her handle Mac for the moment.

"Had you taken the time to investigate, or paid the slightest attention to the world around you, or spent some time with us, you would know that Lawrence does not kill his victims. He takes enough blood to slake his hunger and leaves them alive."

"You expect me to believe that?"

"I know it's hard for a mere dog to understand. After all, whoever heard of a dog eating in moderation? Your kind eats until you're sick! Leave a bowl of dog-food out, and it's gone in seconds!"

With that, Mac pounced into the front seat. He'd had enough from the mousetrap. Lady, who had been watching him as she ridiculed him, jumped at the key moment. Mac found himself on an empty seat with an angry cat flying at him. Lady had rebounded herself off the dashboard to land directly atop Mac. Her sharp claws promptly sank through his fur and into his flesh. Mac yelped at this counterattack. Turning his head at a seemingly impossible angle, Mac's muzzle latched briefly onto her mobile tail.

Lady gave a piercing yowl as she vaulted over onto Lawrence's lap. His shouted commands to stop fighting went unheard by the brawling animals. In his rage, Mac followed Lady onto Lawrence's already crowded lap, heedless of the fact that the driver was now heavily restricted. Lawrence was forced to pull his head back, jerking it spastically from side to side to avoid receiving the missed blows from the melee. Even so, he was having only moderate success at keeping his face untouched by the claws and teeth of the rowdy animals. Finally, a tragically missed bite landed most inconveniently, but not on Lawrence's face. By reflex, his hands both dropped, too late, to protect that most vulnerable of a man's organs, releasing his grip on the wheel.

Lady, who had leapt up to avoid the bite that landed so uncomfortably on Lawrence, came down on the uncontrolled steering wheel. Surprisingly, her supernatural balance allowed her to perch there; but, as she was off-center, the wheel began to roll to the right. Her attempt to maintain the precarious position only served to spin it all the faster. She looked like an odd parody of a lumberjack balancing himself in a well-matched log-rolling competition.

Lawrence had realized the danger and had begun slowing down as soon as the animals landed in his lap, but the rusty van was still doing 45 when it began the sudden right turn brought about by Lady's scrambling balancing act. Even lightning reflexes are of little use when the individual is too shocked or distracted to use them. The three only watched in dismay as the van threw itself perpendicular to their direction of travel and began to lurch onto its side in a squeal of bald tires. By the time Lawrence recovered his senses from the bite and had moved his hands back to the wildly spinning wheel, it was too late. The van was rolling, tumbling down the dark highway.

They flew out of the van in three separate directions as it tumbled. Lawrence bounced a few times on the gravel shoulder of the road before sliding to a halt on his side in the grassy median. He lay there for only a moment before dragging himself up. With the practiced speed of hundreds of years of dangerous living, he assessed his damage as he took stock of the current situation. Knee broken, but functional. Arm also broken, perhaps twice. How many ribs? Don't think about it.

Coming to the decision that he could still walk - though only with great pain - he cast his eyes about, looking for the animals.

Lady he found in the middle of the center lane, mewling piteously as cars roared over her. Their tires, for the most part, were straddling her body, doing no further damage to her obviously distorted form.

The passing motorists slowed to gawk at the dim form of the overturned van. Lawrence took advantage of their reduced speed to plunge into a small break in the traffic. He stooped to pick up her battered form but did not stop moving. He continued his awkward run as he raced to grab Mac. Mac had not been as lucky: as Lawrence approached the dog, he saw another car roll over him, heard the *whump-whump* of the tires on Mac's legs. Even with all the horrors Lawrence had borne witness to through his years, he could not help but wince at the scene, and the disturbingly visceral sound of bones breaking and grinding against each other in their brief moment under the weight of each car. Mac was blessedly unconscious as Lawrence scooped him up; hopefully he was thus spared most of the pain.

Lawrence did his best to run into the darkness as he left the oddly busy night highway, but the best he was able to manage was a rapid walk. His knee would not allow him much better than that as he left the upturned minivan behind, its wheels still spinning fruitlessly in the air.

*   *   *

The next evening, Lawrence found himself playing the strange, mixed role of both animal catcher and waiter. Lady was up and able to catch her own food, though she didn't stray far from the hotel and moved with a very subtle limp. Mac was not so fortunate. His legs had each been broken multiple times, he had several cracked ribs, and Lawrence was pretty sure the dog's spinal cord had been severed at some point. Even with the speed and totality of vampiric healing, Mac would be down for this evening.

Lawrence also had a heavy limp again from his broken knee. His left arm seemed little better than it had last night. Had Lawrence the luxury of considering his own situation, he would have been troubled by it. A vampire of his age should not have been so heavily inconvenienced by last night's accident. The injury itself should not have been so serious, and the mending of his bones would have been the work of a few hours, insignificant damage for his body's recuperative powers. In the back of his mind he had taken note of the problem; although he tried to pass it off lightly, the truth was that it made him nervous...very nervous.

For now, though, his concern was focused on his two fuzzy friends. He had taken responsibility for them by the very act of Awakening them; no matter what they did to themselves or each other, he held himself accountable.

As it turned out, Mac had become a culinary snob.

"I don't *want* a damn rat," he'd growled from his place in the casket. Rather than moving him about, pulling him out from under the bed to eat and then sliding him back under like a hide-a-bed for the day, Lawrence had ensconced him safely in the coffin. Lawrence himself had taken shelter on the bathroom floor for the day, as there were no windows in the small, echoing room that might allow a ray of light to pass between the folds of drawn curtains.

"Well, you refuse to feed on people. That plump little maid that works here looked pretty good, and the little bit of blood you'd take from her wouldn't cause her any trouble."

"I told you I will *not* feed on humans! It's wrong! What kind of dog would I be if I did such a thing?"

"A vampire dog, you gimpy fool. And a well-fed one at that." Lady appeared on the open windowsill from the dark night, seemingly out of nowhere. "Just eat the stupid rat if you refuse to munch on the maid. They're pretty good, actually. Thin blood, goes down smooooth." Her small, pink tongue flicked out, as if savoring some flavor still on her lips.

"A common rat may be good enough for the likes of you, Pretty Boots;" Lady hissed at his taunt as she dropped gracefully to the floor from the window; "but feeding off such vermin offends my dignity."

"Ha! Dignity? Yes, dogs are so well known for their dignity! Leg humping, floor wetting, toilet-bowl-water drinking simpletons! You probably didn't even wait for the toilet to be flushed before lapping it out!"

"Enough, you two!" Lawrence was still holding the unconscious rat by its thick tail. "Your constant bickering has already cost me my van, and the rest of my stuff I had in it! Now, do you want this or not?"

"No. Get me a cat. Preferably Siamese or Persian, but just about any short-hair will do in a pinch, I suppose."

"Oh, don't be such a -" Lady began before Lawrence cut her off.

"Alright, I'll get you a cat, but only because you're an invalid. Don't start expecting star treatment, though. It's your own fault you're all busted up." He turned to Lady. "You, too. I'll not put up with another incident like last night. If nothing else, such behavior is undignified." Lady had the sense to look down at her front paws in repentance. Lawrence threw the rat out the open window, turned on his heel and left to get Mac a cat.

A couple hours later, Mac had finished his meal. Lawrence left the cat, a stray shorthair mix, outside. In a few minutes, it would wake up and wander off. This brought a question to Mac's mind, which he relayed to Lawrence. "I was thinking," he began.

"With what?" Lady interjected.

Ignoring his tormentor, Mac continued. "It's one thing to take what you need and let a cat or whatever go, but aren't you afraid that one of your human victims will report you and they'll hunt you down or something?"

Lawrence was standing at the window, looking out on the dark, empty street below. With a cautionary glance at Lady to tell her to shut up, he explained. "That's really not a concern. People don't remember being bitten, and the minor break in the skin caused by our fangs heals incredibly quick, within a couple hours, at the most. I don't know why it works that way but it does, much the same way that feeding puts the victim to sleep."

"What about that skinny guy, the first night? Will he remember you approaching him?"

"Who?"

"Our first night out, you attacked that skinny guy, the one you offered the leftovers to me from. He saw you a second before you bit him. Will he remember that?"

"Oh, yeah. I was moving pretty slow that night. Probably still wasn't recovered from my old wounds, and I'd also just Awakened you two. But yes, whatever causes them to forget what happened causes them to forget the several seconds before we actually bite, so he won't remember anything."

"Old wounds?"

"Nothing major. A couple nights before I Awakened you, I had a feeding go bad on me."

"How so?"

"Well, the guy was pulling out a gun. He had seen me charging him. I wasn't nearly as fast as I should have been, and didn't notice him reaching for it. When I actually bit him, the guy managed to squeeze off a couple shots. Pain in the ass. I didn't even finish feeding, it hurt so much, and the guy only had five bucks on him. Even he shouldn't remember what happened. Maybe just a vague recollection of 'something' happening, but that's it, and even that much is very unlikely. Really, though, you should know all this."

"It's all that toilet water he drank as a mortal," Lady opined. "It messed with his already sub-par canine cerebellum."

"Toilet water? I thought you were both strays?"

"We were. Man's Best Friend here claims to have lived in a home once, though he refuses to say more about it. I think he got kicked to the curb. Probably peed on his owner's bed. You might want to check your coffin before you get back in after he's been in it."

Mac started to get up, yelped in pain, and relaxed again. He stared balefully at Lady. "You'd be better off not talking about things you know nothing about."

"That's enough, you two." Lawrence had learned patience over his five hundred years. When one has decades, centuries or more to accomplish anything one wants, without having to worry about the degenerative effects of aging, one starts to take the long view on everything. Vampires could outwait glaciers, and rarely lost their temper. Patience was a virtue not created for the flaws inherent in mortality. Humans had no idea what true patience was. They might practice it, they might appear to be patient, but time always bore on their thoughts. The undead knew true patience.

Lawrence doubted any mortal could cope patiently with these two.

He stepped away from the window, sat on the bed next to Lady, and absently removed some lint from his pants. He hated having to concern himself with financial matters, but they were preying heavily on his mind now. One of the things he missed - though not nearly as much as he'd missed companionship – was the easy wealth of his youth. Four hundred years of near-poverty had not erased the memories of those early times, and the simple peace of mind that ready cash brought.

But the issue had to be addressed. "Because the van was wrecked, I'm stuck to preying on the poor people in this area, which means less money. If either of you guys can help get us some cash, it would be appreciated."

"I'm not doing anything. I tell you, I refuse to prey on humans!"

"Yeah, yeah, we've heard your whining before." Lady was grooming herself with her raspy tongue. "I'll do what I can, though I can't imagine what I could do."

"Don't you have some antiques from your youth you could sell or something? You're old - you must have accumulated some ancient junk," Mac commented.

"Even had I 'accumulated some ancient junk', it would have been in the van we left smoking on the side of the highway last night."

"Oh."

"Don't worry. Due to some issues of loyalty a few centuries ago, I did not have anything of real value from my youth."

Mac pushed on. "Why don't you just get a job? That seems the most obvious solution to your money problems. And there are night-shift jobs out there."

"I know, and believe me, I've tried. I don't like stealing. It's beneath me. It lacks dignity. And, it's simply wrong. But at any job, you always wind up having to do something during the day: staff meetings, late shifts, something. It never works out."

Mac looked thoughtful. "Lawrence, why even prey on the innocent pedestrians?"

"Because, Mac, if I feed on a cat or dog, I kill it. They don't have enough blood for me. And like you, I don't crave rat-tat-tailie."

"No, that's not what I mean. Why prey on the poor people?"

"I told you, I can't spend the money every night for a cab, and those with lots of money rarely carry it around. Credit cards are no good – too easily traceable, if they're not immediately reported stolen."

"That's not what I mean, either, Lawrence. There are people with wads of money that they carry around with them, right here in the ghetto."

Lawrence's eyes widened as he finally understood what Mac was getting at. "Drug dealers!"

"That's right. And your fears of consuming blood tainted by drugs probably won't matter, because the drug dealers usually don't use the stuff themselves, especially when they're actually dealing."

Lady sat up, her whiskers twitching. "Well, dog, that may actually be a good idea. Lawrence! Mark the date! 'Mac had an idea'!"

"You just can't stand the thought that I may be as clever as you, can you?"

"No, I can't stand the thought. Fortunately, it's not a concern. Your brief flash of inspiration counts for little." She contemplated her white paw. She was holding it in front or her face, her slitted eyes peering closely at it, looking for any signs of dirt. "In fact, I was just thinking the same thing. I must have let my thoughts leak out to you."

"Cut it out, Lady," Lawrence chided her. "That is a very good idea. A little risky, perhaps, as they all seem to be paranoid and armed, and often have somebody watching out for them as well, but I think I'll give it a try."

"There are a couple of them working about five blocks from here." Mac shifted his legs and bit back a whimper. "I'd actually like to go with you on this one, but my legs..."

"Don't worry, Mac. I'm not quite up to snuff tonight, either. I'm not healing these little fractures as quickly as I should, nor moving as fast as usual. Probably tomorrow."

"What's the problem?" Lady asked curiously.

"I don't know. It's the vampire flu, I guess." Lawrence smiled weakly. "Same thing that slowed me down enough for that guy to shoot me. I experienced something similar in the early 1800's. It went away before too long, though. Nothing to worry about."

CHAPTER FOUR

The next evening, Mac was up and perfectly healthy. His leg bones – or the fragments that remained - had knitted together like new, flawlessly aligned. At the same time, the spinal damage (and Lawrence was sure it'd been serious - Mac could neither move nor feel his hind legs or tail) healed just as rapidly, as did his ribs. Lawrence, on the other hand, was still limping. His right knee continued to plague him. His ribs were still a nuisance, and his right arm still bent in unnatural and painful ways if he wasn't careful.

He had passed this off the night before as nothing of concern, whimsically calling it the effects of the "Vampire Flu". Of course, to the best of his knowledge, no such thing existed. He kept to himself his increasing unease over his condition. Lawrence didn't believe the so-called "Vampire Flu" had affected him with such debilitating effects the last time - if indeed it was the same thing - but he'd never been wounded then. Many years stood between now and then, and it was hard to remember just how much he'd been weakened. He couldn't shake the belief that it hadn't been this bad, or that it hadn't lasted as long. If it went on for much longer, he would have to do something about it. Presuming he could think of what that something might be. Finding answers would itself prove a challenge, cut off as he was from the rest of the vampire world. For now, it was enough to tend to practical matters.

They started hunting the drug dealers Thursday, the night after Mac was fully healed, and Lawrence almost completely flubbed their first attempt.

He had taken up his favored position: in an alley. This one was situated near where he'd seen their 'mark' earlier in the evening, plying his trade. The dealer was a heavily tattooed white man. Dollar signs and a woman were prominently displayed on one arm. The other bore the stylized legend "Every day is pay day." Not even his face was left untouched by the artist's needle: there were two teardrops tattooed beneath the corner of his left eye.

Lady had already fed and was off somewhere scouting future prospects for Lawrence. She had suggested this one last night after noting that he worked alone and followed a fairly predictable routine. Mac had not yet fed. He planned to do so once Lawrence finished here, apparently feeling the need to ensure that Lawrence behaved himself. Mac may not have liked the drug dealers, but they were still human, and worthy of some protection from the beasts of the night.

Mac sat quietly next to one of many overflowing trash cans by the mouth of the alley, where he could watch the proceedings. Lawrence said nothing of the issue, but was of the opinion that Mac did not believe his assertion that he didn't kill his victims, and wanted to confirm the fact personally.

"What do you think, Mac? He should be done soon. Last customer was twenty minutes ago." It was 2:30 a.m., and Lawrence had been standing, waiting since about midnight with the patience of a statue. Lady had left about an hour after their arrival, and with her went Lawrence's best conversation. Mac was not much of a talker this evening.

"Yeah. Soon." Brief though this response was, that was the most Mac had spoken in the last hour and a half. Before that, Lady would simply goad him into joining the conversation, but he'd maintained an almost monastic silence since she went off.

Sure enough, not two minutes later Mac perked up his ears and simply stated, "He's leaving."

Without thinking, Lawrence verbalized, "What?" before reverting back to the secure silence of the telepathic link. "How close is he? I can't hear him."

Mac listened, his head cocked, for just a moment before answering. "He's walking away."

Lawrence quickly moved to the corner of the abandoned store abutting the alley and peeked his head cautiously around. "Damn!" He brushed his hand through his hair and took a quick look around for any possible witnesses. Seeing none, he stepped briskly from the alley, doing his best to ignore his knee's grinding reaction to his swift movements. He had running shoes on, and was treading as lightly as he could while still closing the gap between the tattooed dealer and himself.

Mac, who was following silently and easily behind Lawrence, chuckled to himself at the sight. Lawrence was placing his feet with cautious but rapid deliberation, trying to walk silently. On top of that, he still had a significant limp from the accident in his van - probably part of the reason he was taking such care in his walking. All in all, it was the most amusing walk Mac had ever seen a human do; to Mac's eye Lawrence resembled a stork walking with one leg significantly shorter than the other.

Then the whole situation became very unamusing.

Lawrence was about fifteen feet from his target when the man turned around. Whether Lawrence had somehow made a noise, or the dealer had just succumbed to the usual paranoia that gripped those engaged in illegal activities, it didn't matter. What mattered was that the man glanced back at an inopportune moment to see Lawrence rushing up behind him. His guard was instantly up, and Lawrence had no option but to charge.

The dealer knew how to fight. He had to: his line of work demanded it. Sometimes it came down to kill or be killed. Lawrence was no slouch, either. He'd picked up a thing or two in the last several centuries, and though they were not what they'd been just weeks ago, his superhuman speed and strength still far outstripped a normal man.

Lawrence managed to plow into the man, shoulder first, while the thug was still reaching for something under his silk shirt. Both men fell to the ground, Lawrence on top. The dealer seemed to be unaware that Lawrence was not trying so much to pummel him as to sink his hungry fangs into his opponent.

The human, however, was doing everything he could to regain the upper hand. Punching, pushing, kicking, squirming, rolling, he could not get Lawrence off of him. Neither could he reach his gun, which is what Lawrence felt sure was under the shirt. Lawrence was trying to get a good bite, but the way his adversary was moving, his fangs would literally shred wherever he bit before the power would calm the man's frantic movements.

It was only a matter of time before the man hit one of Lawrence's all too many weak spots. Lawrence had been doing a surprisingly good job keeping his clumsy, broken arm out of the fray and his bad knee from banging into the sidewalk. There was little he could do about his chest, though, and the human inevitably landed a punch there. A good, solid hit to his left side, directly on two of his three broken ribs.

The dealer saw he'd scored a good hit by the widening of Lawrence's eyes. Seizing the advantage he'd acquired, he used his legs to flip the vampire over his head. With Lawrence no longer holding him down, he was finally able to jump to his feet and draw his weapon.

He neither saw nor heard Mac until the dog had his jaws clamped around his outstretched arm. The tattooed arm was pulled down by Mac's weight as the gun fired, causing it to miss its vampiric target. Lawrence looked up as the stray bullet chipped the pavement next to his arm. The dealer was shaking his arm in an unsuccessful attempt to free himself of the dog's toothy grip.

Mustering all his energy, Lawrence pulled himself to his feet as swiftly as he was able and launched himself at the momentarily distracted dealer, grabbing the man's head to clear the way to his neck. A few moments after Lawrence's fangs pierced flesh, the man stopped struggling, his sudden slackness giving him the appearance of being under the influence of his own product.

Lawrence lowered the unconscious dealer to the ground before sinking to the pavement himself in exhaustion and pain. Once there, he pulled the human half onto his lap and finished his feeding.

A human's lifeblood was a vampire's key to life. It was everything a human took in - food, drink, sunlight, vitamins, minerals; all the energy a person took in by day, those of the shadows had to take by night. Some vampires took time to acquire a taste for the thick, salty sustenance. At Lawrence's age, he no longer savored the flavor he'd learned to enjoy centuries before. Even the most exquisitely seasoned, palate-pleasing food will grow stale when nothing else is available year after year, and Lawrence had fed on nothing but human blood for five hundred years.

Different humans had subtle undertones of variety in their taste. Now, Lawrence relished only the sensation of power, of pure, unbridled energy that flowed with the currents of the blood. The pleasure of the palate may have disappeared, but one could never truly tire of the feeling of inward rushing power that accompanied a feeding.

Tonight, it was not enough. He pushed the man's limp form off his lap, letting the human sprawl unconscious on the cracked sidewalk before him. Missing the usual flush of power after a feeding, Lawrence lay back on the ground next to his victim.

Besides being exhausted and hurt, he was angry. Not at his victim or at Mac, but at himself for his string of failures and weakness. The sooner this weak spell was over, the better, but it still seemed to be getting progressively worse. It could very well be the true death of him if his condition didn't improve soon; if Mac hadn't been around to distract the dealer, the street thug could have emptied his pistol into Lawrence. In his weakened state, with his regenerative abilities so retarded, it was conceivable that he would have been rendered unconscious or immobile by the sheer quantity of damage he would have taken. When the sun peeked up some hours later, it would have been his end.

He had barely enough energy for the shudder he gave at the thought of such an unpleasant chain of events.

Mac stood looking from human to vampire before nuzzling Lawrence's good arm. "C'mon, Lawrence. We need to go before this guy gets up."

"We should have at least five minutes," Lawrence moaned in reply.

"I don't know. I already saw him moving. We better get going."

The human groaned. Doing his best not to mimic the sounds coming from the almost still form before him, Lawrence climbed unsteadily to his feet. He held his wounded hand protectively against his front. He shambled the few steps to the slowly waking man and bent over to run his hands through the human's pockets, looking for the money he knew was there. Finding the tightly rolled stack of bills in the dealer's pants, Lawrence started off for the relative safety of the alley.

"Wait a minute, Lawrence," Mac requested. Lawrence paused and turned towards Mac, who was still sitting next to the moaning dealer. "Grab his leftover drugs for me, please. It's kinda hard to do without hands."

Giving Mac a questioning look but saying nothing, Lawrence did as Mac asked, and placed the six baggies containing the vile mixtures on the ground in front of him. Three contained a white powder, two contained something that looked like oregano, and the sixth contained several pills. Mac picked up all six bags in his jaws, trotted over to the curb, and dropped them into the storm drain there.

"Now we can go." He glanced over to where the dealer's eyes were beginning to move beneath their eyelids. "We'd better hurry, too. That 'five minutes' seems to be disappearing more quickly than five minutes should." Even as he said this, he went over to sniff at the man, unconsciously letting out a quiet whimper.

"Come on, Mac. You're right, he's waking up quick. He'll be alright." Without replying, Mac trotted after him.

* * *

Later, in the pre-dawn hours, Lawrence was telling Lady about his first attempt against the dealers. He was lying on the bed, exhausted. Lady was sitting on the closed coffin, listening to Lawrence speak. Mac was sitting on a chair next to the grimy window, looking out at the street below their room. He was doing his best to ignore Lawrence and the looks Lady was casting his way. It had taken Lawrence a while to get the whole story out. He insisted on actually speaking it aloud, which required air, which thereby required inflating his lungs against the broken and re-injured ribs. Because of the discomfort, he took his time relating the tale.

"So, the dog saved the day," Lady mused. "Wow, Mac, you're a regular Lassie, aren't you?"

"Watch it, cat. I won't be as gentle with you as I was with the drug dealer. I can snap your spine if I wanted."

Lady meowed shrilly, echoing it derisively in her thoughts. "Meow. Aren't we catty tonight! I don't know what you're so angry about."

"I do," Lawrence called from the bed. He swung his feet ponderously down onto the floor and stood up. Slowly, he limped over to where Mac was sitting. "Thanks, Mac. You may not have saved my life, but you certainly saved me a lot of pain." He winced as he stepped wrong on his bad knee. "A lot more pain, anyway. And with this Vampire Flu or whatever, I don't even want to think about how long I'd have been laid up, especially on top of the wounds I already have." He didn't mention the worst-case scenario he'd tortured himself with earlier; no need to sow such doom and gloom unnecessarily among his two friends.

Mac looked up at him, the expression on his canine face neutral, and then returned his gaze to the window.

Lawrence continued, telepathically this time. "And I appreciate it all the more because I can understand what it took for you to make even that minor attack on a human. Especially to help a vampire." He put his hand lightly on Mac's head, the briefest pat before turning back to the bed. "I saw his arm. You did fine, Mac. However, you did it, you exhibited incredible control. You barely broke the skin, and even that didn't look like you got him with your fangs."

"What did you just say, Lawrence? I didn't catch it," Lady asked from her perch atop the casket.

"You weren't meant to."

"Whatever." She stood up and hopped lightly to the floor. "Listen. Until you're not so pathetically weak, we should make a few changes in the way you're hunting these guys."

"Okay. What're you thinking?"

* * *

Jamon took another pull on his cigarette and took it out of his mouth, looking at it distastefully. He hated these things, but they were part of the image. When he started, he had been afraid he might grow addicted to the slender cancer sticks, but so far he retained his distaste for them. They were still better than the death he was standing here dealing, though.

He dropped the butt and smashed the spark out of it with his foot. He was a tall man, a shade over six feet. He almost looked as though he'd been stretched, with his lanky frame and long face. His hair was the shade commonly called dishwater blond, and hung just past his shoulders, frequently falling forward to frame his face before he tucked it back behind his ears again. Its light shade matched the paleness of his face. He blamed his rather white skin on all the nights he spent working, leaving him to sleep most of the daylight hours away.

The streets were empty. He was done. For the night, anyway. It appeared people had better things to do on a Tuesday night. Nobody had been by at all in the last thirty minutes, save a black cat. He didn't care much for cats - he was a dog person, though he hadn't had any pets at all since high school. Of course, even cats had enough sense not to touch the toxic shit he was slinging. People could be so stupid.

As he pondered the lack of sense of it all, he patted himself, preparatory to leaving his post. Gun: in place. Cash: in place. Leftover drugs: in place.

Something caught the corner of his eye and he glanced over towards the movement as he made his way down the dimly lit sidewalk to his car. Just a cat. He peered closer. Yeah, the same cat he'd seen earlier, in fact. It was sitting on the hood of some beat-up old station wagon. Freaky critter, it was watching him rather intently, keeping its eyes locked on him as he passed.

It wasn't just that its eyes followed him that gave Jamon the creeps. It seemed more...well, just more. More catlike, he supposed. And, as the cat watched him, there was a part of him, deep down, that recoiled in fear. Some ancient part of his spirit was terrified of the waves of power emanating from this dead animal.

What? Waves of power? Dead animal? Where the hell were these thoughts coming from? The cat was most obviously not dead, and was no more powerful than his aunt's tabby. Damn, he was overtired tonight. Just a stupid cat.

Still, the fear was there. No, Jamon wasn't afraid of the cat, only some long neglected part of him was. Which was silly. It was a cat. Fear of a rottweiler? Okay. Fear of a pussy cat? Stupid. He patted his gun, still under his long black jacket.

He felt no safer.

Later on, at first, he'd blame it on the cat. He kept looking back at the creature, and one time, as he turned back around to watch where he was walking –

He woke up slowly, looking at the dark sky. What the hell? Trash bins? Where was he?

He sat up, his long arms propping him up, and looked about in confusion.

His mind seemed a bit...muddled. He could tell he wasn't thinking clearly.

The last he remembered was...a cat? Yeah, the cat! And now he's... in an alley?

A surge of panic gripped him, and he reached in his jacket.

Ah. His gun was still there. He patted it like an old, reliable pet. That would have been *big* trouble. But wait a minute. He patted his other pockets. Shit! Gone! The whole damn roll! Over twenty-five hundred bucks! And the last of the drugs he hadn't sold tonight, gone too!

Strange. As quickly as he was recovering, he couldn't have been drugged, yet he wasn't sore anywhere either, so he didn't think he'd been beaten.

He paused a moment, taking stock of himself, trying to figure out just what was going on. Something wet, trickling down his neck. He reached up to touch it and his fingers came away wet. It was hard to make out what it was, in this light. He sniffed it, touched it to his lips hesitantly. Blood? He was bleeding? He stood up slowly, continuing the constant, though unsteady, observation of his surroundings. Had somebody hit him with a tranquilizer gun? That didn't feel right. He checked his watch. It was a fashionable Movado, as he had to look the part; it was still on his wrist – the thief hadn't taken it. Hmmm. 2:49. He'd been out for five minutes, at the most. Didn't seem like any tranq he knew of.

Jamon stepped out into the street and walked down to his car. That too was right where he'd left it. He hit his key-fob, de-activating the alarm, and slid into the BMW, a loan from across town. One of the perks of this job, as long as it lasted.

He tilted the rearview mirror, angling his head to get a look at his neck. Light. He reached over and hit the dome light. Yeah, blood. Not a lot. He popped the glove box and pulled a couple napkins out. After blotting out the worst of the blood, he resumed his inspection. Two darts? This just didn't make sense. He'd have to review tonight's surveillance video as soon as he got back to the apartment.

* * *

Lawrence and Lady made their way leisurely back to the Biltmore. Lady had fed her hunger several hours ago, but Mac had yet to return from his own feeding, which he still preferred to do alone.

Lawrence finished counting the cash as they strolled along the dark streets. "Well, there's another twenty-five hundred," he informed Lady.

She was a bit ahead of Lawrence, and had stopped to stand with her front paws on a storefront window, letting the glass support her. "So, what's the plan? Is that enough yet?" She didn't look at him, her eyes perusing the contents of the darkened drug store. Her tail waved lazily in the air behind her. She couldn't see them, but her extra-sensitive ears picked up dozens of mice scurrying around in the secured building.

"Yeah, it's enough." He gave the bars on the window a pejorative glance as he passed by Lady de Winter's position. "We'll be out of this neighborhood right soon. Tomorrow evening, first thing, I'm getting us a new car. Well, not *brand* new, but certainly better than the van was. Then, we check ourselves into a respectable hotel uptown. No more slumming it." He drew in a breath to whistle a tune; he was feeling pretty good. The last few nights had worked themselves out smoothly. This had been their sixth night working as a team in this fashion. Lady had pointed out that cats, as a rule, do not draw suspicion on the street. She could sit out in plain view and no one would really be concerned. Then, with her telepathic link to Lawrence, she could tell him exactly when to strike. He didn't have to watch his victim at all. This more than made up for the disadvantage engendered by Lawrence's still bothersome injuries.

It worked even better than they'd planned. Three nights ago, the dealer had walked off in an unexpected direction, as had happened the first neardisastrous night with Mac. Lady had simply followed him, telling Lawrence where to intercept. When Lawrence said he needed a few more seconds to get back into position, she'd run ahead of the human and stood in his path, hissing angrily at him and easily dodging his pitiful attempts to kick her out of his way. Her supernatural speed made the oncoming boot seem no more than a gentle foot trying to nudge her aside. Easily avoided. There had been no major problems like he'd had on his first attempt.

Lady ran back up alongside Lawrence. Somehow, she made it seem like no more than a casual trot, as though Lawrence had slowed down to wait for her. "And that stupid dog, with all his needless worrying," she commented

"Mac? What was he worried about?" They turned the corner, and could now see the Biltmore, looming at them in all its neglected misery.

"I don't know. He'd gone with me last night when I was scouting our next target. He can be of some use, at times, and I like to indulge him on occasion. Anyway, I found the guy we hit tonight, and Mac said 'No'."

"He said no? Why?"

"I don't know. He mumbled something about the guy smelling bad. Didn't make any sense. Hell, I thought the guy smelled better than most."

Lawrence was just about to ask how Mac could mumble telepathically when Mac spoke up, seemingly out of nowhere. "I said he smelled *wrong,* not bad, you annoying feline."

Lady turned her head sharply, her ears rotating, swiveling atop her head like radar. "See, Lawrence, the problem with this telepathy thing is that you don't always know where the sender is, so you don't know where to claw."

"Well, you stupid cat, if you could rely on that underdeveloped schnozz of yours instead of those twitchy ears, maybe you wouldn't have such trouble."

Lawrence stopped in the sidewalk. "Enough, you two. Come on out, Mac, and please tell me what you meant about the dealer smelling 'wrong'."

Mac appeared from behind a car parked about ten feet ahead of them, looked at Lady, and then pointedly looked away. "I don't know, really, how to describe it in English," he stated.

"Ah, the problems of having a monosyllabic vocabulary."

"Knock it off, Lady," Lawrence commanded automatically, not taking his eyes or attention off of Mac. "Please, Mac, try to explain." He began walking again. Mac fell in on his left, opposite Lady.

"Well, certain things have certain smells, even beyond their individual smells." At Lawrence's puzzled look, he explained. "Okay, for example. If we ever see another vampire -"

"Let's hope not," Lawrence murmured.

"- I'll know him to be one, just by his smell. It's a smell I can label 'vampire'. All vampires have it, under their personal scent. To me, it's like a cross between recent death, a very powerfully charismatic person, and a heavy electrical discharge. That sounds kind of odd, I know, but the three of us have that smell, and I know, by instinct or whatever, that all other vampires do, too."

"Is this how it's always been? I mean, even when you were a normal dog? Not a vampire?"

Mac considered the question for a moment. "No, not really. No. Definitely not. It seems to have something to do with my enhanced senses."

"Okay. So, this drug dealer," Lawrence prompted as they climbed the stairs to their room.

"Yeah, spit it out," Lady contributed.

"Lady, enough. Please, Mac."

"Right, Lawrence. Anyway, drug dealers also have a specific smell. Maybe it's somehow tied into the actual drugs they sell, I don't know. Like I said, I don't claim to understand it. But this guy, he just didn't have that smell."

"Could he have been new to the business?"

They were back in the room. Lawrence had taken off his shoes and sat down on the bed. Lady hopped up to curl around herself on the casket lid, and Mac was sitting on the floor in front of Lawrence. "Well, I suppose it's possible," he began hesitantly, "but he had a different scent on him. I couldn't place it at first. It's kinda reminiscent of oak, with a hint of bear, and a little touch of blue."

"Blue? And how do you know what a bear smells like?"

"Hard to explain. Just... smells like blue. And I just seem to know some scents. Anyway, there's a few other scents thrown in, but those are the major ones. But definitely not the smell of a drug dealer. I really have no idea what that scent is, but it's somehow familiar."

* * *

Stephanie checked herself out before heading out the door. She hoped to turn at least a couple heads tonight, and she'd dressed with that goal in mind. She didn't like to completely expose herself the way some of those kids did, but she had yet to spend any evening in any club dancing alone.

She was keeping it pretty simple tonight: denim skirt, see-through white blouse over a blue tank-top, and flats. She'd considered heels, especially with this skirt, to show off her slender legs a bit more, but she hated dancing in them.

She wasn't vain, not by any stretch, but she could have been, as she was quite attractive. She wore only about 117 pounds on her thin, five foot six frame. Her caramel skin could almost be mistaken for a dark tan in the dim light of the clubs, a gift of her mixed black and Caucasian heritage. It gave her an appealingly exotic look, combining well with her almost innocent looking wide brown eyes. Her thick black hair hung just past her shoulders. When she was going out, which was most nights, she pressed it straight with a slight inward curve at the bottom. She was quite thin, but not unhealthy; when she wished to wear the clothing to reveal it, as tonight, her body curved very elegantly in all the right places, drawing a steady wave of appreciative looks. Her slightly rounded face seemed just wide enough to contain her broad smile. She flashed one of these now, thinking of the evening ahead of her.

Satisfied with her attire, she stepped out of her house and into her garage. She locked the door behind her and slid into her car.

Stephanie usually went to the club a couple of times a week. After all, what good was being eternally young if you didn't have some fun with it? Of course, the music and dance and so much else had changed in the years since she'd been Awakened, but she was adaptable. She sometimes missed her own generation's music being played at the clubs, but the modern stuff was quite fun too, once you got used to it. Well, except for the country.

The clubs were also good places to feed, as long as she stuck with the designated drivers so as to avoid absorbing the alcohol of those that were drinking. Sit in a booth with him, and her feeding looked like just another young couple making out. When he woke up, she could either be gone and leave him - or her, she wasn't picky - wondering, or she could tell him he'd fainted from the heat and activity of the busy club. Often, her target had snuck in a nip or two of alcohol. The little bit may not have affected the victim, but was usually enough to give her a pleasant buzz.

Other thoughts were on her mind tonight, though. Specifically, the Dream she'd had today. The only real question now, though, was what to do about it. The Dreams were her Calling. They didn't happen often, but when they did, she paid attention.

Usually, vampires don't dream. Hers were not exactly dreams, either; more in the line of 'visions', or precognition; but she preferred the term 'Dream'. As a vampire, she no longer had normal dreams. These allowed her, in her mind at least, some link to her lost mortality. Not that she regretted her choice. She enjoyed the advantages, even as an unlawful vampire. Who was the Council to say she could exist or not, anyway? Bunch of ancient, out-of-touch bastards, from what she'd learned of them.

She was ever only able to interpret perhaps a quarter of her Dreams before the events they foretold came to pass. This Dream she largely understood, and it definitely indicated grave danger. A danger which seemed to be coming from three different sources.

One, to her mind the most disturbing, was a hand reaching out. The disturbing part was the rot that covered the hand and wrist: all she could see in her unnatural Dream. The flesh was largely eaten through, and she'd heard wet, plopping sounds as flesh and tissue dropped away from the decaying appendage. The stench of it had been unbearable; she had almost been sick upon waking.

From another direction came a threat she easily recognized. In the dream, it was represented by a braying black hound with only one good eye; the other was just an empty socket. The hound was kept under rein by a very tenuous-looking leash reaching back into the unseen darkness. That one was easy enough to interpret. The Council would soon be unleashing their assassins again.

The third was a complete enigma, and a seeming contradiction. It was a blue shield, and was providing protection from both of the other two threats, alternately. Yet at the same time, the inner surface of the shield was covered with dozens of razor-sharp blades, threatening to destroy even that which it protected.

The individual in the midst of this tangle of danger was no mystery at all. The Council had been after Lawrence for hundreds of years. He'd been able to elude them surprisingly well so far, but she felt sure he'd be needing her help soon. She only hoped she'd know when it was time to return to him.

She buckled herself in and drove off for the club, thoughts of rotting arms squelching unnervingly through her mind.

CHAPTER FIVE

Jamon entered his apartment, locked his door, and put his keys on the key-shaped key rack hanging on the wall by the door. As he walked into the kitchen, he set down the black briefcase he'd carried in and opened the refrigerator. He pulled out a carton of orange juice, turned around and grabbed a glass from the cupboard. He opened the orange juice and stared at the clean glass, then chugged his refreshment straight from the carton, glaring at the glass as though daring it to deride this uncultured behavior. It was too early in the morning to mess with a glass, and besides, he decided to finish off the carton anyway. He felt drained, and the O.J. really hit the spot.

Jamon tossed the empty carton in the trash, picked the briefcase back up, and tossed his wallet on the counter as he walked into his living room. The wallet fell open as it landed. On one side, you could see his driver's license, stating his name, Jamon Schroeder. On the other side, reflecting the kitchen lights on its polished surface, was Detective Schroeder's badge, Twelfth Precinct.

Out of the briefcase and into the player went the memory stick. Detective Jamon Schroeder - now off duty - settled back into his recliner and hit play on the remote. The time/date stamp at the bottom of the screen indicated the start time of 6:41 p.m. The tiny camera itself was located in the wheel well of an old car which had no wheels; it was propped up on blocks and standing silent sentry just down the block from 'his' corner. The camera sent its signal, via radio frequency, to the actual recorder hidden in Jamon's car. He had to ensure his car was parked within about two blocks of the device, with no significant obstructions, like buildings. Or so he'd been told by the tech guys down at the station.

He skipped forward to the end of the recording, to where he had 'closed' for the night. There he was, walking down the sidewalk. He could see the cat already on the TV...and himself, looking at the cat. Watching the cat, only checking where he was walking for brief moments. Still watching that damn cat, then –

There! Some guy, right out of the shadows! What the hell was he doing? Was it a woman? A gay man? Just for a second, he seemed to be trying to kiss Jamon's neck or something before dragging him into the alley.

Rewind it a bit, take another look. In slow motion this time. Walking along, watching the cat...There he is, coming out of the alley like a dark ghost, right behind Jamon... Grabs him... Pulls the head back... and... What? A kiss? It's definitely a man. Gay? And then, the Jamon on the screen begins to go slack, and the guy drags him back into the alley.

Jamon paused the playback and closed his eyes to think. There was no doubt he'd been given some sort of drug. But what? And how? He hadn't seen any point on the video where he'd been hit by anything.

Wait a minute.

He opened his eyes and replayed the scene of the guy kissing his neck. Does he think he's some kind of vampire or something? Jamon had dealt with those odd kids who dressed all in black and played those goofy games before. They were usually harmless, but could he be one of them? He'd dressed the part, all the dark clothes, but that could just be to make himself less visible in the night. Hard to tell if he's opening his mouth to bite instead of kiss. Perhaps he wore some specially made fangs containing a small amount of some narcotic.

Jamon pulled himself out of his recliner and walked to his tiny bathroom to check the spacing on the two neck wounds. He moistened a washcloth to clean the small trickle of dried blood that remained on his neck. Just as he'd seen earlier, two small wounds about an inch apart. Not too bad. They looked a day old, actually, closing up already.

It fit, however. Just the right spacing for some of those Halloween fangs. Well, he supposed that solved one aspect.

He smacked himself on the head with the palm of his hand. He should have gone straight down to the precinct's labs. Let them get some blood to find out what he'd been hit with. He was not thinking straight tonight. Shouldn't be too late to do it anyway; he'd bring in today's surveillance at the same time. Let the tech guys see if they could match the guy's face to any of the files.

He walked out to get the memory stick and go.

* * *

"Whaddya think of the new wheels, kids?"

Lady and Mac looked at each other, their attitudes in sync this one time. Kids?

Lawrence had gone out when he woke to pick up a vehicle he'd seen in the paper. Upon returning, he'd merely spoken their name from the street, but that was plenty loud enough for their supersensitive ears. They had come down from the room to see him standing next to a truck. The truck was obviously not the only purchase he'd made tonight. Lawrence had replaced his discount duds with a new wardrobe. Gone were his cotton shirt and beige slacks. He was now a new man, looking much more comfortable, even natural, in a sharp suit. Fit for a night on the town, and conspicuously out of place in their current locale, much like the truck itself.

"Well, it's certainly... big," Lady noted. And it was. In addition to being a large SUV, a Suburban, it had extra-large wheels, making the vehicle ride perhaps nine inches higher than was normal. It was pure black, even the rims and front grille. "But you look much more presentable in your new clothes. I approve."

"Yeah, yeah. You do look better," Mac conceded. "Of course, getting rid of your slouch helped, too." Lady and Lawrence both looked at Mac in surprise.

"He's right," Lady reflected, returning her attention to Lawrence. "You were slouching. It's like you'd been carrying a weight for some time. I hadn't noticed."

"See what a little money'll do for a human's self esteem?"

Lawrence looked at Mac appraisingly. "Very astute, Mac, and very true. But, it takes more than money." He turned back to the Suburban. "As for the truck, I'd thought about buying something fast and sporty. I even had just the car in mind, a little red thing. But there'd be no room to haul my coffin, so I decided I'd stick with a truck. I saw this, and decided it may as well be a nice one. I was so tired of that minivan."

Mac nodded, his tail wagging easily in approval. "I like it. I hope you've still got enough money to get us out of this dump? The smell is really starting to get to me."

"Indeed I do, Mac. In fact, I already made our reservations at the Hyatt, downtown." He made a theatrical bow, one arm extended towards the truck. "Shall we go?" The animals climbed in, and within the hour they were packed and on the way to their new, temporary digs.

As they pulled into a vacant parking space in the Hyatt's underground parking area, Mac wondered, "Are they gonna let us in?"

Lawrence shut off the truck. "I had to pay a bit extra, but yes, it's all taken care of. Now, we just have to get the coffin up to the room."

"You and that stupid, obsolete coffin. What floor are we on?"

Lawrence looked at his key card as he walked to the back of the truck. "Room 512, so fifth floor. And unlike you guys, I need to use a coffin. If a human vampire goes too long without one, he weakens steadily." He paused, looking at his coffin in the back of the Suburban. "Even at this hour, there's too much chance of being caught in the elevator with this thing, so I guess it's the stairs again." Lawrence pulled it out of the truck and settled it as well as he could to rest on his back. "It's good to not have any wounds slowing me down for a change. Lead on Lady, Mac. Blaze the trail!" he said jauntily, as he sauntered over towards the stairway.

As they hit the first floor landing, Lawrence commented, "This vampire flu thing is really getting annoying. This little thing seems to weigh five times what it should."

By the time they reached the fifth floor, his energy was visibly flagging. Mac couldn't resist. "Your old age and evil ways finally catching up with you?" Lawrence was too beat to even offer a reply. Fortunately, Lady and Mac both knew what needed to be done (Lawrence didn't even think of issuing the commands mentally), and listened very attentively for any of the human noises that might indicate someone entering the hall from their rooms.

Once Lawrence got the coffin situated to his liking, he fell into the hardback chair at the room's desk and they all took in their new surroundings. It was a single suite, with a king-size bed, desk, recliner, 32 inch TV, a separate kitchenette and spacious bathroom. Everything was spotlessly clean and looked new. The wallpaper was a tasteful light blue, with an abstract pattern for trim, and a generic, anonymous, but eye-pleasing print hanging on the wall. The ambient lighting could be a subtle night-light to near-daylight conditions. Lawrence kept it at a very low level; none of them needed more than starlight to see, and the moon served them as well as daylight serves a mortal.

"Much better. You're finally living up to at least one promise, Larry." Mac's tail wagged slowly as he investigated the room, his nose probing everywhere he could fit it.

Lawrence winced. "Please, Mac. It's Lawrence."

"I hear mice. And maybe some rats. That settles it. This place gets my five star rating," Lady decided. "In fact, gentlemen, I'm feeling a bit peckish. I'm going to see what I can round up."

"I'm going to head out to the city to feed. I'll probably hit that last dealer you scouted out. Sure you don't want to go?"

"No, I'd like to check this place out a bit more. Why don't you go to-morrow? Hit one of the guests here for tonight?"

"I want to get some cash. I blew most of the last of it on this room. We've got it for five days, but I prefer to have some extra, just in case. Besides, I'm trying to get enough to get us at least a nice apartment again. Something more permanent." He got up, heading for the door. "No big deal. Mac, would you do me a favor and be my look-out tonight?"

Before Mac could reply, Lady hopped down from the coffin top, quickly but casually, tail held straight up. "Don't worry, Mac. I'll take care of it. You can go find yourself some poor cat or whatever it is you do."

* * *

"I just don't see anything abnormal, Jamon." The lab tech was dressed in a typical white lab coat. No matter where you were, if there was a lab of any sort, its workers would be wearing a white lab coat. It seemed too silly to be anything more than a lame stereotype, but it was the truth. Jamon never saw the reason for it. Why white? Why not blue? If you presumed the coat was to protect your clothes from chemical spills or other accidents, wouldn't blue protect you just as well? Actually, blue would be quite well suited, here. It would match the blonde tech's eyes perfectly. He shook himself, mentally. No good, Jamon. Forget it; you'll just bring yourself trouble this soon after the divorce. Still, though, why the white? It made no sense to Jamon.

"There must be *something*," Jamon objected. "I was out for five minutes. Some kind of drug. Is it possible it left no traces?"

"How long before you got to the lab?"

Jamon checked the clock on his desk. Sara had been kind enough to bring her results by before heading home for the day. She worked the night shift, as did he. She claimed she hadn't been the one to actually run the tests - the day shift had done that - but that it would be no problem to stop by and interpret the results for him; the daytime guys hadn't gotten around to filing their report yet. He was still dressed in his 'pimp duds', as he called them, for his undercover drug sting. His long hair, sharp blue silk shirt, expensive slacks (he didn't know the name - just how much they cost. It was on the precinct's tab). The shoes alone cost as much as his entire wardrobe at home, but they weren't new, they had come out of confiscated goods. They looked just like any other pair of shoes to Jamon – why anyone would spend thousands of dollars for a pair of shoes was beyond him. They weren't even good for running in, which he figured would be a large concern on the streets.

The clock on his desk told him nothing. It was yesterday morning that he'd come in for the blood test. "I think it was about three hours, at most."

"Well, Jamon, the only thing that seems abnormal is your hemoglobin. It's a bit low."

"What's that mean?"

She reviewed the printout she held. "Nothing much, really. It was just a little low, which can sometimes indicate a slightly depleted blood volume. Kind of like you were a bit dehydrated, hadn't been drinking enough fluids, that sort of thing. Nothing really abnormal."

Jamon sat back and pondered this for a moment. He looked up at the sound of Sara clearing her throat. "Sorry, Sara. I guess that covers all my questions, unless you can think of anything useful."

"Not really, unless you can give me some more idea of what happened to make you think you were drugged. It'd give me some idea of what to look for."

He paused. He was trying to keep the circumstances to himself as much as possible. It was a bit embarrassing, in more ways than one. "Well, I think I was attacked. I woke up in an alley, but I don't have any recollection of getting into a fight."

"Oh. Well, you *can* pass out if you get too dehydrated, but these numbers don't really indicate that kind of problem."

"Okay. Thanks, Sara."

"Well, if you need anything else, you know where to find me. Good luck." She gave a little wave and turned to go. Jamon watched her back as she walked off until he realized what he was doing and forced himself to look down at the reports piled on his desk. This mishap was causing him all sorts of paperwork. The loss of money, the loss of the drugs, not to mention the incident itself. He was lucky he had the disc backing up what he claimed. Even then, there could have been suspicion cast on him. His solid reputation and the fact that it was just too weird for him to have tried to pull off helped in that respect.

The report from the A/V techs lay on top of his other reports. Preliminary report, he corrected himself. They were having trouble extracting a good image of his assailant's face from the footage. They'd had no luck matching him to anyone in their files so far, but were still working on it. They couldn't even call it an assault yet. No evidence of physical violence, no drugs; in fact, you could almost make a case, looking at the video, saying the guy had arrived just in time to keep Jamon from falling to the ground. Not quite, really, but it could still hardly be called an assault. They didn't even have footage of the stranger actually robbing Jamon.

He started shutting down his computer in preparation for leaving for the day. As he closed his active programs, he saw that the IT guys had set up a new background for his computer screen. It was a still frame of Bela Lugosi in "Dracula". Cute. Another reason why he didn't want this getting out to the rest of the staff. Unfortunately, there wasn't much he could do to stop it, as they had the video of the incident. That kid was going to answer, not only for his theft, but the humiliation Jamon was enduring as well. Punk kids.

* * *

Two Dreams in the same week. That had never before happened in all the time Stephanie had been a vampire. This almost confirmed her belief that Lawrence's situation was soon to come to a head. The Dream's message seemed even more straightforward: it was time to renew contact with Lawrence. That shouldn't be a problem. She'd kept tabs on him, without his knowledge of course, for the past twenty-five years or so.

When she got to his apartment, however, he wasn't there. His minivan wasn't in the lot and he didn't seem to be home. After waiting in her car for three hours she began to grow concerned as a nagging suspicion slowly filled her thoughts. She walked upstairs again to knock on his door, a last gesture she knew to be futile as she'd have seen him come in.

Back downstairs, she strolled around the building to stand beneath where she knew his apartment to be. She first peered up at its dark windows, and then looked down at herself.

In anticipation of seeing Lawrence again, she'd spent two nervous hours choosing an outfit to wear. She'd settled on a figure flattering, but elegant, red dress with matching heels. She now regretted the choice. Not because it didn't highlight her best physical attributes - the best and fastest way to any man's heart - for it did that with flair. The red contrasted strikingly with her light chocolate skin. No, the problem was that her attire was simply not suited to climbing.

Now was not the time to change, though. She had spent too much time feeding and waiting for Lawrence. Her stolen blood was telling her of the sun's coming. It wasn't about to crest the horizon or anything, but she still had to get home, which was on the other side of town.

As she cast a quick glance around for any early risers, she kicked off her shoes and stepped onto the four foot wide strip of grass that bordered each apartment building, the only concession to aesthetics.

She took one more step to the wall, still looking up at the window. At the wall, she examined the surface in front of her. It was red brick with deep, thick joins, so would provide plenty of foot- and toe-holds, and was easily strong enough to hold her.

With the ease of a mortal climbing a ladder, she scaled the wall up to Lawrence's window. Had someone seen her ascent, they might have likened it to a lizard climbing a wall. With a combination of extraordinary strength, cat-like balance, eyes that could pick out every useful feature of the wall by the dim, stuttering lights of the complex, and constantly adjusting reflexes, she was up the ten feet to the window in a matter of seconds. She lifted her head cautiously above the sill, peering in, feeling a bit like a peeping tom.

Empty.

Her suspicion confirmed, she pushed lightly back, dropping the six feet to the ground below. She stepped back onto the sidewalk, brushed the worst of the dirt and grass off her stocking feet and put her shoes back on. She turned away and walked back to her car while adjusting her dress, which had scrunched up to unlady-like heights from her climb.

For now she had to get home, but tomorrow after sunset would find her back here, trying to find Lawrence's whereabouts from the apartment offices. It was possible that he'd just moved to another apartment within the complex, but she doubted it. She'd find out whatever they knew here, though. If they didn't want to tell her, she'd use her feminine charms. Or she'd lie. If nothing else, no mortal could deny her anything once they'd been ensnared in the power of her gaze.

She only hoped she wouldn't be too late to help Lawrence with whatever he was to be facing.

CHAPTER SIX

Phil woke in a pleasant mood. He was feeling well-rested from his trip, ready to conduct his business and spend the rest of the week enjoying the city. In fact, it was probably time to start getting ready: the meeting was in just half an hour. The representatives from Surinck Technologies should arrive within fifteen minutes.

Rolling out of bed, he glanced over to the wire cage he'd left resting on the desk. George was in his treadmill and William III seemed to be just snuffling around. Expanding his consciousness, a bit, he re-established contact with the two mice and felt his mind connect with theirs. He decided he was going to let them roam the hotel tonight.

First, though, he walked over to the window and removed the black plastic cover he had placed before he slept this morning. The simple device stopped the sun's deadly rays far more effectively than curtains did. He always carried a few of these when he traveled. They could be expanded or retracted to fit in almost any window frame, and completely blocked out the light. A locking mechanism ensured only he could remove the device. Most vampires traveled with these now. Much more discreet than lugging around a coffin, and almost as secure for short trips.

With the window block folded away for the night, he stepped over to his mice. He opened the cage door and set his hand, palm up, in front of it. The two mice, recognizing their master through long association and his near constant presence in their miniscule brains, scurried onto his hand, George going up Phil's arm a bit to make room for his brother.

Phil lowered his hand to the floor, allowing them to run off. Following the connection to them he'd already established, he placed a command in their minds: avoid all people. He didn't want some poor maid freaked out, or worse, harming one of his little friends.

George and William III, being little more than simple white mice, could not recognize any command in English, like 'avoid all people'. Instead, what entered their small, rudimentary mind was desire. Desire and need were what drove simple creatures like these mice. The desire to search for food, the need to eat, the desire to avoid something which caused it pain. What the two mice actually received from their master's command was the desire to avoid all people. 'People', to their mind, was an abstract image of a giant creature associated with certain smells and sounds, and a vague visual representation. This depiction would not have been recognizable as human to any person, but it worked very well for the mice. Phil understood this, but gave it no conscious thought as he issued his commands. He let them run off. They'd be summoned back after his meeting.

The mice immediately ran straight under the bed, exploring the best safe locations, seeking out the secret ways their kind always found or created in human habitations. Phil proceeded to get dressed for his meeting, idly enjoying the small bursts of discovery he received from the exploring rodents. Such simple joys his companions always brought him. Even in times of great stress - which this was not - their very commonness eased his mind.

Phil put on his suit and went downstairs to meet with the representatives. He was negotiating for a relatively minor buyout of one of the Surinck Technologies subsidiaries, a transaction valued at about ten million dollars. This was merely stage one; the meetings were expected to go on for the rest of the week, several hours each night. The Surinck representatives had been easily persuaded to schedule evening meetings to accommodate Phil's claimed jet-lag and other commitments. The ease with which he acquired this concession indicated to him that they were eager to sell, and that he would be returning home with better than expected results. This was always a good thing when reporting directly to the Council.

The meetings themselves were being held in one of the hotel's many small conference rooms. When he arrived, he found that he was to be pitted against just four human men and a woman.

One immortal, with centuries of experience and a supernaturally accelerated mind, against five mortals, one of whom was a female. He kept his face cordial, even when shaking the woman's hand, as though acknowledging her as an equal. He knew his success would be all the greater: women had no place in business. She would drag down their negotiations with her weakness.

They didn't realize it yet, but they were hopelessly outclassed.

Phil actually enjoyed his negotiations and dealings with mortals; it was the only time he ever felt in control. Dealings with his fellow vampires all too often left him feeling woefully inadequate. They considered him a weak, simpering fool. Here, he was the best, and he knew it. A mortal human was simply nothing compared to a vampire's abilities.

Phil had long cultivated those supernatural abilities that gave him an edge in human relations. He'd also studied and practiced manipulation of humans by means now known as psychology. The value of the ability to manipulate the mortals had become apparent to him centuries ago, and he now prided himself as one of the best in that area. He had refined his power over mortals; and the Council valued power in all its forms. This was how the Council's many holdings acquired, and held, so much in so many markets. Power begets power.

He was perhaps an hour and a half into the meeting, little more than concluding the exchange of pleasantries and courtesies, when he felt a surge of fear rush through him. He managed to keep it from his features, and was certain it didn't touch his voice, but the negotiation team from Surinck would definitely feel the change in the air about him. There was little he could do about that.

Mortals were like vampires themselves; they unconsciously fed off the power that radiated from the older undead. This power was often a direct reflection of a vampire's emotional state. When a vampire felt confident, as was usually the case, the mortals around him were simply in awe of his power and at least slightly cowed by it. When a vampire felt joy, those around him were usually inspired to happiness as well. These reactions were generally to Phil's benefit during negotiations like this buyout.

On the singularly rare occasions when a vampire felt fear, however, mortals sensed that as well, and reacted differently based on the circumstances. At this time, their reaction would not likely be to his benefit.

They would sense the fear emanating from him and, if they saw nothing around to inspire such fear, they would allow his fear to bolster their own confidence. Even with the slightly mesmeric state they'd put themselves in by looking into Phil's eyes, there was little he could do to counter the damage this would do to tonight's negotiations, but he could try. First, he must address the fear he was feeling.

His eyes darted around the room only once, taking everything in, too quickly for the mortals to even register it as more than a twitch. He had nothing to fear, personally. The panic - for that was a more apt description of the sensation - was filtering through the link with his pets. He closed his eyes briefly, focusing his attention on the link. He followed it back, tracing the link through the ether to its origin. It was George.

This much confirmed, he opened his eyes. His mind and body were both moving quickly now, an automatic reaction to the possible, though unknown, danger. It appeared to the Surinck negotiators as no more than a slow eye blink.

He spoke. "Gentlemen, ma'am." There was no more panic from the link. Was the danger gone? "I regret that I must, ah..." what's that, now? Is George asleep? Yes, he seemed to be unconscious, "...call tonight's meeting to an early close." Try to wake him up. That should not be a problem through the link.

His guests said something. What was it? Oh, yes. "No, no, gentlemen, ma'am. My apologies." George was not waking up. If anything, he was falling deeper into unconsciousness. "Migraine. It just seemed to hit me out of nowhere." Fear! Fear! From William III this time.

What'd the stupid woman say? "Yes, yes, it's almost certainly an after-effect of the flight." Run, William, run! Into one of those little bolt holes somewhere! "Reschedule for tomorrow evening? Thank you, you're most understanding." Firm handshake; he must not appear weak or overly distraught, even now.

He went suddenly rigid. NO! Dead!? No! Come back, George! Come back! "Oh, your hand! I'm terribly sorry, Mr. Castor. Nothing broken, I hope? My apologies. The pain just hit me all of a sudden. Caused me to tense up. Sorry. Yes, tomorrow."

Phil managed to let the door close behind him before breaking into a full run. He was up to the sixth floor, via the stairs, in less time than it would take to board an elevator and wait for the door to close. The link with George still remained, though faint and weakening rapidly. He followed it like a line being reeled in to find George's body.

It was in a trash can in the hallway. Digging through a small amount of trash, Phil extracted George's lifeless, tiny white body. With red tears welling up he started walking to his room on the other side of the hotel, simultaneously summoning William III. It was obviously not as safe for them here as he'd hoped.

He blinked back the tears as he walked down the hallway to his room. It would not do to be seen crying - tears of blood tended to freak out humans. His eyes clear again, he looked down at poor little George. The frail mouse almost looked asleep. It didn't appear as though he'd been stepped on, or even swatted with a broom. He couldn't hear any bones grinding as his hands subtly shifted the body, so probably nothing was broken.

As Phil entered the room, he set the body down on the table. William III was waiting to be hoisted back to the safety of his cage, as Phil had commanded him. After making sure William III was secure and fed, he sat on the edge of the bed, his hands cradling George in his lap. He let himself cry. He had few friends. His own people, the vampire community, were constantly struggling for power. The vampire women were the same, and tended to dismiss him as a weak player in the never-ceasing political games. Mortal women were notoriously difficult to keep due to the habits his undead nature engendered. Those who did stay with him did so only for his money and power, which were not insignificant by mortal standards. On occasion he'd used his powers over the mortal mind, a basic ability held by all vampires, to try to implant feelings of love towards him in women. Such attempts were hollow and short-lived, and most often left him feeling dirty.

His pets, however, were his friends. He could implant suggestions, yes, but the mice didn't need such artificial impetus to be loyal. He had raised them from infancy, and they saw him as family in their limited way. There was no duplicity to be found in their loyalty to him, no taint of artificial inducement. In his lonely world, they were all he truly had.

The red tears of a vampire, so rarely shed, trickled slowly down his face, dripping on the dark sleeve of his suit coat. He allowed himself this private luxury for several minutes, mourning the mouse even after the tears stopped flowing. He did not find this strange; no more so than a family who has lost a long faithful and well-loved dog mourning its passing.

Finally, he placed his sorrow aside with the intent of deducing the cause of his pet's untimely death. Neither the sensations he'd received, nor the physical evidence of the body, lent themselves to the supposition of a quick, violent death. Neither could it have been due to natural causes. He gazed at the body, seeking any indication as to what might have cost him his friend. There appeared to be nothing. The fur was clean and unbloodied. All the bones felt intact to Phil's sensitive fingers. He looked at its belly. There was something wrong here, he realized. It was only noticeable at all on its almost hairless belly, but it was the only hint so far. It was hard to say, especially on a white mouse, but the critter seemed, well, pale. Rather than the light pink its skin should have been, it could have passed for an albino.

Phil lifted the body and sniffed it. Just as he'd suspected. No blood. He was, after all, sensitive to that smell. He quickly searched for puncture wounds.

There they were. Two piercing wounds. They were almost gone; even in death, a vampire's bite marks heal over.

What was strange about them was the size, the spacing. The vampire who did this could only be in a body that was, by size, that of a child, maybe five or six, if that. To create such a vampire was typically not done. They usually had little to contribute to the community, having neither money nor power of their own, and were limited in what they could do in an adult, human society. There were a few, but not many. He would take the time to investigate and, if at all possible, to punish.

* * *

"Ah, Lawrence, I might have known." The voice was a bit high-pitched and had a perpetually wheedling tone to it. Lawrence recognized the voice even as he recognized the face. He seemed to have been waiting in the hallway just outside of Lawrence's room.

Lawrence closed the door to his room abruptly behind him and leaned against it, facing his visitor. "Phil. Well, this is a surprise. I haven't seen you in, what, three hundred, three hundred fifty years?"

"Yes, something like that." Phil kept smiling while getting a good look at Lawrence. He didn't look good, not to put too fine a point on it. He still had the same dark, good looks, but there was something about him. It took Phil a moment to put words to it, but finally he had it. Lawrence looked tired. This in itself explained his difficulty in applying a label. Vampires simply didn't get tired. Not even when sunset wakens them, or as dawn approaches, calling them to their unearthly, unnatural slumber. When morning is imminent, they simply sense and prepare for its coming. They don't so much as yawn, or grow weary. When a vampire enters his deathly sleep, he is out in less than five seconds. Sleepiness, insomnia, all were left behind with mortality.

Phil looked as he always had, Lawrence thought in the moment of silence as they both appraised each other. Phil had been Awakened a bit later in his life, when he was about forty, so had a few small touches of gray in his short cropped hair. Whereas on some men it would have conveyed distinguished maturity, on Phil it just made him look like he was getting old. He also had what was called in modern times a small beer belly, a bit of a paunch.

In addition to all that he had a tendency, when affronted, of squinting his eyes and lifting his upper lip while tilting his head up a bit. With all this, and his disproportionately skinny arms, it made Lawrence think of a rat. He wondered passingly if Phil's appearance was due to his ability to control rodents. No, he looked that way before becoming a vampire.

Phil had apparently also taken to dressing almost completely in black, even going so far as to wear black nail polish and, Lawrence was pretty sure, black mascara. He wore an Ankh draped on a silver chain around his neck. It was a fashion adopted primarily by certain rebellious youth, and Lawrence could not recall ever seeing a grown man attired in such a fashion. He had heard of this style of attire referred to as 'Goth'. Lawrence preferred 'lame'. "Are you going to turn me in to the Council again? Try to get that reward?" Lawrence asked.

There it was - the rat face. Lawrence had touched a nerve. "Well, Larry," Lawrence closed his eyes in controlled irritation. Phil seemed not to notice. "Times have changed a lot since then. As far as the reward goes, I no longer need it. I've recovered my fortune, and besides -"

"Lawrence! There's another vampire in the hotel! I'm smelling him all over!" Mac came running around a corner down the hall, saw Phil, and skidded to a stop. His front legs already splayed out before him from his sudden halt, he immediately went into a crouch, as though ready to pounce. He growled. "That's him, Lawrence! I knew the smell was stronger, but I thought it might be just you. He's a vampire!"

"Still making vampires out of animals, eh?" Phil couldn't hear the telepathic voice of Mac, but was easily able to deduce the situation. "Well, that would possibly explain something I've been wondering the last few days.

You wouldn't happen to have a cat, or something of similar size, would you?"

"Why do you ask?" Lawrence questioned back warily.

"One of my pets was bitten by a very small set of fangs, three days ago. I thought it was a child at first, but now that I know you're here, a different theory springs naturally to mind."

Sighing, Lawrence opened his door and stepped in, signaling Phil to enter behind him. Inside, Lady sat looking at Lawrence. He wasn't sure how she did it with a cat's face, but she looked irritated. She obviously didn't like having the door shut in her face, but Lawrence had hoped to keep the animals' existence from Phil. No such luck.

"Phil, may I introduce Lady de Winter and Mac. Mac, Lady, this is Phil."

Mac gave a muffled bark, acknowledging the introduction aloud for Phil's benefit. Lady looked at Phil speculatively for a moment before uttering a polite, but reluctant, meow.

"Pleased to meet you both," Phil intoned, bowing slightly.

"He smells of mice," Lady commented.

"Another damn vampire," was Mac's initial response. "And I imagine I have to be nice to him, too. If only I could still pee on legs."

"You may ask her about it, Phil," Lawrence offered, referring to the dead mouse Phil had mentioned outside the door, politely ignoring the animals' comments.

"Thank you. Ms. de Winter, did you happen to feed on a white mouse three nights ago on the sixth floor, disposing of the body in a wastebasket?" Phil was pleased with how steady his voice remained.

"What is this schmoe's problem? Why the big concern about a stupid mouse? It's not like it was a vampire or intelligent or anything. I would have known."

"Please, just answer the question. Lady," Lawrence communicated to her.

"Well, yeah, I fed on one like that. So?"

Lawrence edited Lady's telepathic message. "She says she did, and is curious as to your concern over this particular mouse. She is unaware of your, ah, talent. I'm sure that had she known, she would have refrained from feeding on that mouse. Perhaps you would be so kind as to explain to her?"

"Oh, is that what I said?"

"Close enough."

"I really doubt I would have refrained - as you put it - no matter what his explanation is. This guy strikes me as kind of weaselly. Plus, that was a rather succulent, well fed rodent."

Phil looked from Lawrence to Lady, probably trying to judge the accuracy of Lawrence's translation. "Certainly. Lady, Mac, as you are both probably aware, all vampires eventually develop a power that is unique to them, or at least, incredibly rare. Of course you know Lawrence's unique ability already."

Mac gave a short whine and cocked his head, indicating to Phil that he did not know. Phil looked at Lawrence, who explained it to Mac. "Vampires cannot normally Awaken animals. Generally, they can only make other human vampires. I am the only one who can create a vampire from any creature."

"Well, not exactly any creature," Phil qualified.

"No. You are quite correct," Lawrence said tersely. He turned back to Mac. "I seem to lack the ability to make other human vampires."

"Well, that's rather messed up," Lady noted.

Mac snorted, laughing. "What kind of crappy vampire can't even make more of its own kind? Ha! You're an undead eunuch!"

"My, your vocabulary has reached new heights, Mac! Eunuch, eh? I'm impressed! Or does that word have special significance for you? Did your owners ever think you were broken?"

Lawrence didn't follow that. "Think he was broken?"

"Yeah," she replied. "So they had to have him fixed!" The rapid purring that was her laughter sounded in her throat.

Mac turned back to Phil. "I won't even dignify that with a response."

"Can't think of one, can you?" Mac ignored her.

Phil knew something had passed, but all he'd heard was Lawrence's verbalized question. "I had forgotten how annoying the telepathy is. It's even worse than people speaking a foreign language in front of you. At least with that you can pick up intonations and hand gestures."

"Sorry," Lawrence apologized. "There's really nothing I can do about it."

Phil waved his hand airily. "No big deal. I understand." He turned his attention back to the animals. "Anyway, back to what I was saying. My ability has to do with mice. Well, rodents in general, but I prefer mice. I am able to command any and all rodents within about a mile of myself. There's a bit more to it than that, but the details are inconsequential, except for one thing. Forming this link on a regular basis extends their lifespan significantly for some reason. The mouse you killed the other day - whose name, by the way, was George - had been with me for eighty-seven years."

"He wandered with this stupid mouse for eighty-seven years?" Lady asked, looking at Mac. "This guy needs to get a life even more than Lawrence does, Mac!"

Lawrence managed to sound sincere as he translated. "Lady apologizes very profusely. Had she had any idea what George meant to you, she would have continued hunting, bypassing him, and she hopes you can forgive her a mistake made in ignorance."

Like most vampires, Phil could sense lies; that ability, however, worked only against humans - vampires were unreadable. He looked skeptically at Lady, but replied, "Certainly, I understand. One can't blame her for not knowing, after all. Just so you know, George had a brother, William III. I would ask that you try to be a bit more discriminatory when you feed?"

Not bothering to listen to the snide comment Lady was sending him in response to Phil's request, Lawrence replied, "Of course, Phil. She says she will do her utmost to avoid a recurrence of that horrible misunderstanding."

"Thank you."

"How long are you in town for, anyway? The night is soon coming to an end, but perhaps we can get together later with some more time to talk. It has been quite a while, after all."

"Yes, it has. I'm actually here on business. Council business," he added, a bit smugly. "I'll be available afterwards, though. Say, one a.m.?"

"A Council man now, eh?"

"We are all Council men, Lawrence. Those of us who wish to retain our power and lives, anyway."

"Yes, yes. You spout the propaganda admirably." He smiled, trying to make the words seem less deprecating even as he uttered them. "One o'clock sounds good, though. I'll be expecting you here?"

"That's fine." Phil turned, opened the door, and turned again, his right hand out. After a pause, Lawrence took his hand and they shook. "It really is good to see you again, Lawrence." He sounded sincere.

"Thanks, Phil. Tomorrow."

CHAPTER SEVEN

"I appreciate you meeting with me, Ghost." Detective Jamon Schroeder was sitting across from a short black man. He was about 5'3", but had to weigh in at 180, all of it muscle. He was fairly respectable looking – no visible tattoos, and wore a long-sleeve blue silk shirt. Of course, his tattoos could have been under the shirt, and he did have the gangster's requisite heavy gold chain.

"Steve vouched for you. He said you're new in the area, but a buddy of his on the west coast said you used to be one of his guys."

"West Coast? Eric Castillo?"

"Yeah, that's him."

"Yeah, I used to be one of his guys. He taught me the trade. Wait a minute. Steve? Steve Lopez? Isn't he in the pen?"

"Yeah, but his word is still gold here. He'll be down for seven years, they're saying. So, whatcha need?"

"It's kinda embarrassing, really." He paused as the waitress came by. They were seated in a small cafe on Ghost's turf. Called the Clean Café after its owner and head cook, Jeremy Clean ("It's pronounced 'Klen'," he was always muttering), it nonetheless lived up to its name. Every surface shined, the chrome sparkled, and the serving plates appeared brand new. This was a pleasant change, as all too many eateries in this part of town took few pains to maintain anything beyond what the health inspectors required, if they did even that much. As a bonus to the sanitary condition, the food was very good, too. It was said that Jeremy made the best french fries in the city.

To top it all off, the Clean Cafe was considered neutral ground for anybody, any underground organization in the city. With so many rich young men coming in, the tips were always good, and the waitresses were always happy and discrete after taking their orders. This one, Michelle by her name tag, promptly left them in privacy after noting their orders on her little pad. "That's okay, Jaim, I ain't gonna give you no shit. Out with it."

"I got robbed a few days ago. My cash, my stash. I woke up not knowin' nothing in an alley. Didn't see nobody, nothing. I was wondering if I was the only guy that's been hit like that. I've heard stories, but they's just rumors. You know everyone. Got anything solid?"

Ghost pulled out a cigarette and his lighter. He looked around for an ashtray before remembering the cafe was a no-smoking restaurant. He put the lighter away and tucked the cigarette back in its pack. "Ya think I'd remember, as much as I come here", he muttered. He would have lit up anyway, but he had to set the example. Neutral location or not, this was his turf. He took care of it. He paused, considering Jamon, before continuing. "Yeah, there's others. Seems like one of the guys is getting hit each night for the last couple weeks. So, you're not alone."

"I guess that's some consolation. Did any of 'em get a look at the guy?"

"They all say no, but I think Willy's holding out on something. Far as I can tell, he was maybe the first one to be hit, but who knows?"

They sat in silence for a while, watching out the window at the people walking by. It was not quite five in the evening. Jamon hadn't begun his shift for the night, selling on the corner. He'd wanted to follow up on this lead first. Steve, who he'd personally busted about two months ago, had turned informant, and was doing much to help this bust in exchange for his walking papers. It was Steve's word that got Jamon his own spot in the local hierarchy. It was shaping up to be a huge bust, and it was Jamon's show.

The one bad spot was that freak who robbed him. Neither the video techs nor the lab had come up with anything new for him. Not that he could point fingers; he hadn't gotten any further, either. He still couldn't place why the face seemed familiar. The only thing new that he had was that every time he'd close his eyes to picture the face, he heard a sound in his mind, a muffled pop, which seemed to echo once. It made no sense to him, though.

The waitress brought them their food, refilled their drinks, and left them in silence again. "Ghost, did any of 'em see a cat around when it happened? A black cat?" The cat was still bothering him. The way it had looked at him. No, the way it had *watched* him. Those eyes.

Ghost finished chewing his burger. "What're you, getting superstitious or some shit?" Jamon shrugged. Ghost took another bite. Talking around this mouthful, he continued. "Ya know, though, one of the guys did mention a cat. Don't remember if it was black, though. He said it chased him, goofy sumbitch. And Willy mentioned a dog that attacked him that same night he was robbed, too. That mean anything to ya?" Jamon shook his head. "Oh well."

"You don't think these guys'd mind if I talked to 'em about it, do ya? This punk pissed me off. I mean to get him."

"I suppose it'd be okay. I'll give ya a couple names and let 'em know you're coming around."

"Thanks, Ghost."

* * *

Lawrence figured the sun had been down for about an hour, maybe more, when his eyes opened. The coffin lid was already up; Lady must have woke up before him and opened it herself. An impossible task for a normal cat due to the weight of the lid, Lady almost certainly encountered no problems.

Lawrence had been waking later and returning to rest earlier each day. This was the worst so far. He still had plenty of time tonight to do whatever he wished, but this was getting both annoying and embarrassing.

He sat up to find both Lady and Mac watching a special on TV about the downfall of ancient Greece. Lady turned towards him. "I was wondering, Lawrence. I heard your conversation with Phil through the door when he found you last night. What did you mean about him turning you in to the Council?"

Although Mac kept his eyes on the TV, his ears perked up. He was curious, too. Lady must have told Mac about Lawrence's comment to Phil, as Mac hadn't heard it himself. Lawrence climbed out of his coffin and sat down on the bed. "Do you know what the Council is?"

"To some extent," replied Lady. "It was in the knowledge you passed to us.

"No," said Mac.

Lawrence looked at Mac. The dog should know this; he should know *all* of what Lady knew. "Well, the Council is the ruling group of all vampires. It's comprised of the most ancient, most powerful of our kind. Thirteen of them."

"Thirteen?" Mac inquired.

"Yes. I believe it was considered a number of power several thousand years ago. Or, perhaps that's just how many vampires there were when it was formed. I really don't know. In fact, there's a lot about the Council that isn't known by anyone not part of the Council itself. Membership on the Council is until true death; the final death."

"Considering we're immortal, turnover on the Council must be pretty slow," Lady noted wryly.

"It is, Lady. To the best of my knowledge, the last change in the Council was over six hundred years ago. I'd heard rumors that that vacancy appeared because of a...strong disagreement...on policy. The official story was that the church had gotten a hold of the offending member. In fact, there may have been some truth to that. It would be within the Council's methods to have revealed his daytime location to the Pope."

"The Pope?"

"Yes. There has always been a strong vampire presence near what is now known as Vatican City, and many of our brethren have had close ties with the papacy throughout the centuries. I don't know why, but it's true. As I was saying, this Council *is* the vampire government, and its decisions are law. It has many ways of enforcing its rule, the most simple of which are its mortal and immortal armies. Yes, Mac, armies. They don't call them armies, but that's essentially what they are. In addition to the Council, there are lesser groups, called guilds, which handle specific aspects of the vampire community. For example, one such guild handles the creation of all new vampires. If someone wants to create a new vampire, they must petition this guild, and it is then decided if the creation may proceed."

Mac spoke up again. "Why is that? Why such a big deal about making a new vampire? If it's anything like what you do, it doesn't seem like it'd be such a big deal."

While Lawrence paused to consider how to frame his answer, Lady jumped right in, with no such consideration. "Because, Captain Neuter,"

Mac growled, but listened; "there would be a serious population problem. Think about it. Vampires are functionally immortal. Even if every vamp only created a new one every ten years, the population would grow to, well, a lot. I won't pester your dog-brain with the advanced math, but it would be an exponential growth."

"Wrong attitude, right answer," Lawrence admonished Lady. "She is correct, though. Our population, without this particular aspect of government, would easily outpace the human, and probably animal, population. We would grow like a virus, depleting both human and animal populations by just feeding our large numbers, and then starve. Not to mention that long before that happened, the humans would realize we are among them and systematically destroy us."

"Ha! Let them try! We've more power than they could imagine! We're almost impossible to kill!"

"That is true, Lady, we are. However, we are very easy to destroy." He glanced at the digital clock on the bedside table. "Hang on a second; I want to feed before Phil stops by tonight." He got up from where he was sitting on the bed, picked up the phone and requested room service. "Yes. Ah, I'd just like to order a light dessert, for three please. What do you have available? ... Excellent. That sounds good. Yes, 512. Thank you." He hung up the phone and returned to the animals, who were looking at him quizzically.

"Now, where was I? Ah, yes. We are easy to destroy, if not kill. What I mean by that is...well, you must remember that during the day we are defenseless. It would be as nothing for someone to come to us during the day and destroy our body. You see? Never get overconfident in your own immortality. There are many of us who have paid the price for that."

They sat in silence for a few minutes considering Lawrence's words before a knock at the door disturbed their contemplation. Lawrence got up to answer it. Behind the door was a plump young woman of about 20, bearing a small tray containing the dessert he'd just ordered. "Ah, thank you, miss. If you'll just give me a moment..."

"Oh, is that your kitten?" she asked with a child-like smile. Lady had crept up to the door. "How cute!"

Lawrence glanced over from the table he was getting his wallet from. "She's very friendly. You can pick her up and pet her, if you wish." Mentally, he told Lady, "Be good. For a moment."

The woman scooped Lady up and began to nuzzle her. "She's a sweetie. What's her name?"

"Lady de Winter." Again mentally, he commanded, "Hit her." As the woman slowly rubbed her cheek against Lady's glossy fur, the cat squirmed around and sank her fangs into the woman's pulsing jugular. Almost before the woman noticed the cat's lightning movement, her eyes began to glaze and she started sinking to the floor. Lady rode the woman all the way down, only shifting position to maintain a good angle for feeding and to avoid being landed on. Lawrence had already walked over and closed the door to the hallway. "She was named for an accomplished assassin," he told the unconscious form.

Once Lady was done drinking the little she needed, Lawrence took his turn. "Ah," Lady said, "room service."

"You disgust me, cat," snarled Mac.

"Lighten up, Mac."

Lawrence finished his feeding and stood up. He reached over and grabbed his wallet off the table, where he'd left it again when Lady struck. After pulling out a couple bills, he hunkered down on his heels, waiting for the woman to recover from Lady's bite. It wasn't two minutes before the effects began to wear off and the woman came slowly back to consciousness. "I said, are you okay?" Lawrence asked when he thought she could hear him again.

"What happened? Why am I on the floor?"

"You fainted, miss." Lawrence managed to sound surprised. He tilted her face up to look directly into her eyes. "Did you hear me? You fainted. You're feeling better now, though, aren't you?"

When she spoke again, she did so as if in a trance, which she nearly was. Her eyes, while locked on Lawrence, seemed to be focused on something miles away. Mac and Lady could feel a small amount of Lawrence's power shining out of him, seemingly focused on the unfortunate hotel employee. "Yes, I remember fainting. I do feel much better, though. Thank you."

He stood up, keeping his eyes on her, and helped her to her feet. "You probably need to eat something. Take one of these desserts, along with your tip.'"

Still in a daze, she accepted. "Thank you." Tip and dessert in hand, she left the room.

"What was all that?" Mac asked.

"Just one of our common powers. We can fairly well hypnotize the weak-willed. It's especially easy if we've just fed off them. Kind of like we're connected because of the feeding, like we've got some of them in us, a bit of their essence."

"So, why didn't you do that with all the dealers? Instead of robbing them, ask them to give you their money? Save some trouble."

Lawrence sat on the floor next to Mac, his arms resting on his upright knees. "It wouldn't quite work that way, Mac. When we hypnotize someone, they remember everything that happened during that time. If I were to tell them to give me their money, after they came out of it they'd know what they'd done, if not why, and come after it. I don't think that'd be good.

Besides, most of them are too strong-willed to mesmerize that well."

"Can we mesmerize, too?" Mac asked.

"I don't know. For one thing, you kind of need to talk to them while you do it. And, it's usually a year or so before human vampires are strong enough to do it."

"Well, that's seven dog years," Mac noted. "Or would it be one seventh of a year?"

"Give it up, Kibble-head," Lady suggested. Casting a thought to Lawrence only, she said, "I'm actually a bit worried about the mutt, Lawrence. Well, maybe not worried, but curious. I'm really starting to think he might be brain damaged. Seriously. He doesn't seem to know as much as he should, as much as I do. There have been several other things I've had to explain to him."

Lawrence thought about it. "Mac, you seem to have a significant gap in your knowledge, and I'm a bit concerned."

Mac looked up at Lawrence. "Don't worry. I don't blame you. You probably didn't realize it at the time."

"Realize what, Mac?"

Mac cocked his head to the side. "Why, that you were too weak to make two vampires in one night, of course."

Lawrence closed his eyes. "I should have realized that myself." He looked at Mac. "I'm sorry, Mac. You're right - I remember feeling weaker that night after I made Lady. I didn't realize the 'flu' would make you weaker, though."

"Oh, I'm not weaker. You were strong enough to Awaken me. You just couldn't push all your knowledge into me." He looked at Lawrence, then Lady. "I thought you two realized that."

Lady flicked her tail. "Well, of course I knew."

Mac growled.

"Okay, dog, you got me on that one," she relented.

"In fact, I used to think that decay was part of the vampire smell."

"Decay?" Lawrence asked.

"Yeah. Kind of like a rotting corpse. But Phil didn't have that smell on him, and it keeps getting stronger on you"

Lawrence looked a bit unnerved by Mac's statement.

Lady perked up. "Well, now, how about we go back to my original question about Phil turning you in to the Council?"

"Sure. We've still got some time before he stops by." And he told them about it.

CHAPTER EIGHT

The year was 1603 (Lawrence began). I was a baron, living as a vampire quite comfortably in Eastern Europe. I had been Awakened some 82 years earlier.

It was nearly dawn when I heard the clatter of horse hooves and the rumble of wooden wheels that announced a visitor's carriage coming down the road to my estate. I put my book down, sliding the ribbon in to hold my place. I had an expansive library in those days; it was one of my greatest expenses. Books were not so common, then, and I took great pride in my collection.

I walked over to the window of my study to confirm who I believed the arrival to be. My study was on the second floor of my manor, its window facing east, the front of my estate, so it always afforded me a good preview of who was coming to call. In this instance, the carriage was one I knew well, without even looking at the coat-of-arms displayed prominently on the sides.

The carriage itself had been made to order fifteen years before, and was kept in pristine condition. Drawn by six horses, it was simply huge. The wheels alone stood taller than a man. Resting on these excessive wheels was the carriage itself, which was twice as large as the standard four-passenger style popular then. This surprisingly graceful, undeniably beautiful carriage had room inside for eight to sit. It was the height of luxury and vanity, but its most notable, and unique, feature was the two coffins built in under the seats. Secured from the inside and heavily reinforced, they allowed the carriage's owner to travel in comfort and relative safety even by day.

What was sad was that this represented the last of Phil's wealth and power. Nine years earlier, he had been forced to flee his lands as his castle was taken by a neighboring baron with aspirations of greatness. It should not have happened; Phil had a very good army and competent generals – or knights, as they were then. However, they had grown disturbed over their lord's strange habits and betrayed him. During the day, while Phil lay helpless beneath his castle, a prisoner to the sun, the leaders of his own army opened the gate to his enemies. With this, the battle fought by his few remaining loyal units was short and one sided. Those of his men who remained loyal were fending off enemies from without, while wondering which of their old comrades would next appear to attempt to stab them in the back from within. Phil was fortunate to escape with his life that night, let alone with his carriage and a few handfuls of gold, thanks to those last few loyal retainers.

Since that day, I had taken care to ensure the loyalty of my own troops, ensuring adequate pay and mesmerizing them to ask after their loyalty. This ensured an honest answer. We can usually sniff out the truth when mortals speak, but I was not yet confident of my abilities with this particular talent. Any who were not loyal were promptly discharged from duty with no penalties. This helped keep the men loyal, to see all my people treated fairly and gently. What the men did not know was that I invariably used those I discharged for my next meal. Back then, I was not as kind as I am now. My meal was my victim's last breath. I am sure other vampire lords took similar precautions to ensure loyalties.

Phil had lived these last nine years on the sufferance of neighboring lords and a few of his more well-to-do vassals still loyal to him. He stayed in any one place for only a few months at a time. It is true, it would not have been difficult at all for him to win through on his own and kill the usurping baron in his sleep, but Phil had been forbidden from taking any action against the man by the Council. One *never* went against the Council's wishes. That way laid certain ruin, if not death.

So, yes, I was quite familiar with this carriage. It was still some distance away. I had picked up the sound and spotted it roughly two miles out on that quiet night. With the bell that always sat next to my favorite reading chair, I summoned one of my manservants, Tomás, to attend to my friend. That done, I returned to my book. Tomás would see Phil to my study when he was ready.

While I read, I also listened. Therefore, I was not at all surprised when Tomás rapped on my door. My sensitive ears could easily track everything going on in my home. "Enter," I instructed.

The door opened, allowing Tomás to step in. "Sir, may I present Lord Philip Bulle of Grunemead." Tomás bowed and left the room, his duty done.

He was perhaps my best servant that century. He never so much as batted an eye at my strange, vampiric habits, nor those of my associates. When rumors against me came to his ears, he immediately clamped down on the source. A good man.

I stood up and walked over to shake Phil's hand. "It's good to see you, friend!"

"As always, Lawrence. But tell me, what am I doing here? What was so urgent that you 'required my presence most urgently,' as you put it?"

"Ah, Philip, your late arrival unfortunately precludes any time for proper explanations," I informed him with a grin. I gestured towards the window.

"The sun is almost up. You cut your arrival fairly fine."

"Well, if it came to that, I do have resources in my carriage."

"Yes, I know, but still. Do you need to feed tonight?"

"No, I've no need tonight. Thank you."

"Very well, then," I said, opening the door and leading him out to the hall.

"Allow me to show you to your room."

He grabbed my arm. "But tell me, Lawrence, what is it -"

"Tomorrow will do for that, Philip. Rest well. You know the routine here. If you need anything, the bell is by your door. Good day." I opened the door to his room for him and went down to my sleeping chambers, which I had moved beneath the castle some seventy-some years before.

*　*　*

I woke the next evening eager to share my new secret with Phil. Only one other was privy to this information as yet, and she had left over a month before. It was not becoming, however, to appear over-anxious about anything, and one truth that holds now held then, as well: image is everything. So I left Phil to Tomás' care that evening while I awaited his presence in my audience chamber.

I climbed the dais to the chair behind my massive, almost altar-like desk and awaited him. All of the room was decorated similarly – overdone to the point of being ostentatious. This was done solely to impress visitors. After over one hundred years, it had little effect on me. Everything, from the banners above the chairs that lined the walls, to the delicately carved monstrosity of a table before my opulent seat, was designed and arranged to remind others of my family's power and position. As I've mentioned, image was everything, especially in those times. Even when receiving friends, it was expected that you do so properly. While it's true I'd already seen him when he arrived that morning, it had been informal and rushed. It's difficult to explain today, but there existed many seemingly pointless formalities that everyone accepted as proper. Perhaps it was these small symbols of civilized attitude that kept us from sliding back into barbarism. Perhaps it's the same today, really, only a different set of rules.

I was seated for perhaps a minute before Tomás appeared in the doorway to announce Phil. "My lord, may I present for your esteemed audience and consideration the most worthy Lord Philip Bulle of Grunemead." With that, Tomás stepped back to allow Phil entrance, and walked in behind him to ask, "Shall I be of further service, milord?"

"Yes, Tomás, please pull up a seat for Lord Bulle." This was simply a nod towards Phil's status in my home as an equal, as commoners and servants - or any who were beneath my station - were not permitted to be seated in my audience chamber. I, as befitted my station, had remained seated throughout.

Tomás brought forth a seat, placed it for Phil and waited for further instructions. "Carry on with your other duties, Tomás." Once he had left the room, I walked out from behind my desk and we shook hands again. "Good morning, Phil. Shall we grab some breakfast?" Yes, I know what I said about image and all that, but Phil was an old friend. We tended to cut through all the tedium in private. What little ceremony we tolerated, we did so for the benefit of others, like Tomás.

"Sounds good, Lawrence. It's been a few days for me. How about you?"

"Just over a week," I replied as we walked out of the chamber.

We hunted and we fed.

Perhaps I should elaborate on that a bit, though it shames me today. We chose not to simply let ourselves into some sleeping peasant's home and take the easy prey we'd find within. We walked the streets that evening for a good hour, passing on many targets too old, too young, or whatever other reasons.

It was not a pitch-dark evening. The moon had been full but four days past. It was as daylight for Phil and me, the moon casting more light than we could need, but for the peasantry its pale light only added to the unearthly feel of the evening. The shadows seemed darker in contrast to the dim glow that surrounded the dark places, but even that which did receive the moon's scant light seemed to give the most mundane things a dangerous quality. Trees which were waiting for someone to come within reach; houses that never let those who passed through their doors leave; small depressions in the ground that now seemed to lead to other, horrible worlds. To add to all this, a nearby wolf pack had caught our scent and were howling after us, whether in fear or anger I did not know, nor did it matter.

In short, the perfect night for Phil and I to be out hunting.

We walked boldly along the streets, watching and judging those who shared this night with us. There were various men about, but we saw no gentlemen. And while we saw no ladies, there were a few women. Most of these women plied their trade on the streets, as opposed to the more discreet and respectable ones who waited in their homes for their customers. It was one of the women on the streets we finally targeted.

We observed her, shadowmerging as we waited for her to hook a customer.

What do I mean by shadowmerging? It's another vampiric ability, like knowing truth from lies, that will come in time. I haven't been able to do it very well for a while with this vampire flu thing. We merge into the darkness, and become no more than a shadow to the mortal eye, if that. A shadow in the darkness, a void in the black of night, nearly impossible to see. It's more than just hiding in the dark. A mortal can be two inches away, and his eyes will refuse to see us. Well, that's not entirely accurate. They don't consciously see us, but some part of them sees the danger lurking there. You can hear their heart race every time their eyes drift over you; smell the fear pour off them.

And that's what we did. We shadowmerged in a place she couldn't help but look at regularly, directly across the street from her. We savored her fear. This, to us, was what made a hunt more than just feeding: generating fear before the kill. I think we affected her business, too. There were at least four men who looked as though they were about to approach her, but as they drew near their eyes would pass over us and they would walk right past her, shuffling along a bit more quickly than before, perhaps considering all their other past sins as they slouched into the dark. We didn't care - we had all night, and every taste of fear excited us more. This slow terror would flavor the blood, too, as the adrenaline released adds a taste of spice, energizing the vampire even more with the feeding.

She moved twice, trying to escape from whatever was causing her this sense of dread, but we followed wherever she went. After about an hour and a half, someone finally overcame his own unease and approached her to request her services. They negotiated a price and started back for her home. We followed, unseen. When we arrived behind the illicit, temporary couple at the prostitute's home, Phil and I stayed outside, waiting for our moment.

"I must admit I'm still rather curious as to why you summoned me," Phil whispered as we waited. We were standing in the dark, in front of her house; a pair of dark sentinels guarding the two engaged in private pleasures. We watched what little foot traffic remained on the road, and listened to the sounds of my town at night. The pub was doing a brisk business, and we listened as a fight broke out over a spilled tankard of ale and ended just as quickly as another iron mug was used heavily on the man's skull. A street over, we heard Brian the Cobbler instruct his wife, with the back of his hand, on the importance of obedience.

"Philip, such impatience is most unbecoming, but I'm feeling indulgent." We were safe from detection, our whispers as quiet as a small breeze ruffling the grass of an open field. If a mortal human were a foot away he might have heard something, though he would have been unable to distinguish the words we spoke; indeed, he would have been unsure there were words contained in the half-heard whisperings reaching his ear. I paused a moment, listening. It seemed the festivities behind us were soon to begin in full. "I had my Calling."

He was surprised. "How delightful! What is it?"

"Well, I can't reveal *everything*." He'd had his Calling seventeen years before. I will admit to some jealousy over this. The Calling, of course, is when we first discover our unique power. We feel a calling, an urge, to use it the first time. For example, if the ability was that of flight, one night that vampire would just have an urge to will his body to leave the ground.

Phil had discovered his affinity for rodents, as I said, seventeen years before. He had reached out with his will, not really knowing what he was doing, and shortly found hundreds of rats, mice, squirrels, and other rodentia streaming into his home. His staff, as can be imagined, was appalled, though they never linked it to him. It wasn't overly exciting, as far as powers went, but it was still more than I had.

So I was jealous, but he was still a friend, so I tried not to let it show. We had been chosen for Awakening the same year. I still don't know all the reasons for that, but it was a happy coincidence for us, as he had helped my father at a difficult point, and assisted me as I took the reins of the barony over from my father.

Before any more could be said on the topic, I told him, "I think it's time." We both turned to the door. With a single blow of my fists, it was blasted inward, landing in two pieces on the floor of the kitchen. We rapidly moved to the only other door, which led into the bedroom. This, I sundered in the same manner as the other. The two humans were well into their sordid pleasures. The man, who was on top, looked back over his shoulder at us with an expression that changed from outrage at the interruption to abject fear at the sight of us. We were hungry, and we were hunting. The humans innately, subconsciously, knew this and were terrified. The woman had lifted her head up off the pillow to see us and tried to scream. Nothing came out, her voice frozen with fear.

When we had finished savoring the initial terror, Phil and I moved swiftly to opposite sides of the bed. Our movement was faster than their eye could follow, and for a moment the couple was disoriented, uncertain where we'd gone. When they saw us looming over them, seemingly transported in an instant, fangs fully exposed, they finally moved.

The man leapt off the woman and raced for the door, with her following immediately behind him. Phil took the lead here and maneuvered in front of them, easily outpacing them to cut off their run towards the center of town. Seeing Phil in their intended path of escape, the naked pair turned as one and began running out of town. As they fled, the prostitute's long blond hair flowed majestically behind her, a striking contrast to her pendulous breasts, which flounced about, to our amused delight.

Phil and I continued to herd them like cattle wherever we wished, one of us using our unearthly speed to slide ahead of them and cut off undesired routes while the other loped along behind, maintaining the chase.

We ran them out of the town, then through a farm, across a field covered in animal droppings. They both fell more than once in that treacherously slick footing, to rise covered in filth. We ran them into the forest, where we would occasionally split them up, adding to their terror. Soon their flesh was covered with stripes, like a tan and red tiger, from the countless cuts they'd received from the reaching, clawing branches of the forest.

After about ten minutes of our chase, we knew they would not be able to withstand it much longer, so we herded them to a river. As they stood there, naked, shivering in fear and cold, knee deep in the water, we came at them with all our speed to forcibly dunk them, cleaning the worst of the filth away. As they cried their last desperate screams, praying to an uncaring god, we dragged them a half-mile apart from each other and fed.

Those two humans died naked, cold, exhausted, wounded, filthy, terrified, and utterly alone.

Phil and I considered it a fabulous hunt.

* * *

We returned to my estate, but did not go directly to my manor. Instead, we walked around to the back, where I kept my riding stables and hunting kennels. Since I'd last had Phil as a guest about two years before, I'd had another structure erected. This building stood about eighty feet from my home, situated between the kennel and the stable, its size about halfway between the two. It was of quite solid construction - half of stone, no windows, and a latch which was operated and locked on the inside as well as out. None of my staff tended it except for occasional cleanings.

Phil walked to this outbuilding in almost total silence beside me, knowing the futility of asking any questions, but making no attempt to dampen the curiosity evident on his face. "Ah, your Calling was to construct a barn. Very good," was all he said as he saw the new structure, to which I merely smiled.

I opened the door and we walked in. My eyes widened slightly at the barrage of noise I 'heard'. My reaction elicited a puzzled look from Phil as we stepped in. To his ears it was perfectly silent apart from some movement, and the overpowering odor associated with livestock stables was conspicuously absent. Of course, I was hearing many conversations and several queries telepathically directed at me. Foremost among these was Iron, cursing my very name and existence with his usual colorful and creative, if vicious, style. Iron had a special talent in stringing together seemingly innocuous words to form the most scathing and vituperative insults. There were now five more dogs. None of them hated me like Iron did, but the only one I could say actually liked me was Copper.

There was also Chestnut, a prize horse from my stables, and my only Awakened mount. I didn't Awaken any more horses after Chestnut told me I was no longer permitted to ride him. It was 'beneath his dignity,' he told me, and I didn't want to lose any of my other mounts like that.

I also had a duck. He was primarily a test, to see what would happen. What happened was that I wound up with a vampire duck. He was actually a pretty amusing fellow, and not just because of the way he looked with fangs coming out of his bill. Great sense of humor, although he sometimes irritated the cow. They didn't get along too well for some reason.

I'll always remember the cow. She had taken the name of Jenetta, and turned out to be one hell of a philosopher. Her insights on the nature of man, life, vampires, the universe as a whole, were some of the most original thoughts I've heard before or since. I had wanted to get some of it down on paper, but I delayed until it was too late.

Anyway, there were several other animal vampires, twenty-one in all. This stable, which I'd had constructed after I'd awakened three dogs and a cat, could hold several more, with many separate stalls - or living spaces, as the animals called them. It was made specifically to keep the sunlight out of these stalls, even if the door was accidentally opened during the day.

Phil looked around. "I can feel power in here. Quite a bit, but I can't tell what from."

I considered what would be the most dramatic way of showing him. I settled for visual effect. I called out, verbally, for Jenetta to come to us and she complied, moving with a grace not normally seen in a thousand pound bovine. "Philip, I'd like to introduce you to Jenetta. Jenetta, my friend Lord Philip Bulle of Grunemead."

"Tell him I'm very pleased to meet him, Lawrence," her voice rang in my head.

"I still don't get it," Phil said at the same time.

"She says she's very pleased to meet you, Philip," I told him. "Show him your fangs, Jenetta," I asked her telepathically. When she smiled, it was a moment before Phil noticed, as he was looking at me, still uncertain what was up. He saw where my gaze was resting, followed it, and took three clumsy steps back. Vampires are never clumsy - I'd succeeded in surprising him. I grinned. "All the animals you see in here," I did a quick count, "and a couple more besides, are vampires."

CHAPTER NINE

When he finally understood the magnitude of my ability, Phil was struck with a hopeful inspiration. Using his power, he summoned a few various rodents to him and tried to Awaken them. He reasoned that maybe he could do more than just control them. The experiment failed. He was not able to make them vampires, though I could.

"What about the strictures against Awakening new vampires without authorization?" he asked later. We were sitting in my study, having retired there after his failed experiment with the mice. Had we been mortal men, one might imagine us; two distinguished gentlemen of the ruling class, sitting with a glass of wine each, sipping leisurely in a well-lit room as we discussed matters of politics or the latest rumors of royal infidelity. As it was, though, we two undead creatures of the night sat relaxing in the near dark after an evening of murder and bantered about the legality of making thinking, vampiric creatures out of common, harmless animals.

"I don't think they apply here," I replied.

"How can they not? The rules are rather clear: you shall not create a vampire without the Council's express permission."

"Have you ever seen the rule in written form?"

"No, but that makes it no less valid."

"That's not my point. It is quite possible, perhaps even probable, that the restriction is worded such that it makes reference only to human vampires."

"Oh? Have *you* seen the wording?" Phil asked.

"Well, no."

"In fact, have you spoken to the Council about this at all? I'm sure they could instantly clear up any ambiguities for you."

"No, I haven't spoken to the Council." I was feeling a bit defensive. "But really, that restriction is in place to prevent overpopulation, primarily. I have found that my animal vampires are unable to create more of themselves. They are not even able to Awaken human vampires, so I don't see that the restriction has any place in this." The truth was, I was a bit nervous. I had finally discovered my Calling, and it was quite possible that the Council would disallow me from using it. Of course, they would find out eventually, but I wanted to enjoy this as long as I could.

It was immediately after sunset, two days after this discussion that I stepped from my bedchambers to find Tomás waiting for me.

"We had a problem today, Milord."

"Yes, Tomás? What was the problem?"

"If you will accompany me to the new stable, sir," he responded. A problem in the new stable? This was most curious. My staff was only allowed in once a month, after the animals had left for the night, to do the small amount of cleaning required. They weren't due back in for three weeks. I was intrigued, but not concerned. The Awakened animals kept themselves out of trouble. Most likely someone had gone in when they shouldn't have and seen almost two dozen freshly 'dead' animals.

I was horribly mistaken. My new little stable was a charnel house. The animals - *my vampires* - were dead. Not just dead. As I entered the structure I was greeted by silence. Not so much as a whisper in my mind. It was not an 'unearthly' silence; it was all *too* earthly, for this was the silence of true death. I would have welcomed Iron's acerbic comments right then. I felt none of the power Phil had mentioned when he'd come in two nights ago, and I smelled... ash. When the fireplace had burned itself out and nothing is left but gray and black flakes that fly into the air at the slightest provocation. That is what I smelled.

"What happened here?!" I turned and almost grabbed Tomás by his lapels to throw him across the dead stable in my anger. Almost; I caught myself and pushed it down. I was still just as angry, but I was in control. I lowered my hands back to my sides from where they had half risen. Tomás had exhibited more self control in that moment than I; his eyes had widened, and he positively stank of fear, but he had not so much as flinched from me. "What happened, Tomás?" I repeated more calmly.

"Milord, the first indication we had that something was amiss was at about noon today." Ah, noon. I sometimes miss seeing the sun lording over all of creation. "One of the stable hands, Jorge, thought he heard sounds from the new stable while he was walking the mare, Maple, near it. This was a sufficiently odd occurrence that he rousted Jacob the stable keeper from his other duties to mention it. Jacob thought it was probably one of the maids and a boy on a frolic and called out to them, but he received no answer. It was then that he noticed the holes."

He nodded to me, pausing to allow me a moment to investigate for myself the holes he mentioned. I opened the stall nearest to me, something I had been avoiding since entering the stable, all too certain of what I would find. I touched the door, grabbed the handle, and froze. I wasn't thinking anything in particular. At least, if I was, I don't remember it now. Just the fear of what lay beyond the door. I closed my eyes and eased the door open. The smell of ash only grew stronger, as I had expected. When it was fully open, I let myself see what was before me. I wasn't sure if it was worse or better than I feared.

There was nothing to identify that there were once two cats in this 'living space'. No body; no messy, wet remains. So, I guess that was good. Conversely, there was nothing to indicate that those small piles of ash had once been a pair of very ingenious cats. Chaser and Laina, they'd called themselves. Chaser used to challenge Jenetta the cow in philosophical traps almost daily, and Laina was just flat-out lazy, but very nice to everybody. Even Steel liked her, and that dog had always been an incorrigible cat-chaser. Now there was nothing to show of these friends of mine, these *creations* of mine; not even a twisted shell indicating their agonizing death.

I suppose I was ultimately fortunate in that. Death by sunlight is particularly brutal. The victim becomes partially awake, just barely aware, as they are rapidly and thoroughly cooked. My friends had been unable to escape the rays of light bearing in from the large hole that had been hacked in the outer wall, just above the lower half of stone.

"Each of the other stalls is essentially identical, milord," Tomás informed me.

"What happened?" I asked as I closed the stall door.

"Jacob went straight to Clive, and he came out here with five of the guards, where they caught the man still inside. Jorge must have heard him hacking the last few holes. By the time Clive arrived, it was all over in here. Clive had the man thrown in the dungeon, where he began making various accusations against you. Clive ordered the guards out, and was done with him until I woke up this evening." Tomás kept the same schedule as I, so that he could be at hand whenever I needed him. A good man. I sometimes wish I could have Awakened him, but I'm not sure he would have appreciated this life of ours.

Tomás had more to say on the day's events. "When I awoke a couple hours ago, and after Clive related the day's events to me, I promptly went down to investigate this wretch myself." He paused as we left the stable and I latched it behind me. We started for the manor, my intention to see for myself the ghoul who would do this to my friends and exact my justice. "His first reaction to my presence was to curse your name, swearing that you were an abomination and making various denigrating claims against you." We left unspoken the fact that his claims were most likely accurate. I was the Baron; nothing else was of consequence.

We entered the manor and began crossing to the other side, where my dungeon lay. Directly below us as we entered lay my own chambers. "Did he say anything of consequence?" I asked.

"He informed me that you were his second target. It was his intent to kill one of the guards or otherwise obtain some of the manor livery, steal into your chambers and slay you."

I barked a short laugh. He could not have made a hole into my chambers to let in the sunlight had he two full days available to him. "Slay me how?"

"He carried on his person a large sword, an axe, a wooden stake, and a large canteen of water." He did not have to state that the water had been blessed. We both knew it. "He was also wearing a large crucifix on a chain about his neck and a pocketful of garlic."

This was most disturbing. The man had come in well-armed to deal with one of my kind. Of course, the garlic would not have affected me in the slightest, but he could have easily destroyed me while I slept once he got my sarcophagus open. I suddenly remembered my guest. "How is Philip? Where is he?"

"Lord Philip is being attended by Gregory. I do not believe the assassin was aware you have a visitor." This he spoke in a whisper, as we had just arrived at the door to the dungeons.

"I will see to this fiend alone," I told Tomás after he'd unlocked the thick, wooden door.

"Very well, sir." He went back up the stairs we had just descended.

I walked slowly toward the cell in which the killer had been confined. When I stopped in front of it, he spoke in a heavily slurred, mumbling voice. "Ah, the nosferatu has finally risen. Am I to be your day's repast, then?"

He was in rough shape. His right arm was viciously broken in three places, one of which jutted out from his forearm, poking through the heavily bruised flesh. His face was a kaleidoscope of color, and it was amazing he could speak at all, so swollen was his broken jaw. His hair, matted with blood, hung down to cover his right eye, which had been rendered useless with the swelling. Any other injuries I was unable to see, as he had been left his clothes after being searched. Whether his injuries stemmed from resistance when he was captured or beatings afterward, I did not know, nor did it matter. "Not today, filth. But when I choose, your blood, your very life, shall enrich me." I had more to say, but was unsure of my words' effectiveness - I sensed no fear from this beaten man, only righteousness. "I can make it easy and painless for you if you tell me who sent you, why you have come after me and my pets."

He looked at me for a moment. I was about to speak again to repeat my order when he said, "Spare me your inhuman mercy. A devil as yourself knows no such concept. As for who sent me, it was God. He spits on you and all your kind, as even now he pits you against each other."

"What do you mean, fool?"

"I was hired by your own Council. Two pounds of gold to destroy the abominations you have made of God's creatures, three pounds for you. I will have their gold, then I will have their heads, too."

So, the Council knew of my Awakened animals. That they had hired a human to kill me was no surprise in itself. That they knew of my Calling and were so strongly opposed to me Awakening vampires without Council permission was. I really had been convincing myself that what I was doing was not the same, that it would be okay. Even so, I would not have imagined such harsh retribution.

He began shouting prayers as I left him, locking the door behind me with the key Tomás had left. With nothing else pressing my attention at the moment, I went up to Phil, who was awaiting me in my study.

"What do you intend to do?" he asked when I finished relaying all the details to him.

"I don't know. I suppose I shall have to send a message to the Council, explaining my actions, and requesting a pardon. They've sent their warning, and I imagine they are awaiting my response."

"Warning?" asked Phil.

"Certainly they would not destroy me out of hand for this. Obviously, they only sent one human knowing he would fail. You remember Count Rafael, right?"

"I remember something about him. He placed himself in the Council's disfavor with some transgression, I know."

"He awakened eight of his favorite concubines without authorization. The Council sent three dozen men after each one and had them killed. Three days later, the Count was summoned before the Council and fined."

"Fined?"

"Well, he had to make some kind of reparation. I imagine only part of it was monetary."

We spent most of the rest of the evening discussing the day's events, my options, and other related subjects. It was perhaps half an hour before sunrise when Tomás knocked on my study door.

"Enter, Tomás. What is it?"

I immediately noticed that he appeared uneasy, which was very unusual for him. "We appear to be under siege, milord."

I stood up. "What? By who?"

"They bear no colors, though they appear to outnumber the men we have available three to one. I took the liberty of sending a courier to discover their intent. He was thrown by one of them, perhaps thirty feet, against the main door. He was dead, sir, and rather...pale." I'm sure if Tomás had felt it necessary he would have made mention of two marks on the courier's neck, but both the power of the throw, and the bloodless pallor were enough to tell us: there were vampires out there.

"They just wait there?"

"Yes, milord."

I thought for a minute. "Well, I guess I should go see what it is they want."

"I would really rather you didn't, milord."

"I appreciate your concern, Tomás, but I don't think I have anything to fear, personally."

"As you say, sir."

"Philip, perhaps it'd be best for now if they remained ignorant of your presence." With that, I walked confidently out the door, Tomás following. Before opening the great doors, I signaled Tomás to stand back, in consideration of his safety. I opened the door, framing myself in the opening. "I am Baron Lawrence Hermanson. By what right do you place yourself on my land? What is it you seek?"

"Your head!" someone shouted as two arrows shattered on the stone doorway next to me. I took a step to the right at the sight of a more accurately fired third arrow. It did not strike me in the chest as its firer had intended, but still managed to pierce my left bicep. What caused me the gravest concern was the splash of water that sprayed onto the ground just shy of my feet. I closed and barred the door.

"Tomás, my boots, please." They were thick leather, so none of the drops of holy water which had reached them had soaked through, but it was nothing I was going to fool with. The arrow in my arm I could handle. I sat on one of the benches along the walls of the hall, and while Tomás took care of my footwear, I reached up with my right hand and got a firm grasp on the shaft near the point to which it had penetrated. I steeled myself as best I could. "Hold a moment, Tomás." He looked up, saw what I was about, and prudently rocked back on his heels. I counted to three and pulled.

Yes, it hurt, but not as much as I'd expected. I looked at the tip and saw why, and a shudder ran through me. It was a vampire killer. No barb was necessary, which is usually why you don't remove arrows in the manner I just had: straight back. The shaft and arrowhead were one piece. A long wooden rod sharpened at the tip. It was nothing more than a very slender, long wooden stake with a fletched end. A vampire killer. Had I not moved, it could well have been my end.

Tomás saw what I was looking at, and as he bent back to my boots, commented, "I don't think they're here to negotiate, milord."

"I'm afraid I must agree with your assessment."

"We can go for quite some time under siege, milord. The larders are well stocked."

"No."

"No?"

"No," I confirmed. Both boots were off. I wiggled my toes, gazing at them as I considered my next course of action. I was in a most unfortunate position. "Find two of the guards, and show them to the emergency passages in the kitchen and the dry goods storeroom. I want to be sure they're clear, but tell them to be careful. I'll be in my study. Hurry, though. Time is short."

"Understood." He walked off, shouting for assistance. Time was very short; perhaps twenty minutes remained before I would be completely at the mercy of any who came upon me. The sun approached rapidly, and never slowed in consideration of the needs of us here on earth. I returned to my study.

"Well, we will be leaving very soon," I informed Phil.

He looked up at me from the book he was perusing. "Oh?"

"Yes. Tell me, where is your carriage parked?"

"Out back, as usual, I would presume."

"Do you know exactly where?"

"No. My attendant, Johann, parked it." He closed the book and walked over to return it to its place on the shelves. "I take it we will be leaving in my carriage."

"I'm not yet sure. You might do well to gather your things." Phil left, and

I rang for an attendant. Tomás was busy, so Clive responded. He appeared to have wakened only recently.

"Yes, milord?"

"Assemble my grip for travel. Also, include a few bags of gold from my treasury. Have it all ready in my chambers."

"Very good, sir," he replied and walked out.

Tomás was the first to return, several precious minutes later. "Both passages are guarded. One of the scouts, Sean, was hit by an arrow while he was investigating the one from the kitchen. When we pulled it out of him, it was identical to the one that hit you. He also said someone threw water on him, too. I'm afraid we're fairly well stuck, sir."

"Well, we have - what's that?" I strode rapidly to the window and looked down. "It appears we are no longer under siege," I informed Tomás as I walked out of the room. "We are under attack."

CHAPTER TEN

Even as I announced our new situation to Tomás, we heard the call to arms of the manor, followed by a rush of feet as the reserves rushed to all ports of entry in case any assistance was needed. "Tomás, grab the sword in the study." He turned to follow my order as I continued down the hall to Phil's chambers.

Phil was looking around the room, rubbing his hands, then touching his mouth with a finger, then back to rubbing his hands, muttering, "Is that everything? Yes, I have my clothes, my belt, shoes." When he didn't notice me standing in the doorway, I rapped the open door with my knuckles. He turned towards me at the sound. "I think we're under attack, Lawrence." The last time he'd been in a castle under attack he'd lost almost everything - he was understandably nervous. "And the sun's coming. I can feel it. They're going to get us in our sleep."

He was correct. The sun was very nearly due to make its appearance; it was just minutes away. We had to move. "Come on, Philip. It's time to go." Tomás slipped my scabbarded sword into my hand from behind me, and then walked off to see to other matters.

"Where?" Phil practically shouted. "I heard Tomás. All your ways out are blocked!"

"Not all. Let's go." I started for the stairs, hoping he would get a hold of himself and follow. I wasn't sure I had the time to drag him along if he gave in to the hysterics he was courting right now. As I started down to the ground floor, I heard him coming down behind me.

I left the staircase at the bottom and had an excellent view of the fight for the front door. I couldn't see any vampires, but I figured they'd retreated to safety with dawn imminent. This was fortunate, as my men could probably not have held a defensive line against the combined force of just two vampires. I simply wasn't equipped to defend against the undead.

As it was, they were doing well, considering the numbers they were up against. The bottleneck caused by the doorway and other passages were to the defender's advantage. The attackers were rendered unable to fully utilize their greatest asset: their overwhelming numbers. There were perhaps twenty of my men at this door, but fifteen were standing idle, waiting for a comrade to fall. In the few seconds I watched, waiting for Philip, one did drop. One man promptly pulled his body back to make room as another stepped in, sword already raised, to continue the grisly business.

I had no time to watch, and most certainly not enough to help. We had to move fast. Each minute was clocked against us as the sun rose. "Tomás!" I shouted. I would need his competent, steadfast aid in the daytime. I crossed the dining room, heading for the stairs leading down to my chambers. "Tomás!" My ears picked up his reply, barely, over the raucous noise of the raging battle. "Come on, Philip," I commanded as I turned toward the kitchen, following Tomás' voice.

Tomás was backed into a small storage room to my right as I entered. In there with him were three of my men, holding off thirteen of the attackers who had apparently managed to win through the emergency passage into the kitchen. Again, the bottleneck of the door was serving my defenders well. The remnants of the beginnings of this battle for the kitchen were scattered about. Over a dozen bodies lay sprawled along the floor, some atop each other, some draped across the central food prep table. Some of the dead even had kitchen cutlery left sticking in them, such as the skinny man with the meat-cleaver jutting from his skull. Those implements had apparently been wielded as a last-minute, but effective, surprise weapon.

It was my first close look at the attacking forces, all these bodies on the floor. They wore no distinctive uniform. This led me to believe that they were not the Council's regular forces. All of them, however, were armed with swords of fair quality, so not just common rabble, either. Someone had paid for a competent group of men. They were all shapes and sizes, and none seemed to wear any armor. Very difficult to trace them to any one unit, but I knew who had hired them. The Council hadn't even seen fit to send their regular troops against me.

My own soldiers were good, but there was no way the remaining three of them could hold off thirteen -- yet they were trying. There was also no way they could have kept themselves from glancing up at me as I entered the room. Two of the enemy thugs turned at their looks. "That's him! Eight pounds of gold!" Apparently, my price had gone up since the lone assassin had tried his hand and failed earlier that day. I regretted that I hadn't killed him when I'd had the chance. Too late for that now.

Swordplay is not incredibly difficult. Anyone can swing a sword and hit another amateur with it. Being even moderately competent, however, is a little bit more challenging. I was good. Not great, but certainly good. Unfortunately, so were they. *And* I was outnumbered. Four remained to fight my three soldiers as the other nine turned to me. Phil, still standing behind me, would be of little use. He had only the most rudimentary knowledge of swordplay and no sword anyway. It also seemed he had forgotten our other advantages.

The nine of them swiftly advanced on me, spreading out in my large kitchen in a semi-circle to surround me and enable them all to attack at once. Only eight of them held swords. One must have lost his earlier, as he carried only a wicked-looking dagger, already bloodied. Their maneuvering was fleet, and rapid to their eyes. To my perception, they moved at a leisurely pace, and before they'd reached their positions, they were only eight in number, reduced by one before we engaged in true battle.

One of the dead bodies from the earlier fighting was lying at my feet. He had been wearing a dirk in his belt. I reached down to pick it up to use as a backup weapon, and as I rose, I realized it had the perfect balance of a throwing knife. These were never a specialty of mine, but I had some practice with them, and I could strike my target blade first - that was the challenge - about twenty-five percent of the time. It was a short throw, and either I was lucky, or some dark god favored me that night. The mercenaries may have seen me move, but they did not have time to react before the dirk appeared to sprout from their comrade's chest, a man brandishing a massive, two-handed sword. He fell slowly backwards, looking down, the handle which jutted from his torso his last vision in life. This was how they were brought down from nine to eight before they even started advancing.

The others seemed to take that as the signal to charge, and I was rushed by seven very competent blademen en masse.

Yes, seven. Another had suddenly disappeared from their number. While one might easily dismiss Phil as an incompetent fool in battle - as I had certainly done - that is not necessarily the case. One of the men had remained back, fumbling at his belt for something. He grabbed a small bottle from his belt-pouch, unstoppered it, and was ready to throw the liquid on me when he was struck in the arm by a large black kettle. True, Philip was probably aiming for the man's head, or the hand holding the vial. That he likely missed his intended target was of no consequence, as the twenty-five pound kettle broke the man's arm horribly and sent the holy water spraying harmlessly away from us. It was only then that I noticed several of the men, at least three, had vials of water at their belts, too. Being mercenaries, they most likely relied more on their skill with the blade than such mystical unknowns as holy water.

That would be their fatal mistake.

All of this I was able to observe only peripherally, as I was rather busy in dealing with the seven men surrounding me. They continued to coordinate themselves well, seeming to move forward as one. The daggerman was in the center of their arc, and the swordsman to his left – my right – was the first to feel my blade. I began my swing from my left, coming up across my body. The tip of my sword sliced his neck wide open in this sweep, coming in well under his own upraised sword. Before he even started to fall, his blood geysering from his severed jugular, my sword continued its arc, flowing in a continuous, smooth movement from the swing that had sliced his neck. As it reached the second man, my weapon – moving at vampiric speed – knocked a blade aside that had already begun its descent upon me. This lightning collision of steel on steel also deflected my own sword's path about a foot upwards, causing it to fly over and past the next man's head as I continued my extended swing. I quickly reversed its direction and brought it down, landing the blade at an angle on the man's left arm, just below the shoulder. With my supernatural strength behind the blow, his arm was left dangling useless- ly, attached to the rest of his body by no more than a bloody tangle of muscle and skin, as my sword had sheared clean through the bone. At the same time, I managed to bring the hilt of my sword up to catch his blade, stopping it from connecting with my flesh.

The daggerman had taken this brief flurry of combat to mean I was distracted, which proved to be his last error in this world. My awareness was much more than these humans could conceive; indeed, combined with my celeritous reactions, it was the only thing that was allowing a moderately good swordsman like myself to move with the speed necessary to handle this sellsword scum. I heard his feet splash in the blood behind me as he advanced to dagger range. As soon as he was close enough, even as he prepared to thrust his dagger into me, I reached for him with my left hand and grabbed him by the hair. I yanked him forward and up, placing his neck in the position I required. His struggling, however, caused me to miss my mark. As my jaws were about to snap on his throat, he ducked his head to protect this vulnerable spot, and my mouth instead closed on his chin, my fangs piercing straight into the bone of his mandible. Not caring, I clamped down even harder and tore away, ripping his lower jaw completely away from his face as he screamed. Now, screaming was all the sound he could make, as his tongue hung uselessly down his neck, dangling from the back of his throat, his jaw lying on the floor where I'd spit it out. I let go of his hair. He was no longer a threat.

Even a vampire can move only so quickly, do so much at once, and thus I had been forced to leave myself open to the other three. As I was cleaving the third man's arm and biting the jaw off the other, I felt two swords bite into my back. I turned my head in time to see the third attempting a thrust and managed to arch my now-bleeding back enough that the tip missed its mark, whistling harmlessly through my blouse. This fool had been overconfident and wound up over thrusting as he failed to find the resistance of solid tissue he'd expected. An amateur's mistake. I reached behind myself with my bloody left hand and brushed his arm. Blindly, I moved my hand a touch lower and grabbed his wrist. My hand had been made slick with the blood of the slain daggerman, and I had to squeeze tight to maintain my grip. I squeezed hard, and felt his bones shifting, breaking and grinding beneath my hand. He cried out and I heard his sword clatter to the ground.

Swordsman number two, whose blade I'd deflected, had already recovered. His sword was speeding for my ribcage under my sword arm. As

I stepped to the left, I yanked at the man whose arm I had grabbed. He stumbled forward to where I'd just been standing, bent over at the waist. His face was promptly split open by the other man's upswing.

I continued my movement, releasing the falling man's wrist as I swiveled in to the first swordsman who had split open my back. I slipped a bit in the blood of the man with the slit throat, so as I brought my sword around back-handed, pommel first, I missed crushing his windpipe, as I'd intended. My arm instead rose up several inches as I tried to maintain my footing and balance on the blood-soaked floor, causing me to crunch his nose into his skull. The preternatural force of the blow caused the first inch of my pommel to actually continue into his nasal cavity as well, following his collapsing nose and crunching more bone on the way. My balance restored, I immediately reversed my weapon's direction. It emerged from the dead goon's face with a slurping, sucking sound, and pierced the chest of the man who had twice missed me as he charged the few feet between us.

As I pulled my blade out of his crumpling body I turned to the last swordsman - the other who had managed to land a strike on me - to find him lying on the floor, his throat ripped out in a bloody mess of tissue and cartilage by Phil's fangs.

I looked over to where the last four had pinned my men. Two were down, as was one of my men. I walked over to the final two goons, sticking my sword into the back of one of their fallen comrades on the way just to get it out of my hands for a moment. The sell-swords were preoccupied with fighting my men and failed to notice my approach. I reached out with both hands and brought their skulls together with all the force I could muster. Perhaps this was a bit much, as my hands met in the middle with a muffled, wet clap, only a few fragments of skull bone between them. Their skulls had exploded on contact with each other like a pair of melons, the sheer force of the impact sending gray matter, blood, tissue and bone spraying both me and my soldiers. Perhaps this attack from behind was not honorable, but I had no time for honorable combat; I was on a very tight schedule. Dawn was just a few short minutes away.

I pointed a gore-coated finger at my soldiers, who seemed to be in a bit of shock over the visceral display they had just witnessed. "Tell those who need to get out that there is a passage in my chambers they can use. Tomás, let's go." The orders seemed to reanimate the soldiers. They saluted smartly and ran off. I also turned and strode out, collecting Phil on the way. "Where is Philip's driver?" I called back over my shoulder.

"He was to visit a, uh, woman in the town tonight. I imagine we'll find him still there, milord."

"Excellent. That will be our first stop, with any luck."

We entered my chamber and I approached my sarcophagus. This was no budget coffin. It stood on a two foot tall base which was carved from one solid block of stone. The sarcophagus itself was of marble and gold, and both sarcophagus and base were intricately carved in matching bas-relief. It was enormous and weighed about two tons. It had been my resting place for 73 years, and was the finest I'd ever seen, a cabalistic work of profane art in itself. Its size and weight served to conceal a new exit I'd had made the year before. I knew its existence was still a secret, as those involved in its construction had not lived to speak of the work.

To be honest, I hadn't intended it as an exit, but as an entrance. I imagined it as an escape route from the new stable and into the manor for my vampiric animals in the event of an emergency. All of them knew of it, but it had done them no good in the contemptible daytime attack. Perhaps it would serve us tonight.

I grabbed an edge of the monolithic casket and began pulling it aside to reveal the passage beyond. When the sarcophagus was clear I led the way in. After taking a moment to light a portable oil lamp, Tomás followed.

"Wait." I went back into my room. There, on the large bed that dominated the room along with the sarcophagus was the bag Clive had prepared, and the money I'd requested. I handed the traveling bag to Tomás, grabbed the coins and returned to the dark passage. As Tomás stepped back in with his lantern, I could see every detail of the rough tunnel. It was fairly close to the surface, and so the roof and walls had been heavily reinforced with stone and wood. We walked rapidly along its eighty foot length before it up sloped a bit in the last twenty feet to come to a dead end. Above us was a heavy wooden door, which I knew to be eight inches thick and reinforced with steel. I also knew that there was a catch on the other side that would allow it to drop open, thus allowing the animals to jump down. There was a simple catch on this side as well to close it up again, but this one was currently unlatched to allow it to be opened from the other side only.

Fortunately for us, there was a pair of heavy-duty handles on this side, though I couldn't see what for. Most likely the human workers had left them in, not understanding the use to which this door would be put. I pulled down on the handles. I pulled and hoisted my own feet off the ground, but the door wouldn't budge. "Philip, throw your weight in. Grab that handle." He came out of his daze to do as I requested. The weight of both of us, even with his considerable stomach, did nothing. Not good.

I looked up at the door. Bloody thing. It mocked me in its immobility.

Leverage. That's what we needed. "Philip, one hand on the handle pulling down, push up here." I indicated the stable floor above, which was just as sturdy as the door above our heads. We did so, both of us with one hand gripping a handle, pulling down, the other hand providing a countering force pushing against the ceiling. I heard it creak, felt maybe a slight movement, but nothing else. What I felt more was the inexorable approach of dawn, ready to render us nothing more than unconscious, helpless forms with its cursed advent. In desperation I grabbed the handle with both hands and swung my feet up to push against the ceiling.

That gave us the extra bit of force we needed. I heard the catch above snap with a loud 'CRACK' and fly off as the door crashed down on us. Phil managed to let go and drop to the floor. Due to my position, I was thrown against the dead end, crushed between the wall and the now-open trapdoor. It hurt, a lot, but the door was open, and that was the important thing. I came around the side of the door to see Phil covered in ash. That would be Chestnut. The entrance to the escape tunnel was in his stall. I put the thought out of my mind and hoisted Tomás up. I jumped up after him, easily clearing the seven feet up even with my injuries, followed by Phil.

"Where is Philip's carriage?" I whispered to Tomás.

He pointed. "You should be able to see it through there, milord." The stable had been built without windows, but the holes chopped by the barbarian in my dungeon now served the same purpose. I looked through the one in the stall we presently occupied. There it was. I could barely see the rear of it, as the angle at which I was peering caused most of it to be blocked from my view. It was right behind the stable, opposite the manor, not fifteen feet from where we stood. Almost perfect placement for our needs. The mercenaries that were still outside were farther in, between this stable and the manor. Our way out should be clear.

"Quiet, now," I instructed. I opened the stall door, then the rear stable door. We ran to the carriage, Phil and I getting into the back and opening up his two concealed coffins. We each climbed in; latching them shut as Tomás stepped up to the open-air driver's seat and took up the reins. He got the horses moving, and the last I remember as the sun began to climb above the eastern horizon was the angry shouts of the mercenaries and a couple arrows thudding into the carriage. "We made it," I thought as I lost consciousness.

CHAPTER ELEVEN

"What're you stopping there for? That's not the end, is it? You still haven't said how he betrayed you," protested Mac. He was lying on the floor, having hardly moved from when Lawrence started his tale.

"It's one o'clock, Mac, and I think I heard footsteps," Lawrence replied as he pushed himself up from where he'd been sitting on the floor and walked to the door. He hesitated with his hand on the knob, listening, then opened it just as Phil was raising his hand to knock. Lawrence smiled at him. "Good to see you, Phil. Please come in." Phil smiled back and did as bidden. "I trust your negotiations are going well?"

"Indeed they are. In fact, tonight was the last. I wrapped it up well ahead of schedule. I will be returning to Europe tomorrow with better than expected results." He was beaming with pride at his news, his smile growing as he relished his victory. He sat in one of the available chairs and looked at the animals. "And good evening to you two as well; Mac, Lady." He nodded a greeting to each as he spoke their names.

Mac barked a quiet greeting, a muffled "Woof."

"'Tell rat-boy hello from me too, Lawrence,'" Lady said from her usual perch atop the coffin.

"Lady says hello as well, Phil."

"Ya know, Larry, I didn't even think to ask you yesterday. What are you doing in town? Have you business here as well? Whatever the reason, it's a lovely coincidence that we should be not only in town at the same time but in the same hotel as well."

Lawrence gathered his thoughts before answering, weighing how much he trusted his one-time friend. His impassive face revealed no sign of his irritation at Phil's shortening of his name. "Coincidence, Phil? You know my feelings about 'coincidence'. We are supernatural beings. Coincidence always follows in our footsteps. As for being at this hotel, I live here."

"Here? In the hotel?" He glanced around the room, re-appraising it. "I'd wondered why you'd brought a coffin here, though I didn't expect that model would be your primary resting place," he finished as he eyed the cut-rate casket.

"This is just temporary lodging. I expect to be in more permanent residence in a week or two."

"Moving, eh? Any particular reason?"

"Let me just say that I have been rather...mobile. When the Council is looking for you it is best not to remain in any one place for too long."

"Oh." Phil fiddled uncomfortably with his Ankh necklace. "Look, Larry," his focus on his pendant kept him from seeing the moue on Lawrence's face at the undignified shortening of his name; "I know it's a long time coming, but I'm really sorry for what happened that night. I..."

Lawrence shook his head. "Don't worry about it, Phil. If it hadn't been you, someone else would have turned me in."

"That's not the point, Lawrence. You stood by me all those years after I lost my lands, even arguing against the Council for me. You gave me money when I needed it, you took me in. I was just...well, never mind. There's no acceptable reason. I'm sorry. The least I could have done was stop running away and done you that one last favor you called out for."

Lawrence's eyes closed, an ineffective dam against the flood of painful memories, but all he said was, "That's fine, Phil. Apology is accepted."

"I think the Council's kinda forgotten about you, anyway. I haven't heard your name come up in almost thirty years. They've had a lot of trouble finding you the last few hundred years, for some reason."

"Good."

The group was silent. Phil began fingering his Ankh again. "So," he said, breaking the stillness. "What have you three been up to?"

"Just sharing some old stories, Phil."

He brightened up. "Oh? About what?" He stopped abruptly and looked at Mac and Lady gazing serenely at him. He shifted uncertainly in his chair. "Uh, about that last night?"

"Among other things, yes, Phil." Lawrence looked at him, a small, predatory grin on his face. After holding it for a second, the grin disappeared. "Don't worry. I've also been telling them of your help in the fight at the manor. You weren't all bad. And, of course, they also just heard your apology."

"Um. Yes." Phil cast his eyes around the room, alighting finally on Lawrence's shoulder. "So, I see you've already fed tonight, eh?" he asked, making an obvious - and awkward - attempt to change the subject.

"What do you mean?" Lawrence asked guardedly.

"I see it was a brunette, eh? Some raven-haired vixen?"

"She was blond, if you must know. What on earth are you prattling on about?"

Phil's smile disappeared. He looked at Lady, then Mac. "Well, whose are these, then?" He stretched across and plucked a few loose strands of hair off of Lawrence's shoulder. Lawrence reached up and took them from Phil.

"They appear to be mine," he shrugged, looking at them.

"Ha! Hey, Mac - Lawrence is shedding!" Lady snickered.

"Lady, I'm not sure I like the look on Phil's face," Mac returned.

Phil's eyebrows had gone up slightly and he was sitting quietly, immobile to all appearances. Lady looked over at him to see his brows drop down, giving the impression of a man deep in troubling thoughts.

"Phil?" Lawrence prompted.

"Lawrence, have you had any other problems? Ummm...early to sleep, late to rise? Weakness? Anything?" His tone grew urgent as he asked his questions.

"A bit. Nothing major. Why?"

Phil was silent, his brows still knitted in concerned thought. "Anything else? Uh, slowing down? Your special ability not working quite as well as it should?"

"Yes, yes, and I'm not healing quickly either. What of it?"

"Well, I'm not sure, Lawrence," he began haltingly before ending in a tumble of rushed words, "but I think you may be dying."

There was a pause, and Lawrence burst out laughing. "I'm already dead, you melodramatic fool! And wherever would you get an idea like that, anyway?"

"I'm quite serious, Lawrence. Remember Count Lowenhagen?"

"Sure, I remember him. He's the one that Awakened his wife, too, right?"

"Correct. He's dead. True death."

"What happened?"

"No one knows, but I'm afraid it was the same thing that's happening to you. I didn't personally see him when he was sick, but I remember talking to some of the others about it. It started out like what you have, nothing major, but certainly odd. Then his hair started falling out, his body started to decay.

Other stuff too, I guess."

Lawrence was running his hand down his front, smoothing a tie that wasn't there. "And he died? What happened?"

"I guess one night he just didn't wake up at all. His wife the Countess finally put his putrefying remains in the sun so she could scatter his ashes."

"You're sure it's not just a story? Or maybe the Countess did it - maybe she killed him."

"No, I've heard it from too many reliable sources, including some who were there at the end. And Angela was always faithfully in love with the Count, and he with her. They were the most content couple I ever knew - married for 700 years, after all. No, that wasn't it. He died. And you're showing the same symptoms."

*　*　*

"Look, Mr. Hull, I have questioned witnesses who saw him come in here. Several of them. And I have a pretty strong feeling that if I start knocking on doors, somebody here will have seen this man. He may answer a door himself. Should I start doing that? Knocking on doors? Of course, I could also take you down to the station and ask you at length, and really find out everything about what you do here. Or you could be a bit more forthcoming." Jamon was talking to the man Lawrence thought of as 'Fat Jack', the night manager of the Biltmore Hotel. The corpulent fellow's real name was Richard Hull. Jamon had been led here by some of the street cops who had been showing Jamon's assailant's picture around discretely. It was not a clear photo, being lifted from the video, but they'd received a couple reports of him entering and leaving this fleabag hotel. It was Jamon's only lead, and he was going to make the most of it.

The little TV was still exhibiting mankind's foibles, but Mr. Hull was no longer focused on it. Since Detective Schroeder had flashed his badge, Mr. Hull had paid him cautious attention. He now made a show of looking through old registration cards. They were the size of regular index cards, thrown haphazardly in a shoebox. "Look, Detective, sometimes records here get lost. You see we don't got no computer here, and our registration cards are small, easily misplaced. But I do remember this guy, now I think about it." Jamon smiled at the pudgy worm's suddenly improved memory. "He, uh, kept to himself. Had a couple animals with him. Dog and a cat."

Jamon kept his face professionally neutral at the news. "What was his name? Is he still here?"

Mr. Hull frowned in the unaccustomed effort of thought. "Nah. Checked out days ago. Name was...uh, Terrance. No. Lawrence. Lawrence something."

"A last name would be much help, Mr. Hull. And what did he drive?"

"Uh, Lawrence... Watts! Yeah. Lawrence Watts. And he drove an old green van. Minivan. At least, until his last night here. Then he had a black truck of some kind." Mr. Hull was perspiring with his efforts at recall. Or perhaps it was just the dozens of pounds of insulation provided by his adipose tissue.

"What happened to the minivan?" Jamon was jotting everything down in his notebook. He knew he'd have no problem remembering any of it, but it was taught from day one at the academy: take notes on *everything*.

"Dunno. Just didn't have it. Come to think of it, he didn't have it for a few days before he got his new truck. At least not what I saw."

After a few more questions on Lawrence's habits, clothes, company, and anything else Jamon could think of, he gave Mr. Hull his card. "Mr. Hull, if you can think of anything else that may be of use, please call. Anytime." Jamon knew the man would never use the cell number on the card, but he had to cover all the bases.

It was past time for him to leave: this place was uncomfortably close to his 'turf'. He didn't want anybody recognizing him as the dealer from downtown.

He climbed into his car, a late model Chevy. As he started back home to pick up the BMW, he reflected on the other information he had on

Lawrence. This was not something he'd put in any notebook. If Jamon's memory was finally working properly, he knew that Lawrence should be dead.

His revelation had come to him this morning. Well, this evening, actually - working night shift does strange things to one's vocabulary. He was eating breakfast when a series of images flashed through his mind in quick succession. His spoon had splashed back into the bowl, forgotten as he tried to make some sense of the parade of seemingly random images fluttering like leaves through his still-sleepy head. This went on for perhaps five seconds before the startling array of scenes reordered themselves into one long memory. He originally mistook it for a remembrance of a forgotten dream before recognizing it for what it was - his mind unlocking something that had somehow been hidden in his own head, prevented from being recollected.

It was a memory that had somehow abandoned him - a memory of an evening about a month past. He had closed the Lopez case and received authorization for his current sting. He'd met with some of the guys at the bar to celebrate his success. Afterward he had been walking out to his car after overindulging on soda pop - he never drank if he had duty the next day: if he did, he always went over the top and was still tipsy when reporting in the following morning. He recognized in himself the hiding alcoholic and fought valiantly to keep that enemy at bay.

Walking out of the bar had been his last memory before he had awakened

to find himself in an alley, without a clue what had knocked him out to begin with. Curiously, he hadn't given the matter a thought after waking, not even remembering that aspect of it to correlate with his last attack. Now he remembered it all, vividly. He played the memory through his mind again, reliving parts of it bit by bit, as he did so often with the surveillance video.

He'd turned around, just on a haunting feeling, to see a dark figure emerge from the shadows. Only it was not emerging, not really. Better to say that the form materialized out of nothing, took substance from the shadows. The dark shape immediately rushed him. He felt his memory was still playing tricks on him for it seemed, in retrospect, that the figure had moved faster than was mortally possible.

Jamon responded to this rushing figure with reflexes that had been honed by training to near instinctual reactions. He reached for his pistol. He'd barely pulled it from his holster when the stranger was on him, pulling Jamon's head back. As he felt something pierce his flesh, he'd instinctively squeezed the trigger. His first shot, he knew, had struck true, right to the center of his assailant's chest. His hand was knocked down for the second shot, causing that one to probably hit in the pelvis, maybe a leg. The first shot should have the man dead, or certainly well on his way.

Almost as though he were unaware of the mortal wound he'd just received, the assailant had just continued what he'd been doing. At the time, Jamon had seemed to go into a cathartic state, but he now remembered it all clearly, especially the strange sensation as the man *drank his blood*. Jamon was bleeding freely through the two small holes the man's razor-sharp teeth had punctured in his neck, but his attacker was actually sucking the blood out in a greater rush. It was as though he couldn't wait for the slow trickle of the naturally flowing blood. Jamon could feel his precious fluids rapidly passing out of his system and into the man's greedily sucking mouth. That was only the most visceral aspect of the experience. More disturbing, it felt almost as though his energy, the very force of his life itself, were being taken. This was not just the weariness one experienced with blood loss, but something...deeper. He could feel the grip his body kept on his soul weakening as he felt an almost spiritual component of himself escaping through the holes in his neck.

As if that weren't enough indignity, the man had also stolen the five bucks in cash Jamon had been carrying.

The face of his assailant was instantly recognizable, and he now had a name for it: Lawrence.

* * *

The room was silent. Had a blind man entered, he would have thought it unoccupied. No voice, no movement; no breath nor heartbeat.

To Lawrence's mind, the silence was complete. There were no voices in his head, no messages being communicated with him from his two animal friends. He took this to mean that they were pursuing their own thoughts in the confines of their own minds, as he was. They were not.

"I smell the decay too, Mac, now that I know what to look for."

"It's been getting progressively worse since we first joined him. In fact, it seems to get worse more quickly each day," Mac replied.

"What is it?"

"You heard Phil, Lady. Nobody knows. I just wonder if we can do anything about it."

"I wish we could go to the library or something."

"What are you gonna do, check out *Undead Physiology 101*?" Lady could hear Mac's derision at this idea. "Now who's the dumb one?"

"We might find *something*, you fool! There's hundreds of books on vampires, and not just fictional stories. Some must have some basis in fact. The stories, the legends, sprang from some fragments of truth, obviously. Perhaps there's something out there about this. We have to do *something*!" Neither had any response to this.

Minutes ticked away in pure silence, now for everyone.

Expanding her telepathy to include Lawrence, Lady asked, "So, we've got some time before dawn. Are you going to finish your tale?"

His reverie finally broken, Lawrence turned to Lady. He, too, had been contemplating the veracity of Phil's words, and was worried. While he took some comfort from the fact that he had gone through similar problems about two hundred years before, they had been nowhere near as pronounced, nor had they gone on for so long; two weeks at best. And Phil had no reason to lie to him about such a thing.

Lawrence had questioned Phil at length, probing for every piece of information the pot-bellied vampire could yield. The animals, through Lawrence, had also posited several questions. Most of them Phil did not have an answer for. What knowledge they had was far surpassed by that which they did not have. They learned that it had stricken other vampires in the past, with Lawrence's prior experience apparently the only one that had not proven fatal. It was astonishingly rare, only afflicting one vampire every few hundred years, on average. The Council claimed to have no knowledge of either its causes or its cure.

Lawrence had even considered finding a doctor. This idea was discarded out of hand almost as rapidly as the thought had surfaced. Were the doctor to take a vow of silence not to speak of Lawrence or vampires in general, allowing the truth to be revealed, the physician would still be able to do nothing, knowing naught of vampire physiology.

Lawrence had grown bored over the centuries, but now found that he had no wish to lie down and die. In addition, he'd found companionship again, friends. This, too, weighed heavily on his mind, surpassing even his own desire to live; for if Lawrence died, who would take care of Mac and Lady?

This would soon demand deeper thought, he decided. But not tonight.

"Yes, Lady, let us finish this tale before the sun comes up."

CHAPTER TWELVE

The rest of that day (Lawrence resumed) passed without my intervention, lost as I was in whatever place our consciousness goes when it flees our bodies for the day. Our lives rested wholly in the able hands of Tomás; it was up to him to carry us to safety. He managed to locate Phil's driver, Johann, and pry him from the arms of the prostitute he was so fond of. We now had two mortal aides to assist us against all of vampire kind. Not good odds. Fortunately, our current plan was nothing more elaborate than flight, followed by concealment.

That first night we decided to drive west until we found a large city in which we could hide out amid the anonymous masses. Ultimately, Phil would return to his own life, but he would stay to see me settled comfortably for the nonce. Clive had sent me on my way with a good quantity of gold from the treasury, so I was not in fear of becoming an instant pauper. With Tomás at my side and Phil's assistance, I should have few problems until I resolved this issue with the Council.

Phil and I led the horses west that night, allowing Tomás and Johann time to rest while still putting more space between ourselves and the mercenaries. As we took our turns at the lazy task of handling the reins, I allowed myself the luxury of wondering what had happened to the rest of my staff after our hasty departure. I had always considered myself a kind lord - how easy it was for me to disregard the brutality of my feedings to think this - and earnestly hoped my people had managed to escape the brutality of my attackers. I later discovered from Phil that much of my staff did get away at first. Those that did not were questioned by the human mercenaries. They did not survive this barbaric process for long. At that, they were the lucky ones. The Council's Seekers found much of the staff that had escaped. The Seekers have been known to question mortals for days. Indeed, I am told it was they who trained the priests of the Spanish Inquisition in questioning heretics. With the greater resilience of the undead body, the suffering is only greater - I hope to never come under their power. Perhaps they no longer operate the same way; I prefer not to investigate this first-hand, even now.

After a few weeks of largely uneventful travel, we settled in Dunkirk, a coastal city in France. It was many times larger than any of my own small villages. Indeed, all combined, the few little villages of my lost barony could not match the population of this one city. Likewise, I was certain they could not match its wealth, prosperity, and variety; nor could they match its squalor, crime, or filth. One would think that, being so close to so much water - a whole ocean of it - the city should at least be somewhat clean. This was not the case. Cleanliness was never a major civic concern back then. It was not even a *minor* civic concern. Granted, in the wealthier district there were men whose sole function was to keep the streets clean, and they did a fair job. Anywhere else, however, one could wonder if a broom had ever whisked its way past. The problem, of course, was waste removal: there wasn't any. Removal, that is; there was always plenty of waste. So people often simply dumped their garbage and...bodily wastes...into the streets or alleys right out their windows. Remember that the phrase "neither a pot to piss in nor a window to throw it out of" has very literal roots.

As much as I would have preferred to room in the more luxurious – and clean - section of the city, I had two concerns. One was that my funds, though ample, were limited. Clive had packed quite a bit in my bags, but I had no idea how long I had to make it last, and I was no longer collecting new taxes to refill my coffers. The other item on my mind was something I've forgotten at my own peril a few times only: luxurious living is conspicuous.

I repeated these reasons to myself as I stepped over the drunken body sprawled at the inn's doorway as we went in to claim a couple rooms. The inn we chose was rather typical of the city. Far from the affluence of the wealthier district, it was likewise distant from the worst of the ghetto.

We got a room on the ground floor of the two-story structure. The common room seemed to have fewer than the normal number of drunks, and Tomás later reported the food as being rather good, if bland. It was called "Three Signposts" for some obscure reason probably known only to long-time residents of that area of Dunkirk. It was a nice enough place, I suppose, but even after almost two years of residence there I looked down on it, remembering the easy, expansive comfort of my manor.

Anyway, as I said, we were in France. I was not French, but could speak the language passing fair. Tomás, however, had been raised by a Frenchwoman before he ran away and joined my household as a young teenager. After a week of re-immersing himself in it, he was speaking the language like a native. This had been a factor in our choice of France, as we needed to blend well with the populace for a time. I despised hiding, but the Council gave me no other choice.

Hiding was easier in those times than today in many ways. No one carried any form of identification - such a thing was unheard of. You could take any name you wished - if there was no one there you knew, there was no way for anyone to know otherwise. There were no computers tracking your purchases, your vehicle permits or your location by your residential registrations. There were no fingerprints being detected or DNA analyzed to find out who you were and where you had been, no face-recognition software finding your face among crowds.

We settled in easily. I took the name of Lawrence Prill for the duration of my stay in Dunkirk. The first month was spent in a calm state of near paranoia. By this I mean that we were always on the watch for anything that might indicate we'd been found, or even suspected, while remaining outwardly serene. Tomás was pressed into giving me lessons on how to behave as a commoner. Had anybody seen Phil or I strut into our rooms that first night, the whispers would have traveled rapidly across the land until the Council and the Seekers knew of the 'royalty' staying at the Three Signposts. The only thing more conspicuous than living well is living in mediocrity while appearing to be above such mean standards. Image is everything - even when it is a lowly image you seek.

After six weeks in Dunkirk, Phil set off to return home - or to one of the many places he was accustomed to stay in. We had discussed what he was to do at great length, though there wasn't much to it. He would attempt to gauge the mood of the Council towards me. Based on this, we would then decide how I was to proceed in getting my name cleared with the Council and, hopefully, getting my lands back. I would be sorry to lose his company while he returned to his transient life, but there was no need for him to stay; to the best of our knowledge, the Council was unaware he'd been with me at the time, and did not view him as a co-conspirator or any such thing.

It was to be almost two years before Phil was to return to Dunkirk, though I'd received a couple of messages from him updating me on his doings. Neither message was very hopeful, though he'd tried to make them sound optimistic. There was a bounty on my head, raised again to fifteen pounds of gold. There was no reason given for this apart from "Crimes against the community." Rumors regarding the nature of my offense abounded: from me killing a Council member to revealing our existence to the world at large. Some of them even had the facts right: that I had Awakened several animals without the Council's permission.

As it seemed the Council was not open to negotiation, I remained in hiding. Those first two years would have been impossible were it not for the patient, watchful company of Tomás. I had lived as a baron for over a hundred years. It was not easy, at first, to change my ways. Tomás showed me what it was to be a commoner. Not one of those dirty, sodden drunks that littered the streets all too often. He showed me the best of the common folk. I was molded by his careful, patient tutelage into a respectable commoner, still able to carry myself with pride, if not such hauteur, as more fitted my tastes and style.

While I was kept quite busy for the next twenty months, there isn't really all that much that bears repeating.

The evening in question, the culmination of this tale, came in the middle of February, in the year 1606. It may not have been the worst winter of my life, but at the time you could not have convinced me otherwise. For one thing, the snowfall seemed to be unending. To all appearances, the inn should have been buried by this boundless frozen precipitation. The reality of the situation was that the wind coming in off the water was constantly blowing the snow around, but such details were beneath consideration at the time. It was cold. Oh, cold doesn't even begin to plumb the depths of the sub-arctic, mercury-scoffing depths to which the thermometer plunged.

A night of this would not have been bad. Two nights, I could have tolerated. This abysmal weather, after which I would have welcomed the unending furnace of hell, went on for three weeks. Perhaps I had been pampered up until then. My own estate never experienced such hard winters, and vampires do not pay heed to normal fluctuations in temperature. Turn up the heat to one hundred degrees Fahrenheit; we will not break a sweat. Likewise, drop the thermostat to freezing, thirty-two degrees, and we will not reward you with so much as a shiver. The temperatures that year were enough to make me feel as though I'd soon go numb. In addition, it kept the people indoors except for necessities, making my hunting a bothersome process.

I had just fed the night before everything came apart, and so was near the peak of my strength - or should have been - when I rose that night. Instead, I woke up to a sharp pain in my chest and the knowledge that sunset was already an hour gone. My third realization was that my now-open eyes were viewing the rough timbers of my room's ceiling, not the smooth wooden underside of my coffin's lid. I remained in my supine position, listening, trying to pick up some clue as to what was going on. I heard breathing: two humans drawing air, one laboriously. Past my room, toward the common area was the usual smatterings of noise that accompanied the evening meal, and the other normal sounds of the inn for this hour. But, two people in my room? I could not imagine that Tomás would have been so unrefined as to bring one of his women - he had managed to win several admirers with his charming, refined ways - to our room.

I also heard a drip. Like a drop of water falling into a puddle, but not quite. Closer to a drop of oil, or something of similar viscosity. This prompted me to draw a most uncomfortable small breath, aggravating my chest pain, to gain a taste of the air. As I'd suspected, the warm, coppery scent of blood was strong. Much had been spilled, recently, in my room. If the dripping was any indication, it was still being shed, albeit slowly. I could think of nothing else to do, so I sat up.

Oh yes, there was blood. Were it spread more evenly, the floor could have been painted with it, and there would still remain enough to start on the walls. So much from two people, and still they drew breath? It was then that I saw Tomás. Obviously the source of a significant quantity of the fluid, he sat back in a chair against the wall. His left arm ended perhaps two inches below the elbow, a jagged amputation. He cradled what remained of his arm against his body. It was from this wound that I'd heard the blood drip.

His pallor could have been caused by shock or blood loss; I had no way of knowing which at the time. Indeed, shock was not a known problem in that period's medical lexicon; physicians were still treating what were called 'humours'. Tomás, however, had somehow had the presence of mind to tie off his stump in a makeshift tourniquet. The severity of the wound and his appearance gave me grave doubt over whether he would survive the injury.

I decided what I had to do even as I climbed out of my coffin. Though I should have been crying out in pain for the injury I had, in truth I had forgotten my own wound - whatever it was - in my sudden concern for Tomás: my steadfast, able, and true companion. I had realized only then what his death would mean to me. His passing would be more than the loss of a loyal servant; he had become, I discovered with a gripping intensity, a friend. The last two stressful years in hiding had slowly and powerfully solidified a relationship that had been curtailed decades before by his decorum and my natural distance from the 'hired help' as the lord of the manor.

I could save him, perhaps. Though I lacked the ability to Awaken him, the bite of all vampires has the ability to heal mortals. As I've mentioned, our bites are easily missed due in part to the fact that they heal so rapidly. Even in death, the punctures made by our piercing fangs disappear. This ability also works, to a limited extent, on other injuries a mortal may bear.

With this in mind, I crossed the short distance to my bleeding, dying friend. He tried to speak. I silenced him, saying, "Speak not, dear Tomás. And do not fear. I am not coming to swallow your life. My bite has healing properties. Allow me to aid you." At the barest hint of a nod from the mortally exhausted man, I sunk my fangs into his neck, taking no more than a few drops of his blood and hoping my power was enough to save him.

It was. Almost before I pulled my head back, the slow dripping ceased. I sat myself on the floor next to him, disregarding the half-congealed blood in which my ankles were resting. Even as I watched, the color came back to his face and the jagged flesh on the edges of his stump began to close in. The arm would never grow back, but he should no longer be in danger of dying from the wound.

While I waited for Tomás' healing to progress, I took stock of our current situation. Apart from the hole in my chest, and its accompanying pain, I noted the man lying on the floor near my casket. I had nearly stepped on him in my haste to reach Tomás. Judging from his present condition, he would not have noticed. He had a deep, penetrating wound in his back, which was still adding to the blood on the floor. His breathing was irregular and had a bubbling sound to it - I didn't expect him to live long. Judging by his accoutrements, that would be no loss to me. He was well outfitted for vampire hunting, much like the assassin who had intruded on my manor almost two years before and set the current *Sturm und Drang* into motion.

I also saw what had caused my late rising and the bothersome hole in my chest: a large wooden stake was lying on the floor next to the casket.

It had obviously been used, judging by the trifling amount of blood still resident upon it. The evidence indicated to me that the would-be assassin had come in and staked me; a rather simple deduction, given the facts at hand.

A common misconception among mortals is that a stake through the heart kills us. This is not so. In fact, what it does is send us into torpor, or what the modern world might call suspended animation. We will remain in that state for years, until the stake is removed or we are more permanently killed. Tomás must have removed the stake, allowing me to wake up some time later.

As his vigor returned, I told Tomás my view of the events and he confirmed them.

"Yes, milord, it is even as you say. I had just come back in from having a meal to see this lout standing over you with his axe upraised. I believe he was going to finish the job of destroying you with the removal of your head. I grabbed my knife, which I had kept handy on my belt per your instructions, and stabbed him directly in the back. He turned around with the axe and brought it down on, and through, my arm. I must have somehow gotten in a lucky blow when I successively struck him in the head with the hilt of my knife, for he slumped to the floor. I seem to have passed out for a moment myself. When I woke up on the floor alongside him, I tied off my arm and passed out again. The next time I awoke I clubbed him again: I didn't want him waking unexpectedly, you see. Then I pulled myself up to check on you. I yanked out the stake, sat down in the chair, and I must have passed out a third time. I awoke the last time to see you rising. I am only thankful I was able to return in time to keep that savage from finishing you, milord."

This was perhaps the longest speech I'd ever heard Tomás utter. He spoke all of this with his usual aplomb; this brief tale of his devotion to my safety, his self-sacrifice, he spoke as though referring to some simple errand such as fetching my pipe for me. I could see in his eyes he only did as he felt he should, expecting no greater reward than to continue in my service.

Oh, how I miss him.

He finished his explanation. "I felt it would be best to leave him alive. I doubt he would reveal anything to you under questioning, but I believed it likely your injuries would renew your appetite."

"That is, as always, most thoughtful, Tomás."

"I only strive to do as you require, milord. I shall step out for a moment to give you some privacy as you dine."

I could have told him then, after those words, that he'd always done more than I required; that he had become more to me than just the hired help. But I was hungry and weakened: I needed to feed. I would tell him how much I valued his companionship when he returned. This I thought as he turned and walked out the room, removing the tourniquet from his brutally shortened but healing arm as he did so.

I set to feeding. It would have been possible to draw my sustenance through the wound Tomás had rent in his back, but it was messy and I would have received things other than his pure blood. I flipped the body over, fed as normal and was strengthened. I could feel myself being refreshed as I drew his vitality into me. I felt the final, brief surge as his heart beat its last and sent me its last pulse of life. This boost, so soon after my feeding the day before, would certainly aid in my recuperative process. Besides that, it gave me a feeling of warmth, a sort of smooth high.

It was as I was basking in the effulgent glow of my repast that I heard the clatter of several horses drawing a carriage up the icy road to stop in front of the inn. I paid it no heed, reveling in contemplation of my own powers over death. Instead, I cast the focus of my acute hearing above me to a business man discussing with his equally roguish partner how they were going to bilk a third man out of his share of the profits in some venture. I found this discourse much more entertaining.

There was a knock on the door, followed by a tentative, "Milord?"

I came back to the moment. Much still needed to be done tonight. We had to clean up this mess without attracting undue attention. It was also, perhaps, time to change our home, as someone had finally tracked us down. I also meant to ask Tomás how he knew to remove the stake - he'd obviously spent some time researching my state. "Enter, Tomás." It was time to give him my long-overdue thanks.

He opened the door and stood in it. I tried not to wince at the sight of his freshly amputated arm, giving him my polite attention. "Milord, Philip's carriage has just pulled up out front. He appears to be accompanied by someone. No one I recognize, sir, as his face is partially hidden from the wind with a scarf. He wears a cape, carries a sword, and I expect he's —" He looked down as I did at the same moment, witness to a sword tip that was suddenly protruding from his chest. I'd seen the man approaching behind him, but thought nothing of it until he drew his sword and thrust it in one smooth, otherworldly swift movement. Tomás dropped to the floor.

In the second it took for the caped vampire to retract his blade from Tomás' chest, I'd reached into my coffin to extract my own sword. The intruder stepped over Tomás. We stood just yards apart, each with a bare blade, studying each other. I recognized him, even under his scarf. His name was Sandoval, and he bore some sort of title in Spain. He was also known to be close to the Council. I had never seen him fight, so had no idea what I was up against. This would not be the easy victory I had against the nine mortals: as another vampire, he would be my equal - or close enough as to give me no notable advantage - in speed, strength, and reaction. I could only hope I was his better at the sword, but I did not believe that was to be my fortune. We each stepped forward, and without further preamble began to cross blades.

Within the first seconds I could tell our skill level was about even. This put me at a disadvantage, as I was already hindered by the wound the assassin's stake had left. Our swords clashed back and forth, each of us doing our best to deflect the other's blows while landing our own, but neither took a true advantage. The assaults grew heavier and harder as we both strove to mete out the decisively crippling blow. On one particularly mighty stroke, which I scarcely managed to block in time with my own sword, both blades snapped from the abuse. With a pair of distinct ringing tones, the blades went spinning off to opposite corners of the room. We gazed at each other over our now purposeless hilts.

Sandoval was the first to recover. Dropping the useless sword handle, he surged at me, grabbing me by my arms. I managed to get my hands up and began to dig my thumbs into his eyes. Unable to force my arms down far enough, he jerked his head back and flung me across the small room with a light toss. I flew only fifteen feet before crashing down upon my coffin, my body staving it in from the force of my landing. I scrambled back to my feet amidst the splintered remains. As I did so, my eyes caught on a vial on the assassin's belt. I recognized it for the weapon it was and grabbed it as I stood. The glass of the vial was thin, delicate; instead of unstoppering it, I threw it at my opponent with all the speed and strength I could muster.

This form of attack caught Sandoval off guard, and as with the dagger not two years before, my aim did not fail me. The vial struck true, shattering the fragile glass on the bone of his high forehead. Most of its contents splashed harmlessly away, but a large quantity wasn't really needed: each drop of holy water acted on his flesh like acid on mortal skin. Sandoval screamed as the first drops of holy water made contact with the sensitive flesh of his face, the first of only two times I ever heard a sound from him. By reflex, he raised his hands to wipe it away, but this accomplished nothing more than to irritate the rapidly deepening wounds and to spread the blessed water onto the palms of his hands. As his hands began to smoke and burn with pain he pulled them away and I saw the destruction I'd wrought.

The holy water had wreaked its burning havoc rapidly upon him where it hit. Some of his flesh was deeply scored, small holes in his skin revealing the tissues beneath. What immediately caught my eye, though, were the deep, wide swaths of damage. His forehead had become little more than a window to his bare, pitted skull, so much of the sanctified liquid had spilled there. A large splash of it evidently landed on his right eye, as both lid and eyeball were eaten through, some of the eye's jelly-like aqueous humor running down his cheek. His left eye had fared better, but not by much - it appeared that while the eye itself was untouched, the lid had absorbed a small runnel of the water from his forehead. There was a slim channel of dissolved flesh running from the left side of what remained of his forehead to the eyelid. The water had melted through much of it, leaving the lid dangling uselessly, flapping monstrously whenever he tried to blink or close his eye.

The holy water was still working its blessed effect on him when he went into a rage. I paid no more heed to his damaged face, though there was more being done to it even then by the wasting effects of the water, some certainly where I couldn't see it, under the scarf covering his mouth. With a roar he came at me, reached out and turned to throw me at the wall next to the room's door.

Ordinarily in a mature, healthy vampire, our bodies can withstand staggering amounts of blunt trauma. Our accident in the van crippled me as it did because of my weakening. The youth of a vampiric body also leaves it more susceptible to damage. It takes some time for a vampire's body to fully realize its physical potential, and even then, you grow stronger as each decade passes.

I was over one hundred years old, and my body could take a lot of punishment. Sandoval was, I believe, over two hundred, and could dish out a lot of punishment. While I didn't go through it when he threw me at the wall, I left some dangerously splintered beams behind me. Consequently, when he came up to me and I reversed our positions, pitching him at the same wall, he sailed clear through it. By this time, the pain from the holy water had already propelled him into a nearly berserk rage, and my only recourse was to match his ferocity to defend myself. Our bodies flew about, crashing through walls, missed punches and kicks splintering support beams.

Yes, perhaps you can see where this fight was going. After perhaps five minutes of non-stop supernatural wrath, the inn of Three Signposts could take no more, and began collapsing around us, a section at a time. I don't know how many humans were still in the building when it fell, but I have to imagine the smarter ones had already evacuated by that time. Bit by bit, as a portion of the structure collapsed, we were exposed more to the keening snow storm outside that had been roaring almost continuously for the past weeks, annoying me with its almost constant wind and frigid temperatures. This storm is perhaps the only thing that allowed me to survive the night.

As the last wall fell, a fresh gust of wind kicked violently up. Sandoval, peering down at me with his one good eye, was soon to finish me. I was on my back, exhausted, lying in what remained of the common room, as he reached out for me one last time. The wind kicked up, a near gale it felt like, the snow stinging my eyes and numbing my hands, and blew Sandoval's fancy cape not once, but twice around his pitted and gouged head. Recognizing this as my last chance, I groped blindly through the rubble next to me as he fumbled with his cape. My questing hand found what it searched for and I lunged up, driving the wooden shard deep into his exposed chest.

It did the job. He toppled over backwards, the improvised stake jutting from his breast just as his murderous sword had poked out the front of Tomás

I had no time to rest, to revel in my victory, or even to finish off Sandoval: I knew the wound Tomás had taken was also mortal. I hoped fervently, even praying, that I could repay his years of dedication a second time tonight and save his life.

I waded through the wreckage of the inn, casting my eyes about, forcing them to pierce the wall of the storm until I could see where my room had been. Its location approximated, I began hurling lumber out of my way, digging through the wreckage, searching desperately for Tomás. I refused to consider the possibility that the building's collapse had finished what his other wounds had begun.

I found him pinned beneath a fallen support, still breathing, though he was deathly pale and deeply unconscious. I flung away the remaining debris that held him down and dropped to my knees beside him. Gently, with as much care as I could, I turned his head, exposing his neck. For the second time that night I bit him, piercing his flesh and desperately sharing my contempt for death with him.

As I tasted his blood, I knew he was beyond my meager abilities. His multiple wounds, compounded with exposure to the killing temperatures, had sent him past any hope of recovery. I looked up, seeking empty solace in the power of nature storming around us, and saw the silhouette of a figure standing in the rubble not far off. It was then that I remembered what Tomás had said about the identity of the arrivals.

"Philip!" I shouted. The figure moved, taking a hesitant step, though I knew not if that step was towards me or away from me. The constantly swirling snow made it impossible to tell. It might not even have been Phil. I reached out, picking Tomás up in my arms, his life still pulsing, but so weakly. He would not live another ten minutes, no matter what was done. But if he was going to die, he could die in a manner of *my* choosing; he could die to live again! I may not have the ability to Awaken humans, but Phil did. As long as Tomás' heart beat and his lungs drew air, he could be Awakened.

Cradling his dying body gently in my arms, oblivious now to the bonebiting cold around me but still hindered in my actions by the wind and snow, I shouted the name once more. "PHILIP!" The figure moved again, but I had closed the distance and could see his motions better - he moved away from me. Then I realized the full import of the circumstance, logic finally winning past my grief. Phil had led this vampire, Sandoval, to me. He was the only one who had known I was in Dunkirk; it stood to reason that he, for some reason, had revealed my location to the Council. It was his doing that led to two men nearly killing Tomás.

But, he could *save* Tomás as well. His betrayal I could readily forgive of him if he would but save Tomás. If only he'd do it. "Phil, Tomás is dying! Awaken him! You can save him!" I shouted, my voice booming to be heard above the storm. I paid no heed to the pain within my own breast as my wound protested each shout.

He turned and started picking his way through the remains of the inn, away from me. I moved, too. As quickly as I was able, doing all I could not to jostle Tomás overmuch, I threaded my way through the worst of the timber. I gained several yards on Phil. "Philip! He can still be saved! Awaken him!" my voice cracked in desperation.

Phil had reached the street now, and began walking away more briskly, ignoring his carriage. I reached the street seconds after he did and set off after him. He broke into a run.

"Damn it, Philip! Come back! Please!" I cried out to him. "Just save Tomás! He still breathes! He still..."

It was no use. Phil was gone. His betrayal was complete. I couldn't catch him in my state even if I *could* see him. I looked down at my only friend. He drew his last breath.

I was alone in the world.

I cried, kneeling in the whirling snow over his body.

CHAPTER THIRTEEN

The animals were both silent.

Lawrence was silent, too. He sat slouched on the floor, his legs straight out in front of him, arms sitting limply at his sides, chin resting on his chest. Mac, who sat in front of him, watched as red tears of blood slowly dropped, to be absorbed into the fabric of his dark shirt.

Lawrence spoke. "I don't think he understands to this day that he betrayed me twice that night. Once by revealing me to the Council, the other..." he shook his head. "I don't think he gave a second thought about Tomás. Just another nameless mortal to him. From that day forth, in memory and respect of my all-too-mortal friend Tomás, I never killed to feed again." He reached up to wipe under each eye with a thumb, drying his face before raising his head to look at Mac. "I took Phil's carriage. He'd left it because one of the horses had been struck and maimed by a falling timber. I woke up a hostler and bought a replacement, and for the better part of a year that carriage became my home. I had to modify it, trying to make it less ostentatious, less noticeable, but I valued it for the same reason Phil had - the built-in coffins. Eventually, I had to get rid of it – its size alone made it too memorable."

When he realized Lawrence was done speaking, Mac asked, "What happened to the Spanish vamp?"

"Either the villagers finished him off or the sun got him in the morning. One way or the other, it doesn't matter."

"Phil didn't seem like such a bad guy when he was here. An idiot, yes, but not a bad guy. Why did he reveal your location to the Council?" Lady wanted to know.

"Well, he was always a weak person, easily manipulated. How he held his lands as long as he did was beyond me. And," Lawrence scowled, "I found out ten years later, my lands had a new lord."

"No!" both animals cried simultaneously.

Lawrence grinned sourly. "Yes. The Council gave Phil my lands, a 'reward for his steadfast loyalty to the Council and services rendered'; namely, fingering me. Oh, sure, I was mad. But I eventually decided, better him to rule my people than some fiend I didn't know. And Phil was so lost without his title as to be pathetic." Lawrence pushed himself up and stepped to his coffin. "Excuse me. Lady. I need to climb in. That's all for tonight."

Lady jumped down from the lid. "You're getting worse, Lawrence. It's well over an hour till sunrise."

"I know," he replied without turning. He climbed in, leaving the lid open so Lady could get in when she wished later on. In five minutes he was no longer truly with them, gone to wherever vampire's spirits went during the day.

*   *   *

Jamon had finished talking to the dealers the previous night after seeing Mr. Hull. Almost all of them had seen a cat. Jamon postulated that those who hadn't just didn't remember it; after all, who pays any attention to a stray cat? The one really notable exception was Willy. He'd seen, and been attacked by, a dog. A very scruffy-looking, rust colored dog. The same one the witnesses near the Biltmore had reported seeing.

The detective tallied up his meager supply of facts:

In most of the cases, that freaky black cat was present.

The money was always taken.

Any leftover drugs were taken.

Nothing else was taken: jewelry, etc.

The victims wake up with no memory of what happened.

The attacks always seemed to be preceeded by a bad case of the nerves.

Only Willy reported the dog.

Lawrence Watts was not in any database: DMV, Social Security, nothing. They were still looking for where else he might be, calling around to other hotels.

Finally, none of the other victims seemed to be having flashbacks.

They weren't really flashbacks. More like bits of memory coming back to him. Unlike the last time - when it all came to him in one big jumbled flood and reordered itself in his mind - these images came a bit here, a bit there. He was pretty sure he could now remember Lawrence grabbing him from behind as he walked, looking at the cat. He originally attributed it to a false memory created by watching the video so often. He no longer felt this was the case.

His cell phone rang, interrupting his musings. He pulled it out to look at the caller ID: Zim. Zim was a dealer who worked an area about two miles away. Zim wasn't his real name, of course. It was a nickname given him due to his strange fixation on some obscure cartoon. He had even gotten the title character - a goofy looking green humanoid with two small antennae and large eyes - tattooed on his left bleep. It takes all kinds, Jamon supposed. He answered the phone, slipping neatly into his persona as 'Jaim'. "Jaim. What's up, Zim?"

The voice on the other end sounded a touch tremulous, though quiet. "Jaim. That cat. I swear, it's watching me. Am I going crazy? Paranoid? I swear I'm not trippin' on nothing." Jamon had asked the dealers who'd been 'rolled' by Lawrence to call him if they saw either a man fitting the description he'd given them, or the cat. They hadn't questioned how Jamon had a description of the guy. This was fortunate, as he couldn't tell them about the video - it'd give away too much and make them suspicious, blowing his sting. He had planned to mention his flashbacks to explain away his knowledge of Lawrence's appearance if they'd asked. This might also have given him more information, if one of them was having the flashbacks, too. Nonetheless, he was relieved that they hadn't asked about the description, for simplicity's sake.

"Be cool, Zim, be cool. You're sure it's the same cat? Do you see that guy anywhere?"

"No, man, no. He ain't nowhere. And...and I moved before I called you to, ya know, make sure the guy wasn't around to hear me." His voice dropped completely to a whisper made hoarse by years of cigarettes. "That spooky-ass cat followed me."

"Alright, man, tell ya what." Jamon checked his watch. "It's 1:30. This place is dead. I was fixing to leave anyway. How 'bout I swing on by? Where ya at? Maybe we can get the bastard."

"Uhhh...I'm at Kilbourne and 21. You comin' by?" Zim sounded deeply spooked, but hopeful at the prospect of some assistance.

Jamon was already walking to his car. "Yeah. I'll be there in five. See ya." He ended the call as he slipped behind the wheel.

As Jamon pulled the blue BMW up, it was obvious that Zim had a bad case of the nerves. His head was constantly in motion, jerking every which way as he paced in a tight circle. When his right hand wasn't fidgeting with the gun in his waistband, it was clasped in his left. Only the sight of Jamon stepping out of the car seemed to calm his frantic movements any.

"Jaim," Zim called as he quickstepped over to Jamon. "It's gone, man. It... it must've heard I was calling in reinforcements. It was watching me when I was talking to you." His eyes were still darting around, but the rest of his nervous movements had ceased.

"Whaddya mean?" Jamon asked, though his trained eyes told him the simple fact: the cat was gone. Whatever the reason, he was too late. "Did the guy get you?"

At the realization he'd escaped whatever fate might have been awaiting him, relief flooded his face and his eyes stopped twitching. "No, man, no. Like I was saying, I hung up the phone with you and the cat took off."

"It ran?"

"No, man, no. It just hopped offa that car and walked in that alley." He pointed to a small walkway between a pair of old apartment buildings.

Jamon started to walk toward it. "Did you follow it? Look where it'd gone?" he called over his shoulder. Zim hadn't moved from where he'd been standing by the curb next to Jamon's BMW.

"No, man, no. I, uh...wanted to make sure you didn't miss me. I knew you were coming straight over and didn't want you to think I'd gone."

Jamon let the obviously false justification pass. "Cool. I'm gonna check it out." He walked back to the passenger side of the car and pulled a small penlight out of the glove box. "Maybe the damn cat's gone hiding back there somewhere."

The light cast its sharp but narrow beam into the blackness, revealing nothing dangerous. Jamon stepped over an unseen border, entering the alley proper. It contained whispers of residual evidence of two denizens of the dark. But these intangibles - the sense of unease, the unidentifiable smell of old death, the deeper than expected darkness - none of these could be catalogued, recorded, by the methodical detective in his little book. There was no current presence about, only the lingering essence of great power in a semi-enclosed space. As he looked back into the ever-darkening depths of the alley, the scant beam from his mini-light offered little comfort, and only slightly better visibility. *There's more to this than drugs and money*, Jamon thought to himself as he walked cautiously down the alley.

* * *

Jamon would have no luck finding the mysterious black cat or Lawrence. By the time Jamon was pulling up in the seized BMW, Lawrence and Lady were already in the black Suburban, driving off. They had no particular destination in mind, but Lawrence still had to feed tonight.

Lady cast a glance over at Lawrence from her position in the front passenger seat. He looked more like some fabled, mindless, rotting zombie than the unstoppable, immortal vampire she knew he should be. Waves of power still rolled off of him, but it was now more in the unhealthy way greasy sweat rolls off a fat man in the sun than the natural perfection of a healthy athlete glistening with perspiration after a strong workout. It was a sickly dispersing of his power, an uncontrolled loss of vitality. Mac had pointed out this radiation of power two nights ago, and it had only gotten easier to detect. Lawrence was dying. There could be no doubt. He was still waking at least an hour after sunset, and yesterday he'd retired to his coffin three hours before sunrise. His hair was still thinning, but not terribly obvious yet. What was obvious was the weary look that never seemed to leave Lawrence's features now. He had appeared to age ten mortal years in the last week, with bags under his eyes and lines of use on his face.

Right now, he was gazing almost sightlessly at the road, seeming to drive without seeing, a lifeless automaton behind the wheel.

"What do you think happened back there, Lawrence?" Lady asked, trying to draw him out of his stupor.

There was a measurable lag between Lady's question and Lawrence's response, as though he were giving it grave consideration. His blank face gave the lie to that belief. It would be closer to the truth to say his mind had to wake up before answering. "I don't know. They're on to us, I guess." His words came out slowly at first, gradually returning to a normal speaking cadence. "I guess we can't feed on those guys anymore."

"So, you want to stop feeding on the dealers?"

"No, we do need that better income. I just think we should expand out a bit. Why don't you and Mac see if you can find some more dealers besides the ones we've been hitting?"

"I told you getting them twice was not a good idea," Lady stated petulantly.

"Actually, it was Mac who said that. I'll have to tell him he was right; thank him for good advice poorly heeded. In the meantime, I still need to feed. This looks like a good place," he said as he pulled up to the curb. "We needed to stop anyway. Feeding twice on someone is okay, but you don't want to do it more than that."

"Why is that?" Lady asked, more to keep him talking and aware than as a quest for information. She already knew the answer, having received his knowledge at Awakening.

He answered, not realizing in his befuddled state that she already knew. "You've heard of the old stories about three bites and you're a vampire. Not true, but it does give humans some strange abilities. No, I really don't know exactly what they are, just that it's to be avoided. It's not usually a problem, as almost all vampires kill as they feed. That's why little is said or commonly known about it."

"Oh." Lady glanced around as she hopped lightly to the ground from the truck. "I don't see a good alley around."

She was right. The buildings along this strip were butted right up against each other. "I don't *have* to hunt that way, skulking in some dark alley. It's just easier sometimes," he replied indignantly. "It gives me a place out of view of others, preventing accidental discovery."

"I know, I know. I was just saying you'd be out in the open while you fed." This was mostly true; she was also concerned about his weakening abilities lately. She and Mac both felt that Lawrence was unaware of how much his condition was worsening, far beyond the obvious physical manifestations. Their telepathic link with Lawrence gave them valuable insight as to his very thought processes. With his ebbing control, more of his thoughts were discernible besides what he specifically communicated. The pair felt it best not to mention this failing to Lawrence.

"Besides, I can go between cars for a bit of cover while I actually feed." He began walking down the sidewalk in an attempt to look less conspicuous. "Let me know if you see or hear anything."

"Sure." Lawrence never seemed to speak much of his problems. Was it pride? Denial? Lady and Mac had spoken of it often since the night four evenings ago when Phil disclosed what he knew about the nature of Lawrence's illness. The two were at a loss. Every time they tried to bring Lawrence into the discussion, he'd give a few half-answers and abruptly change the subject. Even were his attempts to dissemble on the subject not so pathetic as to be transparent, they would have had a hint at his true concerns on the matter; his stronger feelings had begun to seep through the telepathic link to them. They easily picked up his anxieties over the matter, and even some helplessness. This, Lady could understand. What could they do? Their best possible source of information, the Council, was closed off to them. Phil had already told them all he knew. None of them had come up with anything, and Lawrence's condition was degenerating with alarming speed.

Lady cut off these thoughts at the sound of someone approaching. She stopped in the sidewalk ahead of Lawrence, her ears swiveling as she searched for the source of the sound. "Someone around that corner, Lawrence," she reported. By an almost indefinable change in Lawrence's step - largely a more deliberate pacing indicating a heightened alertness - she could detect his readiness to attack the approaching human. They saw their potential victim, a husky man of about thirty, round the corner and continue walking towards the pair. Lady easily noted the difference in the way the man carried himself when he spotted Lawrence. They were well out of the bad neighborhoods; one was not perpetually afraid for his life if caught out after dark. Nevertheless, the man's defenses went up. Whether this was due simply to common sense in seeing a lone stranger after dark, or his reaction to the power still tangibly pouring uncontrollably off of Lawrence, Lady didn't know.

Lawrence walked to the far right of the sidewalk as he approached the stranger, as though to provide a wide berth to his fellow pedestrian. This allowed the man to relax a hair, Lady observed. They passed each other, each offering the other a "hello"; the simple, strained greeting of two strangers passing in uncertain circumstances.

Lawrence turned and attacked.

Rather than finding the man's back, as Lawrence had certainly expected, the man had seemed to sense the change in the situation and turned
to face his attacker. To Lady, it was almost slow motion. The stranger had
moved quickly, yes, but no more so than any other mortal. The speed of
a vampire's reactions and thoughts made any human movement seem
leisurely. While the reaction of the mortal was nothing extraordinary,
though quick, Lawrence's speed was little better, so low had he been
brought by his sickness. The stranger's first instinct was to raise his hands
to guard his face. This also served to block Lawrence's access to the
jugular.

As Lawrence used his left arm to bat the man's hands out of the way,
his mouth opened, preparing to strike. The hapless pedestrian saw this,
saw the bared fangs gleaming in the dim lamplight and knew true panic,
possibly for the first time in his life.

His actions grew more desperate as he fought to fend off his unnatural
assailant. His terror-stricken body sent adrenaline coursing through his
veins, pumping the mortal with greater strength and speed in an attempt
to preserve his life. Lady knew this spiced the blood, but it seemed that
Lawrence was no longer able to cope with the fresh energy this gave his
victim. The two struggled in what should have been a one-way battle,
Lawrence trying to maintain a firm hold on the man, while the human
hammered furiously on Lawrence's face and shoulders. Throughout the
scuffle, the man uttered nary a cry, the fear which Lawrence still inspired
locking all sound out of the man's throat.

Lady had just decided to leap into the fray and deliver her own bite to
end it when Lawrence finally locked his jaws on the man's neck. Even
then, he was subject to half a dozen more blows to his head before the
man's eyes glazed over and his body yielded to the somnolent effects of
the bite. Lawrence, near exhaustion by the brief spate of exertion, fed.

Finished, he let the man's limp body drop to the ground and staggered
off to the truck. In silence, the two climbed into the vehicle for the trip
back to the hotel.

"I don't know how much more of this I can take," Lawrence confided
to Lady. This was the first time he'd spoken since feeding, ten minutes
before. They'd driven most of the trip in silence. "He refused to go
under when I bit him. I thought for a moment he'd be conscious for

the whole feeding. And he seemed to move so fast. It felt like fighting another vampire. I know, it was me that was slow, but that's how it felt, like...like when I fought Sandoval."

Lady almost told him "Don't worry," but she realized the hollowness of such a sentiment in these circumstances. And, Lawrence was not one to worry needlessly, she'd found.

"If this gets much worse, I won't be able to feed myself." His hand moved in a vague, uncertain gesture as he spoke.

Lady kept her own counsel, and did not mention the small sore on the back of Lawrence's hand. Just a spot of discoloration, really. It could be nothing more than a small wound from his fight with the man tonight. That's probably all there was to it.

CHAPTER FOURTEEN

Again, the large stone table. In the center a single, slender, lit candle. The dancing flame gave off the faint scent of vanilla, a concession to the room's inherent mustiness. There was no electricity on this level, the lowest floor of the building, to power even the dimmest of lights. Not so much as an elevator - the only approach was the heavily guarded stairway. It was not that electricity, or modern convenience in general, would somehow interfere with the power of those in the room. It was certainly not concern over cost. The concern was tradition. For those who have personally weathered eras of human time, sometimes even participating in - or precipitating - the events that defined those eras, tradition was venerated. They were not backwards throwbacks for it; witness their corporate empire, the gleaming capital of which rose majestically and imposingly above them. But tradition was to be appreciated, respected. After all, most traditions had an origin, a reason, even if that reason was lost in the mists of time.

The room was large, the light of the small candle too feeble to combat the gloom. A human visitor would have seen no more than moving shadows. This was of no consequence: no human had been in this room in recorded history, and only one short-lived storyteller's apprentice had ever so much as stood outside the room and looked in. Even that event had been incorporated into tradition. Before each meeting, a moment of silence as the assembled beings listened for the tell-tale breathing of a mortal, as they gazed across from themselves, searching for unwelcome visitors.

What a human eye would have called shadow in darkness moved slightly, preparatory to speaking. "I raise the issue of Lawrence Hermanson."

The language spoken was one long forgotten by the mortals crawling the globe like so many short-lived insects. Again, tradition.

Were the men around the table mortal men, lacking the quiet, powerful dignity held by all present, a quiet, interested murmuring might have been heard. The issue of Lawrence Hermanson had not been raised in over twenty-five years, and then only briefly, a failed endeavor so uncommon here. Even among the immortal, to broach a subject after such a hiatus indicated something new and potentially interesting. Had one the supernatural vision needed to penetrate the shadows, he might see a few eyebrows quirk up the smallest fraction of an inch, the most expression these eternal Visigoths allowed themselves amidst their brooding peers.

The one who spoke pulled a sheet from the thin, black leather notebook sitting before him on the stone table, though he never once referenced it in the discussion to follow. "He has been found. Visual confirmation." He paused once more. To his senses, honed by eons, the surprise was palpable: a slight flux in the controlled power emanating from each member of the circle. Normally their power was tightly reined in, but here they could relax their hold a little. Besides being the only accepted means of loosening up, it was also a way of reminding one's peers of one's level of power.

"Who claims to have seen him, Berengol?" came a voice from across the table.

"A reliable source, who has proven valuable in the past," Berengol replied with only the faintest trace of smug self-satisfaction. Berengol had been the one to cultivate the original betrayal over four hundred years ago.

"I think we know who this source is," another voice chuckled darkly.

"Enough." The command was deep, resonating. "Continue."

"Yes. He is living in the United States now, as we'd known. Surprisingly, he is in Milwaukee."

"Milwaukee?" the commanding voice demanded.

"Yes, Lord Rabus." A circle of equals, ostensibly, but only one of whom was addressed as lord. "I can only say that perhaps our prior scout somehow missed this rogue, or that perhaps he has only recently relocated there. My information claims Lawrence himself says that he has been 'mobile'."

"Shall I send forth an assassin?" This voice was almost nasal sounding, not what one would expect in such an august council. "We can finally be done with this little annoyance."

"Yes, and that silly prophecy." This utterance earned a pressing look from Lord Rabus, the speaker nearly flinching under the powerful, weighty gaze.

"We will not 'be done' with the prophecy, ever." Rabus steepled his hands together. "As you are young and new to this Council, I shall overlook your shortsightedness." The slightest upward motion of the lips indicated the barest hint of a smile on several of the others. Candiano had been on the Council for one hundred fifty years, and was perhaps nine hundred years old. He was the newest and youngest member. "Something you must understand. A prophecy, any *true* prophecy, not just some foretelling or clairvoyance, will strive to make itself true. In a case like this, it will try repeatedly throughout the ages, forever reappearing as the world trundles on. Lawrence Hermanson was not the first one through which this prophecy has tried to manifest. When we destroy him, the prophecy will attempt to make itself felt again, though probably not for several hundred years." He leaned forward intently, his palms flat on the stone table. "Do not ever let your guard down. Discipline and caution at all times." His hands returned to rest, clasped together, on the table as he sat back. "Did this informant of yours bring any further news?" he asked, returning his attention to Berengol.

"Yes, Lord Rabus." Berengol's gaze traveled slowly around the table. "He has Awakened two more animals: a dog and a cat."

Another of the thirteen spoke; a rough, gravelly voice. "Damn. We *must* send an assassin. We cannot allow this."

Berengol turned to the speaker. He had a swarthy, yet somehow still pale, complexion. His beard was maintained in Arabic fashion. "Actually, Hojani," Berengol began, "it seems as though the abominations may soon be the only things we need to terminate." The faces around the table looked up or turned to face Berengol again, expectantly. Lord Rabus gave him a signal to please continue. "Lawrence Hermanson appears to be dying." He allowed a small smile to grace his usually staid face at the reactions this claim engendered.

"How can he possibly be dying?" The very precisely enunciated words came from Berengol's left, voicing the question plaguing the thoughts of most of them. Vampires were either alive (in their limited sense), truly dead, or in very rare cases, in torpor - such as with a stake through the heart. Vampires did not get cancer, age, or anything else that might indicate the use of the word 'dying'.

"The same manner in which Count Lowenhagen met his end," he answered with just the slightest hint of satisfaction. Nods of understanding came from around the table.

A new voice, also resonant in its innate authority, sounded out directly across the table from Lord Rabus. This speaker did not sit at the table, as the others did, but two feet removed from it, almost aloof from the discussions. His head rested against the back of the chair as though it needed support, yet he maintained the aura of idle strength, his position only serving to greater emphasize his hauteur. "Destroy Lawrence nonetheless. We will not rely on the whims of fortune to supply us with our needs. That is the behavior of those who lack the ability to make the world bend to their will, and the path to decadence and failure." None had looked towards the speaker; most had humbly cast their eyes down at the table in the age-old sign of acquiescence and respect. Only Lord Rabus had the strength of character to hold his head up, though even he gave every sign of respectful attention.

Lord Rabus spoke. "Let us unleash our hound. Finish this matter."

* * *

Jamon slowly poured the second glass of wine, reflecting. This was a good way to spend a night off. He'd just returned home, but for the first time in too many weeks - no, months - he'd not been alone as he crossed the threshold of his small apartment. Sara was currently waiting for him on the loveseat in the living room.

He walked out to give Sara her drink, and sat down next to her. They sat in a comfortable silence, sipping their wine and simply enjoying the company of each other. Jamon had finally taken the plunge last night and asked her out. Truthfully, it hadn't been much of a plunge, as she'd made it fairly clear over the last couple weeks that she would welcome an evening out with him. He'd gone in to the office after he was done on the street to catch up on his paperwork last night. His sting was almost finished, and he would soon be reduced to shuffling paperwork on the case, the scourge of all police work, successful or otherwise. He'd not been doing anything when she'd stopped by his desk on her way out. Not doing anything, that is, aside from gazing at the box of 'Count Chocula' cereal that some jokesters had thoughtfully placed on his desk.

He looked up at her chuckle. "I think my favorite was the stuffed doll of 'The Count' from *Sesame Street*," she claimed with a smile.

He couldn't help but grin in spite of himself - no frown was safe against her smile. "Yeah, although their call for emergency back-up for a blood bank robbery was amusing as well, in retrospect. I dragged myself out of bed and all the way across town for that one, expecting a hostage situation or something. I didn't recognize the address, and never stopped to think why they were calling me in on it until I was halfway there."

They'd just looked at each other in silence until she asked him about his sting. He gave her a brief rundown on its status, ending with, "It'll still be nice to just kick back tomorrow night."

"Oh, you have tomorrow off?" she inquired pleasantly.

"Yeah. First night in a while, actually."

"Oh. Me too."

More silence, before he realized the opening she'd deliberately given him. "Um, would you care to do something? Tomorrow? With me?" Yeah. Suave.

But suave or not, here he was, just after one in the morning with a lovely woman. Due to their nocturnal schedules, they'd scheduled the date for late in the evening.

She smiled at him over her glass. "Whatcha thinking?"

He grinned back. "Nothing, really. I was just -" His phone rang. He recognized the ring tone he'd assigned to a particular set of numbers. "Damn. I'm terribly sorry, Sara. I have to get this. Work." He looked at her apologetically and checked to confirm the caller ID. He was right. It was work related. Ordinarily, he considered answering phones at times like dinner, or especially dates, to be the height of bad manners, but his line of work sometimes made it necessary.

"It's okay," she told him. She got up to give him some privacy.

He put the phone to his ear. "Jaim."

"Jaim. It's K.P. I'm looking at a big sell tonight, thought I'd let you in on it."

"I'll be there. Give me thirty minutes. Your usual spot?"

"Yeah. Later."

Jamon ended the call. K.P. was being watched by a black cat. No. *The* black cat, Jamon was sure. After the concerns Zim had given about being overheard, Jamon had elected to use a simple code phrase if anyone saw Lawrence or the cat. He didn't believe the *cat* had overheard Zim, but perhaps Lawrence had. During the daylight hours, or in a well-lit room, he believed that. When he pictured those green, slitted eyes, staring intelligently at him in the night, though...

Suppressing a shudder he got up and stepped into the kitchen, where he found Sara. "That was one of the dealers. He thinks Lawrence is around. I have to go check it out. I'm sorry. More than I can say, I'm sorry. Can we reschedule? Pick up where we leave off tonight? Or start over? Which ever?"

She stopped his babbling with a light kiss and her irresistible smile. "If you'd like, I can even go with you," she suggested.

He considered the option, as it would allow them to continue their date after he cleared this up, especially if there was nothing to it. But there were at least two strong arguments against it. She wasn't trained in field work, and he didn't know what he might find. This was just too weird to bring her along on. "No, I don't think that'd be wise." His brow furrowed deeply in consternation. This sucked. "Can I give you a ride home?"

"What, and leave my car here?" she chuckled.

"Oh. Yeah." She'd driven herself over rather than have him pick her up.

"Don't worry. We *will* do this again. Soon." She gave him another kiss, this one intended to convey her desire for a repeat. Jamon happily reciprocated. "Good night, cutie." Jamon collected his wits enough to instigate a kiss as he showed her to the door.

After throwing on clothes more typical to his persona as 'Jaim', he drove out to where K.P. kept his trade. K.P. had not been among the group of dealers already robbed by Lawrence. After last night's missed chance with Zim, Jamon had spread the word to a large portion of the other dealers in the city. Actually, Ghost had spread the word for him, agreeing that the robberies were a bad trend to allow to continue. Jamon was pleased by the call from K.P., even though it had interrupted an atyp-ically wonderful evening. He had not really expected results so soon, but apparently the criminals were keeping their eyes open.

He turned onto K.P.'s street and had to force his eyes back to the road. *There it is!* he thought as he corrected his poorly handled turn. The cat still spooked him, still drew his eyes. It was lying on a rusted-out old blue Honda four cars down from K.P. Just lying there like any stray might, but Jamon knew it was no innocent street cat. He still hadn't come to terms with just what he thought of the cat, but there was definitely something... abnormal.

Jamon pulled into an open spot directly across the street from K.P. He got out to introduce himself as K.P. had already crossed over to him. "K.P. Good to meet you in person. Jaim." He put out his hand to shake as he logged K.P. in his mind. A short, extremely muscular black man, he could have passed for Ghost's brother. While he could see tattoos cascading all across his skin, he could not make out anything definite; the dim streetlamps did not give off enough light for him to differentiate the details in the blue ink from the man's dark skin.

As they shook, K.P. leaned forward and whispered, "Is that it? The right cat?"

Jamon had kept one eye on the cat since he saw the freaky little beast. He nodded in answer to K.P.'s question, but hissed in a short breath. The cat's ears seemed to have canted towards them when the dealer whis-pered his question. It was hard to tell in the dark, and it could have been chance, but it still unsettled Jamon.

He could not have called any of his buddies on the force for backup on the drive over, though he'd considered it - not and kept his cover intact. "Get my back," he requested, taking what he could get in the way of assistance.

Keeping his right hand near his own weapon - a Colt .45, not his reg-ular service automatic - he began walking in the direction of, but not straight towards, the cat. Almost directly next to the Honda the cat was sitting on, just across the sidewalk, was an alley. *What is it with the damned alleys?* he wondered. His movements were those of a trained profession-al, ready for almost anything. His 'backup' was content to follow behind, gun held in the air in both hands, the classic position of TV gunmen everywhere.

As Jamon drew nearer the cat and the alley, his palms began to sweat lightly. His gaze shifted steadily between the cat and the alley, as though watching a high-speed tennis match.

"This is fucked up, man," came the dealer's less-than-steady voice behind him. Jamon made no reply. Why bother? K.P. had pretty succinctly summed up the situation.

Jamon's current goal was to acquire a peek down the alley. The last thirty feet seemed the longest he'd ever walked, his feelings of unease mounting with every step. When he was ten feet from the Honda, the cat stood up, looked at him and meowed. He froze, surprised, and then continued moving. Stupid cat, that's all it was. He was having trouble keeping his eyes off the animal and on the alley, where any true danger was sure to be lurking. A quick glance behind him showed him his erstwhile partner, K.P., had his dark eyes riveted on the cat, so should it try anything funny...

He shook his head. What kind of 'funny business' would a cat try? Try as he may to retain a cool, logical slant of mind, he still felt better knowing the cat was being watched.

He turned his eyes to the alley. Time to take a peak, see what's down there.

Nobody in the street, and the sidewalk was clear. Now to check the alley.

The building to the right of the alley seemed to be abandoned.

Jamon frowned, wondering what his problem was. Twice he'd intended to look down the alley, twice his eyes had passed right over it. Was it somehow due to the deep, clenching fear that crawled through his entire being? But he wasn't afraid to look in the alley, much as he might be growing to dread what he might see in it. Enough of this. He looked once over his shoulder at the cat, who was focused intently on him, drew a deep breath, and forced his eyes down the dark alley.

He let out his breath. Nothing. Though it was dark and shadowy in the narrow passageway, he could see well enough to know there was nothing, at least not near the mouth. He took a step forward and realized his mind had changed tacks. Instead of his mind screaming at him to run, or making him ignore the alley entirely, his eyes were drawn toward a murky area against the wall. It scared him. He didn't know why - there was nothing there - but it scared him.

And the veil fell from his mind. Suddenly, he could see. Most of the alley was unchanged, but the murky area was suddenly opened up to him. Standing there, plain as the moonlit night allowed, was Lawrence.

* * *

"Something's wrong, Lawrence," Lady cautioned.

"What is it?" Lawrence asked telepathically from his location in the alley. He was using his ability to shadowmerge.

"I don't know, but the guy who just got out of that white car is familiar, and he keeps looking at me." Jamon had just pulled up across from K.P. in the BMW.

"Familiar? How?"

"I think it's one of the dealers we hit before."

"Hm. Well, let's just be patient and see what he's doing here."

Lady did as he suggested, though her tail switched irritably from side to side, counter to the relaxed state she tried to project as she lay on the car's roof. She didn't have long to wait before something got her attention.

"They're talking about me."

"How do you know?"

"You see any other cats out here?" she snapped. "Besides, the one who introduced himself as Jaim is watching me."

"Well, watch him back," Lawrence casually suggested.

"They're walking this way. And they've got their guns out."

"Don't worry. They won't be able to see me, and they'll ultimately dismiss you as just a cat. Do something...catlike."

"I think we should go," she said, but did as Lawrence suggested, something 'catlike', for lack of anything better to do. She stood and meowed. "Ooh, they're antsy. You should've seen them jump when I meowed." Lady was momentarily amused. "You'd think I roared and pounced on them, by their reaction." Her amusement faded, her tone serious again. "I still don't like this. I don't trust them. Let's go."

"Too late. I'm not up to running away, and I won't be very good sneaking away, either. It's taking all I've got to remain hidden. What's going on?" Jamon and K.P. had stopped on the cracked sidewalk between Lady and Lawrence. "They should be far too nervous to stand so close to me." Jamon's eyes passed over Lawrence, continuing on to look down the street.

"Is he trying to find you?" Lady asked.

"Yeah, but his eyes are going right over, like they should. There he goes again. He seems pretty determined, but we're fine." Lawrence waited patiently as Jamon tried again. As Jamon's eyes stopped, looking into the alley, Lawrence felt that something was wrong. This mortal was being awfully persistent; he should have left by now with chills coursing down his spine. Damn. He was looking straight down the alley. He shouldn't have been able to look down it at all; the whole alley was part of his cloak of darkness. Lawrence was now watching Jamon intently, warily, and so he saw the instant the blonde man pierced the magic, his eyes widening in shock. "He saw me," Lawrence informed Lady.

"Shit!" she exclaimed. "What do you want me to do?"

"Nothing yet." He stepped out of the alley. Jamon reached for his gun. It was a fruitless attempt, as he'd already drawn it some time ago. Panic, Lawrence decided, could be an amusing tool at times.

"Stop right there," Jamon commanded, the pistol now pointed at Lawrence.

K.P. turned at the sound of Jamon's voice. "Where the hell did *he* come from?"

"Gentlemen, gentlemen, no need to get all excited," Lawrence soothed. He put the force of his personality behind his voice and his gaze, which flicked back and forth evenly between the two mortals. "Why don't you two just ease up a bit." He should have their minds now, but it was hard to tell. Normally, it was obvious. Usually, he could feel that tendril of his own spirit which had somehow snaked into their mind, could feel his power dominating their will, but not tonight. It was always harder with multiple people, but Lawrence had found long ago that he, like Phil, was particularly talented in this art. He believed it had to do with the empathy he had cultivated with humankind in general. He didn't like to use it, as the victim remembered what had gone on - though they didn't know how or why - but this was an emergency. "Just go back to your own cars and head home," he instructed.

K.P. immediately turned away and started off. Jamon caught his motion out of the corner of his eye. "K.P.! What the hell are you doing?"

Lawrence tried again, focusing all his will on Jamon. "Go on, Jaim, he's got the right idea. Just head home, don't bother about me."

"It's not working, Lawrence," Lady called from atop the car.

"I can see that. I'm too weak, and he's too strong willed. Any ideas?"

With his only back-up gone, Jamon got desperate. This was getting weirder and weirder, and he wanted it ended. "I am Detective Jamon Schroeder," he said, fumbling out his wallet from his jacket pocket and flashing his badge at Lawrence. "You are under arrest for assaulting an officer," he began.

"Yeah, I remember this guy," Lawrence told Lady, not realizing he'd spoken aloud in his agitation.

"Who are you talking to?" Jamon shouted, his nerves starting to get the best of him. Then he realized: when Lawrence had spoken, his mouth had opened enough to reveal his fangs. "Holy shit. Th-those things aren't fake."

"Lawrence, trouble," Lady called.

"Yeah. I think he knows what we are," Lawrence replied.

"Ideas?"

"It's all up to you. Get him!"

The exchange between Lady and Lawrence came and went faster than words, taking almost no time at all. Lady immediately launched herself from the car, seeming to fly the eight feet to Jamon. She allowed her claws to scrape on the metal, providing more distraction for Lawrence. Jamon did not turn at the sound, and she landed solidly on his back. Her claws dug in for purchase in his clothing, though she knew Jamon would now come out of this with at least a few scratches on his back, as well. More evidence left behind, but with any luck they'd heal quickly enough not to be noticed. Nothing deliberate, but she had to hold on somehow, and the claws were her only option.

Jamon fell forward, propelled by the momentum imparted on him by the flying cat. Lawrence took a short step up and grabbed the officer's gun arm. At the same time, he bared his fangs and struck. Jamon's struggles were strong, but short-lived, and Lawrence was able to hold him at bay until the effects of his bite took hold. He fed, then eased Jamon's limp form to the ground for Lady to partake as well.

Back in the truck they discussed what had happened. "Did you hear what that Jaim guy said? He's a cop. That can't be good," Lady was arguing.

"Yeah, I've been thinking about that." Lawrence turned the truck onto the highway, merging easily with the light traffic of the late hour. "He must have been called there by the other one, what's his name."

"K.P. I told you they were watching me." Lady's claws were flashing in and out, extending and retracting repeatedly, though she had the presence of mind not to dig them into the upholstery. "And the cop seemed to be specifically looking for you. How did he see you, anyway?"

"I'm just growing too weak. My powers are waning, just as Phil said. The cop simply penetrated the illusion." The next few minutes passed in a thoughtful silence, then, "Lady, wasn't that guy Jamon the one Mac cautioned us against? The one he claimed didn't smell right?"

"Yeah," Lady grudgingly admitted. "But what was he doing selling drugs?

Is he a dirty cop?"

"It's possible," Lawrence conceded, "but unlikely. It's too dangerous. He'd get caught too easily, I'd think, standing out on city streets selling drugs like he was. He was probably undercover or something."

"Well, he's obviously warned most of the dealers to look out for us. This K.P. guy wasn't anyone you'd fed on before. We're going to have to try something new."

"Actually, Lady, I think it would be best to stop targeting them at all for now. At least around here. It's getting too dangerous, and I'm just not up to it anymore. We have enough cash to last for a while."

"We don't have to tell Mac he was right about the cop, do we?" Lady asked hopefully. Lawrence just looked at her. She lay down in the seat, resting her head on her paws dejectedly. "I figured you'd see it that way."

CHAPTER FIFTEEN

Stephanie's slim, caramel fingers drummed on her steering wheel. No specific pattern to it, just a steady, rapid drumming as she looked at the elegant doorway across the street. She was going to see him tonight; after twenty-seven lonely years, she would speak to Lawrence again.

At least, she would if she could get herself to step out of the car and up to his room.

She was sitting in her Audi across the street from the front entrance to his hotel, the Hyatt. It was a pleasant evening, a light breeze off the lake blowing through the streets of the city, chasing away the smell of yeast from the breweries, but she took no note of it in her preoccupied state. Earlier, she'd once again been plagued with indecision over how to dress for the occasion, as she'd been two weeks prior. The issue was decided by settling on the same outfit she'd worn that last time, when she had expected to see him. After all, he hadn't seen her in it then, so it was still new to him, if not her. She could be pragmatic about such things, more so than she might have been twentyfive years ago. The wisdom of age with the vigor of youth - a delightful combination, or so she thought.

She looked up at the stately hotel rearing up across the avenue. Lawrence had seemingly had a reversal of his fortunes to have moved from his little economy apartment into one of the city's better temporary lodgings. The Hyatt stood about thirty stories, capped with one of the finest restaurants in the city, which rotated to provide a view all around.

This was perhaps the last place she'd expected to find Lawrence. After she'd discovered his old apartment had been vacated, she had spent a significant portion of each night calling hotels and apartments throughout the area. It was quite possibly the most tedious two weeks she'd ever spent, but she had no idea how else to proceed. A nice precognitive Dream telling her where he was would have been most welcome, but her Calling simply didn't work like that, was never so accommodating. Even in retrospect, she couldn't think of any Dream she'd had which might be interpreted in such a way as to lead her here. So, she'd had to do all this legwork.

He hadn't left a forwarding address or any other clue that might have aided her search. She had been growing more and more concerned that she wouldn't find him at all. Even in modern society, it was easy to make oneself disappear, especially as practiced as Lawrence had become in the art over the course of four hundred years.

She had relied on hopes that he had not changed his name again, and that he had not left the general area. Her hope had grown thin as the nights passed with no success. Her dismay grew in inverse proportion to her hope's recession; what would she do if she couldn't find him? What if she was too late? She couldn't bear to have waited for her love for twenty-seven years, to have left him questioning her disappearance, only to utterly fail him at the end. It would be too much; and immortal or not, she didn't know how she could survive such a travesty of fate.

As she timidly put off stepping out of the car for another minute, she thought back to the last evening she'd spent with him, a cool October night in his apartment. As it had for much of their last few days together, much of their talk that night had revolved around the topic of vampirism. He had told her of the many troubles - he called them adventures, not wanting her to think he was looking for pity - he'd had in his five hundred or so years, and the causes behind them. By that time, she'd already known his claims to be true. Not so, the first night he'd made his revelation. When he'd first told her he was a vampire, sitting in her car by Lake Michigan, she'd laughed it off, though such a joke had seemed very out of character for him.

She stopped laughing when he'd proven his claims to her by lifting the car above his head with her still in it. She was already in love with him by then; how could she not have been? Besides his darkly handsome appearance, he was the best conversationalist she'd ever met - having centuries of experience to draw on, she supposed. He treated her well, and even though he never let it drop his nearly regal manner, he was obviously enchanted by her and overjoyed to be in her company. He was certainly not rich; indeed, his finances seemed spotty at best, but he always gave her a pleasant evening, and never gave thought to the looks they got as a mixed-race couple.

She'd asked him, on that last night in his apartment, to make her a vampire too: to 'Awaken' her, as he'd told her it was called. He'd looked down at his hands, thinking, then raised his gaze to her again and told her he could not. He confessed to her that he had never acquired that ability, to Awaken humans. The look he gave her was as though he'd just revealed he'd been castrated.

After a short period of awkwardness, the rest of the evening had passed well, but that was the last time they'd ever been together.

While it was the last time he'd ever seen her, she had kept tabs on him over the intervening years, sneaking a peek at him when she could do so without danger of being seen. She often wondered if he thought she had left him because of his inability to give her that one thing she had asked for. He probably did - that was so like a man, no matter how old that man may be. That was yet another reason for her trepidation over seeing him again. Hopefully, now she'd have a chance to straighten all that out, to explain what had happened the following two nights, what had caused her to leave so abruptly.

She turned off the car. Enough daydreaming and procrastinating. She was not some timid schoolgirl waiting for her first date - far from it. It was time to go. She opened the door, stepped out of the car ...

And stopped. There were perhaps a dozen police vehicles pulling up in front of the hotel. *This can't be good,* Stephanie thought as she slipped back into her seat to watch the spectacle. She was disconsolately certain that this had something to do with Lawrence, and that their glorious reunion was to be delayed yet again.

* * *

The pounding of the footsteps in the hall was the first sign that something was going on. It was still early in the evening, perhaps two hours after sunset, but Lawrence hadn't heard such a ruckus in the halls since he'd been staying there. So he sat where he was, on the edge of the bed with the TV on, listening to their rapid progression up the hall. He had woken to an empty room again tonight, with Mac and Lady already off doing their own things. He muted the TV and listened to the commotion outside his door. Apart from the actual footsteps, there was far less noise than what he would expect from a group of people as large as the sounds indicated - very little talking.

The multitude of feet stopped abruptly outside his door. Almost before he could wonder why, there was a solid knock and a shouting voice informed him that it was the police and that he must open up.

There was little he could do in his weakened state. Even the usually blazing speed of his mind had been slowed to near-mortal levels. In a mild daze, he walked over and opened the door.

He immediately found himself overwhelmed by a flood of people. Like a true flood, the flow forced him back, though it was a flow of arms, legs and faces - all nothing more than a jumble to his senses - which pushed him back into the room. As he staggered back they circled past and around him. Lawrence found himself surrounded by grim-looking men and women in police uniform, most with obvious body armor and drawn weapons. The silence of the group in the hallway was left to memory as commands, acknowledgements, and information bounced rapidly back and forth among the mass of professionals. It was almost more than his ears could keep track of.

One particular voice in the babble demanded his attention. He came out of his fugue to see a familiar face on the tall, blond man standing before him. At the same time, he realized dimly he'd been maneuvered back to sit on the end of the bed. Sometime in all the rush he'd also been cuffed. Automatically, he tested the strength of his steel bonds. Not surprisingly, they would require more strength than he could bring to bear in his enfeebled state. Lawrence ran through all of this as he looked up. He was being asked a question.

"Where are they? Your room assignment says one cat, one dog."

The chaos around Lawrence was almost overwhelming. He searched his memory. "Jamon, right?" He smiled serenely up. He was trying to think fast, but it was as though his mental batteries were drained; rather than coming lightning quick, his thoughts moved with all the speed of an old settler's wagon train. A stray thought ran through his head: *A weak vampire is the most pathetic of creatures.* His brows came down together as he tried to focus. "What is a police officer doing looking for animals?

Doesn't the Humane Society handle that?"

He heard someone snicker behind him. "Just answer the question," Jamon replied obdurately.

Instead, Lawrence looked around. Several of the officers were clustered around his coffin. From their discussion it seemed as though they were having difficulty believing it was real, and that he used it. He looked back at the detective, Jamon, who was still waiting for an answer. It was going to be a long night. And he hadn't even fed yet.

* * *

Stephanie briefly considered taking up smoking, just for the night. It was said to soothe the nerves, and cancer was no longer a concern for her. The question arose, however, whether it would have any effect with her undead physiology. She didn't normally breathe, so would the chemicals from the smoke get into the bloodstream to be transported to the brain? Since her veins also didn't pulse, she didn't think so. Something to ease her anxiety would be welcome, though.

She'd been sitting impatiently in her car for a few hours, now. Earlier, shortly after the arrival of the police, she'd ventured into the stairwell on Lawrence's floor and let her ears pick up what was going on. It didn't take long. Even after so many years, and in the present unpleasant conditions, Lawrence's calm, self-assured voice was just about as she remembered it. What she didn't understand was why he was subjecting himself to such indignity. With the power contained in him, he could have easily made his escape.

Rather than intercede and give him a breakout he didn't need and might not want, she'd decided to be patient and wait. For now.

But it was difficult for her to sit and wait. She'd thought, with eternity before her, and twenty-seven years to grow used to it, she'd have learned patience. Apparently not. Three hours since her reconnaissance, and no sign of his grand escape. She was growing anxious. Two of the squad cars had left, but Lawrence still seemed to be up in the room with the majority of the officers.

She almost missed seeing him. Lost in her own thoughts and reminiscing, her gaze had slowly wandered from the area in front of the hotel and drifted down the empty street. She turned, snapped out of her mental wanderings by barely seen movement, and there he was. Even from her distance, and with the brief glimpse she had as he was bundled into the back of a car, she knew he was just as handsome as she remembered. That could have been her bias speaking, but she ignored such an unflattering possibility. The casual suit he wore suited him perfectly. Even when he couldn't afford the best clothes, she remembered, he made what he wore look like far more than it was on its own. Still, with his good looks, his style, there was something detracting from it now. She couldn't quite put a finger on it. The humans certainly wouldn't notice it, as they were unaccustomed to the raw power and anima exuded by a vampire, but she could sense it, even from such a brief look. It concerned her, but there were more important things to deal with right now.

As the car with Lawrence pulled out, she started her own car's engine and followed from about a block back - easy to do on the open, early morning streets. She had driven about half a mile before she realized she was not the only one following the police car. For a while, rather than the intense watch she had kept on the police vehicle, she watched the two animals who were relentlessly following the same path as she, but from the sidewalk. One cat, one dog, running together. Side by side, not chasing one another. They, too, were keeping a reasonable distance from the apparent object of their pursuit.

At one point, there was a small rush of traffic, coinciding with a large number of cars parked along the road. Stephanie came very near to hitting the suddenly stopped car ahead of her. Not because of slow reactions, but because she was distracted by the cat's nine foot jump. Obviously, their view was momentarily disrupted by the obstructing vehicles, and so one of the duo jumped to maintain sight of their quarry, but *nine feet*?! She shouldn't be surprised, she realized, as she had already surmised they were two of the vampiric animals Lawrence had long ago mentioned he could Awaken. What other explanation for such single-mindedness, speed and stamina over two miles?

She considered picking them up, but who knew how they'd react to a strange vampire? And from what she remembered of Lawrence's stories, they'd have no way of communicating with her. They might even mistake her for a minion of the Council. No, best to keep her relative distance for now. And, whatever Lawrence's reasons for allowing himself to be taken in like this, the two animals were probably in on it with him. She'd watch and wait for Lawrence to reappear.

* * *

The truth of the matter was that neither Lady nor Mac had any idea of what to do next, and they knew that Lawrence didn't either.

They had been on their way up to the room when they heard numerous human voices coming from it. Not recognizing them, sensing something was amiss, they halted. "Lawrence?" Mac called from the hallway, "what's going on?"

"Don't come in, guys. There are about ten cops in here," he warned them.

"Aw, come on, Lawrence. The three of us can take a dozen humans easily!" Lady's tail was whisking behind her, her claws already extended at the thought of a fight. "You took on nine yourself once, remember!"

"They're armed and edgy, and I'm cuffed and weak, and those are guns, not swords. Someone could get hurt, and I will not condone it," Lawrence admonished.

"He's right. Lady. It'd be too easy for us to hurt one real bad if we had to fight all of 'em."

Lady looked at her canine companion and snorted in disgust, a sound easily mistaken for a sneeze. Mac's tail was down between his hind legs, and he was prancing nervously from side to side with just his front paws. "Bah. Coward," she said.

Mac stopped his shuffling, his tail came up, and he growled, head dropping low. "Watch yourself, you blood-thirsty little savage. I'll rip your throat from you without even trying."

"Knock that shit off, Lady!" Even muffled by distance, the command rang in their heads. "You too, Mac. You should know better than to react to her needling. We don't have time for it."

Mac's posture immediately relaxed. "You have a plan, then?"

Lawrence's response came slow, and was not hopeful. "No. Not yet. But just hang out, follow, and see if a chance presents itself. And I don't want any humans seriously injured." He let his words sink in. "Got that, Lady?"

She agreed, with a sullen, "I got it. Don't see why, but I got it."

And now, an hour and a half later, they were following Lawrence to some police station, jail, they weren't sure what. The two watched forlornly as the car carrying their master disappeared into a secure garage under the building.

"Shall we crawl under this car?" Mac suggested. They had stopped across the street from the heavy garage door.

"Why on earth would we do that?" Lady's scorn carried easily across the link.

"So that we aren't seen by anyone," Mac reasoned.

"What do we care if we're seen? They'll dismiss us as stray pets, Bowser."

"Did you see who it was that had Lawrence?"

"Some human. What's the difference? They all look alike to me," she purred with an air of indifference.

"No, they don't. If you had been paying the least bit of attention, you would have recognized him. It's the same cop you guys ran into last night." He gave her a contemptuous look. "And you call me dim-witted."

"No, I call you stupid and foul. Now get under the car before someone sees you." She was already crawling under it herself. She found it disgusting. The pavement itself was filthy, but the worst part was the gunk on the car's undercarriage sticking to the fur of her back. Her next grooming was going to go down hard. She could guess the taste by the overwhelming smell of grease, oil, gas and dirt that almost caused her to choke as she drew in an experimental sniff.

"Actually, Lady, I'm going to walk around the building. The cop's never seen me before. Why don't you stay and watch in case anything happens."

"Yeah. Great," she said, her tail rippling in agitation. *Why the hell am I taking orders from a mutt all of a sudden,* she wondered. As her up-to-now clean tail hit a particularly sticky splotch of grease, she meowed in angry frustration.

Mac was already halfway down the block, but still heard her yowl. He allowed himself his chuffing laugh as he imagined the prissy feline's discomfort under the car's grimy chassis. He'd suggested hiding after he smelled the mess under the automobile, though he'd already been thinking it would be a good idea. He put his pleasant thoughts aside. The immediate problem was how to get Lawrence out. It was obvious that Lawrence could do little for himself; he'd weakened far too much. His strength was little better than that of a mortal strongman, his speed was also at near-human level, and his other powers were nearing uselessness with a frightening rapidity.

Conversely, while Mac and Lady were far more than a match for any small group of humans physically, they were little better off than Lawrence for several reasons: they were not to harm any humans; they could not mesmerize, not being able to communicate with humans; and they were simply not adapted to the human world. Their strength and intelligence allowed them to deal with most obstacles they encountered day to day, like doorknobs, but a secured environment like a police station was bound to be far trickier. They would likely need to resort to a lot of brute strength, and leave obvious evidence of their passage. Even with that, Mac wasn't sure he and Lady together would be able to bend prison bars, or get the best of any other obstacles that stood in their way. According to Lady, their strength would still be increasing for a year or so, but that did no good now.

As he completed his tour around the facility, he found himself hoping that Lady would be able to come up with something; he had seen no good options. "Seen anything promising, Lady?" he called as he came up on the car.

"No. How about you? Find anything on your stroll around the block? Any fire hydrants to pee on?"

Mac could see her angry green eyes practically glowing under the car. With a bit of surprise, he noticed that they actually were green, not one of the many shades of gray he was used to seeing in. Lawrence had never mentioned he'd undergo such a change, nor had Lady. Perhaps Lawrence's past dogs had never informed him of this particular enhancement. He paused to admire the green. Very pretty, though he'd have to be sure not to let Lady know he thought so. He looked down the street at the stoplight. Oooh. Red. Lovely. He'd never known what he was missing. He admired the colorful new world around him for a moment before turning his attention back to the cat and her affronted dignity. "I can always tell when you're irritated. You get so catty." He chuffed amusedly at his own, poor joke. Realizing Lady had either failed to see the humor, or didn't appreciate his sharp wit, he went on. "No, there wasn't anything where we could get in easy. Do you have any ideas?"

"Of course, you lop-eared fool. Crawl on under here and I'll tell you."

He shook his head, his dangling ears waggling. "Why don't we take a walk, instead? We can't do anything more tonight, unless your plan includes literally dragging him out."

"True. He'll be asleep soon. Speaking of which, we need to find a place for ourselves. I don't want to chance the hotel room tonight." She heaved a mental sigh of relief. His response saved her the embarrassment of either admitting she had no idea how to get Lawrence out or pulling a half-cocked plan out of nowhere.

"Me neither," Mac replied as Lady emerged from under the car. He wisely refrained from commenting on her matted pelt, though he wore a grin beneath the fur of his rust-colored muzzle.

* * *

Two hours later, the red Audi that had been parked discretely down the street came to life and rolled off. Behind the wheel, Stephanie wasn't much clearer on the situation than she had been when the police first converged on the hotel. She had watched the animals watching the police station. She'd seen them staring at each other - she could only presume they'd been 'talking', then the dog patrolling while the cat watched the garage door. They'd both left some time ago, and based on the late hour, she had to conclude that nothing would be done before dawn today.

She looked one more time at the garage door Lawrence had disappeared behind. "Be careful in there, Lawrence," she whispered as she drove off. She'd be back after sunset tonight. If his little companions couldn't get him out, she'd have to do it herself and risk the consequences.

CHAPTER SIXTEEN

There was silence on the phone line for the space of two heartbeats, then, "Dead? You're sure?"

"Yes, Detective, I'm sure. There isn't much question with no heartbeat, no breathing, and a steadily dropping body temperature. Of course, if you doubt my competence to judge such a *difficult* matter, the M.E. will be in tomorrow to render his professional judgment, but I doubt it will be much different from mine."

Jamon rolled his eyes at the sarcasm. "Look, Dustin, I'm sorry. Your call woke me up, and I'd only fallen asleep..." he checked the clock; it was a little after noon, "about three hours ago after a long night. I'm just trying to wrap my brain around this. Can you tell me what happened?"

"Alright." Jamon could hear paper rustling on the other end. "Ummm, let me see. Okay, here's the report. Okay. Uh, he didn't get up for the ten o'clock count and -"

"Never mind, Dustin." Jamon rubbed his red eyes. "I'm going to come in. I want to see him, and I want to talk to whoever found him. What a pain in the ass this guy is. Even dead." He had really wanted to get some answers from this guy. He'd caused Jamon too much trouble, and in such... problematic ways. The man had refused to talk last night. He had never asked for a lawyer. He just didn't answer questions. Jamon knew they'd get something out of him eventually. Well, they would have, had the guy not up and died. "Alright, Detective. I'll let them know you're coming in."

"Thanks, Dustin." He hung up.

Another hour and a half later found him staring at the corpse laid out in the prison morgue. It was a small room, with only one exam table.

Apart from the small size, it was like any other morgue, filled with bright, mobile lights illuminating every corner of the sterile, utilitarian environment. No one was ever surprised by the smell of death that permeated this room. It was not the stench of decay, but rather the antiseptic odor of modern, clinical death. This was expected. What tended to make people uncomfortable was all the other, subtle aspects of the room, many of which even a trained observer such as Jamon could not put a finger on. Every facet of the room cried out to the senses that it was just a brief stopping point, a pit stop on the all-tooshort road to the grave. The chill air, the scent of chemicals, the austerity of the room whose only color was provided by the grim anatomical charts, and the lack of any sound save his own breathing. He was an intruder here.

Somehow, he felt that this body before him was also an intruder, a trespasser in this room for the dead. Oh, there was no doubt it was dead, but there remained some elusive hint of vitality that Jamon could not quite put his finger on. This hidden vitality had such force that he had even felt for a pulse on the cadaver. Dustin had merely looked askance at him, raised an eyebrow, and turned back to his notes as he walked out.

Jamon looked at his copy of the report again. Among the usual mundania, it noted that the fangs seemed to be real, at least superficially. Jamon had observed them earlier that morning as he interviewed the subject at the hotel, though Lawrence had managed to keep them from being obvious as he spoke. With one last, affronted look at the body, he left the chilly room. "I'm done with him, Dustin, if you want to stick him in your freezer."

"It's not a freezer, Detective," he admonished.

"I know, I know. Anyway, I'm done. Do you have a cause of death? I didn't see one listed on here," he noted, lifting the report to indicate it.

Dustin's expression smoothed as he turned his face away from Jamon and looked down at the papers in his own hand. "No, not yet. It's kind of odd. No severe trauma, no obvious medical problems. He's quite young, maybe 35." He turned back to Jamon, an almost hopeful look on his honest face. "We're having trouble with some of the equipment, though, so maybe we'll have a better answer for you when it's working right."

"Trouble with the equipment? How so?"

"It's listing his blood type as all possible types. It keeps switching the results every time we run it. You know: A, B, O, AB. Like it can't make up its mind what kind of blood the late Mr. Watts had. Quite impossible. By the way, you'd asked earlier about drugs. If the other results are to be trusted, which I don't believe they are with the way the machine is misbehaving, he was clean of any drugs."

"You said the Medical Examiner will be in tomorrow?"

"Yeah. He doesn't work weekends. He'll do the autopsy first thing in the morning."

Lawrence looked back at the door to the morgue he'd just come through. "He won't come in to do it today? Did you ask?"

"No, he wouldn't do it. No need. The body'll keep fine. And it's not like it's going anywhere." A ghoulish grin crossed Dustin's face at his own macabre humor.

"Heh. Yeah. I guess not. Okay. Thanks for your time, Dustin, and the call. I appreciate it." He started for the stairs.

"No problem. I knew it was your case, and the death struck me as odd enough that you might want to know about it right away."

"Yeah. Later."

Upstairs at his desk, he reviewed the reports for the fifth time, the last time before he went home for a few more hours of desperately needed sleep. According to the documentation, after Jamon had left at about three a.m., Lawrence had been speaking with the inmate sharing his cell when the officer on duty heard the sounds of a fight. The Response Team rushed in to break it up. Neither party was significantly injured, but they were both still sent to the 'hole' as disciplinary problems. The 'hole' was a special set of cells used primarily as punishment for troublemakers. They held one inmate per room. The rooms were smaller even than the limiting confines of the normal cells. In addition, there were no windows to the outside, very limited options or time for recreation, and various other small things to make the 'hole' more punitive than an ordinary cell. It was the closest equivalent in modern America to the dungeons of old.

Upon questioning, Lawrence had claimed the other man said something offensive, but refused to elaborate. His cellmate, a Mr. Sean Cooke – in for auto theft - claimed he'd done no such thing. Mr. Cooke stated they'd been talking about the different types of jail cells and Lawrence had asked if there were any that had no windows. Sean had told him only the disciplinary ones had none. Lawrence had then jumped him with no warning.

Sean's protestations of innocence were no surprise: most convicts involved in a fight denied any culpability. They hoped not to garner additional punishment and typically tried to pass themselves off as blameless. It was like dealing with children. This time, however, Jamon felt Mr. Cooke was telling the truth. Not that Jamon placed any faith in the auto-thief's dubious integrity. It was due more to the strange feeling Jamon had gotten from Lawrence each time he'd encountered the odd man. The feeling that Lawrence did things for reasons beyond Jamon's experience.

Whatever the reason for the scuffle between the two inmates, both participants were promptly sent to the hole. The guards on duty reported nothing else of significance until that morning's ten a.m. count. In fact, the report stated that Lawrence had seemed to go almost immediately off to sleep, with no other entries in the log until the stand-up count, except that he refused to take his breakfast tray which had been placed in his cell through the door slit.

In all prisons and jails, the inmates are counted several times a day; at some of these 'counts' the prisoners are required to stand. This prevents them from just putting something in their bed to give the appearance of it being inhabited. Many escapes in the past used this very tactic to good effect, sometimes delaying pursuit by days. The stand-up counts alleviated this concern. The counts have other purposes as well, like the current issue Jamon was confronted by, identifying a suddenly dead inmate, but escapes were the initial reason for the procedure.

At the ten a.m. count, which was a standing count, Lawrence failed to rise. After a few shouts through the door telling him to stand up, another guard was summoned for support and they investigated. When he failed to respond to their prods, his pulse was checked. Finding it absent, they immediately called the resident Physician's Assistant, Dustin Rider. Cursory attempts to revive were made, though with little hope. Based on his body temperature, they had already approximated the time of death at six hours earlier.

Jamon tossed the report back on his desk and ignored the goosebumps as he thought, *What if?* He knew he was being silly to even consider the possibility, but *What if?* This last incident, Lawrence's convenient, unexplained death, on top of everything else...

He shook it off. His rational mind reasserted itself. He was not so gullible. It could all be explained. Case in point: Dustin had declared that while the fangs *appeared* natural, there were several reasonable explanations. He claimed he'd be able to tell what they really were after the M.E.'s more thorough investigation. Everything else could likewise be explained away normally, Jamon reassured himself. His training told him that Lawrence Watts was just another freak. But training was not everything; he felt in the depths of his gut that Lawrence was not just a common wacko. Jamon felt that he was seeing something in Lawrence that mortal man was simply not meant to see. He was not so melodramatic as to question if his very soul was in peril, or any other such silly thing, but something here was tugging at his inner being. In fact, he'd felt different ever since his last encounter with Lawrence in the alley the night before. Nothing he could put his finger on, but different, somehow. Something... unnatural. Had he been tainted in some way? Was he becoming whatever Lawrence was?

He considered sitting up in the morgue as the sun set tonight, or tasking someone else with it. A glance at the box of Count Chocula cereal still sitting on his desk decided his mind against the idea. He'd never hear the end of it if he were to do such a thing. "Fuck this," he muttered as he got up out of his chair.

After a short visit to a supply locker, he was back downstairs in the lifeless chill of the morgue. He casually spun the padlock around on his finger as he looked at the drawer holding Lawrence's body.

Ordinarily the roll-out shelves were easily opened, even from the inside. The latch which held them closed bore a disturbing similarity to that common on walk-in freezers, or 'meat lockers'. Looking at the drawer in which Lawrence's body had been placed, he felt jittery. His mind was calling on his legs to leave, but Jamon clamped his will down on such treasonous thoughts. His unexplained fear decided him, and he snapped the lock on the cabinet with no further hesitation. "Just in case," he said to himself as he exited the room, shutting off the light behind him.

* * *

Even in the darkest of nights, police stations tend to be well-lit locations. This could be due to an attempt to remind criminals that police are always on the job, or to act as a sort of beacon to those who need their help. Perhaps it is simply because the electricity bill is covered by the taxpayers and therefore not a concern. Whatever the reason, the fact remains that it is difficult for anyone to loiter unseen near a law-enforcement facility. Anyone human, that is. Lady de Winter and Mac had little trouble at all with it. Their small size enabled them to take advantage of the tiniest of shadows near the garage; their ability to remain unnaturally still enhanced their hiding abilities; and the fact that they were just a couple of 'dumb animals' caused anyone who did see the duo to disregard them as a non-concern.

They had been waiting for about 45 minutes for a car to either enter or leave the garage. At such a time, the secure door would open briefly, giving them a chance to scurry in. There was almost no discussion between them tonight; Lady refused to reveal any details of her plan for getting Lawrence out. Besides that, there was little to discuss for the moment. Neither was keen on talking about their accommodations for the past day.

They had taken refuge from the sun in the basement of an abandoned tenement. A far cry from their almost luxurious accommodations of the past few weeks, it could not even compare favorably with the seedy room at the Biltmore they'd started in. Their primary concern while searching for a suitable resting place was being found as they lay helpless during the day. Should someone find them, dead to all appearances, it was all too possible they'd be tossed into some outside trash bin, exposed to the sun. They tried not to consider what else might happen if they were discovered. They were all too aware, from their days as mortal animals, of what some juveniles considered entertainment.

With those unsettling thoughts lodged in their minds, they found a condemned building. The one they settled on didn't even hold the usual complement of unsavory tenants who used such unwanted buildings either for shelter or for hiding in. The reason for this vacancy became apparent as the pair entered through a broken window: the decaying structure seemed ready to collapse down around them. Even the light weight planted on the floor from Mac's jump through the broken window was too much - his left front paw splintered through one of the rotten floorboards as he landed. Lady took this opportunity to regale

Mac with an almost endless run of fat jokes at his expense. This comedic performance lasted until he launched a single, stinging comment on her filthy, matted fur.

In addition to the structural concerns, the odor was unbearable. Mac was constantly sneezing and complaining about the smell until Lady exasperatedly suggested he simply stop breathing. The source of the odors became clear as they reached the basement of the dilapidated structure. Piled garbage of every description - and some that defied description - littered the floor. It was in this inauspicious locale, beneath a few concealing stacks of cardboard, that they had laid to rest for the day.

Now, Lady suddenly stepped from their shelter in the shadows near the garage. "Excuse me a moment," she said as she started down the sidewalk.

"What's going on? Where're you going?" Mac asked. He peered around into the darkness, ears perked up, sniffing the air for any disturbance.

"Nowhere. I'll be right back," she replied, not looking back at his shadowy form.

"Where are you going?" Mac demanded again.

"My own business," she snapped. "Shut up and keep watch. I'll be right back." She turned the corner down the sidewalk.

Moments later, Mac heard a long series of guttural hacking and choking sounds. At first concerned, he relaxed when he realized their cause, and allowed a satisfied smile to grace his long canine snout. When it was finished and Lady came back around the corner, he called to her. "Couldn't you hack up your hairball at that disgusting building this morning?"

Primly, she replied, "I wasn't done grooming that mess off of me. You'd understand, if you ever -"

"There's a car coming!" Mac interrupted.

Lady bolted, and was at their post in a flash. "Where from?"

"It's in the garage, coming out." As Lady settled back into her position the door began to open. Mac got up from his sitting position and canted down in a crouch, ready to run. "Now?"

"No. Wait until it's closing, so they won't see us as easily." Plus, she thought, if they were seen, it'd give them more time to hide before the car could get back in. Hopefully the police would think it not worth the bother in that case.

The door opened to reveal a squad car. Lady looked to make sure that Jamon was nowhere to be seen. Not because she'd grown afraid of him and his uncanny ability to pop up when least expected to cause trouble. It was only in case he were to recognize her and do something stupid, that's all. After the car pulled onto the road, she waited until the door was a scant eighteen inches from the ground.

"Go!"

They made it to the door at the same time. With twelve inches of clearance left, Lady's sleek body fit through much more readily than Mac's.

"Damn it, cat, I almost broke my spine! Again!" Mac whined.

Lady ignored him, eyes already scanning for a place to hide should the need arise. When the door hadn't gone back up a minute later, she proclaimed them in the clear. "Now, we pick out an air vent and go in."

Mac groaned, rolling his eyes. "An air vent? That's your great plan? You're kidding. How cliché!"

Lady began exploring as she defended her reasoning. "Cliché, perhaps. But that's only because it's a good idea. It wouldn't work for humans like they show on TV, because their oversized bodies wouldn't fit well in the vents. And that's a problem on just the simple, straight lengths of conduit. Imagine them trying to negotiate the corners. We, on the other hand, are a more convenient, compact size. We should have no problems with our more reasonably proportioned forms."

"Why didn't we just use one of the ones that lead outside? There must've been some on the roof or something."

"My, what a clever dog you are. Remind me to give you a biscuit when we're done. Yes, there most certainly are some on the roof, but this being a prison, they are probably blocked up pretty well with heavy-duty bars or something. I figured the ones in here, being still inside the building, would be easier to get to and not be so heavily blocked." Actually, she hadn't thought of trying the roof, but the excuse she gave Mac sounded pretty valid to her. No need to spoil his belief in her intellectual superiority. Especially since it was true. "Now, which one shall we use?"

"They all seem to be up pretty high," Mac noted. He, too, was walking the perimeter of the large room, looking high and low for all options.

"What's the matter, you can't jump a mere fifteen feet?"

"It's not just that. I have yet to see one that's not covered. Or are you

going to just cannonball yourself through the grill? That, I'd like to see."
Mac paused in his investigations, closing his eyes to enjoy the mental image. He could see it vividly; in color, even. Lady runs, picking up speed before launching herself into the air, perhaps uttering some catlike war meow. She curls up into a ball and hits the grating, headfirst. Of course she leaves a small dent where her dense skull connected with the metal, but falls to the ground. Oooh - she'd have to remain conscious for proper heckling to immediately follow. "Yeah, why don't you try that? It sounds like a great idea."

Lady paused in her prowling, casting a piercing glare his way. "You really are a fool, dog, if you think I'd try that." She sat in front of the wall opposite the garage door, gazing up at a vent high above her. "By the way, you need to learn to control your telepathy better. I saw the little scenario you just imagined." She tossed another withering look over her shoulder at him, her whiskers twitching in agitation. "And, you need to have your vision checked. I'm not nearly that fat."

Mac cocked his head, his ears lifting a bit as he did his version of a shrug. He trotted over to Lady's side, sat and looked up at the vent with her. "That's the one you wanna try?" It looked exactly like the other five vents he'd seen in the garage. Perhaps nine inches tall by twice that wide, it was covered by a rather solid looking steel grill. Very solid looking, in fact. Mac couldn't see how they'd be able to rend it enough to pass through. "I don't know if this is going to work, Lady."

"Yeah, you've got a point," she commented thoughtfully. Mac enjoyed the warm sensation of vindication. Lady turned her head towards him again, her ears canted forward. "Let me know when *your* brilliant plan comes to fruition," she finished, the sarcasm so thick it seemed to leave a residue in Mac's mind. His warm feeling instantly chilled. "Now, watch out, and see true animal cunning."

She walked back, away from the wall, and crouched, eyeing her target. Her tail swished back and forth. With eight running steps, she launched herself into the air. She didn't curl into a ball, to Mac's disappointment. Rather, he saw her flex her claws out, front and rear, as she approached the grill feet first.

Perhaps it was Mac's mental shout of "Cannonball!" distracting her as she soared towards the grill, perhaps it was just chance, but when she struck the grill, only one paw found purchase in the steel slats. She dangled fifteen feet above the floor from her one paw as she scrabbled furiously for purchase. She was able to hold on for the few anxious seconds she needed to get all claws locked solidly in the screen of the vent. Once secure, she spared a second to cast an angry look down at Mac. He was sitting patiently, watching her progress in silence. She turned back to her work without comment.

Slowly, she began to force the grill's horizontal slats apart. This was not the common, flimsy grill used for covering most home and commercial vents. Always with an eye toward security, or perhaps just durability, the police used a heavy-duty grill. The steel was still no match for the strength of even a young vampiric cat, and began to yield beneath her forceful ministrations.

Suddenly there was an angry meow, and her upper body flew back from the wall. For a moment she leaned back, sticking out perpendicular from the wall, only her hind claws still holding the grate. She held this undignified position for just a fraction of a second before her back legs pushed off and ejected her from her position at the wall.

As she fell to the ground, Mac's enhanced eyes watched intently as she performed an uncomfortable-looking but rapid series of intricate twists in the air. At the end of the acrobatics, she landed easily on all fours, her back still to the wall. *That's a handy trick*, he thought to himself. "There's no way you can fit through that little gap, and I certainly can't."

Lady had sat back on her haunches, and was licking one of her white paws. At Mac's comment she looked back up at the vent. "Oh? Hm. I thought it was enough," she claimed indifferently. "Of course I should have realized: if you're fat enough to crash through floors, you certainly couldn't squeeze through as easily as I can."

Mac walked over to her. "Kiss off. That was not intentional, no matter how you try and play it off. You fell."

Lady rolled her green eyes, her long whiskers twitching. "Fine. If you *must* know, I broke a nail." She held up her left paw, displaying the jagged end of the damaged claw.

"Bloody female," Mac muttered.

"What?! I heard that!"

"That's alright. Sit back and the man will handle this." His boast proclaimed, he performed the same run and jump Lady had done to get up to the vent. As he landed against the grill he thrust his gray and rust-mottled front paws through the gap Lady had coerced from the metal slats. Mac looked around, his head swiveling to take everything in. Now that he was up here, hanging by his forepaws, he wasn't entirely sure how to proceed. He saw Lady gazing complacently up at him, certainly only waiting for him to fail. He turned his shaggy head back to his work and considered. He could probably bend the slats another inch or so. Lady could possibly fit through then, but though Mac wasn't fat, he still massed at least double what Lady did. The slats would never part enough for him. On reflection, none of this struck him as a particularly well thought-out plan.

It was still better than the nothing he'd come up with, though, so he refrained from tossing a sharp comment at Lady.

With a flash of inspiration, he remembered Lawrence's story about the escape from the manor under siege, and his flight through the trap door. Leverage. Bending his paws down to ensure a firm hold on the vent grill, he planted his hind feet against the wall below. Once he was comfortable with the stability of his position, he began to pull backwards on the grill. At the same time, he pressed his hind paws against the wall for the leverage he needed, much as Lawrence had done when hanging from the trap door beneath the stable.

The first thing to begin giving was simply the slats he was pulling against. They bent outward an inch or two under the pressure he exerted. He was considering giving up for another plan when he was encouraged by the sound of groaning metal. He redoubled his efforts and was rewarded by a popping sound, and the feeling of his body jerking back as one bolt after another came loose. Only as the last bolt popped did he realize the precariousness of his position; he was holding himself up by the very thing he was removing. An image flashed through his mind; a man sawing off the tree limb he sits upon. With a yelp, he flew backward, much as Lady had done, but with his prize - the vent grill - in his paws. He threw it away from him, and did his best to mimic the convoluted twists he had earlier seen Lady perform with such ease.

To his surprise, the writhing contortions worked. He felt briefly like a pretzel, but he found himself coming to rest on all fours as the grate clattered loudly to the ground about eight feet away.

Lady simply watched as Mac landed in front of her, her expression unchanging, though one ear ticked as the grate landed.

When the echoes from its impact died away, Mac asked, "How do you expect Lawrence to fit through there?"

"Relax, dog, I've got this covered." This statement was, simply put, a lie. Lady de Winter had no idea what they could do when they found Lawrence. Mac was right - Lawrence certainly wouldn't fit through the ventilation system. That sort of escape only happened in bad movies, as she'd mentioned. She had never really thought that would be how they'd get him out. She couldn't come up with a viable plan without knowing what they would be facing. Of course, she couldn't let the poor dog know her plan only went as far as how to get themselves in; he was putting all his faith in her superior planning skills. A wise decision, she readily conceded to herself, but even she could do only so much.

More importantly, to admit otherwise to Mac would make her look bad.

"Let's go, Mac." Five running steps, a jump, and she vanished into the musty darkness of the ventilation ducts, followed closely by Mac.

CHAPTER SEVENTEEN

The vent system was a maze. The ducts seemed to go on forever, turning and angling through room after room, coming to dozens of dead ends and even more intersections. Mac was completely lost in just minutes; he knew his hyper-acute sense of smell would not be sufficient to lead them out of here. He found it eased his mind if he didn't worry about it, that a blind faith in Lady's abilities to get them out again took a load of weight off his mind.

For all this wandering, there seemed to be nothing of note on the ground floor. Mac got no strong scents, but they wandered the entire span of the first level of the complex nonetheless, peeking through almost every grill they came across. As they drew near the center, where they'd be able to switch levels, Mac finally detected a familiar scent. He drew in a deep breath, confirming it. "I smell that cop that caused all this, the one you said is named Jamon. I recognize the smell from when I told you to leave him alone."

Lady acted nonchalant, but Mac grinned at the way her tail instantly stopped its slow side-to-side movement. She turned back to face him. "He's here?"

"No," Mac replied, waving his snout forward to indicate his desire to keep moving. "But he must work in that office there, outside this vent. I can smell his residue."

Reassured, Lady continued leading them in their tour of the first floor. "I think that's pretty much it for this level, Mac. You haven't got a good whiff of Lawrence anywhere?" They paused at one of many intersections. Lady claimed they'd been everywhere, but Mac couldn't tell the difference. All the passages looked the same to him.

"No. I can smell him, but it's faint, and I can't tell where it's from. All these ducts make it tough to pinpoint, the way they interconnect."

"All right. We'll start heading up. It looked like that's where most of the prison cells were."

They arrived at the central vertical shaft and Mac turned his gaze upward, peering into the dark, square passage above him. "How are we going to get up there?" The vent went straight up, the walls perfectly smooth aside from the occasional coupling. There was no way they could position themselves to jump up to the top, as they had done in the garage. It was also too wide to wedge themselves against opposite walls, allowing them to squeeze up it. It would have been difficult to reach such a position at any rate; the shaft also sunk straight down, making any attempt to enter the upper reaches difficult. No matter how they chose to go about it, just beginning their ascent would prove a daunting task.

"Piece of cake," Lady asserted confidently, almost cheerfully. "We claw our way up. The metal's pretty thin, so we shouldn't have much trouble punching our claws through. It'll be just like climbing a tree. Even your thick, dull puppy-paw-claws should be able to get a purchase if you hit the metal hard enough. Of course, if you can't manage, I might be willing to drag your dead weight up with me, but I'd rather not."

Mac continued to look up the forbidding shaft as he listened to Lady's plan. This did not sound like one of her better ideas. "I know you think everybody else is deaf compared to you, but humans *can* hear - even mortal ones. Don't you think they'll wonder what all the noise is as we're slamming our claws into the metal, hammering away like a pair of construction workers?"

"Once again, I'm eagerly awaiting the revelation of *your* brilliant plan."

Rather than answer, Mac stood against the side wall, close to the vertical shaft on his hind legs. He put his head into the shaft and thrust his snuffling nose as far into the duct above them as possible. He tested the air thoroughly, and then dropped back on all fours. He hunched down so he was nearly lying down and scooted right up to the drop-off. Here, he dropped his nose over the edge as far as he dared, giving the air below an even more complete sniffing. "I think he's downstairs, anyway."

Lady had watched him as he let his nose do their exploring for them. "I thought you said you couldn't tell where he is?" She had a skeptical look about her, as her own nose and whiskers twitched once, but her voice in Mac's head sounded hopeful. Mac guessed she didn't relish the risk of climbing so many floors, either.

"It's hard to tell, and it's a very small difference, but the scent seems just a bit stronger, a bit fresher, down below." His voice carried the confidence of one speaking on his field of expertise. He scooted cautiously back and reared up to nose at the upper shaft again. "He might have been up there at some point, but I don't think he still is." He dropped to all fours one last time before asking, "How do we get down?"

"Jump."

As Lady gave her one-word plan, they heard a motor start up, the noise coming from somewhere far up the shaft above them. They felt the sudden push as the air conditioner forced its air through the shafts, ruffling their fur as the cold breeze blew past.

"Well, at least we know we won't be jumping into the belly of the air conditioner," Mac snorted, blinking against the artificial wind. "So, how are we gonna get down?"

"I was serious. We jump. The trick is going to be catching ourselves on the right level."

"What do you mean?"

"Well, it's quite possible that this shaft continues down past the next floor. So, as we drop we're going to have to snag ourselves on the next level of air ducts."

"You're kidding, right? This is another one of your lame 'stupid dog' jokes, right?"

"No, but I could easily turn it into one. That's never a problem," she snapped.

"Never mind, I can see you're serious." And he could. Between the stillness of her tail and the way her whiskers seemed to droop, it was all too obvious she was not looking forward to this dangerous exercise in dexterity and timing, either. He felt the need to reassure. "I'm quite sure he's down, not up, though." He wasn't quite clear on who he was reassuring: Lady or himself.

"Yeah." She paused, gazing down the shaft. "I can see better, I'm more nimble, I have better claws. I'll go first."

Mac thought he heard her repeat that statement, almost as though she were reciting a mantra, trying to convince herself. It seemed neither of them was completely confident in how to proceed. Mac wasn't sure if he was pleased at this show of Lady's lack of self-confidence or wished it had come at a more opportune time. Confident or not, she stepped promptly off the edge, her eyes the only betrayal of her fear, looking a little wide to Mac. They had little idea of what they were stepping into: the distance down, if the shaft narrowed, where exactly it ended up, et cetera. It looked perfectly safe, but the light in the shaft was dim by even the animal's standards; they couldn't be sure.

Mac listened attentively as she dropped, his head hanging over the shaft. He was rewarded by a brief but loud yowl and the sound of her claws screeching on sheet metal. The sound was akin to - and had the same effect on the nerves as - someone dragging their nails down a chalkboard.

"Are you okay?" he called after her. In his anxious state he broadcast his thoughts to her at the telepathic equivalent of a shout.

"Shut up!" was the equally voluble response he received. Her response carried with it an undercurrent of panic. Something in her jump had not gone as she'd hoped. How badly it had gone wrong he was unable to tell. She was obviously focused on fixing the problem and didn't want the distraction of his voice in her head.

As he was running numerous potentially catastrophic scenarios in his mind, he heard a pair of thumps from down below. Each one had the sound of a small, cat-sized body hitting the duct. It was all Mac could do to wait for Lady to tell him what was going on, or even if she was okay.

Finally his patience was at least partially rewarded as she told him, "Okay, your turn. The next level is about twelve feet down, and the two ways into it run crosswise form the one you're sitting in. You'll need to turn ninety degrees in either direction to catch a tunnel. Do you understand what I mean?"

"Yeah, but what -"

"Good. I'll be waiting for you when you're ready."

With her instructions still ringing in his head, he followed her down. The layout was just as she'd informed him. Catching the next level was not an easy task, even with her guidance. As he plummeted to the opening on the next floor down, he shot his paws out to catch the ledge. With nothing to grab onto aside from the smooth metal surface of the duct, he paws immediately began to slip back as the momentum of his body tried to carry him farther down the drop. His paws were holding on to the last two inches of ductwork and still sliding when what felt like a dozen needles jabbed violently and simultaneously into them. This did nothing to ease his state of mind, already slightly panicked by his pending fall. He let out a yelp even louder than Lady had voiced earlier, though his was not nearly as brief as hers had been.

"Shut up, fool!" he heard, and promptly cut off the noise. He looked up into Lady's concerned eyes, and realized it was her claws holding him where he was, stopping his descent. Gulping back a last whimper, he allowed her to assist his scramble out of the shaft.

Once he was secure again, he spared a look at his new environment. He was not surprised to see what appeared to be the same scene as above. His welcome to this level was another unending labyrinth of metal ducts paired with another contumelious comment from Lady. "It's about time. I thought it'd be dawn before you got up the nerve to jump." Mac ignored this obviously false jibe. He'd jumped less than two seconds after she told him to. It struck Mac that she intended to ignore, for now at least, the problem they'd each had. He was amazed to realize that she must be somewhat embarrassed over her own difficulties with catching the ledge. This policy of ignoring the problem suited him just fine.

Instinctively, Mac sniffed the air. "We're definitely closer to him."

"Is he on this floor?"

"I dunno. Are there any floors farther down? His scent is still rather faint. How about you? Can you smell him yet?"

Lady looked up from her grooming, an apparently unending process. "Of course."

Mac lifted one ear, his equivalent of a raised eyebrow.

"Well, maybe not quite yet," she conceded.

"See, if he was on this floor, I'd think even your dwarfish nose could smell him," he said, flaring his damp nostrils to accentuate his point. He could be just as snide as she, if he wanted.

"Well, we're not finding him just sitting here." Lady got to her feet and started down the steel pathway that stretched out before them.

*   *   *

Lawrence's first thought on waking was that he was home in his coffin. There was no light at all to see by, but he could sense the confines of his surroundings pressing in on him. As his mind cleared, he knew that was not likely. He was resting instead on something hard, something that felt to his back like metal. In fact, it felt as though there were metal on all sides, though he didn't reach out to touch anything. He had not yet moved, assessing his situation as best he could before committing himself to anything, even opening his eyes. He could sense the bare metal around him nonetheless. It was also cold, damn near freezing. His weakness revealed itself to him again as he lay in discomfort. It couldn't be below freezing, yet his body was feeling the low temperature most acutely.

And he was naked.

That was the last straw. How completely did they need to rob a man of his dignity? By the assembled facts - including his nudity - he knew where he was. Even as he'd realized he was not in his coffin, the events of last night had come back to him. It was a bit disconcerting, this slow return of awareness; too much like the waking of a living human for his liking. He could not afford a mortal's mental sluggishness. His mind would have to be sharper than that if he was to get himself out of here.

He hoped the animals were doing okay without him.

The facts at hand had led to his realization of his current circumstances. His gaolers had obviously found him and presumed him dead. The only logical thing to do with a dead man was to put him in the morgue. This was not a terrible predicament; it could have been far worse. Most of the alternative possible outcomes of his situation had involved him not waking up at all.

With that cheery thought, he began to feel out his resting place. He was obviously in one of the drawers in which they store bodies for further evaluation or disposition. He was not completely naked: a sheet of some sort was draped across him. Not much better, but there was nothing to be done about it for now. It was the least of his pressing concerns, yet it bothered his sense of propriety deeply.

He put such thoughts out of his mind and listened intently. It did not sound as though there were anyone in the room outside. He had to proceed either way, but it was good to know he'd not have to deal with anyone immediately upon exiting his drawer.

Movement was terribly restricted; Lawrence found the dimensions much more constrictive than he was used to in his coffin. It took some maneuvering, some tight bending of his arms to get them above his head to push open the drawer.

It was stuck. He was stuck. The drawer refused to open. It should have been a simple matter to push it open, but the roll-out slab refused to give an inch. At his prime, it would have made no difference; he could have torn his way out with very little effort, he was sure. Such was not now the case. Weakening him even more was the fact he'd not fed yesterday. He should have gotten a bite on the car-thief he'd been stuck with.

The thought crossed his mind that if he yelled for help, he would certainly be answered eventually. That, however, would land him in a whole new, fresh mess, and likely bring to raise many questions best left unasked by the authorities. Better to disappear and leave them to wonder about a stolen corpse. He feared it might come down to calling for help anyway. He had little to work with, and less room to do it in. Apart from the police, he could not expect any aid from outside. His only friends were a pair of bickering animals who would certainly not be permitted entrance to this facility.

He was stretched out as much as possible, trying again to force the drawer open when he thought he heard someone. He stopped straining, putting all his attention to listening. He heard it again, rather faint. It sounded like someone calling his name. He debated with himself whether or not he should reply. They could be calling for someone else named Lawrence, however unlikely that was. He wasn't quite sure yet that he wanted to give himself away to the police.

The full truth hit him, and he started yelling back - telepathically. "Mac! Lady!" The voice calling him had only been in his mind. He'd been so certain those two would be unable to get in that he'd not even paid attention to what his addled senses had been telling him. "Can you hear me? I think I'm in the morgue! I'm stuck in one of the drawers!"

"We're on the way!" He could tell it was shouted, but he heard it only faintly. Did he hear laughter, too? No, that must have been his imagination - it wouldn't carry well enough over the distance. So he hoped, anyway.

"Where are you guys?" he mind-yelled.

"Not far. We'll be there in a few seconds. We know where the morgue is. We just passed it, but we didn't see you in there," Lady replied. She hadn't answered the intent of his question. How had they gotten into the building and been allowed to roam it freely? Whatever the answer might be, he could freely admit he was happy to see them. He only hoped they weren't going to be in their own trouble because of this. He imagined it'd be hard to catch the pair of them if they were set on evading capture, though. Before he could ask for a clarification of their location, Lady informed him, "Okay, we're at the morgue. Mac's going to get us in." She was no longer shouting. As she finished her update, Lawrence heard a loud clattering, as of something metal falling to the floor in the room beyond his drawer.

"What the hell?" he exclaimed.

"All right, Lawrence, we're in. Where are you?" Mac asked.

"I'm in this one," he responded, knocking on the end of his drawer.

"Oh. Ah, slight problem, Lawrence. There's a padlock on your drawer. Someone didn't trust you to stay put."

Lawrence sighed. He supposed it had been too much to hope that no one believed him more than human. He'd tried to keep any hints as to his true nature concealed, but there was only so much he could do. It was probably that bastard, Jamon. "I don't suppose there's a key out there somewhere?"

"Lady's looking for one right now. No luck so far."

Lady chimed in. "It's not looking good, pal. I'm not sure it matters. How would we use a key if I find one? Stupid non-opposable thumbs. Evolution ripped us off."

Out in the morgue itself, she was scampering everywhere, seeking keys. She hung over the edge of the counter she'd climbed upon to pull its top drawer out. "Ha! Keys!" She reached a paw into the drawer and fished out a ring of perhaps half a dozen keys. "Mac, come get these," she ordered, knocking them to the floor with a flick of her paw.

Before they hit the ground, Mac had them caught in his teeth. He tossed his head about in small, deliberate movements, reaching up with a paw to help control the keys. When he had a single key perched precisely between his teeth, he walked over to the drawer. A quick glance at the pattern of the lock's keyhole revealed the futility of his efforts. The key would not fit. He let the key ring drop to the floor, where they jingled on the clean tile. His shaggy nose held just inches away from the ring, he perused his other options. A quick comparison convinced him that the ring held no keys that would fit the troublesome lock.

Lady had since jumped lightly off the cabinet and stood on the other side of the keys from Mac. She looked up into his face, only inches from her own. "Those are the only keys in here."

"Any other ideas, Lady?" they heard Lawrence ask from within his steel tomb.

"Well, we could...um...no. I got nothing, Lawrence. Sorry."

Mac stepped back over to the drawer which held Lawrence, his eyes on the lock. He reared up on his hind legs, examining the lock and handle from a closer perspective. "What are you thinking, Mac?" Lady asked.

Mac made no response, instead taking the lock in his jaws. He lifted his hind legs off the floor and put them against the cooler unit. The appearance he gave was of standing on the wall unit, perpendicular to the floor. His muscles bunched, notable even under his straggly fur coat, and a low growl escaped from his throat.

"Mac? What are you doing?" Lawrence called out. He could hear Mac's growl coming in from outside the drawer, right next to his head. "Lady? What's going on?"

Her response was slow as she watched Mac's struggle against the lock. "He's...trying to break the lock, I think."

No sooner had the thoughts left her mind than Mac flew backward. As in the garage, he tried to twist his way to a four-footed landing. The short fall was not enough for his amateurish attempt. He ended up on his side as he hit the ground. He was apparently unhurt, though certainly irritated. Lady looked from Mac, where he lay with a tangled chunk of metal in his jaws, to the slightly mangled drawer. "Try now, Lawrence," she calmly suggested.

This time the drawer slid open with little effort, only briefly catching on something at first. Lawrence got out, carefully keeping the sheet he'd been under wrapped around him. The reason for the hitch as the drawer opened was obvious: Mac had been unable to break the lock, but the handle itself was not made to the same standards. It had been twisted about and largely wrenched from its duty of latching the drawer. Its mangled remains had snagged on themselves. Mac was spitting out bits of metal fragments from the destroyed handle still caught in his teeth.

"I think I chipped a tooth," he complained.

"Better than contracting lockjaw," Lady commented brightly.

Mac and Lawrence both looked at her with pained expressions. "I think I prefer your sarcasm," Lawrence claimed.

"Okay. I love your new duds, Lawrence. What's the new look you're going for, Halloween ghost or Greek revival?"

"There's a lab coat hanging in that corner," Mac said, indicating the location with a raised paw. The metal fragments he had dislodged from his teeth were scattered on the floor in front of him.

As Lawrence dropped the sheet and hid his nakedness under the lab coat he asked, "I don't suppose you guys have a plan to get us out? Can we get out the same way you got in?"

Mac and Lady both glanced at the open access to the ventilation system. Lawrence followed their gaze, and then looked for the falling metal he'd heard as they'd entered. The grill lay off to the side of the room, where it had passed unnoticed by him until now.

Lady responded to Lawrence's question first. "Sorry, Lawrence, I don't think you'll quite fit." Lawrence wordlessly nodded his agreement. "But, I doubt the morgue will be as heavily secured as the jail area. It should be much easier to get out from here."

Mac picked up the disregarded keys. "These might be helpful, too," he suggested, bringing them to Lawrence.

"Somehow I doubt it, Mac, but thanks. Well, no need to stick around here any longer. Let's go." They stepped into the empty hallway outside the morgue's door.

"What about your plan for getting Lawrence out, Lady?" Mac asked.

"Well, we didn't find him in a jail cell as we'd expected," she evaded.

"Alright then," Lawrence said as he started down the hall. "We'll just follow the 'Exit' signs, unless you two have any better ideas." Nobody had any better ideas, so the trio followed the signs for the exit. The first door they came to was unlocked; the second was not. After trying all the keys on the ring Lady had found earlier, they stared mutely at the locked door.

"You wanna try biting this lock off too, Mac?" Lady suggested.

Lawrence answered instead. "I don't think that will work, Lady. I don't think Mac's jaws are big enough to get a firm hold on the handle. Maybe if he'd been a great dane, but as it is, he's too small."

As they descended into silence again, Mac had a vision: his earlier fantasy of Lady cannonballing into the vent in the garage. With one last look at the door to confirm it opened away from them, he trotted back down the hallway about thirty feet. "Stand clear," he commanded. As the other two stepped back, he launched himself to as fast a run as he could manage. A few feet from the door, he jumped three feet into the air and turned sideways, slamming into the middle of the door with the solid mass of his body. There was a sharp "CRACK" as the door flew open, its lock broken.

"Our own furry battering ram," was Lady's comment as they continued their search for the way out.

Fortunately for Mac's bruised side, there was only one more door he had to ram before they emerged into some sort of lobby. Through the glass door opposite the windowless one from which they'd emerged, they could see the dark street outside. They drew no relief from this sight, though: a dozen uniformed officers stood around the room, guns drawn.

As Lawrence and the animals took in the situation, Lawrence's eyes caught new movement outside. What he saw would have stopped his heart, had it still beat. Running at the door, almost faster than Lawrence's eyes could follow, was a figure that he had not seen in four hundred years; a figure he had thought never to see again.

As the caped form smashed through the glass door, sending shards flying at Lawrence and his companions, there was no mistaking the gruesome face that even now bore the marks of that encounter of centuries past: the face, half the flesh eaten away, an empty eye socket, raw muscle showing through in many other places, sometimes nothing covering bone at all. Holy water damage could not be healed by a vampire's regenerative abilities. Lawrence shouted for Mac and Lady to run as Sandoval came charging at him, eager to finish the job he'd failed those years ago, the elimination of Lawrence.

CHAPTER EIGHTEEN

Sandoval had landed in Milwaukee the evening before in one of the Council's private jets. At the same time that Lawrence was discussing windowless rooms with his temporary cellmate, the felon Sean Cooke, Sandoval was walking the five flights up to Lawrence's room. He was greeted by the sight of yellow police tape crossing the doorway, which he ignored as he slammed the door open, breaking the latch. As he'd expected from the police tape, the room was empty.

Back downstairs at the front desk, he pulled back the deep hood he wore when he had to operate in the mortal world. The clerk, a twenty-one year old local college student, blanched at the sight. Hours later, Tony - the clerk - would convince himself that it was just elaborate make-up. He would convince himself the leaden ball of fear in his belly that had almost caused him to lose control of his bladder was nothing at all, just surprise at the unexpected sight. Such lies to self were necessary if he wished to retain his sanity. But for the next week, his nightmares would remind him of the truth: he had been stared down by the only true predator of mankind.

When Sandoval pulled back his hood, Tony was instantly caught by the vampire's eye. Even though Sandoval had but one eye, he still commanded the full mesmeric power of any vampire. At times, catching humans in his trance was easier for him than others of his kind. Mortals' gazes were drawn towards his mutilated face, his deformed eyes.

There was a sharp 'Click' as Sandoval placed a flat, rectangular object on the desk in front of Tony. At the sound, Tony managed to flick his eyes down for a fraction of a second, long enough to identify the item. It was the numbered plate from the door of one of the hotel's rooms. His eyes snapped back to lock again on Sandoval's good eye. He heard himself speaking, almost as though he had no control over his own tongue. More than that, the information he gave, he would not normally have been able to recall with any amount of conscious effort.

"Lawrence Watts...Room 512...arrested by 12th Precinct cops." Tony conveyed the information as tonelessly as a computer, with the measured precision of a metronome.

In the silent space following Tony's few words, Sandoval reached into a pocket of his suit-coat and withdrew a business card. He placed it on the desk, sweeping aside the room number.

"Yes, Mr. Sandoval, we have a suite reserved in your name. Your key." The boy's voice marched as it had earlier as he handed over the key card.

In most major cities, the Council kept safe houses for its emissaries. Milwaukee was hardly a major city, though, so they had been forced to rent a room for Sandoval, as they had for Phillip. Sandoval did not mind. It was just a place to wait out the day until he tried again tomorrow to move in for the kill. He pulled his hood back up and walked for the elevator, leaving a confused desk clerk already questioning the truth of what his memory claimed he just saw.

* * *

Before leaving the following evening, Sandoval ensured he was fully prepared, going over his various implements, inspecting and cleaning everything to perfection. It had been about a week since he'd last fed, so he found a pleasingly plump blond maid. She'd just delivered room service a few doors down. He broke into an unoccupied room and left her lifeless body there for later disposal.

While Mac was yanking the lock off with his teeth, Sandoval hailed a cab, which he had drop him off a block from the precinct. He was halfway around his initial circuit of the building when he saw his target through a glass door. Lawrence was making it easy for him. His fleshless upper lip pulled back in a hideous grin. The grin turned what was once merely ghastly into the truly horrific.

The time for revenge was at hand. He let his hood fall back. He charged.

* * *

Lawrence's command to run went unheeded by Mac and Lady. While they realized the action was almost certainly futile, they positioned themselves in front of Lawrence. From there they could guard against both Sandoval and the now lesser threat of the police.

Sandoval's first action on smashing through the window was to shoot.

With a hitherto unnoticed small pistol in his hand, he fired three precise shots in rapid succession. His targets were the security cameras that otherwise could have been used to identify him at a later time. This action performed, he tossed the firearm aside in contempt. Two other shots rang out as a couple officers decided to chance a shot within the close quarters. One managed to strike Sandoval in the gut. Having already visually confirmed his true prey's weak state, Sandoval chose to engage the greater threat. For the first time in his experience, this was posed by mortals. So many weapons could do enough harm to make him distinctly uncomfortable. He attacked.

Lawrence paused. Mac looked up at him. Though no telepathy took place, they still knew, and shared, each other's thoughts on this matter.

They attacked. As one, Mac and Lawrence leaped upon Sandoval just as he was reaching out an arm to rip the throat out of his second victim. Mac's teeth clamped firmly on the outstretched arm at the same time Lawrence grabbed hold of it. Sandoval's one good eye looked scornfully at them, the half-detached eyelid twitching uselessly above it. A whip-like motion of his arm sent Lawrence crashing against the far wall. Mac, through the strength of his jaws, managed to stay on though he feared another flick like that would snap his neck. He could feel his teeth tear easily through the fabric of Sandoval's shirt and into the far more solid mass of his steel-muscled arm.

Rather than repeat an attempt that had failed the first time and risk the torn flesh that could result, Sandoval reached over and pried Mac's jaws apart before throwing him across the room as well.

Mac hit the wall sideways, as he'd been doing when slamming the doors open. He fell to the ground, leaving a visible dent in the wall where he'd struck it.

Lawrence had missed the wall and flown through the door they'd entered through. Mac saw him picking himself up, eyes again locked on their target. Off to the side, in the hallway not four feet from Lawrence – but completely unnoticed by him - was another cop, though she wore civilian clothes rather than a uniform.

Mac's attention was ripped back to the action by the sound of several gunshots. Sandoval jerked back slightly with each shot, due simply to the velocity of the bullets. He was closing on two rather hefty officers who were the source of the most recent shots. Sandoval closed on the over-massed pair, grabbing each man's gun hand. His crushing grip forced them to drop their weapons, though one managed to fire a round straight into the monster's chest before the bones of his hand were crushed.

"Let's go!" Mac heard, and found himself again at Lawrence's side, at-tacking the killer. As before, Lawrence did no damage at all before being thrown back, though Mac managed to tear off a small chunk of flesh. Mac shook himself off after yet another jarring collision with the wall to see Lady de Winter hissing at the non-uniformed woman. Lady was doing her best to keep the woman in the hallway.

"This stupid woman has no weapon and she wants to charge in!" Lady explained as she continued hissing and making threatening swipes with her paw. Had the circumstances not been so dire, the sight would have been nothing short of comical. The woman, having witnessed the effec-tiveness and strength of Mac, was not underestimating the cat. She stood back, but continued to try to go around Lady. She was obviously very confused, in a panic.

Mac and Lawrence pressed their attacks, with similar results each time: Lawrence tossed aside like a doll, Mac abused in various ways. Through-out it all, the thundering of pistols echoed in the enclosed space. As the sharp scent of the discharging weapons soon overwhelmed all else, Mac quit breathing. He wondered how the mortals could get enough air through all the gun smoke.

While the scent saturated the air, Mac could still see quite clearly through the haze; between the steady barrage of lead and Mac's own attacks, Sandoval was taking heavy punishment and slowing down. Now, after a total of five assaults, Lawrence was down, and not getting up again. Mac knew he himself had several cracked ribs; he could only imag-ine how Lawrence was doing in his weakened state. There were also at least two slugs in his own torso. He didn't think Lawrence had taken any stray rounds, but it hardly mattered at this point.

Their own injuries aside, there were only two officers still up, and the woman with no weapon. She was no longer trying to plunge into certain suicide. She was just crying, muttering, "What're we going to do, what're we going to do?" over and over. Finally, the last of the noise died with the two cops who were making it.

The vampire turned his head to take in the four survivors. His incomplete face was rendered even more maleficent by the wounds of several well-fired bullets. Mac could tell Sandoval was weakened. He was far from top shape himself, and he didn't think Lady, with all her bluster, would be enough help to make up the difference. Lawrence was not even conscious. Mac took a step towards Lawrence, preparing to fight to the death for his friend. Lady was doing the same thing.

Sandoval's one-eyed gaze roved past the undead trio and settled on the slumped form of the human, who had dropped to the floor and descended into complete mental withdrawal. He took a slow step toward her, disregarding the animals entirely.

"Protect the human..." It seemed Lawrence was not completely out. Mac and Lady looked at each other and shifted over the few steps necessary to place themselves between the human and the slowly advancing atrocity. He paused, considering the new situation. Even without the fresh wounds, Sandoval's face was more devastated than Lawrence had said. The scarf he'd been wearing those centuries past had concealed from Lawrence's eyes the killer's lower jaw. The holy water had eaten through all of its flesh and meat, leaving only bone. The scarf had apparently held the holy water against his jaw, eating it all away, along with the skin of his upper lip and the tip of his nose. His lower teeth rested in bleached bone, his mandible exposed fully to air, back almost to its hinge in front of the ear. Even without his supernatural presence, his face could probably have driven mortals over sanity's edge. Looking at Sandoval's wild, kill-crazed eyes, Mac thought it more than possible that the beast before him had jumped that edge himself.

The woman looked up at Mac's growling to see both animals doing their best to stare down the image of death which was slowly advancing on her. It grinned: a terrible, gaping parody of human joy. She screamed, but stifled it almost as it escaped her throat. "Vampires. All of you. Vampires," she mumbled almost inaudibly behind them. Sandoval was just three feet away from the crouching animals when they heard her voice again, a little stronger this time. "I hope this works. Watch out, little guys." Mac cast a quick look back to see her clawing frantically at her shirt as she rose unsteadily to her feet. They had no time to wonder what she was rambling about; they were watching, waiting for Sandoval to make his move.

Suddenly the room erupted in light. It was as if the sun had suddenly appeared and paid no heed to the walls surrounding them. An uncomfortable heat sprang up from behind them. Sandoval's mouth opened silently and he cringed back, fear joining insanity and bloodlust in the battle over bodily control; fear won. He backed off, slowly at first, cowering behind his arm and moving faster as the woman stepped forward.

Mac and Lady, too, felt the fear, though they could see no reason for it. It was not the pure terror they saw reflected in Sandoval's lurching motions. It was more of a strong discomfort, an urgent desire to be somewhere, anywhere else. They looked back over their shoulder to see the human holding a cross aloft, still attached to a necklace which had been hidden under her shirt. She was cupping one hand beneath it, as though to block the animals' view of the holy symbol. This precaution obviously helped, but was not completely sufficient. They felt the holy might radiating out from the cross, driving them back and weakening them, sapping their strength. The short glimpse they took of the cross alone was enough to cause them physical pain. Seeing this peripherally, the woman covered their view of it more completely, while still keeping it focused on Sandoval. The heat and light, though very tangible to Mac and Lady, seemed not to affect its wielder in the slightest. She started chanting. "The power of Christ compels you. I exorcise you from my sight!"

"She... seems to have... her doctrine... a bit mixed up," Lady noted haltingly. Attempting to escape the presence of the crucifix, they slunk cautiously over to where Lawrence was lying unconscious. "But the cross seems to be working anyway. Agh!" The last was simply an involuntary expression of her own discomfort, significant even with the crucifix completely out of sight. Its power filled the room. Where it was not visible, its presence was felt - by the undead - as a draining heat and powerful psychological aversion. The effect of being under its full presence was evident in the haste with which Sandoval was presently fleeing.

The woman stood in front of the shattered door for several seconds holding the cross well over her head. Its chain had broken at some time during her display. Finally, she fell to the ground, overcome with exhaustion or grief. Mac stepped warily up to her motionless form. "It looks like she fell on her cross," he notified Lady.

"Good. Let's get this galoot out of here. Use your disgusting slobber-tongue and wake him up."

With no better ideas, he cast a pained look at Lady and gave Lawrence a few of the wet licks that dogs are so known for. Lawrence's eyes didn't open, but he spoke to them. "I hear breathing. Help them." He then seemed to slide back into unconsciousness; Mac could get no further response.

"Help them how?" Lady wanted to know. "We've got to get ourselves out of here."

Mac knew what Lawrence wanted. "Our bite heals, remember? Bite the ones that still breathe, but don't take more than a drop or two of blood. Maybe they can be saved."

Mac found two that still lived, and did as he'd instructed Lady. Lady raced around to find three more.

Their task completed, they met again over Lawrence's still form. "We don't have time to wait for him to wake up. We've gotta get out of here." Lady looked appraisingly at their maker. "Alright, I guess we'll have to drag him out. Grab on, Mac." Lady grabbed hold of the collar of the lab coat Lawrence was wearing. She immediately started pulling, her feet sliding on the floor as she fought for purchase. Mac took a piece of the coat next to her, and together they got the dead weight of Lawrence's body moving toward the door.

Scrabbling as hard and fast as they could, they got him across the room in just thirty seconds. As they pulled, they swept the ground in their path clear of glass with their tails. It felt like ten minutes to them, knowing that someone else was bound to show up any minute. It had been just two and a half minutes since they entered the room with Lawrence.

At the door they paused to consider the logistics. Should they lift him over the three inch lip of the door, raking his back across the jagged glass fragments sticking up like so many teeth? They were discussing how to remove the shards and whether or not they could even pull Lawrence over the door's lip when a red car pulled up to a stop just outside the door. The woman behind the wheel cried out in dismay, "Lawrence!"

* * *

Throughout the city, the police were in uproar. Nine of Milwaukee's finest had been not just killed, but slaughtered. The other three were listed in critical condition in Mt. Sinai hospital. The only witness was lying in a shockinduced state of catatonia. She had come around just long enough to provide a rough, almost delirious description of one of the attackers. Due to the sheer number of killings and the nature of the crime scene, it was believed that there were at least six professional killers involved.

The manhunt underway was huge. It would be national headlines in the morning. They were practically begging for any witnesses or those with any knowledge of the events to come forward.

Jamon was curious over another, almost unnoticed aspect. Lawrence's body was missing.

Current theory in the precinct held that the men who'd assaulted the station had somehow escaped with the body. Nobody had any theories yet as to why, but the assumption was that it was somehow tied in to drugs. To Jamon, the facts didn't add up, at least not to the commonly held answer. Right now, most of the force was too emotional to view the situation objectively, but the truth of the evening was plain to Jamon.

One of the cameras caught a back shot of what appeared to be Lawrence - in a lab coat - walking away from the morgue accompanied by a dog and a cat. To Jamon's mind, there was no question of *which* cat. There was no footage of anybody entering the morgue. Others on the force overlooked this fact and claimed the man was simply a member of the team that attacked the facility.

On the floor of the morgue, Jamon found a ventilation grill, obviously from the morgue's air duct. While he was not yet certain what it meant, he had a rather disturbing suspicion. Also, the lock he'd placed had apparently been yanked forcibly off. By teeth. He shivered.

He knew what had happened. Somehow, Lawrence had risen from the dead, rescued by his freaky-ass animals. On the way out, he was caught by the officers in the lobby. Apparently they had seen him in the camera or something and set themselves to ambush him there. They must have had some idea that this was something beyond their usual experience, hence the number of officers involved. One of Lawrence's companions then burst through the door from outside as he entered the lobby and the pair of them - possibly aided by the beasts - attacked, killing all but three, and the woman. They were finally driven off by her crucifix.

Jamon was now taking the steps he felt were necessary to track them down and bring them to justice. They killed nine tonight. Not just co-workers, not just friends, but his brothers and sisters of the blue. He was arming himself in ways he'd never before considered. He'd bought a crucifix. Through a specialist arms supplier, he was getting silver bullets. Finally, he'd sharpened up some wooden stakes. Just in case the unbelievable, the impossible, were true.

Just in case.

* * *

Her first problem had been convincing his...pets?...that she was a friend, and there to help. She had no idea what, or how much, they'd understood, but they'd finally let her put Lawrence in her car. She'd caught a brief glimpse of the carnage inside and the urgency she'd already felt doubled. She left the area as rapidly as she could without being conspicuous. When she was finally able to stop the car to assess Lawrence's condition, she was stunned at what she saw. He looked like he'd aged fifteen years since they'd last been together. Yes, that had been twenty-seven years ago, but he shouldn't have aged at all. The beating he'd apparently taken hadn't helped matters any.

It was still Lawrence. He was still handsome, and the lab coat with nothing underneath was rather sexy, she conceded with a smile, but it was obvious something was going on. Whatever her Dreams had been telling her about, he was already in the middle of it. She found herself hoping again that she wasn't too late to help him.

In the backseat were his animal companions. The cat was adorable. So was the dog, in his own scruffy way. It was all she could do to keep from reaching back to pet them or pulling them onto her lap to snuggle. The looks they seemed to be giving her dissuaded any such action. Besides which, the dog seemed to have taken an appalling beating as well. Instead of snuggling them, she tried talking to them again.

"Any ideas, you two?" They stared at her. "What can we do for him?" Staring. "What's wrong with him?" Well, they had the staring thing down pat. Perhaps yes or no questions. "Has he fed today or yesterday?" Ah! They both shook their heads. Given Lawrence's condition, that should probably be her next priority. She was almost afraid to, but she'd need to wake him up. This was not at all how she'd imagined their reunion. Gently, she caressed his face as she called his name.

After several seconds of this, his eyes fluttered, and then opened. His voice was very soft; a little raspy, as though his throat were parched. "Stephanie? Is that you? You look very good for 54. The years have been most kind." His face reflected his relief at the sight of the animals as they gathered closer to him, trying to squeeze up from the back seat. "I have a few questions for you, Stephanie." He held up a shaking hand to forestall the objection she was about to voice; "But I feel certain you'll tell me something rather banal, like 'explanations will have to wait.' Am I correct?'

Stephanie grinned sheepishly at his assessment. That had been exactly what she was about to say.

Lawrence continued in his weak voice. "I could really stand a bite to eat about now. Know any good eateries?"

CHAPTER NINETEEN

"Mac is wondering what you're doing, Stephanie," Lawrence informed her.

What she was doing was tucking a ten dollar bill into the purse of the woman Lawrence had just fed on. It had been a team effort. Lady, acting the stray in order to get close, jumped and bit the woman, rendering her unconscious. Stephanie had caught the woman as she fell, and then Lawrence was able to feed. Mac had been unable to assist, due to his extensive injuries. Two gunshot wounds, along with some probable broken bones. The ASPCA would have a fit, he thought.

Stephanie smiled bashfully up at Lawrence in the manner of someone caught in an embarrassing act, or engaging in one of their secret guilty pleasures. "I always give some money to the people I feed off of. Kind of paying for what I've taken. It's just...something I do." She shrugged selfconsciously.

Lawrence smiled at her as she stood back up. "I like it, Steph. That's a great idea." He paused as thought listening to something. "Mac and Lady agree." The foursome started the short walk back to Stephanie's car. "If I may be so intrusive, where do you get the money to do that? Have you managed to keep a job as a vampire? I don't remember you being rich, or having a rich family." He paused. "Of course, if it's too personal a question..."

She smiled. "Maybe it's time to tell you my story. Let's head over to my place. Don't worry," she added, forestalling the objection she could see Lawrence forming, "I'll start the tale on the way over." The smile on his face told her she'd guessed his objection correctly. He didn't want to wait any more to hear her tale. So much for the patience of the undead.

Lawrence had already told her all of his story, everything that had been happening to him the last few weeks. Not surprisingly to her, the facts he gave her corroborated quite nicely with the Dreams she'd had about him. She could now clearly see the real-world counterparts to the three threats the Dreams had warned were after him: the rotting disease, the police, and of course, the Council, in the form of Sandoval. She supposed the woman with the cross was why the police were represented to her as a savior as well as a threat.

She began her story. "I was born to a dirt-poor, widowed woman in South Alabama, not far from where my great-grandfather had been freed from slavery on the plantation after the Civil War."

"I thought your parents were happily married teachers, and that you were born here in Wisconsin, down in Kenosha?" Lawrence wondered with a puzzled look on his face. "Besides, are you even old enough for a greatgrandfather to have been a slave?"

She favored him with a mischievous grin. "Yeah, I know, but you get to start off *your* life story by saying, 'I was born a baron in East Europe...' How else am I going to compete with that? But, I guess I'll stick with the truth and save the story-telling for my memoirs. I think I'll call them, 'Interview With the Vampiress'."

"Please tell her to stop, Lawrence. I want to believe she's a good person, but I can't with bad jokes like that," Lady complained dryly.

Mac, on the other hand, was chuffing quietly at her humor.

Stephanie, oblivious to the animals' reactions, contented herself with Lawrence's good-natured groan and went on. "But I'll skip the inconsequential, and tedious, details of my ill-spent and misbegotten youth, and answer what I'm sure has been eating away at you: what're nice fangs like these doing in a girl like me?

"As you may recall, after our last night together, we'd made no plans to get together for the next few days, as my work schedule had gotten busy. The next night, I found myself visited by another vampire. Apparently, he'd been watching us for days, because he knew all about our relationship and all about me. Before you ask, no, I don't think this was Sandoval. I can't be sure because I never saw his face, but this guy didn't behave like I think Sandoval would. He seemed to be focused on politics, whereas Sandoval, from what you've told me of him, is nothing more than a killer. Whoever he was, he claimed to be someone of power within the vampire community. He never gave me his name. I asked if he was of the Council, which seemed to catch him a bit off-guard; perhaps he was surprised I knew of their existence. Whatever the reason, he denied that he was. Rather, he claimed to be against the Council. I told him I had heard that none were against the Council, citing what you told me about them ruling all of vampire kind. 'Ah,' he replied, 'of course I am not *openly* against the Council. That would be...most unwise at this juncture."

"Then he told me of his plans, and asked if I would be willing to help him in his endeavors. I saw how they could benefit you, so I readily agreed, on the condition that there would be no double-dealing where you were concerned. My biggest concern was that he would just use me to get to you, and then destroy you. In retrospect, that was a silly fear - he had no need of me to get to you. He already knew where you lived and everything. He said that for me to truly be a force on his side, he would have to Awaken me, but that I would have to come with him to Europe for a few days. He didn't specify why, claiming he'd tell me more of his plans later, but he needed me as a witness or some such. He claimed my closeness to you would be a big help, especially if I was Awakened. I told him I wanted some time to think about it. I know I had already asked you to Awaken me, but I had actually kind of done so rather recklessly. Earlier that day, after asking you, I'd thought about what becoming a vampire would mean to me; specifically, I contemplated the fact that if I did it, I could never be a mother. That's probably why vampires, from what you've told me, are mostly male. A woman wants to have her family. Anyway, I told him to come back sometime before dawn, give me a chance to think about it.

"He reluctantly agreed, and I gave it some very serious thought. What ultimately decided me was that you couldn't have children anyway, Lawrence, and it was you I really wanted to be with for the rest of my life. I had some fanciful thoughts that maybe, if we really wanted, we could adopt... but I think those were simple justifications for what I had already decided to do - I know it would be a difficult thing to adopt and raise children in our state.

"Just before dawn he came back and I gave him my answer. I would help him. I would allow him to Awaken me. Before he did so, I asked if he had the Council's permission to Awaken another. He laughed. 'Of course not, silly woman. I am planning a revolution. What would I ask them to supply my army for?' This made sense, which indicated to me he was being honest.

"He bit me. I need not tell you three the agony of dying my mortal death, but I'll share my own impressions of it. The pain, I think, must be the very worst that any mortal can experience. I've been told what a heart attack feels like, and a stroke, and the final stages of cancer. I think that Awakening takes them all, makes them ten times worse, and rolls them into one great ball of mortal misery. Then it takes this and rolls it over you like a bowling ball. It sucked. Had I known what it felt like, had I gotten a taste beforehand of the indescribable agony I would undergo for just fifteen minutes, I might have given him a different answer. Well, probably not, but it would certainly have given me even more pause. I do know that I never want to go through that again. But, by then it was too late, and I honestly have to say that even so, I do not regret my decision.

"As I'd taken most of the night to think it over, it was almost immediately time for my first sleep of the dead. He had thoughtfully brought me a coffin. 'A gift I always provide for those I Awaken,' he claimed. He even brought it up to my room for me. A real gentleman.

"That night - or day, rather - I Dreamed. I knew as soon as I woke up that I had discovered my Calling."

Lawrence broke in at that point. "Your first day as a vampire, and you had your Calling? I had to wait almost a hundred years for mine!"

"I know, Lawrence, and it was fortunate for us both that it happened this way. What I Dreamed that night was of death - for both myself and you. And I understood as soon as I rose that this was not some fanciful story my sleeping mind entertained itself with. You had already told me that vampires don't dream. This was...l don't know. Clairvoyance? Whatever it was, what I Dreamed was a representation of what could, or would, come to pass."

She paused, gathering her thoughts again. Lawrence filled the heavy silence. "I've always been of the belief that we don't dream because as we rest during the day, our minds, our souls, or whatever, are no longer residing within our physical bodies. That is why we are completely dead during the day."

Stephanie nodded agreement. "I think that's the case, too. With that belief in mind, I've sometimes wondered where my Dreams come from. I have no idea, though. At least, none that I wish to believe. Anyway, this first Dream told me two things. One was that if I stayed in contact with this vampire who had Awakened me, he would kill me. If my interpretation was correct, he was going to take me before the Council. They, in turn, would be the ones to put me to death for my status as an illegal vampire.

"The second part troubled me just as much, perhaps more. It indicated that were I to return to you, have any contact with you, you would be killed. I had to immediately lose myself, hiding from my own vampire master, and my vampire lover as well. I left my apartment, quit my job, and fled to Chicago."

"So that's what happened to you," Lawrence mused. "All these years, I thought..."

"You thought what?" she prompted.

"Well, I thought you left me so abruptly because I couldn't Awaken you."

She barked out a laugh. "Ha! I knew it! Stupid men - all the same." She flipped the center mirror down so she could see Lady sitting in the back, forgetting for a moment what a fruitless attempt it would be. The mirror reflected an empty seat. "Lady - keep in mind that all men are inherently stupid and that they believe we can do nothing if they don't do it for us. Every little failing on their part spells the end of the world for us."

"I already know that men are naturally inferior. They are useful to have around on certain occasions, like if you want something broken. I finally have these two understanding my mental superiority," Lady agreed. Lawrence sat in silence following this little diatribe until Lady snapped, "Tell her what I said, Lawrence!"

Lawrence sighed. "Lady said she already knows, and she thinks she has Mac and me - as she puts it - understanding her mental superiority."

Stephanie nodded as if all was now as it should be. "Once in Chicago, I knew I would tear through my meager savings rather quickly. So, I went job hunting. It was horrible. I cycled through an unprecedented number of jobs. The problem was that no matter how nocturnal the job seemed, some form of daytime activity would always end up being required."

"Been there."

"Yeah. When you were explaining your meager resources to me, I remember you saying you'd had the same problem. Silly baron, you never understood I didn't care you were broke." Her smile reinforced her assertion. "Anyway, my savings kept dropping. Just as I was beginning to panic about what I was going to do, I remembered a Dream I'd been puzzling over the week before. It suddenly became clear to me - I finally realized what the Dream meant. I promptly raced up to one of the Milwaukee area casinos and came back $38,000 richer. I could have won more, I think, but I'd only understood parts of the Dream. Five months later, I had a similar Dream, went back, and won $682,000.

"It happened a couple more times since then, years later. Most of my living income now comes from investments, interest and such. I had made a couple of good investments with the money I won, so I don't rely on the uncertainties of my Dreams for money anymore. As long as I live modestly, I won't have to worry too much about money. I think I predicted a horse race once, and maybe a couple of big sports games. I didn't understand those until it was too late. That's how it usually is with my Dreams; they're so obscure I don't realize what they refer to until it's already over. They really aren't very reliable, but once in a while, they... well, you can see. We're both alive and together again!"

"So, why are you here?" Lawrence flushed. "Shit. That didn't come out at all right." He gently took her right hand from the wheel, kissing it softly as she drove with her left. "What I mean is, I thought you said it'd be my death if you returned?"

She laughed, and reluctantly took her hand back to turn into her driveway. The community they'd been cruising through, and which her home was a part of, was comprised of lovely, unpretentious but elegant homes. Reinforcing the image of a well-funded neighborhood was the preponderance of German cars when they were visible and not closed off within the attached garages - always an obvious outward indicator of financial comfort. Stephanie's home matched the general style of the rest of the community. It was a sprawling one story home, perhaps with a basement, situated on just over a quarter-acre of land.

"Well, I had another Dream that I interpreted as saying it was time to return to you. I had long since moved back to Wisconsin. I didn't care for living so close to Chicago, the 'big city'. I much preferred it back up here, so I came back as soon as I thought it safe to do so. I'd been keeping tabs on you, just waiting for when we could be together again, and paying close attention to my Dreams, hoping and waiting for the one that would indicate it was time. Your last move caught me off guard, though, and I spent the last two weeks just looking for you again."

The discussions stopped as they piled out of the car and made their way into her home. It had an elegant but simple quality to it; Mac compared it to their room at the Hyatt, only without the police tape and more personalized, homier. The decor was of the sort you could never find in a bachelor's home unless he'd paid a professional to come in and design it for him; it was definitely the home of a single woman.

There was plenty of color, all subdued and matching perfectly. The animals explored the house, discovering in her downstairs bedroom and master bath Stephanie's near obsession with things bearing star and moon patterns. The home had two guest bedrooms in addition to the master, though one was made into a sort of general-purpose home office. This was for managing her various financial endeavors, Stephanie explained when the animals asked through Lawrence.

After a brief guided tour, everyone settled in the spacious living room. Lawrence and Stephanie got comfortable on the couch, leaving plenty of room on it at the far end for other occupants; such was their close proximity to each other. Mac opted for a chair, while Lady took the elevation offered at the top of Stephanie's entertainment center.

"Lawrence, she mentioned her master vampire had plans for you," Mac remembered as he settled himself into the chair. "What were those plans? It might be important."

Lawrence nodded. "Good point, Mac. Steph, Mac was just wondering what were the plans this other vampire had in mind for me?"

"Honestly, Lawrence, I don't remember all of it, and he really didn't tell me much. Basically, he intended to put himself in a position of power, which he swore to use to help you, by bringing the prophecy to bear against the Council. Afterwards, I began to believe I might have been just a little mesmerized to have thought it sounded like a good idea for you. He obviously wasn't trustworthy, but I think he was honest about his plans, which is why he told me so little of them."

"Wait a minute, Steph. What prophecy?"

"You mean you really don't know? I just figured you'd never told me about it out of modesty or disbelief."

"No, I don't know. What is it?"

"It's the reason the Council is so hot to get you," she began.

"You mean they're not after me because I Awakened animals without authorization?"

"No. Well, yes, but there's more to it. The reason why they want you completely dead. Apparently it's some old prophecy. According to this prophecy, you and your animal vampires are destined to destroy the Council."

CHAPTER TWENTY

The dark form prowled along the edge of the single-story home. It circled around the back before finding what it sought. It amazed him, in this age, that so many people still left such unsecured portals into their homes. Quietly, easily, he slipped in.

His first priority was to find the animal. He knew at least one was here. Quickly, but still in complete silence, he surveyed the home. In the master bedroom he found them: a dog and a cat. Two animals. No matter - they were both asleep. The dog was sleeping on the floor; the cat slept with its masters. There were two people here, a man of about 35 and a woman some years his junior. The prowler didn't think it right that the cat enjoyed the comfort and warmth of the bed while the dog went unappreciated on the floor. He knew he was biased, but it still seemed unfair to him. He shrugged: no matter. All were safely sound asleep. He could do what he came for.

He slipped back out through the bedroom door, leaving it open a crack so he could hear any movements. His explorations had already revealed the computer in a small study. The room seemed to serve double-duty as a guest bedroom, as it had a day-bed situated against the far wall. The room was presently unoccupied.

The silent invader entered the room and settled into the chair. The green light on the computer indicated it was already on, but the screen was dark. He nudged the computer mouse. The monitor sprang to life at the activity, and the trespasser began his hunt for information.

His practice over the past weeks had improved his skills, but the mouse was still awkward for him to use. The keyboard was no better, but that only rarely came into play. An hour passed; an hour of clumsily manipulating the mouse, of gazing steadily into the bright glare of the screen in the unlit room. Finally, his diligence was rewarded. He found what he was looking for. It was not everything he sought, but it was certainly the ever-important first step. He would have the truth. It was within his grasp. He clicked links and read, read some more and fumblingly clicked another link.

So engrossed was he that he didn't hear the first stirrings of trouble.

From the sound of it, the man was already out of the bedroom by the time he noticed. Even then, the rapt intruder wouldn't have heard, but the dog's low growl of suspicion was marginally loud enough to penetrate his rigid focus on the material before him. He immediately closed the program and left the room. His way out was in the kitchen. As he entered the kitchen, he could hear the man close behind. The man's slow pace indicated to the invader that he wasn't entirely sure there was a trespasser, yet. The dog knew - its growling grew steadily louder, more threatening.

His eyes, still not fully adjusted to the dark after an hour in the steady glow of the monitor, deceived him. He nudged one of the dining chairs in his uncertain flight. The gentle scrape of its foot on the tile floor was enough evidence for his pursuer, and the furtive figure heard the unmistakable sound of a gun being readied. His egress in sight, he lunged for it in desperation.

The owner of the residence entered his kitchen. He'd passed by the study and seen his computer screen on. He knew he had an intruder; the sound of the moving chair confirmed it. He was tensed up, the trigger half-depressed. At the sight of motion by the door, his nervous finger twitched. The shotgun seemed to explode, the noise deafening in the confined space of the kitchen, the muzzle flash almost blinding. His dog, standing at his side, jumped at the noise, but made no sound. Over the booming shotgun, he could barely hear the 'yelp' as the doggie-door came swinging down behind the now-wounded intruder.

* * *

It was midnight, and Lawrence had only been awake for about an hour. Stephanie was growing more worried as she grew aware of the severity of Lawrence's mysterious problems. She had given him the use of her coffin. Hers was a lovely ivory-toned casket, trimmed all about in gold and cushioned in a durable yet pleasing white satiny fabric. After his spirit retreated last night, some three hours before sunrise, she had sat at his side and studied the face she'd never forgotten. It was changed, as she'd known when she saw him being escorted out of his hotel.

She had perused his appearance at her leisure as he'd rested. He was still the handsome man she'd fallen in love with, just...aged. If anything, he looked more distinguished. His apparent age was now approximately forty- five, as opposed to the twenty-five she remembered. The most obvious cause of this semblance of advanced age was the faint lines now evident on his face. Visible even in his relaxed, sleeping state, these were identical to the lines all mortals received as a badge commemorating their past years. He had the typical crow's feet alongside his closed eyes. His elegant forehead bore the faint tracings of several horizontal lines. His lips as well were surrounded by the barely visible etchings of age.

More than aged, he looked tired. The bags under his eyes were the most visible sign, but there were other, subtle nuances she was able to detect when he was awake. Slow-downs and greater caution in his movements, pauses when he would normally be invigorated, a slight stoop in his ordinarily upright posture.

Her hand reached out to caress his long, black hair. There, too, were signs of his...weakness? aging? sickness? Whatever it was, the signs were here as well. His hairline was not receding, but it was noticeably thinning.

The most distressing physical signs of his condition were the discolored patches on his skin. There was a largish spot, perhaps an inch and a half in diameter, on the back of his right hand towards the wrist. Other, smaller spots were visible under his chin, on the back of his neck, and who knew where else. Lady de Winter had first pointed them out to Stephanie as Lawrence slept. Ever image-conscious, Lawrence did an admirable job of keeping them out of sight.

The whole situation would be easier if she could communicate directly with the animals. She was certain they'd help all they could to find a solution to what was afflicting Lawrence. Their dedication to him was evident to her as she watched them interact, overriding whatever competition there was between them. The rescue mission alone was a sign of their loyalty to him.

Lawrence was little help. He was loathe to talk about his degenerating condition. She'd gotten *some* information out of him last night, after the 'Great Escape', as she had taken to calling it. Now, sitting in the living room, she was pulling every detail she could out of him. Somewhere, there had to be an answer to this problem, if she could only find it. She refused to believe the situation was hopeless.

While she couldn't be certain, she was pretty sure Lady was also prodding him to share all he could about this disease, or whatever it was. Lady had been gone for an hour shortly after they'd all - with the exception of Lawrence - risen for the night at sunset. Stephanie thought it was adorable how Lady curled protectively around Lawrence's head when she went to sleep in the morning. Stephanie had the sense not to say anything about it.

Her bedroom was in the basement. It was specifically designed so as to not give any opportunity for outside light to intrude. This made the bed safe for sleeping on. Her coffin was full, so she shared the bed with Mac. The dog slept curled at her feet, just like the puppy she'd had as a little girl. Stephanie wondered idly how good a vampire 'old Daisy', that dog from so long ago, would have made. Probably not much of one - she was a notorious coward.

Mac's wounds of the previous night had about half-healed through the day. At sunset he had again gone his own way, much as Lady de Winter had. Unlike Lady, who returned shortly thereafter, Mac had yet to return. Lawrence was telling her this was his usual behavior.

"Where does he go for so long? It can't take him *that* long to feed," Stephanie said.

His pause indicated Lawrence was listening to Lady. "Lady has some rather unflattering ideas as to where he goes, but the truth is, he has never shared that information with us."

Lawrence and Lady didn't seem concerned about Mac's behavior, so she filed it away for later investigation. Not much later - when Mac returned tonight she intended to find out what he'd been up to in very short order. She turned the conversation back to their earlier topic. "You mentioned that others have come down with the same thing. You survived once; has anyone else? Anyone we can ask about it?"

"No. According to Phil, no one's ever survived it. The last known case was a guy named Count Lowenhagen. His wife finally left his body in the sun, it was decomposing so badly."

"What?"

"Well...she did. It makes sense. He'd been dead for over a week."

Lawrence didn't like talking about this at all. Really, neither did Stephanie. She hated to push him into doing so, but they had to have all the facts. A thought struck her - they may not have any survivors to question, but maybe Count Lowenhagen's wife could help. After all, she had been witness to the whole thing, and probably knew as much or more about what the Count had gone through. "Lawrence, this wife of his. Is she someone we could talk to? Someone so close may have seen something we're missing."

Lawrence considered the idea. "I knew Angie and the Count. Good people. I think she might be willing to talk to me about it."

"No. Not you. Me." she said, placing a hand on her chest to emphasize her point. "Look, sweetie, you're just not up to a trip like this. I'm sorry, but if anything happened, you couldn't even run away effectively. If you could just set up an appointment with her for me, or tell me where she is, I'll find out what I can. Besides, I'll probably get more out of her, woman to woman, without you there."

She waited for his response, watching the expressions fly across his face as he argued it with himself. "Yes, yes. You're right, of course. I just worry about you. You've finally come back to me, and now you want to go haring off to Europe. If one of their Seekers discovers you're an illegal vampire, they'll destroy you."

He looked so mournful, his eyes wide, mouth turned down slightly, face downcast. Stephanie almost laughed. He looked like a sad little lost puppy to her eyes. "That's why we simply don't mention it. I'm sure Angie doesn't know every vampire, does she? I didn't think so."

"I don't know how to reach her."

"Phil does. Call him. I'm sure he'll be happy to set it up for us."

"Yes, I'm sure he will," Lawrence conceded.

"Good. It's decided. Be a dear and give him a call."

"Now?"

"Yes, now," she confirmed. "I'm very much afraid your condition is deteriorating rapidly." Her hand stroked his cheek, softening the bluntness of her words. "I want to leave by the night after tomorrow."

She saw by the resigned look on his face she'd have her way. It wasn't what she wanted; she didn't like to be right about this, but she was determined to take care of Lawrence. He walked morosely over to the phone and dialed the number Phil had given him. Stephanie's supernaturally charged senses allowed her to hear the other end ring until Phil's voicemail picked up. "I forgot the stupid time difference," she muttered to herself. Louder, addressing Lawrence, she said, "Leave him a message, my baron. Tell him what we need, and ask him to leave a message for us confirming the appointment and location."

Lawrence left the message as she asked and started back to the couch when they heard a scratching at the door. Lawrence smiled. "We might want to think of getting a pet-flap put in the door." Lady meowed at him, apparently sending him something telepathically, for he replied back to her, "Don't worry, Lady, we know that you -"

The sight of Mac as Lawrence opened the door caused him to leave his sentence unfinished. Even without seeing the wounds, it was evident that something was wrong. The dog didn't move with his usual simple energy. He limped slowly in, his tail down over his bloody haunches. He curled back to lick a particularly irritating wound and something dropped. It hit the hardwood floor of the doorway with a metallic clink and rolled off. Mac watched the pellet drift to a stop, a pained look on his scruffy face.

In the silence, Mac eyed the richly carpeted floor of the living room, then Lawrence, his mute request obvious. The old vampire stepped into the kitchen, returning with several paper towels. These he spread out on the floor in the middle of the room. Gingerly, Mac plodded over to them to lie on his side upon the absorbent layer of towels.

"Oh, Mac," Stephanie finally cried, "what happened?"

* * *

For Stephanie's sake, Lawrence agreed to repeat aloud everything Mac said.

"Are we finally going to hear about where you've been traipsing off to each night?" Lady asked.

Mac's chest expanded like a round bellows and dropped again as he let out a long-suffering sigh. "Yes, that's part of this. It's not like it's any really big deal, anyway."

"Then why've you been so secretive about it?"

A large, quirky smile slowly made its way down the length of the mongrel's muzzle despite the pain of the buckshot. "Primarily to irritate you," he taunted. Lady's irritated hiss gave even Lawrence a small, slow smile of amusement as he translated the exchange for Stephanie.

"What have you been up to, Mac?" Stephanie prompted.

"Research," he summed up. "When we were staying at the Hyatt, and the Biltmore before that, I'd found a couple houses I could get in easy. They had computers, and I'd go on the internet to learn what I could about our kind, to make up for the knowledge I didn't get when Lawrence Awakened me."

Mac gave Lawrence a chance to relay this to Stephanie. She asked, "Did you learn anything good?"

"Well, a few days ago I finished reading 'Dracula' on some Project Guttenberg site. Besides that, I wasn't really looking for anything specific at first. The last week, however, I've been trying to find out what I could about Lawrence's problem. I hadn't found much of anything. Then, when we came out here to Stephanie's place, I had to find a new place to go – the other houses were too far away, and her computer here is password protected. I found this one place; it had one of those pet-doors that made it easy to get in. So, I checked the place out and got on their computer and onto the internet. I was on a message board, and there were some old postings by people who seemed to have heard of this disease. About that time, the guy that lived there woke up and shot me as I was trying to get out."

"Ha! Shot you in the butt!" Lady de Winter seemed to be the only one to find this so amusing. She stopped laughing when she realized she was alone in her mirth. "Hm. Yes. Please continue."

"That's about it. Um, yeah. That's it."

"Fine. But what did you find out about Lawrence's condition? You said some people were posting about it on a board of some sort?"

"Message board. Really, there wasn't anything we didn't know, and the posts were pretty old. My real surprise was that they even knew the condition existed, though most are doubtful that it's true. They called it 'Premetamorphic Malaise'. I was getting ready to post a couple questions when the fat man with the gun woke up and chased me out."

"Sounds like you might have been on to something, Mac. If I got you on my computer, could you find the site again?" Stephanie asked.

"Sure."

"I'll log you in, but I'll also give you all the password. Then you can do your research here, from the safety of home."

Mac liked the way that word sounded - 'home' - and the easy way she implied it as his home as well. "That sounds great. Thank you."

"Aww...no more pellet-butt," Lady complained.

* * *

The next evening, everyone marched into the study, Mac's figure bringing up the rear of the procession. The pellets had come out during the day, leaving his wounds - including those from the 'Great Escape' - almost completely healed.

Stephanie took the seat in front of the keyboard. "All logged in, and you all now have the password," she noted as she brought up the web browser. "Do you remember what the site's address is?"

"Not the exact address for the messages I was reading, no," Mac informed her through Lawrence. "But if you go to vampcentral.com, click the message board link - I think it's labeled 'blood board' - and go to the message thread labeled 'Dr. Bandenarii's Writings', you should be there."

"Dr. Bandenarii? That name is familiar," Lawrence mused quietly.

"How so?" Lady asked.

"I don't remember. Was he a vampire?" he mused to himself. Everyone was silent as they waited for Lawrence to catch his elusive memory. "Ah! He *was* a vampire. He was executed in...well...sometime around 1550 or so. It was during the height of the witch scare in Europe, and the Council had him accused as a witch. Being a vampire, there was no way he could deny the charges, so he was burned one night at the stake by the peasants. I believe the Council did it as punishment. Revealing the details of our existence to some mortal or something. I don't remember exactly. I don't think I ever knew the details, in fact - I was still a young vampire, in too much awe of myself to pay attention to much else."

Stephanie clicked the appropriate link. She read the screen and summarized its contents as she scrolled down. "According to this, he claimed he was a vampire doctor."

"Vampire doctor?" Lady repeated. "What did he mean by that?"

"Hmmm. He said he was trying to use the 'modern medicine' of the sixteenth century to treat the few problems vampires had. I guess he meant things like holy water burns and such. Ah! Here! This guy mentions Lawrence's problem. He says, and I'm quoting, 'But what about this "Premetamorphic Malaise" Bandenarii goes on about? I've never seen reference to anything of the sort in any reputable vampiric literature.' Blah blah blah...this guy is long winded...' I mean, a sick, weak vampire? This guy Bandenarii was obviously F.O.S.'."

"F.O.S.?" Lawrence asked.

"Full of... ah... crap," she smiled up at him.

"I don't remember the word 'crap' starting with 's'," he countered, smiling back at her.

"Now, now, Lawrence, mind the children," she said, indicating the animals with a brief tip of her head.

He chuckled. "If you could hear Lady's response to being referred to as a child, you'd wash her mouth out with soap."

"Or kitty litter," Mac contributed. Lawrence relayed this to Stephanie, eliciting another chuckle. Lady had nothing more to say on the subject.

Lawrence turned back to face the screen. "What is the deal with these people?"

"What do you mean?" Stephanie asked.

"Well, the way they talk, this site...do they know vampires exist?"

"For the most part, no. In fact, if you asked most of them, they'd reply that 'of course vampires don't exist.' Many of these people just view this as an intellectual exercise, or something similar to a realistic extension of the books they read. Some do actually think vampires exist, but even then I wouldn't say they *know* we exist; they just think that we do. They're by far the minority and not believed by the others, anyway."

"Okay. Now, how about this book they're talking about? Can we get a copy of it?"

"I've been looking around this posting, and it seems like an incredibly rare work."

"I saw the same thing, Lawrence. I was going to post a message asking where I could find a copy when I was, ah, asked to leave the house," Mac claimed.

Lawrence repeated Mac's suggestion. Stephanie clicked a few links. "We're going to have to register to post anything."

"Mac says he's already done so."

"Okay. I need his username and password."

Lawrence listened for a moment, a grin stealing across his face. "Okay," he said to Mac before turning back to Stephanie. He leaned over, about to whisper in her ear. He looked up to see Lady's ears swiveled toward him and thought better of it. "If I may, doll," he requested, reaching over her slender shoulders to the keyboard.

Slowly, with the deliberation of one not accustomed to typing, he picked out the letters for the username Mac had given him. As he looked at the screen to check for any miskeyed letters, Lady jumped up on the desk to where she could easily see what he'd entered for the username.

She promptly fell back off the desk, unable to control her laughterin-duced seizures. Seeming not to notice her own fall, she kept repeating the name she'd seen on the screen. "Vampup? Ha! VAMPUP! *VAMPUP!*"

*   *   *

A half hour later found the four mismatched vampires sitting again in Stephanie's living room. After posting their query about Dr. Bandenarii's book, they'd browsed the website a bit more, though they found nothing pertinent to their current needs.

Stephanie settled back into Lawrence's outstretched arm. "Mac, it just hit me: how did you manage to use a computer? You have no fingers."

Mac's head tilted, a floppy ear quirked up: a shrug. "I managed. Mostly I used the mouse. I can move it with a little difficulty, and I've been getting better. The keyboard was always troublesome. I tried using my tail to press the keys at first, but it was too hard. My snout didn't work either, it was too big. Now I use my longest claw to carefully press the letter I want. Just like everything else in the human world Lady and I have to deal with - we find a way to adjust."

Stephanie nodded as Lawrence relayed Mac's words. "Pretty impressive." Mac nodded his thanks, glowing inside with the warmth of the compliment. "Well, I had better get packing." She placed a hand on Lawrence's leg as she prepared to get up.

"Wait, wait now. Are you still planning on leaving tomorrow?"

"Yes, Lawrence. Nothing's changed. Hopefully Phil is already setting up my appointment, and will call sometime today. Either way, I leave tomorrow to hunt her down myself if I have to. If we can get the information we need from the book, so much the better. But we can't rely on the possibility of that. Your condition is not getting better. I can almost see you deteriorating before my eyes." She turned her head away from him. "I fear our time is almost run out."

Lawrence reached for her hand, picked it up from his knee and kissed it. With his other, he brushed her thick, black hair back so he could see her profile. "If you say so, dear. But, can you wait to pack and arrange your flight? I will be going to rest again soon. Already, it feels to me as though dawn is just over the horizon, though I know it is not close at all. I would like to spend some, um...quality time together before I rest and you leave."

Faintly, a blush spread across her features, barely noticeable on her dark skin. "Certainly, my baron." Together, they rose and left the animals alone in the room.

* * *

"I'm just not sure where to go with this, now. We have rewards offered for any information leading to the guy who attacked the station, but the captain refuses to entertain the idea that Lawrence Watts is alive. I'm telling you, Sara, I know he's the one behind it all. I've been conducting my own search for him, but frankly, I've gotten nowhere." Jamon leaned over to kiss her. "Wake up soon, Sara. The doctors say you'll do so as soon as you're ready to deal with what you saw. In the meantime, I'll get the guy who did that to our men and put you in here."

He left the light on for the nurse who was coming in as he left Sara's hospital room.

CHAPTER TWENTY ONE

" - to my message." Lawrence rose to consciousness with Mac's voice in his head. It was possible he'd heard the first part of the sentence, but his muddied mind could not recall it. As it was, there was a gap of several seconds before he understood what he'd heard, how he'd heard it, and who the speaker was. It was almost as though the puzzle pieces of his mind were having more trouble reforming each night as his 'Premeta-morphic Malaise' progressed,

"I'll be right in," he heard Lady reply. By now, his mind had finished as-sembling itself, or whatever it was that happened when a vampire awoke. He awoke much more slowly than natural as of late, but he was fairly certain the process was the same, just slowed. As was often the case anymore, his thoughts on rising turned to his condition. Now, at last, he had a name for it. As his hands reached for the sides of his coffin, he considered that name. Lawrence toyed with the word 'premetamorphic', dissecting its meaning in his mind. It must indicate something specific, he thought as he swung his legs over the rim of the casket.

He was momentarily distracted in his musings. Something snagged his finger as he swung his legs over the side of Stephanie's coffin. A quick look revealed that his pants leg had caught his right thumbnail. The nail had fallen completely off under the meager pressure. There'd been no pain associated with it; the nail must have been about to come off al-ready. Lawrence inspected his other digits. A couple other fingernails felt as though they might be loose, but it was difficult to be sure. Enough pressure to be certain would likely tear a loose one off. He would simply have to take care.

His gaze wandered to the large spot on the back of his right wrist.

More than a spot of discoloration, it seemed to be taking on an almost leprous quality. The center of the strange flaw had begun to suppurate. A thick white ooze was evident on the surface. His left hand rose as if to scrape the gunk off, then fell to his side without taking any action. He didn't want to know what was under the puss; nor did he want to possibly make it worse by messing with it. Delicately, he tugged his sleeve down until it covered most of the unsightly spot.

Intellectually, he knew he should be in a panic at the rate the disease was progressing, but he just didn't seem to be able to generate any strong feelings about it. All of his emotions seemed dampened. He was used to reigning them in; it was necessary on occasion to maintain a proper decorum. Lately it had been almost unnecessary. Even his feelings for Stephanie and the animals - strong as those feelings still were - seemed dulled, blunted somehow without being diluted. The 'malaise' part of his condition was certainly accurately named. This brought his wandering mind back to 'premetamorphic'.

Rather than let his thoughts roll around in the loneliness of his mind, he decided to pose his newly forming hypothesis to his quadruped companions.

"Guys, I was thinking about the word 'premetamorphic'."

"Welcome to the world of the living, Lawrence," Lady greeted him.

"Lawrence, come into the study. I got a response to my query,' Mac added.

Lawrence walked into the study. "Do you guys want to hear my idea?"

Lady looked up at him, then back to Mac sitting at the keyboard. "Sure we do, Lawrence. But first, wipe off your cheek."

Lawrence followed Lady's suggestion, his hand coming away with a light red smear. "What's this?" he asked, cautiously sniffing the slightly oily smudge.

"Lipstick. Stephanie made sure to give you a kiss with fresh make-up. She said she wanted to be sure you knew you got a kiss before she left. I think she put on the make-up just to leave her mark. Pah. And I thought dogs were bad enough, marking their territory as they do. Overly sentimental tripe, if you ask me."

"We didn't ask you. And besides, cats mark their territory, too," Mac pointed out.

Lawrence's eyes lingered longingly on the smear of color on his hand. "When did she leave?"

"She left here a little after eight," Mac said. "She set up a charter flight last night. It's going to follow the sun, so she'll be in the night all the way." "Phil called right after she left," Lady informed Lawrence.

"Did you let Stephanie knew?" Lawrence asked.

Mac barked in reply to Lawrence's question.

"Ah. Right. Forget I asked. I'll listen to the message and call her cell in a minute. What time is it?"

"Your sense of time is slipping too, eh?" Lady asked solicitously. "It's just after 11:30. So, what's this big thought of yours?"

"My sense of time has been slipping for a while. And, it's no big thought, really. I was just considering the meaning of the word 'premetamorphic', and what it implies in this situation. My thought was that it indicates, perhaps, an actual virus or something. Its mutation, or metamorphosis, is what triggers the next stage."

"Next stage?"

"Um...death," Lawrence clarified.

Mac looked up form the computer screen. "Did I just hear you call *death* a *stage*?"

Lawrence saw the irony. "Well, yes. A rather permanent stage, I admit. But you see my point, right?'

"Yeah, I suppose. But what do we do with this knowledge?"

"I'm not sure yet. And it's not yet knowledge, just a theory. But if we can somehow keep the virus from going into that next stage - or, if it's already there, revert it back - we may have a chance." The three friends considered the implications of Lawrence's hypothesis. Lawrence walked to where Mac was sitting before the computer. Mac himself was a unique, rather amusing sight. He sat upright on his haunches upon the chair, his left paw propping him up on the desk while his right paw dexterously manipulated the mouse. His paw rested on the top of the mouse, the ridged pads providing enough grip on its surface for him to move it. At the moment, he was idly moving it in random patterns on the screen, his mind elsewhere. When he needed to click on something, his whole paw would tilt forward to press the button.

Lawrence spoke again, breaking the silence. "What was it you'd found,

Mac?"

The dog's eyes refocused as he turned his muzzle towards Lawrence. "I didn't actually find anything new, yet. Someone replied to what we posted yesterday."

"Well, dog, what did your brilliant idea reveal for us?" Lady's sarcastic tone did little to conceal her interest. She'd been casting surreptitious glances at the screen since Lawrence walked in.

"I'll read it to you. 'Dear...uh...poster,'" he began. Mac watched Lady's reflection in the glass of the monitor. She failed to react to his omission of his screen name, to Mac's relief. He continued reading. "'The meandering work you refer to comes from the only documentation of this self-proclaimed vampire expert ever known to have surfaced.'"

"This guy is a wordy, condescending snob, isn't he?" Lady commented.

"Do I detect a note of appreciation in your voice?" Lawrence gently jibed her.

"Most message board posters are," Mac answered her. "Half of any given board is usually given over to a bunch of name calling and nay-saying. You'd do well in these communities. Lady. This guy does get to the point eventually. Here, I'll skip ahead. Um... 'Only five copies of the book exist, and it hasn't been reproduced by any means, the owners being greedy, righteous,' um... skip ahead again... 'three of these are in private collections in the United States. No surprise, with those selfish rebels.'"

"What?" Lady asked.

"The poster isn't American, he's British," Mac informed her. "And not one of their more polite citizens, either. He goes on quite a bit about Americans. His views on Dr. Bandenarii are not so unique, though. Most of the posters hold him up as a fraud, because some of the topics he writes about, like Premetamorphic Malaise, appear nowhere else in any vampire literature. Anyway, he goes on. 'One is held by,' uh, some name I can't pronounce, 'in Chula Vista, California; one by an unknown party in Florida, and the third is owned by Michael McFarland in West Allis, Wisconsin.'"

Lawrence and Lady both perked up. Mac, who had read the message before summoning Lady, managed to appear smug underneath the fur of his canine face. "What was it you told Phil about coincidence and vampires, Lawrence? Here's another for you. West Allis is practically right next door to us."

Lawrence spoke. "Right, Mac. Can you find his address and phone number on there?"

"You mean Michael McFarland? Of course. Not a problem."

"Good. Do that, please. I'd like to pay this guy a visit, see if he won't grant us some time to look over his book."

"If it's that rare, I doubt he'd let a dog near it. Maybe not even a cat," Lady said.

"Good point, Lady. I'll probably have to go in alone. I'd still like you two to come with me. How did Stephanie get to her flight?"

"She took a cab so you'd have her car if you needed it," Mac informed him.

"Good. You two can wait in the car, then, if he won't let you in." Lawrence turned to walk out of the room. "I'm going to listen to Phil's message and call Stephanie. I'll be right back."

"Why do you both still use a landline instead of a cell? Get with the times, already!" Lady complained.

Lawrence paused at the doorway, turning back to Lady. "Vampires tend to stick to their times, Lady. Even those who are catching up probably still have landlines. We're not as bad as a bunch of grandmas, but we do adopt new things more slowly than most humans." He paused for a moment, thinking. "And Stephanie has one, but she still uses her landline for most things when she's home, too. I should probably memorize her cell number, though. Might be useful." He continued to the phone.

After listening to the message, he returned to the study. "Phil came through. He gave me Angie's address and set up an appointment for later today, our time." Neither Mac nor Lady bothered to remind him they'd heard the message when it was left on the answering machine earlier that evening. "I didn't get through to Stephanie's phone. The message said it was out of range. She's probably still over the ocean or something. So, I left a message on her voicemail - she should get it when she gets over Europe. If she heads straight for Angie's place, she'll get there just in time." He stepped over to see the computer screen. "Did you find this guy's information?"

"Yeah, I got it. Are we going to go tonight?"

"I'd like to call him first, rather than just dropping by unannounced. If he says we can come right over, we will." He'd brought the telephone's handset in with him. "Where's the number?" Mac used the mouse to highlight the correct number on the screen. The phone beeped as Lawrence keyed each number in. After the ringing, he was greeted by voicemail. "Does no one actually *answer* their phones anymore?" he asked rhetorically.

Lady chose to answer anyway. "It *is* midnight, Lawrence."

He requested her silence with a wave of his hand as the recorded voice finished its message. "Hello. My name is Lawrence Wa...Hermanson. I was wondering if I might be able to arrange for a viewing of your copy of Dr. Bandenarii's book. Unfortunately, I'm only available around this time, late night, due to a particularly busy schedule. I'm in town for a limited time on business, so I was hoping to do this soon. Thank you." He finished the message by giving Stephanie's home number to reach him at, and ended the call.

"What's with the Hermanson name?" Mac asked.

"That was my true last name. I think it's time I gave 'Watts' a rest. Until I choose a new one, I'll go back to Hermanson." Lawrence bounced the phone distractedly in his hand. "With any luck, Mr. McFarland will call back sometime tomorrow or tomorrow night, and we'll go over and have a look at what Dr. Bandenarii has to say."

"What if he doesn't call back?" Mac asked.

"I don't see why he wouldn't."

"I don't know, Lawrence. From what I read, it sounds like these guys value the fact that they own such rare books. It's like they're trying to hoard the information in them. It's a prestige thing."

"That would be rather rude of them. If it comes to it, we'll find another way, but there's no need to borrow trouble just yet. Lord knows, we've got enough already. Now, have you two already fed? Yes? Okay. I'll see you in a bit, then. I need to go feed, myself."

Mac turned around, locking eyes with Lady. "Lawrence? I'll go with you," Lady volunteered. "Uh, I don't wanna be cooped up with fleabag."

"Do you ever have a nice thing to say about poor Mac?" Lawrence asked. "By the way, Mac, thanks for all the research you're doing. I appreciate it."

Lawrence's words went almost unheard by the animals, engaged as they were in private communication.

"Thanks for taking him, Lady - I had a few more things I wanted to look up," Mac was saying.

"Not a problem. I'm more comfortable than you helping him hunt, anyway. We both do what we're best at, and we'll get him through this. Then I can get back to mocking you and your testes-licking mannerisms full time."

"Right. Take care, Pretty Boots." Mac smiled, but it was forced humor, the gravity of the situation weighing on the both of them.

*   *   *

"This is really not looking good, Mac."

Mac didn't respond. Lady had stated the obvious; no response was necessary. It was 1:00 AM, and Lawrence had still not risen. Last night, the night of Stephanie's departure, Lawrence had woken at just a little before 11:30, and had returned to the coffin at around 2:30. They had been looking at perhaps two and a half hours to look at Dr. Bandenarii's book, if Mr.

McFarland were to call back.

Now, they'd be happy if Lawrence would rise at all.

Mac sniffed the air. "He doesn't smell all that different from last night, but I don't think he's gonna wake up."

Lady jumped to the open rim of the coffin. "He doesn't look very different either. I mean, he's still getting worse, losing hair, sores growing, all that, but no extreme differences. Nothing to account for this."

Several minutes passed, each of the two furred vampires standing mute sentry. Finally, Mac broke the anxiety-laden silence. "Shall we check the messages?"

"What's the point? Without Lawrence, we can't exactly call anyone back now, can we?"

"I know that, Lady, I just wanna hear if that McFarland guy was willing to set up the appointment."

"Fine. Listen to the messages. I'll stay here - I'll be able to hear them just fine." They were loathe to leave their erstwhile master completely untended for even a moment, in case there should be even the briefest period of activity or change in his status.

Mac padded upstairs to the living room, where the answering machine was. He had no need to check the message indicator - it was still register- ing one message, as it had all night. For easier access, he jumped up onto the divan positioned next to it. From this position it was no trouble to tap the playback button with a furred paw.

Stephanie's voice flowed from the speaker. "Hi Lawrence, Mac and Lady. I got your message, and I'm on my way right now to see Ms. Lowenhagen. I forgot to ask - do I address her as 'Countess' or what? Oh well. I'll bluff my way through it. Take care, and love to you all!"

The machine beeped, indicating the end of the messages. Mac dropped disconsolately back to the floor.

"So, the loser didn't even return Lawrence's call," Lady noted as Mac returned to the subterranean basement.

"It wouldn't have mattered anyway, like you said. Lawrence is not ex- actly able to keep any appointments tonight. So, what do we want to do about this?"

"I say we raid the guy's place, get the book, and see what it says about Lawrence's current state. It still may not be too late."

"What do you mean, *may* not be too late?!" Mac snapped. "It's not like he's dead! Of course it's not too late!"

Lady could hear desperation edging into Mac's voice. "Of *course* it's not too late yet," she soothed him. Lady was not certain, however. If he didn't wake up at all, did it really matter if he was dead or not? If he never rose, what was the difference? Dead, or permanently asleep, they boiled down to the same thing. Besides, from what she could tell, his body was still breaking down. This was not what Mac wanted to hear, though. "That being the case, we should still try to get Dr. Bandenarii's book."

"How? Lawrence wasn't able to set up an appointment. Even if he had, we'd be outta luck. You really think this McFarland guy is going to let a couple 'animals' paw through his treasured book?"

"You're such a goody-good, Mac. I'm surprised you were able to dredge up enough civil disobedience to break in to use people's comput- ers, much less to bust into the jailhouse with me. We're not going to *ask* the guy. We're going to go in and take it!'"

"We're going to steal this guy's priceless book? Why don't we just go in and read it at his place, while he's sleeping or something?"

"Yeah - that worked so well for you last time. Sorry, I don't fancy a butt full of buckshot. Secondly, we don't know it's priceless, or even valuable. Just because something is rare doesn't make it valuable. If that were the case my hairballs, of which very few remain in existence, would be worth thousands. There must be demand for an item in order to drive up the price. Thirdly," she continued, drowning out his protest, "we're not stealing it. I have every intention of returning it when we're done. Heck, I'll even throw in one of my near-priceless hairballs to sweeten the deal for him. We're just *borrowing* the book."

"Without asking."

"A technicality I choose to overlook."

Mac pondered the idea. "I don't know that I like it, but we have to do it. We should really let Stephanie know about Lawrence, too."

"Great idea. I'll dial; you tell her what's going on. Would that be two 'Woofs' or three?"

"I said we *should*. Besides, we could text message her phone from the computer."

Lady perked up. "Really? You can do that?"

"Weeelll, I could, if I knew what her screen name was. I might be able to find out online, anyway, but I don't know."

"What about Phil?" Lady asked.

"What about him?"

"Well, the card he gave Lawrence had his email as well as phone. You could email him, give him Stephanie's number, and have him call her."

"I can do that. Where's his card?"

"Ummm...I think Lawrence has it."

"Lawrence has it? Where?"

Lady looked up at the coffin. "In his pocket."

Mac let out a small, disappointed whimper. He didn't relish the idea of rummaging through Lawrence's clothes. It seemed...disrespectful. "Do you think you can get it?"

"I'll try." Lady leaped gracefully up to the lip of the casket. Gingerly, she stepped down into its snug confines. *It's probably in his wallet, in a back pocket*, she reasoned. Rolling him over to reach the back pocket would not be difficult with her vampire strength, just awkward for her and undignified for Lawrence. And, she could admit to herself, she didn't feel right flipping his probably-dead body around.

As she had guessed, the task was very cumbersome. When she finally got him in a position from which she could check, she found his back pockets empty. Gently, she maneuvered the body back to its usual position of rest, preparatory to checking in his front pockets.

"Lady?" Mac called.

"What? I'm kinda busy here."

"It was in his wallet."

"I know," she told him as she delicately probed a front pocket with her paw.

"Well, I have it right here."

"What?"

"Yeah - his wallet was sitting on the dresser."

Lady allowed a few choice words to roll through her mind. She refrained from sending them for fear of upsetting Mac's delicate sensibilities. "Well, let's go fire off that email."

Several dozen laboriously placed keystrokes later, Mac announced, "It's sent."

"What did you say in it?"

"Basically, I said that Lawrence did not wake at all, and asked Phil to relay the message to Stephanie. I gave him her cell number to do so."

"Good enough. Now, can you pull up Michael McFarland's address on that thing, so we know how to get there?"

"No problem." Mac fiddled with the mouse, clicking away. "Alright, I'm bringing up the map now, but it's a few miles from here. I don't think we'll have time to get there and back tonight."

"Tomorrow then?"

"Both of us?"

"I think that'd be best."

Mac hesitated. "I hate to leave Lawrence, but you're right. Too much could go wrong for there to be just one of us doing this. We both go."

CHAPTER TWENTY TWO

Lady woke from her forced slumber in her customary position curled around Lawrence's head. Immediately on opening her eyes she popped her head above the lip of the casket. She'd left it open for the day. She could have closed it by herself, but didn't see much point. She'd decided Stephanie's basement bedroom really was quite secure against the day. Stephanie had warded it far beyond the simple expedient of putting the room in the center or the basement with no windows. The frame of the room was steel-reinforced. The walls were six inches of concrete under the oak veneer. The only door into the room - right next to the foot of the stairs - was solid steel, secured with an automatic, independent-ly-powered time lock. This lock could only be over-ridden from the in-side with the proper authorization code. Lady hadn't realized Stephanie could be so paranoid. Stephanie called it 'securityconscious'.

Mac was already sitting up on the bed looking expectantly at her when she popped her head up. This was a regular game they'd played against each other since the first days of their Awakening. Every sunset, it was a contest as to who would rise first. Lady had done so only once in that time. The difference was measured in seconds, and neither animal truly had control over the outcome, but she hated losing anyway.

"Are you ready to go?" Mac asked.

"No, please give me a minute to gather up all my belongings," was her sarcastic reply. "Of course I'm ready."

Mac was unfazed by her morning attitude. "Actually, I wanted to do one thing before we go. I'll be right back." He dropped off the bed and moved rapidly up the stairs.

She wondered what he was doing. Rather than appear curious, even with no one watching, she took the time for some always-needed grooming. Just because her companion was a scruffy vagrant didn't mean she had to match his ways.

She could hear the dog clicking and tapping at the computer. She'd know why soon enough, she thought as she preened.

The clicking stopped. Mac reappeared, coming down the steps holding a sheet of paper grasped gently in his mouth. He walked up to the casket and stood on his hind legs against it. "Take this and lay it on Lawrence's face."

"On his face?" Lady frowned down at him.

"Yes. That way, if he wakes up even briefly he's sure to see it," Mac explained patiently.

Lady took the sheet from him and laid it out as requested, reading it as she did so. 'Lawrence, you didn't wake up at all last night. Lady and I have gone to get Bandenarii's book. If you wake, move this somewhere so we'll know you rose tonight.'

Mac's optimism seemed endless. Last night after he'd agreed they should both go, he still half-heartedly argued for it to be a solo journey. Only the knowledge that the chances of success would be greatly improved by having the skills of both of them convinced him. Lady was quite sure that Mac fully expected Lawrence to pop right up around midnight.

Lady was under no such illusions. There'd been no sign of life from him last night, and the external signs of his condition indicated a steady deterioration. If it kept up, she wouldn't be able to stand sleeping in the coffin much longer. She wouldn't yet quit trying to save him, but by all appearances it was already too late.

She set her skepticism temporarily aside as she accompanied Mac out the door and into the night.

* * *

After a fast walk of about fifteen miles along sidewalks and alongside the streets, they arrived at the address listed for Michael McFarland. They stood before a small apartment building. The two-story structure held perhaps eight apartments. "Well, that was a nice little walk," Mac commented contentedly. It was, indeed, an equable night, but Lady had been complaining, without justification, that her footpads would be worn down to nothing from so much running. She bristled at his comment. Not actually wanting to start her off on a diatribe, he added, "This is the place."

"An apartment? What is a priceless book doing in a cheap, weather-beaten apartment?" Lady was bewildered by the seeming incongruity.

"As you so eloquently pointed out, it's not necessarily priceless or even valuable. Besides, he may have sunk his savings into it as an investment, bought it from someone who didn't know its value, received it in an inheritance, or many other possibilities."

She sighed. "Whatever. What was his apartment number?"

"Three."

"Well, then, it should be a ground-floor apartment, don't you think? Which one do you think it is?"

"Probably one of the back two, presuming the numbering starts at the front, by the door. Let's go check them out." They walked towards the back of the building. "Lady, why don't you jump up and see what you can see through the windows." The apartment they were outside of had no major lights visible - the tenant was either asleep or out for the night.

"See what I can see? What are you expecting? A big neon sign saying 'Mike's Place'?" She stood looking at him, waiting for his reply, but he calmly returned his gaze, saying nothing. Heaving an overly dramatic sigh filled with eons of imagined suffering, she moved under the first window. An easy, graceful leap found her balanced on the ledge, peering into the window. The room within was an ordinary kitchen with an attached living room. "No neon signs here," she said, dropping back to the ground. The next window opened to the same adjoining rooms, on the living-room side, so she walked past it without bothering to peek in.

At the third and last window of the apartment along this side wall, she leaped up again. As her feet alighted on the sill, her fanged mouth drew back in a startled hiss. One paw completely slipped off the edge as she backpedaled a step in surprise. As if stepping out of the water, she shook herself, the shudder going from head to tail. "This is him. This is the right apartment." She had regained her usual composure and delivered her message in a matter-of-fact tone.

"What makes you so sure? What did you see?" Mac knew that pushing the issue of her startled reaction was pointless at the moment, though he was curious as to what had caused it.

"Move more to the left and you'll see."

Five steps to the left and he saw it. Just to the side of the window, looking obliquely out of it in an endless paper stare, was a life-size cardboard cutout of Bela Lugosi in his famous role as Dracula. Mac chuckled softly as he thought of Lady coming to rest on the ledge inches away from the classic Dracula's leering, fanged face. Mac recognized it from pictures he'd seen while researching vampirism on the web. He didn't know if Lady recognized its origin or not. Either way, it wasn't important right now except as definite proof that this was the apartment they sought. "I don't suppose he was kind enough to leave the window unlocked for us?" he asked.

"He did us one better," Lady replied. "He left it open for us."

"You're kidding."

"Not at all."

Mac jumped up to balance unsteadily on the narrow ledge. He assessed the open window behind the screen. "There's no way I can fit through that. We'll have to open it a bit, but no big deal."

Lady extended the claws of her right paw with a theatrical backward flick of her paw. She ran the claws horizontally along the screen, opening a hole large enough for Mac to slip through. She stole through the hole, squeezing flat to slither under the open window.

Mac ducked his snout through the screen and under the open window. He pushed gently upwards, trying to raise it. The window did not yield. He pulled his nose back. "It's latched in this position. Can you work the latches?"

Lady went up on her hind legs to find the latches. Finding them, she hit the catch that locked the sash in place and pushed the window up to a height more accommodating to the dog's greater size.

Mac entered, and they both looked around in wonder. "This guy is a fruitcake," Lady decided.

Mac could not, in good faith, disagree with her. He could have described the place in several ways: collection, museum, shrine, sanctorum. The walls were covered with movie and television stills, posters, and pictures: from an image of the deformed vampire of the silent French film 'Nosferatu', to an autographed picture of the cast of television's old

'Dark Shadows' program, to a movie poster for a contemporary vampire flick released in theaters just three months ago. Two bookcases were filled with hundreds of books on vampires, both fact and fiction. Other shelves held various memorabilia, from fake plastic fangs to religious symbols and sharpened, lethal-looking wooden stakes. The room's only light came from a computer monitor. The screen had an image depicting a cartoon vampire being impaled by a wicked looking stake, writhing on his back. A second image next to it showed him sitting up, a thought balloon appearing near his head saying, "Oh, it's only particle board!'

One shelf in the corner held their goal; three books were each enclosed individually in glass-fronted display cases custom fitted for each book. In the center was a very old-looking copy of Bram Stoker's classic. To the left was a book whose title was in a language foreign to Mac. On the right was a third book whose cover bore no markings aside from the name engraved in the lower right-hand corner, 'Dr. George Bandenarii'.

"George?" Lady asked incredulously. "His name was George?"

"George was a very common name back then. It might not have even been his real name. Many vampires took different names as the decades passed to help alleviate the suspicions of the people."

"It's still a lame name."

Mac considered questioning her dislike of the name. He mused on the possibility of repressed feelings of guilt over the killing of Phil's mouse of the same name. Instead of questioning her, he chose to let the discussion die where it was. There was nothing to be served in pursuing that line of questioning. Not right now, anyway. Later, when he had more time to antagonize her.

He turned his attention to the case containing the book they sought. It had a latch to keep it closed, but no lock. Ideally, they would leave it in the case as they took it, keeping the book protected as they traveled. If there was a way to do so and still make decent time on the way back, it escaped Mac. "Any ideas Lady? I'd like to keep it in the case, but don't see how we can."

She studied the case thoughtfully. "Hm. Mac, open your mouth." Mac, seeing where she was leading, ignored her request. She delivered her punch line, anyway. "Naw, not even *your* mouth is that big."

"Enough jokes, cat. I don't like this place. I wanna get moving."

"Whiner. What's not to like? Besides, he's probably got a ton of good, valuable vampire info." She looked around. "Maybe if we stuck the book and case in a bag?"

"That might work," he hesitantly agreed. They began searching the room for a bag big enough to hold the display case. If they found one the right size, they could tuck the book into it and Mac could grip the bag in his teeth. If they lay the slim case in the bag horizontally, it wouldn't drag on the street, though Mac was fairly certain it would be bumping steadily and annoyingly against his front legs.

The best they could find was a cloth sack. Embroidered on it in a deep red were the words 'Hunting Kit'. They dumped out an assortment of stakes, various holy symbols from a dozen religions, vials presumably filled with holy water, an empty box that reeked of garlic, another small box packed with tiny mustard seeds, and other common items of vampire folklore.

Lady surveyed the scattered paraphernalia. "Seeds?" she wondered.

"It's a rather obscure bit of lore. Supposedly if you were running from a vampire, you could scatter seeds behind you, and the vampire would be compelled to stop and count them."

"You've got to be kidding me," Lady accused skeptically.

"True story. Obviously, it doesn't actually work...although you do tend to be easily distracted..." Lady glared at him. Mac continued, "Most modern vampire enthusiasts have never even heard of it. This guy is pretty thorough."

"You sound impressed with the fruitcake, Mac. Remember, the stuff from this bag is used to destroy us."

Mac tried to fit the case into the bag. "It's not going to fit," he announced. "The book alone might fit, but not the case." He stared at the case as though willing it to shrink. "Keep looking for a bigger bag in here. In other words, cat, stay with the book. I'm going to see if I can find anything anywhere else." He walked out of the room.

It took all of two seconds after Mac left the room for Lady to decide she didn't like following orders, especially from a dog. After a cursory glance around the room to make sure they didn't miss anything obvious, she began the laborious process of transferring the book from its case and into the sack. She knew Mac wouldn't find anything better to carry it in. Again, she cursed evolution for not granting her opposable thumbs as she wrestled the book into the bag. It was during this struggle that she knocked the nowempty case off its low shelf.

"What was that?" Mac's voice rang in her mind.

"Just me. Settle down. Scruffy."

"I thought cats were supposed to be such quiet animals? And what's all that other noise?"

"That's me, too, trying to fit this stupid tome in the sack."

"Hang on. I told you I'm looking for a bigger bag," Mac admonished her.

"Whatever." She continued her struggles. Her back was to the door, but she felt his presence as he entered the room. "Give up already? Told you that you wouldn't find anything out there." Finally, the book slid into the bag.

"What?" Mac replied. He did not sound like he was in the same room as her.

She stopped her adjustments to the bag and turned slowly around. A man stood in the doorway with a small pistol. He was in his bathrobe and looking straight at her. As she saw him, he reached for the light switch and flicked it on. Lady's eyes reacted immediately to the harsh illumination, and she assessed her potential quarry.

The man, obviously Michael McFarland, was a husky man of about average height, still just on the friendly side of forty years old. The curly mess atop his head was a very light brown, and he appeared to have last shaved a couple days past. His tattered robe barely covered his plaid boxer shorts.

Lady stood frozen as she calculated whether she could get to him before his gun went off. "Mac, problem."

"I see that, Madam Noisemaker."

She had no response. He was right, this time. She watched the human's eyes take in the status of the room, pausing on the window, followed by the empty case and bulging bag. He'd seen her meticulously stuffing the book into a sack, and the unlatched window through which they'd entered. Lady watched his eyes widen as he arrived at the only logical conclusion a vampireobsessed paranoid could be expected to make. His hand flashed out to grab the nearest crucifix, setting the gun down in its place. The holy symbol immediately came alive in his hand, luminescing with a painful brilliance.

Over the discomfort caused by the glowing symbol of power, Lady could hear McFarland speaking silently to himself. "Oh my god. It's true. It's all true. Vampires. A vampire cat, of all things." She was being pressed back into the shelving, unable to control herself under the direct attention of the man bearing the crucifix. Faintly, she could hear Mac say something, but she was unable to make it out. It was as though the mystical energy was generating some form of static, interfering with their communications. She could sense only Mac's own fear of the cross over the link.

Her eyes turned away, she didn't see what McFarland was doing. Instead, she heard as the vampire expert slowly shuffled to the window to close it, his attention still apparently riveted on her. Over the sounds of his unsteady footsteps, she heard his continued murmurings of disbelief. His task completed, he returned to block her way out of the room. Not that it mattered; she was unable to move anywhere, completely at the human's questionable mercy.

* * *

"A red Audi? You're sure?"

"Well, it was dark, so it might have been some off-red shade. Do you really think it might be important?"

"It would be more important if you could remember the plate."

"I only remember part of it. Would that help?"

"Yes!" Jamon exclaimed, and was instantly sorry. The woman was already nervous; his outburst sent her flying into the back of her chair. She was a mousy, timid woman of about thirty. She claimed to have been on her way home. She'd been sent home early from her midnight shift at the hospital, and witnessed the car in question. "These men sound dangerous," her voice quavered out. "Will I be put in the Witness Protection Program?"

"I assure you that that won't be necessary. Miss Toole."

"You're sure?"

"Yes, Ma'am. Now, what of the license plate do you remember?" Jamon's pen was already poised in readiness over his notepad.

"I only remember the first three letters," she apologized meekly. Jamon had spent most of the interview leaning forward, half over his desk just to hear her. She came in at such a strange hour, she'd explained, because she always stayed up on her nights off in order to maintain her 'biorhythm'. Jamon could easily commiserate with that. She'd just tonight put together what she'd seen that night with the news reports of the attack on the precinct station. "I only remember any of it because the woman was driving very recklessly at first and I thought she might be drunk. Did I mention that? That was after she threw the drunken man into the car with the animals." Her eyes grew even larger in realization, reminding Jamon of a lemur. "Maybe he was wounded, not drunk!" she squeaked.

"That is quite possible," Jamon conceded. "And yes, you did tell me about the erratic driving as she, ah, 'peeled out'. The letters you remember?" he prompted her.

She gave him three letters, allowing Jamon to conclude the interview. Running the make and color of the car through the computer, along with the numbers she'd given him revealed only one possible match. Stephanie Roberson.

* * *

The phone rang, and a hand reached out to get it. As the fist opened to grasp the phone, the palm became visible, had someone been there to see. Most of it was simply a raw, angry red color, as though the owner of the hand had placed it under scalding water for several minutes. Parts of it, however, were burned clear through, rendering visible the tendons that tightened as the fingers closed over the small cell phone.

Sandoval lifted the phone to his ruined face, pressing the speaker against his ear. Saying nothing, he waited as the voice on the other end spoke, providing him with further information he would need to fulfill his mission. Still saying nothing, he closed the phone's cover, ending the call as the individual on the other end did the same.

The remnants of his upper lip curled back in a mockery of a smile that could have chilled a mortal's blood, even without the gruesome sight of the bare mandible beneath it.

CHAPTER TWENTY THREE

The light was almost blinding. He squinted his eyes and tried to ignore both the fear and the way his very bones ached deep in their marrow. In this manner, his eyes no more than slits, Mac could just make out Lady huddled into the shelf beneath the two remaining cased books. If she was trying to say anything, he couldn't hear it - his mind was filled with a roar, akin to what he imagined the sound of an onrushing tsunami might be. Under the tidal wave, he could feel, rather than hear, the deep pulsing of Lady's fear. It surpassed by far his own; she was the sole focal point of the crucifix's powerful attention.

Lady may have been reduced to a near-unthinking panic, but Mac was feeling only the peripheral effects of the religious symbol. Mr. Michael McFarland was unaware of Mac's presence. So oblivious was the vampir-eobsessed human to the possibility of another intruder, he stood in the doorway, his bathrobed back to the vampiric dog.

Lady was helpless. Lawrence was not around to come to their aid. Neither would Stephanie be pulling up in her Audi for a timely rescue. Mac had nowhere to seek help but inward. This he did. Thought was difficult over the roaring in his head. This was far worse than his last exposure to religious iconography, in the police station. There, the woman had been deliberately trying to shield them from the trauma of her cross. Whether it was her physical attempts, or the force of her will, she'd at least partially succeeded in suppressing its effects against them.

Logically, Mac knew the fear he felt was an artificial one. Intellectually, he was aware of the dangers the cross represented to his undead body, and he respected its power; but the fear that rooted him to this spot had nothing to do with his knowledge.

This insight did little to aid him. The sight of the cross held out-thrust before the man, visible from Mac's position, wielded with such fervent belief in its power, held Mac nearly paralyzed.

Nearly paralyzed only; he could still move, if painfully and slowly. While the human stood motionless, apparently pondering what to do with his newly captured prize, Mac inched slowly to his left. The ponderous, sluggish pace he was forced to set gave him grave concern, but his reaction to the crucifix would not allow him to move faster in any direction but directly away. He needed to go to the left. It took all he could muster to manage as little as he was moving.

Steadily, Mac's movement caused the man's own body to eclipse the crucifix. Mac relaxed. The pain was still deep in him, but the surcease from the worst of it was a welcome relief. The burning light of the cross was likewise dimmed. The static still filled his mind, but he could think far more clearly. His first thought in this newfound relative clarity was that they were screwed.

He shook off such troubling concerns, literally: he wagged his head as though encouraging his positive thoughts and ideas to cross the synaptic gaps of his brain with greater speed and efficiency.

He had no time to think of a clever plan. Plans were not his strong suit, anyway - that was more Lady's forte. He wasn't dumb, but Mac was more a brute-force guy, and he knew it. Speed, strength, and surprise were what he'd have to rely on now.

The moment he thought it, he acted. Remembering his vivid imaginings of Lady curled in a cannonball, Mac went on the offensive. He ran a few rapid steps to get up to effective speed before he hurled himself across the remaining seven feet to Michael. As his ascent hit a height of about two feet, the cross came back into view and worked its divine magic on him once again. This time he was ready, already in the position he needed. Were Michael to have seen the object flying at him, he would have been unable to identify the oversize, scruffy, rusted cannonball as a dog.

The curled body of Mac hit McFarland square between his shoulder-blades. Almost immediately Mac felt the effects of the cross vanish. Still in the air, he straightened his body and opened his eyes. Remembering also what he'd learned from watching Lady at the police station, he managed to do the contortions which allowed him to land neatly on his feet. He landed soft. Under his paws was McFarland's back: the man had sprawled out face-first, arms outstretched. The cross lay almost innocuously dormant on the floor at Bela Lugosi's feet.

"Grab the book, Lady! Time to go!" Mac shouted in her mind. He repeated his performance of two seconds prior, taking two steps off Michael's back and throwing himself at the window in a cannonball. The shatter of glass and tearing of wire mesh announced his passage through the window and screen. He shook himself to free the glass fragments from his pelt. Pebble-sized shards of glass flew off in a corona-like spray around him.

Lady landed beside him, audible only because of the bag holding the book. It dangled clumsily from her tightly clenched jaw to strike the ground. It looked fully half her size, and probably weighed more than she.

"I'll take the bag," Mac offered. "Now, let's get out of here before -" he broke off, and both animals started running. Behind them, they could feel the crucifix flare to life again, though it did not hold its full power over them yet.

Only seconds after it flared up, they felt the power abate. McFarland must have set the cross aside. Their sharp ears picked up the human's anguished plea, already fifty yards behind them. "Please, come back! I won't harm you!

Just make me one of you!"

"Fruitcake," Lady reasserted. "Doesn't know whether to kill us or beg us."

"He was probably just scared," Mac replied. He willed himself not to chew; the bag was already beginning to make his mouth uncomfortably dry. "How often does he wake up to find a vampire cat rummaging through his stuff? And by the way, I have to say that I'm getting rather tired of using my body as a battering ram. Everywhere we go; it seems I'm slamming through something." As soon as he let the thoughts go, he regretted it, knowing Lady would have the perfect cutting remark just waiting to be used.

She surprised him. "Well, at least you get the job done."

The two raced along the lit streets, running for the safety of home.

*   *   *

The house was as dark as they'd left it. Mac remembered a comment Stephanie had made a couple days earlier. She'd claimed that vampirism was great for her electrical bill. "No need to run the refrigerator or freezer, rarely use the heater or air conditioner, the lights are almost never on...I'm the electric company's worst customer!"

Now, the darkness seemed foreboding. "I don't like it," Mac noted as they approached the house.

"Don't like what?"

"I don't know. I just don't like it." He cast his eyes over the front of the house, then around the neighborhood. Nothing was wrong, but he was still spooked.

"Dog, you're being paranoid. Don't get your fleas in a riot. Everything's fine. Just look. Nothing's changed."

Still unsettled, Mac could see no concrete cause for concern and grudgingly agreed with Lady.

They entered the house through the back door, which had a handle they could easily manipulate. No sooner had the door latched shut behind them than they scampered down the steps to check on Lawrence. Lady leaped up on the coffin, launching herself from halfway across the room in her desire to check on his condition.

"Did he rise at all? Has my note been moved?" Mac inquired anxiously. His tail wagged uncertainly, and he still held the bag in his jaw, forgotten for the moment, the bottom almost dragging on the floor.

"No. The note's right where we left it," she said with a resigned air. She hated to admit it, but she, too, had been hoping the note would be moved. She wasn't expecting it to be; she would in fact have been surprised had it been. Still, against reason, she'd quietly hoped. Her ears pivoted. "Stephanie's home."

Mac reared up to place the vampire hunting bag, containing the precious tome, on a low dresser. His own floppy ears perked as he listened. "Yup. I hear her now. She's a quiet one - I didn't even hear her close the door."

"She used the back door. Must've forgotten her key. What're you doing?" she puzzled at him. Mac had dropped into a crouch, ready to attack. He faced the bedroom door and the stairs beyond.

"That's not Stephanie," he explained. His nose was sniffing furiously. "It's -"

"Sandoval," Lady finished. She caught the scent, faintly, now that she deliberately sought it.

"I'm gonna close the door," Mac said, starting forward. "It's reinforced."

"Not enough to stand up to Skeletor out there," Lady countered. "Leave it and get into position."

"Right."

"Any ideas, Mac?"

Mac could easily hear the worry in her telepathic voice, even had he not been able to feel the fear pouring over the link. He could do nothing to assuage her fears. He, too, knew the situation to be hopeless. "Die fighting," he replied grimly. "Actually," Mac mused, "we're supposed to overthrow the Council, right? This one vampire shouldn't be too much to handle. And if we are to overthrow the Council, we obviously have to survive this, right?" Hope returned, building up the force of his voice as he talked.

But not for long. "Remember Stephanie's dreams? Not all of them come true, she said."

"You suck, Lady." They listened as the intruder quietly found the stairs. "Alright, cat, new plan. No need for both of us to get killed here. Do what you can, but when you can't take any more, I'll cover your escape. Just help me tear him up some."

"You're still an idiot, Mac. Your first plan was the right one. Die fighting. Scarface can have Lawrence over my true dead body."

And then the time for talk was done. Sandoval stood in the doorway. His grotesque face was shadowed by the hooded top of his cape. Lady and Mac could see his marred features easily, even in the dim light of the room. Their eyesight was as much better than a human vampire's as a normal cat's was above a normal human's. The abomination lowered his hood, his one eye darting between Lady, who was on Lawrence's coffin, and Mac, on the floor. The eyelid above fluttered ineffectually. The animals, in turn, watched him. The three stood motionless, everyone waiting for the other side to take the first action.

Sandoval's leg moved almost imperceptibly, preparatory to taking a step forward. Mac and Lady jumped, both animals homing in with unerring accuracy on their target.

Sandoval had time to react to just one of the furry projectiles speeding at him. He chose to deflect Lady, sending her spinning back across the room to slam into the far wall. Mac was allowed to land on Sandoval's upper chest. The dog used his location to reach up with his jaws and grasp Sandoval's bare mandible. This close, he could easily see the exact nature of the damage wrought centuries ago. As he'd noted before, the bone of the mandible was fully exposed. From his position looking up from Sandoval's chest, he could see the inside of the old vampire's mouth. The palate was visible through the open, horizontal arc described by the curved bone of the jaw. Mac could only presume much of the tongue had been burned away, as it was not blocking his view up. "Gross," he thought before he chomped down on the bone.

He promptly found himself flying across the room. As he was tossed, Lady landed herself on Sandoval's back. She had run around behind him while he was distracted by Mac. As their ghoul-faced tormentor reached back to pull her off, his cape flared wide. Mac's attention was drawn to the various implements worn about Sandoval's person. He was well outfitted for his task, loaded with a variety of stakes and knives.

Unable to get a good grasp on the cat from his angle, Sandoval pulled off one of the razor-sharp knives. "Lady! Knife coming!" Mac warned.

"I can handle a little - Aaahhh!" she yowled as the knife cut a gash along her ribs. "What the hell?! That burns!"

"It's probably silver. Watch out!"

Sandoval plunged the blade back again, forcing Lady to jump off. Mac waited for her, and they repeated their initial assault tactic: jumping the intruder simultaneously. This time it was Mac who was knocked aside. The difficult part when pouncing was to avoid landing on the silver knife Sandoval brandished. Lady quickly jumped from her landing point on his shoulder down to his knife hand. Her attempt to force him to drop it proved futile when he simply switched hands. She was forced to retreat from his arm as the knife whistled through the air at her. The blade bit into her tail, nearly severing the last two inches of it.

They followed the same pattern for over a minute of furious combat, teaming up for their assaults. Sandoval seemed tireless, and they each took multiple silver-infected wounds. These burned deeper than the cut alone would seem to indicate. The struggle was astonishingly silent; Sandoval made no noise, and only an occasional yelp or yowl of pain was audibly emitted by the animals.

Even in the quiet of the battle, all parties were too focused on their immediate tasks to hear the newest home invader until he slapped on the lights and shouted, "Freeze, police!" from the doorway.

Jamon stood at the foot of the stairs, his pistol pointed at Sandoval. As the vampire turned to face him, Jamon paled at his first exposure to the largely bare skull. Mac, who had successfully landed on the most recent assault, made use of Sandoval's distracted hesitation. He stretched from the man's shoulder to lock onto the exposed chin. Mac had noticed such attacks seemed to particularly annoy him, so he'd been spitefully making it his primary target.

Mac dropped as he saw the blade come flashing at him. He pivoted around, dropping from the shoulder to dangle from his lock on the assassin's mandible. Using the move he now had nearly perfected, he braced his legs against Sandoval's chest and gave a ferocious, wrenching yank. To his own surprise, he found himself flying backward in a small spray of blood through the air, the now-fully-detached jaw clutched firmly in his own teeth.

"Gross!" was Lady's only comment.

Shots rang out loudly in the small room. Sandoval staggered back under the kinetic energy of the slugs that found their mark. "Ha! Silver bullets, you freakish asshole!" Jamon screamed triumphantly, almost hysterically, as he fired. Even at the short range, Mac figured no more than four bullets had found their mark.

Mac spit out his osseous trophy in disgust. Not having been fully secured by muscle and other tissues, the mandible had detached relatively easily and was still fully intact. He looked back up to see that Jamon had already dropped his expended pistol, rather than waste the precious time to reload it with a fresh clip. He was now fumbling in a pocket for his next weapon against the angrily advancing Sandoval. Finding his prize, Jamon held it aloft like a shield. By conditioned reflex, all three of the conscious undead creatures flinched back before realizing the six-inch cross bore no power over them. It remained as dark and cold in his hands as a rock.

Jamon was unaware of its ineffectiveness. Seeing Sandoval's initial flinch, his grin was victorious. "Back, you damned beast!" He turned his smiling countenance to where Mac and Lady sat licking their wounds in the brief respite afforded by his intervention. "You're next, you filthy, cursed hellspawn!"

"Now, that was simply uncalled-for," Lady commented, running her raspy tongue along her left flank.

Sandoval recovered his poise. He saw there was nothing to fear from the usually potent instrument of the believers, and continued stalking towards the cop.

Jamon's grin disappeared as the partly dismembered face drew closer. His eyes grew round. He looked at the cross in his hand, thrusting it farther forward in a futile attempt to enforce its power. Still seeing no effect, he desperately shook it, as though trying to make a defective piece of technology work. Now completely mystified as well as terrified, he afforded no resistance as Sandoval contemptuously batted the crucifix out of his hand. Belatedly, Jamon made a feeble attempt to keep Sandoval's hands at bay. His actions had little more effect against the old vampire's might than total passivity would have rendered.

Shirt and belt provided the handholds as Sandoval tossed Jamon easily across the room to crash into the occupied coffin, which very nearly fell atop him.

"Well, there go my hopes for a timely mortal rescue," Lady noted, genuinely concerned.

"Yeah, but what was the deal with the cross?" Mac wondered. "I felt nothing from it."

Jamon struggled slowly to his feet. His eyes furrowed as he saw the occupant of the coffin he'd smashed into. "He's really still dead?" he muttered confusedly to himself.

Sandoval had turned around and was marching at an almost leisurely pace towards Jamon. Jamon raised a hand up, ready to ward the blow he felt was coming. His defensive motion revealed to Mac, through a gap in Jamon's button-up shirt, an inordinately bright pendant in the shape of a six-pointed star. Mac's eyes watered in discomfort just to look at it.

"No wonder! Lady! He's Jewish! No wonder the crucifix held no power! He has no faith in it!"

"Well, how are we gonna let him know, and would it make any difference if he knew, anyway? Your stunning revelation goes straight to the top of this moment's useless knowledge list." She cringed as the first of a series of slaps rang out. Sandoval had his left fist balled in Jamon's shirt, supporting him. His right hand delivered one head-rocking open-hand slap after another. "He's toying with the poor human," Lady observed. "I think it's time we rejoin the fight."

Lady jerked to her feet in a startled response to Mac, who suddenly let loose a fusillade of barking and growling. At the same time she could hear, as though he were shouting in her ear, his amplified voice.

"Star of David, you fool! Use it like a cross! It's your faith that powers it!"

Both men had looked over at Mac's suddenly furious barking. Jamon appeared as though he were listening intently to it, and then looked down at his chest. Sandoval, reminded now of the animal's presence and his true goal, retrieved a second knife from his belt. With casual indifference, he began to stab and slash Jamon in the gut with it.

Sandoval ignored Jamon's hand as it fumbled underneath his shirt, poking him twice more with the knife. Unlike the casual slashes, each thrust was done with almost loving care. The blade was slowly eased in, almost leisurely parting the flesh. He stopped only to bat the animals out of the air. They had resumed their own attack. Their close proximity in their pounce caused Mac to knock into Lady when he was batted aside by Sandoval's easy swipe. Both went sprawling against the wall, falling behind a dresser that had been knocked loose from the same wall.

Before he could return his attention to Jamon, Sandoval's fist went slack, relaxing its grip on Jamon and leaving him to slump to the floor.

Mac didn't need to see the scene to know what was happening. The now-familiar heat, along with the associated light and pain told him the situation. Still, he couldn't help but force his protesting body up to peek over the top of the oaken dresser. Recoiling from the power before him, he nonetheless took in the scene.

Jamon, too weak and battered to stand under his own power, sat with his back against the half-fallen coffin. His hand held the Star of David before him, thrust forward to the limit of its short chain.

Sandoval was doing his best to fight the effects of the Star, but had already been forced back twelve feet. He was using his cape to shield the remains of his face from the power before him.

Jamon's faith was renewed in mystically-backed fighting methods. His hand went for a stainless-steel flask riding his hip. Carefully, with the hand holding up the Star, he slowly, deliberately, unscrewed the cap. Sandoval's eyes - the mangled one and the empty socket - both widened. It was clear that the flask would not hold whiskey tonight. Sandoval retreated two more steps.

Jamon made a feeble attempt to splash some of the contents onto the cowering vampire. The water went no more than five feet, but Sandoval's leap back to the doorway elicited a vengeful smile on Jamon. As Jamon moved, preparing to crawl forward, Sandoval's nerve broke. He turned and fled up the steps.

"You were right, dog," Jamon slurred before falling forward on his face.

The water spilled out of the flask to mix with the pooled blood around him.

"Lawrence!" Stephanie cried from the doorway.

CHAPTER TWENTY FOUR

The Dream had shown a heart. She'd known, in the way one some-times knows things in mortal dreams, that this was her own heart. It was beating steadily. This simple image went on for an immeasurable time before stopping. In the same way she'd known it was her heart, she'd known that, although it had stopped, it was not dead; it was merely rest-ing. Stephanie had surmised the Dream's obvious meaning even before getting the call from Phil. Her heart, her love, her Lawrence, was alive - in the vampire fashion – but unresponsive.

The second Dream she'd had that same day. Two in one day! Things were really coming to a head. Even before she understood its meaning, the Dream chilled her. A fish flopped, gasping for breath in the sands of a desert. Two vultures circled low overhead. Sitting next to the dying fish were a pair of puzzled young children, no more than toddlers. Each was armed with an unloaded gun. Piles of ammunition lay at their feet. They tried to load the weapons, but their young minds seemed incapable of grasping the mechanisms of the weapons' action.

This second Dream had plagued her mind for the whole trip back to General Mitchell Airport. Again, she followed the sun. This trip was much easier than coming in to Europe, as she crossed only part of West-ern Europe before soaring over the international airspace of the Atlan-tic. The trip into Europe had been much more complicated. The expens-es alone were enough to boggle the mind; bribes for foreign officials throughout Asia were enough to buy a comfortable house back home. It was necessary - she had little time for bureaucracies and international clearances and all the other problems her pilots warned her about. Fortu-nately, their warnings came with solutions - expensive solutions, but they knew who could be bought, and speed was her only concern.

Pulling up to her home in the taxi, she still hadn't figured out the Dream, and she'd still not come to terms with Phil's message from the animals. Her first Dream gave her some reassurance, but even the knowledge he still lived, whatever his appearance may indicate, provided faint hope.

Her first sight on arrival was an unfamiliar car parked haphazardly in her driveway. Worried, she left the driver to get her bags and made her way quickly up to her front door. The back door slammed shut just before it came into view as she walked through the house to the back stairway.

Her fear for Lawrence was not at all assuaged by this unexpected noise. She considered running to see who just left, but her concern for Lawrence led her downstairs to the bedroom instead.

At the top of the stairs she heard a male voice, though she could not quite make out the words. No matter: The only voice that should be there at all was Lawrence. That was not his voice. The car in the driveway had indicated there'd be someone, but she'd hoped the animals would have had the bedroom door closed and locked. She could see from the top of the stairs that this was not the case. They'd better have a damn good reason for such an appalling breach of security.

Ha! How would she know their reasons for anything without Lawrence to interpret? Well, they'd figure something out. Perhaps Mac could type on the computer what they were saying.

The sight that greeted her was nothing she'd expected. The room was trashed. The bed was torn up, long slices down the material of the mattress; none of her prints or pictures remained in place on the walls - all had crashed to the floor; her coffin, Lawrence resting crookedly in it, lay canted off its stand; everything seemed moved or damaged. Lastly, there was a human body lying in a pool of blood in the middle of the room. The air carried the tantalizing scent of the blood, but there was an unfamiliar, powerful scent mixed in that made the air unpleasant to taste.

There was no sign of the animals.

She was aware after the fact of having called her love's name. She avoided stepping in the blood, skirting the puddle as she ran to the coffin. Gently, awkwardly, she placed it back on its low stand. The awkwardness was due strictly to the size of the load - the weight was not enough to strain her enhanced musculature.

She looked up from her work to see both Mac and Lady crawling out from behind a dresser. "You were hiding?" she shouted. She prepared to open the floodgates of her worries and fears in a tirade of wrath at their cowardice and carelessness. Her mouth closed. Both were limping in ways a biped can scarcely contemplate. She saw wicked-looking cuts crisscrossing their bodies.

Then Mac started barking.

It was not the sound she normally associated with a dog's bark. Usually, they sounded eager, threatening, angry, or somehow urgent. This had a calmer, measured cadence, interspersed liberally with non-threatening growls and other similar sounds. It was almost a conversational tone.

More spectacular, she understood what he was saying.

At the moment, he was probing, feeling out the possibility of communication. "Can you hear me, Stephanie? Do you understand what I'm saying? Testing, testing, one, two, three." He turned his muzzle towards Lady, but he continued barking, and she heard, "Is this thing on?"

His barking noises were still just that: barking noises. However, it was as if she'd suddenly learned a new language. She was able to interpret the growls, barks, and other noises as words.

Shaking off her shock, she replied, "I heard you."

Both animals turned to her. Maybe they'd had reason to believe this method of communication would work, but they both looked as surprised as she felt.

Lady started meowing. It sounded no different to Stephanie than an ordinary cat. "I can't understand you," Stephanie said, guessing her motive.

"Odd," Mac barked, "but first things first. We were attacked by Sandoval. The cop, Jamon, joined in. Sandoval whupped him bad. Stabbed him repeatedly. I can hear him breathe, so he's still alive, but he's gotta be almost dead. We need to try and heal him."

Stephanie could see the wounds on the animals still trickling blood. That was not normal. "I'll do it. I'm still fresh, not carved up." She stepped over to the motionless form, trying to ignore the way her shoes squelched in the blood-soaked carpet. She squatted down at his side, careful not to let her knee drop to the sopping carpet and rolled him over. "Did either of you two bite him?"

"No," Mac barked.

"Did Sandoval?"

Mac and Lady turned to look at each other; Stephanie guessed they were discussing the answer to her question. "No, not that we saw. Why? What's wrong?"

"Probably nothing, I guess. I just thought his wounds looked a little older than they should. It's probably just been too long since I dealt with mortal injuries. Maybe Sandoval didn't get him as bad as it looked. No matter. I'll give his healing a boost, anyway - he's certainly lost a lot of blood."

Stephanie jerked her head back from Jamon's neck, spitting disgustedly, distaste evident on her face. She stopped spitting, looking vaguely uncomfortable. "I haven't felt the need to vomit in almost thirty years. I can't -" She clamped her mouth shut. Her hand automatically rose to her lips, ready to stem the flow should she lose whatever may have been in her stomach.

Slowly, she relaxed. "What was that all about?" Mac asked. He and Lady had come to sit at the edge of the blood-soaked area's radius, staying on the dry fabric.

"I don't know, but his blood tasted horrible. It made me want to be sick, almost like that...stuff. That stuff that makes you throw up, uh... Ipecac."

Mac's nose wrinkled. He was gathering the scent, drawing breath for the first time since the battle. He didn't like it. His head dropped down, his nose half an inch from the soggy carpet. He inhaled again. Its odor forced a sneeze from him, sending a few stray blood-droplets into the air from the floor, some splattering his already bloody muzzle. He announced his verdict.

"There's something wrong with his blood."

"Did Sandoval do anything weird that could have tainted his blood?"

"Not that we saw. He seemed to be using an ordinary knife. Well, it was silver, but normal otherwise. I don't think it was poisoned or anything. Burns like crazy where he cut us, but that's just a normal vampiric reaction to silver weaponry; it shouldn't matter to a human."

Lady craned her neck, peering at Jamon's wounds without leaving dry carpet. Mac turned his attention to her. Stephanie waited while they conferred. Mac re-examined Jamon's wounds from where he sat. "Lady and I agree: his wounds look too old. We have a -"

MEOW!

"Er, Lady, has a theory on that. She thinks Lawrence may have infected him with his bite."

"Infected him?"

"With Premetamorphic Malaise. Perhaps it is transmittable, and he gave it to Jamon, and it has the opposite effect on humans that it does on vampires."

"And I just bit him."

Mac whimpered as he realized the implications of Stephanie's words. If the disease was contagious, she may have just caught it by biting Jamon. In her desire to help, she may have doomed herself. "Um, did you find anything out in Europe? Any idea for a cure?" he asked hopefully. If she'd found a cure, it would be no big deal.

"No." Stephanie's voice was barely a whisper. The three sat motionless, staring at the newly introduced unknown quantity lying before them. Was it Lawrence's disease?

"There's another thing," Stephanie began. "When I bit him, I could feel my...uh...the magic being, well, turned away. Like, I was trying to push my power into him, to help him heal, but it hit a wall and bounced back at me.

It was as though his body was immune to my power, or refused to accept it."

"Um," was all Mac had to say in response to that.

Stephanie began divesting Jamon of his weaponry. "Well, nothing more we can do for him right now, it seems. Mac, tell me about Lawrence."

Lady settled on the lip of the coffin and Stephanie took a seat on the mussed and nearly shredded bed. Mac righted a chair in the corner with his muzzle and took up residence on that. The three did their best to ignore the devastated room as Mac brought Stephanie up to date. Mac would pause in his narration on occasion; Stephanie presumed Lady was reminding him of a point he'd missed. Mac would then usually backtrack the story to add a detail he'd passed over.

Stephanie had arrived home around four o'clock. At around 4:45, Jamon began to wake up. "Good," Stephanie commented. "I was hoping he'd be up early enough for us to take care of him."

"What're we gonna do with him?" Mac growled.

"I don't know yet. We'll have to see how he behaves."

Apart from Jamon's breathing, and his sporadic groans, the room was silent. His eyes opened slowly, as though it were a Herculean task to lift his eyelids. When his eyes appeared to have a steady consciousness behind them, Stephanie said, "If you start going cliché on me and ask 'Where am I?' or some other crap, I'll be severely disappointed."

This request halted the words Jamon had already been forming. He closed his mouth. After some thought, he asked, "Would you please tell me what's happened since I lost consciousness?" Stephanie started to speak; Jamon cut her off to add, "Actually, if you could start shortly before I lost consciousness

- my memory seems somewhat unreliable as of late."

She smiled. "Mac, care to enlighten him?"

Mac began to relay the evening's events and Jamon whipped his head around. "Oh shit. It's true. You did talk." He paled. "That means…" He looked around the room until his eyes alit on Lady. "You! Back! Back!" he commanded the cat. He began scooting frantically away from her, his hands desperately seeking any of his weapons.

As his scrambling brought him by the bed, Stephanie reached out a reassuring hand. "Relax, Jamon. Lady won't be doing anything. " Seeing him flinch from her own touch, she added, a bit less warmly, "nor will I nor the dog." She held up the weapons she'd earlier removed from him, including the chain with his Star of David. "And neither will you."

"Lady? You call that black freak *Lady*? Wouldn't Mephistopheles be a bit more fitting?" His voice rose slightly in pitch as he grew more excited.

"She wants me to tell you her full name is actually Lady de Winter," Mac barked. "She used to be known as Pretty Boots, though," he chuckled. He proceeded again to tell Jamon of the end of the battle, Stephanie's timely arrival home, and their attempts to revive him. He left out Lady's disease theory. "Do you have any idea why your blood has such a foul odor? Is it some sort of new weapon or defense you've come across?"

Jamon appeared dazed as he absorbed the short retelling of the fight. He looked at his blood congealing on the floor. "No. It doesn't smell any different to me, and it didn't bother your dead friend there. He seemed to rather enjoy it, in fact," he said bitterly. "He bit me three times, after all. Hey, what's the deal with him, anyway? He is a vampire, right? Why is he still dead?"

Nobody answered him, their minds grappling with Jamon's revelation. "Did you say he bit you three times?" Stephanie asked.

"Yeah. Hey - I've been wondering. Doesn't that mean I'm going to turn into a vampire, or is that curse averted because he's dead?" He hooked his thumb back at Lawrence. He was oblivious to the surprise the vampires exhibited in response to his announcement he'd been bit thrice.

Stephanie did her best to keep her cool over his cavalier attitude towards Lawrence's condition. "When did he bite you the third time? No - tell me about each time he bit you."

Jamon listed each time for her: the first, when he shot Lawrence in the chest and leg; the second, when he was undercover as a dealer; and the third, when he confronted Lawrence in the alley.

"That's what's doing it," Mac barked. Stephanie nodded. "Jamon, you're not going to turn into a vampire, but being bit three times evidently gives you some protection from being fed on by other vampires."

"Oh. Well, I guess that's good," Jamon replied. "But it'd be even better if it kept them from stabbing me, too."

"It does seem to be accelerating your healing process," Stephanie noted.

Jamon looked at the knife wounds on his stomach. "Yeah, I guess. They do look several hours old already. Maybe even a day old."

Stephanie stood up and extended a helping hand to Jamon. "Well, it's been just great having you over, but it's time to go. Unless, of course, you want to be stuck here all day."

"What?"

"This room is heavily armored and the door has a time-activated lock." She omitted the fact that it could be over-ridden from the inside. He was still too befuddled to give the matter much thought.

"But it's not sunrise yet," he protested.

"Right, but we have things to discuss. Vampire business. No mortals allowed."

"I could have you arrested," he threatened.

"Oh? For what? For coming home to find you've illegally entered my house? Or do you have a warrant? Didn't think so. Don't worry, though, we will definitely be in touch. I've already got your card," she finished as she flashed one she'd removed from him earlier.

He stood up, accepting her assistance. "I'll be back tomorrow night, then."

"I wouldn't recommend it. Now that Sandoval knows where we are, we're vacating. That's one of the things we'll be discussing. Now, good morning," she said by way of dismissal. She indicated the door. "And don't try to be sneaky - our senses are far better than any mortal's. Especially the dog's nose and the cat's eyes and ears. They will hear and smell you no matter how good at covert surveillance you may think you are. And the house has a rather expensive, top-of-the line security system, which will be on to back them up."

She smiled. "I trust we have an understanding, my good detective?" Jamon left, and Stephanie closed the door behind him.

"Alright, Mac. Finish your story."

He told her the rest of their exploits, including the raid on McFarland's vampire room. He ended with Stephanie's arrival home.

"So, where's this book, then?" she asked. There was a minute of frenzied searching. Their concern that it had been stolen or destroyed in the course of the fight was alleviated soon enough. It had simply fallen and been knocked under the dresser Mac and Lady had ended up behind. Stephanie took it out of the bag for a brief examination. "It's in French, I think. Shit." Lady and Mac both looked over her arm. She had the book lying open on the bed.

"Crap," Mac agreed. Lady looked up at him. Mac turned to Stephanie. "Apparently, French is another bit of knowledge I missed out on during my Awakening. Lady claims she can read it just fine."

Stephanie instantly understood. "Of course. Lawrence lived in Europe for a couple hundred years or so. Some of it he spent right in France.

He mentioned a long time ago that he speaks fluent French. A few other languages too, I think. Good." She slipped the book back into the bag. "Take this, Mac. It's time to go. I'll get Lawrence."

"Where are we going?" Mac asked. Stephanie pulled Lawrence out of the coffin and hoisted him over her shoulder.

"One of the places I keep my money in is real estate. I have a house that's been vacant a couple months. It's bigger than we need, but it's better privacy than one of my apartments. We'll pick up a couple coffins tomorrow," she said, climbing the stairs. "I don't think this place is safe any longer. We won't be returning until this mess is over with. In the meantime, I grabbed a couple things that the vampires in Europe are using to cover windows with while on trips. Very handy, especially since we can't fit the coffin in my Audi, and I've only the one coffin anyway. I bought four window covers, so we should be good for tonight."

They went directly into the garage, where Stephanie arranged Lawrence's unconscious form in the passenger seat of the red car. Mac placed the book in back. Stephanie backed the car out of the garage, got out and tossed her luggage - which the cab driver had left on the front doorstep – into the trunk.

From the back seat Mac asked, "So, what did you find out in Europe?"

Stephanie pulled out of the driveway. "Not much at all. My trip was cancelled a bit quickly, so I only had time to talk with Countess Lowenhagen; I had actually hoped to do a little more research while I was there, but I barely had time to speak to her. Countess Lowenhagen lives in Italy now. As you know, Phil set up an appointment for me to see her. She never suspected I was an illegal vampire, at least not that I could tell. Nor did I let her know I was talking about Lawrence. I just told her my 'consort' – her word, not mine - wished to keep his weakened state hidden for now. She understood and accepted that.

"She revealed little we don't already know. One thing I found interesting was that the Count also came down with the same, smaller scale sickness two hundred years before he died. Just like Lawrence described happened to him. Too much of a coincidence. It must be part of the disease.

"What really struck me was this: the Count - that's how she always referred to him; I still don't know his name - anyway, the Count fed without killing, just like we do, just like Lawrence did. Does," she corrected herself. "Now, get this. The Count started feeding without killing in about 1482, almost exactly *four hundred years* before he died."

She let her statement sink in before continuing. "Obviously, this is caused by feeding without killing."

Mac started barking. "That's stupid! What kind of divine power would sanction killing, and punish compassion? Yes, Lady, I do believe in God," he said in response to her look. "Otherwise, why would religious stuff work against us? Nothing else makes sense!" He paused; she was asking something else. 'Well, then you're just stupid. How else do you explain -'"

"Mac, that's enough. Now is not a time to argue; especially a topic like that."

"We're truly damned," he whimpered softly. Louder, he asked, "Anything else?"

"She waited almost two weeks before putting him in the sun. She said the smell had become unbearable, and she felt certain by then that he wasn't coming back. She'd tried to feed him repeatedly, but it didn't seem to change anything."

The rest of the ride passed in near-total silence. Shortly before sunrise, they pulled into the garage of the home Stephanie had mentioned. The house was a large, furnished, three-story home with an attached three-car garage. Stephanie got the window blockers out of the trunk. A second trip back to the car was made to retrieve Lawrence. She laid him on a bed and took the room next door for herself after blocking the windows of both rooms.

Lady stayed in Lawrence's room. Mac took up his position at the foot of Stephanie's bed.

Three minutes before the sun rose, Mac sniffed the air, detecting a salty, mildly coppery odor, very faint. An almost silent sound revealed the source and cause of the scent. In the two minutes remaining before sunrise, he stood up and walked up the mattress to the head of the bed. As he lay down, he snuggled up close against Stephanie. He was not at all surprised to feel her thin arms wrap tightly around him, nor to feel her wet tears as she buried her face in his fur.

CHAPTER TWENTY FIVE

"You're awake!"

Sara was sitting up in her bed, an empty breakfast tray pushed to the side. "I came out of it around midnight, and I've had no rest since. Although, since I've apparently been asleep for a week, I can't see why I'm still tired at all." She smiled weakly. "It's good to see you again. I heard you've been by almost every day. Thank you."

"Well, I've never been that patient, and I wanted that second date you promised."

Her smile broadened. "You're sweet. Look, Jamon, I'm glad to see you for another reason. I told the investigators what I could, but I left out some of the stranger stuff. Even leaving out the really off-the-wall stuff, they still don't believe me. They think I'm blanking part of it out, or something. They're absolutely certain that several people were involved in the attack. I've been waiting to tell you what really happened. I know you'd understand and believe me after what you've experienced yourself." Her eyes were almost pleading in her hope that he, at least, would believe in what she had to say. Someone needed to tell her she wasn't crazy; her tale was enough that she almost doubted her own sanity.

"I've already been working on it. The guy with the animals, Lawrence, is finally dead for real. I'm still working on the guy with his face half-eaten away. He was the other guy, right?"

"Jamon, the guy with the animals, your man Lawrence, I presume, was *helping*. I don't think he's as bad as you think he is; nor are the animals. Please, let me tell you exactly what I saw."

* * *

"I'll say one thing about being a vampire: jetlag no longer has any meaning. When the sun comes out, it's all taken care of!" Stephanie's cheer was forced, but it was better than perpetual doom and gloom. She, Mac and Lady were sitting on the floor in Lawrence's bedroom. Bandenarii's book was open in the middle of their huddle. Lady was skimming through the pages, looking for the writings concerning Premetamorphic Malaise.

"Here it is," Lady announced to Mac. Mac was dutifully relaying Lady's words to Stephanie. They'd gathered in Lawrence's room 'just in case'. 'Just in case' of what, none of them could have answered with any degree of certainty; nonetheless, all of them felt better being near Lawrence.

"Dr. Bandenarii came to the same conclusion we reached about it being caused by 'deviant feeding' - that's how he puts it. But get this: 'The vampire who has passed this stage is forever restricted from the pleasure of taking life with his blood when feeding.' He's talking about Lawrence's small sickness two hundred years ago. 'Once the two hundred year sickness has passed, any feeding in which the affected vampire kills his prey will see the vampire's own death within a fortnight. I have seen no way around this most aggravating obstacle.' Fortnight? Who actually uses that word? Umm... yammer, yammer, yammer. He goes on listing all the symptoms we've seen. He talks about all his experiments in reversing the process, none of which apparently succeeded. Gah. Some of these things he tried...he was one disturbed blood-sucker.

"Let's see...ah. He says that true death actually happens after thirteen nights, and theorizes that any cure must be administered on the last evening, the thirteenth."

"How many nights has it been so far?" Stephanie asked. "My hurried trip threw off my time-sense a bit, with following the sun so much."

"This is just the third night," Mac replied.

Lady was still reading. "Whoa. It says here a stake through the heart would kill him instantly. We definitely need to keep Psycho Sandoval away. I'm not too sure about that cop, either."

"Does it tell how to fix it? How to save him?" Mac asked impatiently.

"According to this, the good doctor himself never succeeded, but he 'gave the final use to the last of his test subjects' before he was able to test his last theory. 'Gave the final use.' I guess he means he killed the last of his test subjects with one of his demented experiments." She slid the page with a paw to flip it. "Hm. He lists his last theory. I guess he was killed before he got another subject to test it on. If we wanna try this, we're going to need our useless cop friend. He'll need to...let's see... oh. Damn."

*   *   *

It had been three nights since he faced off against the killer vampire, Sandoval, in Ms. Stephanie Roberson's basement vampire haven. For the last two days, every time he thought of Lawrence, he felt a gentle tugging, an urge to move in a certain direction. Tonight, he decided to see what would happen if he submitted to this easy pull. He had a good idea that he already knew the answer to that, but a theory was little more than a guess until it was tested.

A half hour of driving took him to a newer residential development just outside of Waukesha. He circled for about ten minutes in the car to get a precise fix on where he was being pulled. He stopped in front of an expensive looking three story house.

He considered going in, but it would be another illegal entry, and he didn't want to push the vampire Stephanie too far. He was not yet ready to slay her, either; she'd saved him - or at least, hadn't killed him. And, according to Sara, Lawrence and his associates might not be so bad. He hadn't yet decided on that score.

He wasn't about to be invited in, either; it was just after two in the afternoon.

He found himself halfway up the front walkway, staring at a window on the second floor, before he realized it. Perhaps Lawrence wasn't *quite* dead.

Enough of this mumbo-jumbo, he thought as he returned to his Chevy. As he fitted the seatbelt around him, his hand absently ran over his shirt across the lightly puckered, pink scars on his midsection. Sara was fascinated by the rapid healing he was exhibiting. She liked to speculate about what could be done in hospitals if they could reproduce it. Over his protestations, she'd run every test she had available. Not all the results had returned yet, but she was starting to agree: it was simply magic. Nothing they'd be able to reproduce with technology.

He noted the address of the house and drove off.

*   *   *

Five nights later, Sara knocked on his door. He answered the door talking on his cell phone. "Just let me finish this call and we'll be out of here," he requested, covering the receiver with his thumb. Into the phone, he protested, "But I don't even *believe* in that stuff! I'm Jewish! Didn't Mac tell you about my failure with the cross? Well, it doesn't make any sense to me - in fact, it seems rather dangerous for him...Okay, okay... No, I'll do it...Yes, I'm sure. Alright. Bye."

He hung up and gave the wide-eyed Sara a kiss. "Was that him? The vampire?" she asked excitedly. She thought meeting real vampires was the coolest thing, with the exception of Sandoval. She positively adored Mac and Lady. She was eager for a chance to talk to them herself. Jamon kept putting off her request; with Sandoval possibly lurking about, it was too dangerous. He still wasn't sure how he felt about Stephanie or the animals, either. After all, they may not kill, but they still preyed on those he was sworn to protect. Stephanie protested they did no harm, but it seemed wrong to him - else, why their aversion to religious regalia? Besides, anyone mixed up with Lawrence got an automatic black mark in Jamon's book. He sighed. "No, it wasn't him; it was her, the female vampire."

"The black lady you told me about?"

"Black *vampire*, yes."

"What'd she want?"

"Well, first, she finally explained what the deal was with Lawrence."

"And?" Sara prompted.

As they left his apartment behind, Jamon described the conversation he'd had with Stephanie. She had finally come clean with him, explaining most of the details of Lawrence's condition. At the end of his monologue, he asked,

"You're Catholic, right, Sara?"

"Well, I was raised Catholic. I haven't been to Mass in a couple years."

"Good enough. I need your help getting something."

"Sure babe."

"And, could you explain something to me?"

"Anything, babe," she said with a smile.

"Tell me about Transubstantiation."

*   *   *

"I can't believe I just lied to a priest," Sara lamented semi-solemnly as she got in the old Chevy.

"You got it, though?"

"Yeah. I told him my grandmother was too sick to come, and that I would administer communion for her. That, and I'm sure the $500 donation helped." She snickered.

"What?" he asked curiously.

"I just find the thought of a vampiress donating $500 to the Catholic Church amusing. I mean, it'd be like a career criminal donating money to the police retirement fund." She giggled again. "$500 is a lot for a little bit of wine and some bread, if you look at it like that."

Jamon had to smile. "Yeah. Cute." He'd not smiled all day. Tonight was it: the thirteenth night since Lawrence went into his coma, or whatever it was. He'd been brooding about it all day, warring with himself over what was right. Sara thought it was great that they were saving a vampire's life. He just hoped it didn't turn out to be a mistake.

It was already after dark. He was supposed to be at Stephanie's by now, but something had come up and Sara wasn't available as early as she'd planned. They'd wanted to be done with this errand in the afternoon, so Jamon could be at the new Munster Mansion by sunset, but it just didn't work out that way.

There was still plenty of night left. Jamon wasn't that concerned.

"You're sure you don't want me to come?"

Jamon mentally translated her request to, "Please can I come? Pretty please?"

"I still have to thank Mac and Lady for doing what they could at the precinct that night," she said.

"I've already given them your message, and you'll see them as soon as I know Sandoval is no longer a threat."

"You're sweet, but remember, I've got this," she protested, pulling her crucifix from under her shirt. "He can't get me as long as I have it."

"I know, doll, but..." He had no valid argument against this, so he let his sentence trail off.

"I know, you're just a big, macho sweetheart. Fine. But soon, promise me?"

"I promise."

They pulled up to Sara's apartment. "I'll walk you to your door," he offered.

She kissed his cheek. "I'm always so well protected with my brave man around," she swooned playfully.

* * *

The last ten nights had been the longest of Stephanie's life. She'd seen no sign of Sandoval, so it appeared he didn't know their new location. Jamon, on the other hand, had simply shown up one night ringing the doorbell. He explained how he'd found the place, which actually served to ease her mind a bit; it seemed to indicate that Lawrence was still alive somewhere behind those closed eyes. Otherwise, how could he be pulling his minion to himself?

Lady had stopped sleeping in Lawrence's room a week before. The odor of decayed flesh had gotten too much for her. Its potency was such that she tasted it without even drawing breath. The feeble air current within the room sent enough of the odor to her sensitive nose and mouth with no effort of her own. Mac could barely walk by the room without gagging. Nevertheless, at least twice a night he still checked on his master.

Lady was reading through the rest of Bandenarii's book, but it had told them little else of value at this point. Stephanie had bought a new computer for Mac and got it hooked up online. He'd been searching all over the internet, and had posted dozens of messages, but had also come up with nothing of value.

Between the two animals, Stephanie had felt almost useless. Mac and Lady were constantly searching for answers, using their skills to aid Lawrence. Stephanie had contributed nothing. Mac had empathized with her feelings without her even discussing them with him. One night when she was feeling particularly down, he'd explained to her that she was the reason any of them were alive at all; she'd supplied a place to live, twice, among other things.

That was of little consequence. She knew she wasn't doing enough.

She paced in front of the door, looking out its window for Jamon's car every third lap. He had called to tell her he'd be late. She was not happy about it, but there was little she could do. She couldn't exactly stroll into a church herself to get what they needed. According to the book, one of Lawrence's thrice bitten had to do the feeding, so they'd still need him anyway.

She'd been pacing for twenty minutes when she saw the splash of Jamon's headlights on the window. "Did you get it?" she asked anxiously, ushering him in.

He pulled a flask from his pocket. It was blued metal, like a gun's barrel, and had a filigreed cross emblazoned on it in gold. He ignored the involuntary flinch induced in Stephanie by the Christian holy symbol. "I got it. But I'm still not entirely sure why I should be concerned about whether or not Lawrence wakes up." He felt some pity at the despair that crossed Stephanie's face, but remained outwardly impassive at her concern. He had the public to think about.

"Look, Detective Schroeder, he may be a vampire, but remember that the reason he's in the position he's in is because he does *not* kill to feed, as opposed to standard practice among our kind. He has not killed in four hundred years. In fact, he is destined to make some significant changes; changes which will almost certainly improve the lot of humanity at the hands of vampire kind."

"Destined to make changes? What's all that?"

"You don't need the details. In fact, it's better if you don't know, but it's the reason Sandoval is trying to kill him. Lawrence is a good man."

"Fine. Let's get this over with." He still didn't know if he was making the right choice. Ultimately, if he decided Lawrence had to be destroyed, Jamon was confident in his own ability to do so. He could find Lawrence without trouble now, just by thinking of it. With his tools - the Star of David, holy water, silver bullets, and wooden stakes - he could destroy the nosferatu if the need arose. Jamon was fully armed that very moment, just in case he decided it was best to take such action tonight. He was sure the weapons would be able to destroy the animals as well.

He'd hate to have to kill Stephanie, though. She actually seemed like a good person. Vampire. He wasn't sure he could do it, unless she attacked someone first with killing intent.

Stephanie led Jamon up the stairs, stopping outside Lawrence's room. He was almost knocked back by the odor that billowed out as she opened the door. "How do you stand living with that smell?" He could barely get the words out, for fear of what might follow them up his throat. He gagged in his efforts to keep his stomach's contents down.

"We just don't breathe."

His smile froze half-formed as he realized she was serious. "Oh. You're sure he's not dead?" It sure smelled like he was. It smelled, in fact, like he'd died three weeks ago and had been putrefying in a warm, poorly-ventilated room.

"According to our sources, he will continue to decay until he's healed." She stopped in front of a casket situated next to the door of the large bedroom. A solid-looking coffin, it nevertheless lacked the refined styling of Stephanie's own, in the next room over. Even without hers for comparison, it was evident that Lawrence again rested in a budget box. Stephanie saw Jamon look the casket over. "I know it's not much of a casket, but we decided we would destroy it and get him a nice, new one when all this is over. It'd be too much to get the, ah, odor cleaned out of it." Actually, she was having a coffin specially made; one which was large enough for the two of them to rest comfortably. She'd commissioned a well-respected custom casket building shop for the project. When she'd asked, they'd informed her it was an unusual request, but not at all unheard of.

Stephanie lifted the half-lid covering Lawrence's upper body. Jamon had thought the odor already unbearable, but his shallow breathing did nothing to dissipate the rank odor that fountained up at him with the opening of the lid. He had been to crime scenes before - that was why he was familiar with the odor of decayed bodies - but nothing natural could create an odor such as this. It defied his powers of description. It seemed to take the very worst of rotting meat, burned flesh, curdled milk, and bloated corpses washed up on shore, and mix them in a sickening mishmash. It was too much for his already agitated stomach. He ran for the attached bathroom.

After emptying his stomach's contents and rinsing his mouth, he returned sedately to the room. Mac and Lady were sitting on the floor: Mac at the head, Lady at the foot of the coffin. Nobody commented on his embarrassing reaction. Nor could they blame him; he was only a mortal, forced to breathe. They would have fared no better were it not for their supernatural advantages. He'd steeled himself as well as one could expect against the anticipated odor, but nobody could have handled the stench that had billowed up at him.

Mac was obviously nervous, shifting his weight repeatedly from one front paw to the other. "Can we get this done?" he barked.

"Do you guys really believe this is the blood of Christ?" Jamon asked skeptically, holding the blued-metal flask up.

"We don't have the privilege of choosing what we believe," Stephanie asserted, a bit agitatedly. "That's why the Crucifix and the Star of David work equally well against us - it's the faith of the wielder. In this case, the Roman Catholics believe that when the bread and wine are blessed by a priest for communion, they actually *become* the body and blood of Christ. The priest's belief is what matters here, much like with holy water. What is in your flask, for all our purposes, is the actual blood of Christ."

"As you say." He stepped up to the coffin. He raised his flask as though making a toast. "This is the blood of Christ," he intoned solemnly before sipping the blessed wine within. Sara had told him that's how it was done in church. He turned to the casket. "This is the blood of Christ," he repeated for Lawrence's benefit.

He reached down. Ignoring the numerous festering sores, he applied pressure to Lawrence's chin, forcing open his mouth. He placed the flask next to Lawrence's lips and began to tilt the vessel; he would have to gently pour it into his mouth.

The large window opposite the casket on the north wall of the room shattered inward in a spray of glass. Jamon was protected from the flying shards by Stephanie; she'd been standing between him and the window. He knew she'd taken a lot of it instantly: her face betrayed the pain she felt. It struck him as odd for a moment; vampires being the immortal beasts that they are, he forgot that they could still feel the pain, even if it didn't kill them.

Past Stephanie, he could see a nightmare creature that could only be Sandoval land gracefully on the carpeted floor. The monster had jumped up to and through the second floor window. He appeared to be carrying something large. Jamon couldn't make out what it was: Stephanie's body and Sandoval's billowing cape concealed most of it from his sight.

Stephanie turned to face the attacker. Jamon could now see her back. His suspicions were confirmed. Her blouse and slacks had been shredded by the flying glass. Red slashes were visible on her dark flesh, marking her from her neck to her slim ankles. "Finish it, Jamon! We need Lawrence!" she shouted.

She crouched, ready to fight.

No longer concerned with neatness, Jamon rapidly upended the bottle, allowing almost half the contents to gurgle into Lawrence's mouth. He spun the cap back onto the bottle and set it in the coffin, freeing up his hands again.

He heard a loud crash. He looked up to see Stephanie picking herself up from inside the bathroom. The shattered door provided evidence of the force of the toss which had sent her through it.

He glanced back at Lawrence. There was no change. It appeared this experiment was a wash. In fact, he had probably destroyed whatever may have remained of Lawrence's life, feeding him such a powerful religious icon.

Jamon realized with surprise that neither animal had attacked. They were holding back for some reason, though both were ready to pounce, faces locked in the age-old animal expressions of aggression. Jamon began to reach for his Star of David. He pulled his eyes from the animals and turned away from the coffin. He forced his eyes up to the creature in front of him and saw why no more attacks had come. He dropped his groping hand, leaving his Star untouched.

Sandoval stood behind his hostage, a knife to her neck. Sara was terrified, her beautiful blue eyes shooting with panicked speed all about the room. She trembled as though standing naked in a winter storm. She was what Sandoval had been carrying as he jumped through the window.

With his other hand, the one not about to end Sara's mortal life, Sandoval pointed to Jamon, then the floor at his feet. Seeing the lack of comprehension on Jamon's face, he repeated his order. Jamon understood. He was to place his vampiric weaponry at Sandoval's feet. Without his special gear, he stood no chance against the immortal power of Sandoval. From what he'd seen of the amoral creature, Sandoval would have no problem dealing with the three young vampires present.

Sara squeaked a cry of fear and pain. Jamon's hesitation had given Sandoval an excuse to pull the gleaming blade tighter against her pale neck. He saw blood where the blade had parted her skin. In a moment of visual acuity, he could see the pulse of her carotid artery beating against the skin of her neck. It was directly under the knife's path. "Alright, you win!" he said as he began to remove his gear.

First to go was the holy water, which Jamon kept in another flask. Sandoval eyed Jamon closely as he placed the metal container on the floor. The detective stepped back and watched as Sandoval forced Sara to stoop down with him. He picked up the flask and opened it very cautiously with one hand. One step back took him to the jagged window. The contents of the flask went gurgling down to the ground outside as Sandoval upended it at arm's length. Now empty, the flask was tossed out as well. The stakes Jamon then laid out were smashed single-handedly into splinters. Most of the fragments were scooped up and joined the holy water on the ground outside, useless even if retrieved. The gun with the silver bullets received a bent barrel.

Jamon considered brandishing the Star of David, the last weapon of his divine arsenal. He was well aware of how helpless it rendered the undead. He didn't think Sandoval would be incapacitated quickly or fully enough to save Sara's life, however. It would be too easy and quick for Sandoval to carry out his threat. Jamon would not, could not, gamble with Sara's life. Holding it by the chain, he lifted the Star of David over his head and tossed it to the floor. When Sandoval finished with it, it was an unrecognizable mangle of twisted metal.

Sandoval's gaze stayed on Jamon. His one eye hadn't left the officer at all as he disarmed himself. Also in the abomination's field of view were the animals. Jamon could only presume the beast was listening intently to Stephanie's movements. His knife didn't waver from Sara's throat. "That's it! That's all I've got!" Jamon protested. To prove his point, he lifted his shirt and raised his pant legs, showing the ghoulish figure that he had nothing hidden.

It was only at this point that he realized Sandoval had his lower jaw back. It seemed impossible for it to have grown back so quickly. Of course, it was difficult to accept that it could grow back at all. But that was the only explanation that fit the facts before him. He'd seen the detached jawbone sitting on a coffee table last week when he'd come by. He'd asked about it, and it turned out that Lady had kept it. She'd been trying to convince Mac to keep it as a trophy, or at least bury it in the

back yard or something. Mac was not so keen on the idea. Jamon doubted Sandoval's new jaw was fake; it looked exactly as Jamon remembered
it from Stephanie's basement.

Amazing as this revelation was, it had little bearing on the situation
at hand. Sandoval seemed to accept that Jamon was now unarmed and
contemptuously shoved Sara aside. The force of Sandoval's shove propelled her out the room's open door and into the hallway beyond. She
cushioned her crash into the opposite wall with her raised hands.

Feeling helpless, unarmed in the midst of such powerful creatures,
Jamon looked around the room. "Go," Mac barked at him.

Stephanie, standing in the bathroom's doorway, nodded her agreement.

Jamon stepped cautiously toward the door. As he stood between the
room and hallway, he watched as the two sides of the coming conflict
eyed each other. What chilled him was that Sandoval's eye held no fear,
not even a tinge of concern. Only confidence. Sandoval, like Jamon,
knew how this battle would play out. The three young vampires stood no
chance against his aged power.

"Run," Jamon whispered to Sara. She took a step but paused when she
saw that Jamon was not directly behind her. "I'll be following. This is way
out of my league now. Go. I'll follow soon."

There was no time for a lingering, romantic embrace. This in mind,
Sara stepped up to deliver a quick but firm kiss on Jamon's lips that conveyed everything he knew she wanted to say. With one last, apprehensive
look towards the open door, she ran down the hall for the stairs.

A loud crash brought Jamon's attention back to the bedroom. An epic
battle between good and evil? No. A one-sided fight between evil and
notquite-as-bad? Probably closer to the truth. He glanced in. Sandoval
had not moved from where he'd been standing, but Stephanie had been
smashed against the outside wall, leaving a heavy imprint where she'd hit.
As Jamon watched, both animals were thrown across the room, smashing against Lawrence's coffin, almost knocking it off its stand. Only the
fact that the coffin was pressed up almost to the wall kept it upright. The
impact merely wobbled it and dropped its lid closed.

Several more assaults were launched. Sandoval easily stood his ground,
seeming to toy with the trio, occasionally slicing someone with his knife.
What remained of his cheeks, the remnants above where his lower jaw-

bone gleamed whitely, was pulled up in what might have been a smile on someone with a whole face.

Mac was the only one to make notable progress, but it cost him. His fur was already caked with his own blood by the time he was again able to pull off Sandoval's jaw. He'd tried the same maneuver as in the basement, several times, but Sandoval kept knocking him aside. This time, Mac had acted as if he were going for a leg. Just as Sandoval kicked out, Mac leaped straight up to latch on to the bony jaw and tore it off. The muscles once attached to it could be seen dangling uselessly and twitching as they tried to move a bone no longer there.

Infuriated, Sandoval snatched Mac out of the air on the mutt's next attack and threw him against the wall. Following immediately behind him was the knife Sandoval loosed. Even as Mac thudded into the wall, the trailing knife sank into him. With a piercing yelp, Mac was securely attached to the wall.

His position was such that he was unable to free himself. The brilliant, razorsharp blade, which entered his chest from the right side, cut through to pin him sideways against the wall. The silver composition of the blade made any movement all the more painful. Mac passed out.

Sandoval didn't even seem to be trying. The fight was decided before it had begun.

CHAPTER TWENTY SIX

Mac was out of the fight. Lady's legs appeared to be broken. Stephanie was barely able to move. There was nothing Jamon could do. He'd been watching the battle from the doorway, racking his brain to come up with some miraculous, last-minute, save-everything sort of plan.

Nothing. He was a mortal, with not even a regular pistol to use against this timeless beast. Sadly, regretfully, he turned and started down the corridor. He knew that as soon as Stephanie was completely incapacitated, Sandoval would finish them all off.

He'd taken three steps before he felt it. In the part of his mind that felt the pull toward Lawrence before, he felt a building...something. Rapidly building. A feeling of power. Light. Life. Strength. Maybe he hadn't killed Lawrence. But if he hadn't killed him, why hadn't he woken up? And what was this he was now feeling?

He chose. He could still run if he had to...he hoped. He had to know. He stepped back to the door and peeked in. He was not a coward; years of police work had taught him that caution was simple prudence. Unnecessary risks were just that - unnecessary. He therefore remained as unobtrusive as possible, ready to make a hasty retreat as soon as needed.

Sandoval was leaning over Stephanie, who was slumped against a wall. He was slapping her with such force that it would have broken a mortal's bones and possibly snapped her neck. Sandoval looked up as Jamon peeked in, ceasing his torture of Stephanie. For a moment Jamon thought the halffaced monster was walking towards him, but he instead went to stand before Lawrence's coffin. In the hand he hadn't been slapping Stephanie with, he brandished a knife. It was time for him to complete the task and remove Lawrence's head. He reached out to open the coffin and reveal the helpless vampire within.

To Jamon, it felt like his head cracked open. He thought he heard a large explosion, but like the flash of light he also thought he saw, he was not sure if the source was external or whether it came from his own reeling mind. Along with the rush of euphoria he felt and the accompanying, countering pain, it was all too much. He passed out.

* * *

Where she lay, she could see the whole room. She wasn't sure that she liked that. From what she could see, everything had gone to shit. All four of her legs were broken. That was actually the least painful of her injuries. Wounds inflicted by silver weapons *burned*. Lady had heard of pouring salt in a wound. She imagined that it was probably similar, in the way that letting a match burn down to one's fingers was similar to complete bodily immolation. The silver wounds from the last fight had only just healed over the last couple days; not only did they burn, injuries caused by silvered weapons healed with near-mortal sluggishness.

She debated whether Mac was the lucky one or not. He'd fallen unconscious after Sandoval had pinned him to the wall with a knife.

Stephanie was holding up better than Lady would have initially given her credit for. She was topless: her blouse and brassier, already in tatters, had been torn off in some of the earlier scuffling. She was covered with slashes from the knife. Lady believed Stephanie may have taken more abuse than the animals put together. She'd reached her body's limit, though. Sandoval's slaps were not knocking her out, but she was dazed into inaction. She was directly on the perilous edge of consciousness, but didn't seem inclined to lose it completely. That she was aware at all was a tribute to her sheer tenacity.

And that stupid cop still hadn't left! There was nothing he could do - all his weapons were destroyed. But there he was, peeking around the door. *The asshole probably wants to make sure none of us make it out so he only has Sandoval to kill later. Bastard.*

Sandoval finished abusing Stephanie and stood up. He began walking to the coffin.

She heard it. The sound had been building for some seconds, but she only took notice of it now. A growing sound, like a turbine engine winding up. Perhaps not that high pitched, but holding the same promise of power. She looked around for the source of the sound. It might have been originating in her own head, but she wasn't yet sure. It was hard to tell. Her gaze paused on Sandoval, who held his knife at the ready as he prepared to open Lawrence's casket. He seemed oblivious to the rising noise.

Out of the corner of her eye, Lady saw Jamon's eyes roll up as he fell to the floor. Lady did not pass out. She saw the whole thing.

Besides the sound, the first thing was the light.

The bedroom had been lit enough for the mortal detective to see well enough to do his job. The light that shot out from the joins in the lid was as bright as a spotlight streaking its beams across the night sky. Unlike beams of a spotlight, they were wide and narrow rays, coming from the places where the lid met the coffin or the two halves of the lid met each other. They were like blades of light, cutting through the room, yet damaging nothing.

She decided at this point the noise was strictly in her head. At the same time, she knew it came from an external source. She prayed that external source was Lawrence.

Sandoval paused in the act of reaching for the lid, unsure about the light emanating from the casket.

The box exploded.

The room was suddenly a vampiric death trap. Slivers and stakes and everything in between rained out in every direction. The shards of wood seemed to fill the air for a moment. Lady felt one the size of a pencil stab her in the right thigh. None seemed to hit Mac, still pinned to the wall about five feet up. Stephanie was struck by several, but none were so dangerously accurate as to strike her heart.

By the energy of the explosion and the force of several dozen wood shards, Sandoval was driven back. He looked to Lady like the voodoo doll of an overly vengeful Houngan - wood slivers of all size stood out all over him. He was still standing, so his luck appeared to have carried him through this storm as well.

What Lady saw as the hail of wood chips died made her question if she'd taken too many blows to the head tonight. Lawrence was standing - no, floating - above the remains of his coffin. His very skin seemed to glow. The dark Armani suit Stephanie had dressed him in seemed better than new, and was rippling almost as though it bore its own power. She could swear she felt a powerful wind coming from his direction, but her fur was unruffled. Lawrence's eyes were still closed. His toes, in their wingtip shoes, pointed to the ground as though he stood on tiptoe. His arms were slightly extended laterally from his sides, palms inward, hands relaxed. All this, and he hovered perhaps eighteen inches off the ground. He *was* power.

Slowly, he dropped to the floor. As his toes came in contact with the ground, his eyes snapped open, instantly focused on Sandoval. Lawrence's *silver* eyes. His *angry*, silver eyes.

Sandoval charged.

Moving once again with the speed a five hundred year old vampire should exhibit, Lawrence casually blocked the knife Sandoval swung at his neck. He shoved the mutilated vampire back against the far wall. Lawrence stepped forward, out of the rubble. Sandoval sensed the power flowing from Lawrence and advanced cautiously. Lawrence looked every part of the dignified, ancient vampire: immaculately groomed, pressed suit (no longer rippling, though Lady still felt the nonexistent wind of power spreading from Lawrence), handsome, dark features, radiating the energy of the vitalized undead.

Sandoval looked the monster he was: one eye no more than a yawning cavity; the other rendered a mockery with its half-detached, flapping lid. Holy water had scoured his face all about, including the almost rectangular patch of bone showing through where his forehead once was. His mouth could no longer be called as such; with his entire lower jaw removed, all that remained were his upper teeth, half-melted upper lip, and what appeared as torn flesh leading back to his throat from where his mandible was forcibly removed. Disconnected muscles still hung, twitching, from underneath the skin. One could see the beginnings of his esophagus behind the stunted, melted remains of his tongue.

Like Sandoval, Lawrence spoke not at all. Lady, on the other hand, was a veritable chatterbox, filling Lawrence's mind with the events of the past two weeks as the two vampires stared each other down. She could only presume he heard her - he gave no indication, either verbally or mentally, that he had. After her quick summation, she ran out of steam and watched the two nemeses watching each other.

Lawrence made the first move. He leaped forward, reaching for Sandoval's neck. Sandoval, 100 years older and just as fast, grabbed Lawrence's hand before it connected and gave it an ugly slice with the knife he still held.

Lawrence's follow-up attack was a feint. Rather than the punch Sandoval attempted to block, Lawrence managed to knock the dangerous blade from Sandoval's hand. It went spinning out the fragmented window into the dark, moonless night. Sandoval had come prepared for such losses. He reached for a third knife from his belt, but snapped it back into its leather sheath. He reached instead for the sword which had been riding at his hip. It was a long, slender blade. As it slid with a ringing hiss from its sheath Lady could see that it, too, was worked entirely in silver.

Lawrence was forced back by the menacing, flickering point of the sword.

He stumbled, falling backwards onto his hands in the shattered remains of his cheap coffin. He seemed to bounce back up like a ball, rising almost the moment his hands touched ground, almost mocking gravity itself.

He stood only to receive a long gash slantwise down his chest and abdomen. His own upward momentum imparted half the damage, his rise running the sword down the length of his body. He moved back as he rose to avoid the worst of it, but through the slashed suit Lady could make out a couple of ribs. Lawrence could not win bare-handed against this centuriesold swordsman. The only other weapon Lady could see in the room was the knife pinning Mac to the wall.

Movement from an unexpected quarter. Lady watched as Stephanie rose to her feet. Whether she was doing that much better or managing by sheer force of will, Stephanie's movements were rock-steady. And she was quiet. Sandoval, his attention on Lawrence, his back to Stephanie, appeared oblivious to the woman's reanimation. Doubtless he had written her off after the beating he'd given her. She was made of sterner stuff than the brute would believe. Lawrence must have seen his love rise to her feet, but did not so much as blink to give her away. His attention remained riveted on Sandoval and the deadly, dancing blade.

Was that even Lawrence? Who knew what might have happened to his mind while he lay for thirteen nights, dead for all purposes? Perhaps the wine, said by the Catholics to be the actual blood of Christ, had done something horrible to him? He had not said a word, verbally or telepathically, since his amazing reviviscence. He had not so much as acknowledged his companions, those friends of his who had sat with him, guarded him, *saved* him, since his withdrawal from the world of the living and undead. There was no way to tell what those silver eyes held behind them - surely they showed none of the compassion Lady knew him to possess, and there'd been no reaction to her earlier monologue or Stephanie's rising. Through the link, Lady could feel nothing but anger; a cool, controlled anger. Was it him?

That was something to worry about later.

Stephanie stood directly behind Sandoval. His elbow cocked back as he prepared for another sword thrust. Stephanie slid her arm through the crook of his elbow, catching it behind his back. At the same time, she grabbed his other arm, pulling it back as well.

In an eye blink, Lawrence stepped up. The flask containing the sacramental wine appeared in his hand. He had picked it up when he'd fallen amidst the rubble of the coffin. A flick of his thumb sent the screw-cap spinning. So fast did it spin that its momentum sent it three inches into the air at the end of its threads. He placed the small spout directly into the exposed top of Sandoval's throat. Stephanie could not hold the elder creature for long; Lawrence acted with swift, sure movements. His right hand reached up to squeeze the open throat, effectively sealing it around the mouth of the flask. Smoothly, his left hand crushed the metal flask.

With nowhere else to go, the blessed wine - transubstantiated by Catholic ceremony and faith into the holy blood of Christ - was forced down Sandoval's throat. The assassin now knew fear. He knew a fear surpassing even his centuries old phobia of holy water. It showed on the remains of his scarred, beaten face. Stephanie and Lawrence both stepped away from the terrified and doomed vampire.

The crumpled, empty flask fell to the carpeted floor. Sandoval lurched; his back hunched, his neck moving his head forward like a chicken; his attempts to induce vomiting failed to yield results.

The sound which followed was not what is normally associated with an explosion. By contrast, Lawrence's coffin had let a somehow satisfying, though muffled, boom. The only sound that accompanied Sandoval's last moment was similar to that of a large quantity of cooked noodles dropping to a tiled floor; an organic, wet, almost sticky sound. Certainly nothing to draw the attention of close neighbors or people passing by on the sidewalk outside; certainly not what one might have expected to accompany such a violent reaction.

The spontaneous separation of Sandoval's body parts was more to what is expected to accompany an explosion. Unrecognizable chunks of meat from various unknown regions of his body flew about the room, a fleshy recreation of the exploding coffin earlier witnessed. The odd piece would have a strip of fabric clinging to it, but most of the clothes were just as shredded as his organs. Some extremities, or parts thereof, remained intact. Later on, while cleaning, they would find an intact finger here, a foot there. Random pieces, reminders that the wet mess of inanimate tissue and bone had once been a dangerous, living creature.

Surprisingly, the remnants of his head retained cohesion, though it still lacked its lower jaw. As they were being doused with sprays of blood and various internal tissues, the three witnesses watched in morbid fascination as the head rose straight up, bumped lightly into the ceiling, and dropped back to the floor. The unnatural explosion had imparted no spin to the head; for its entire trip up and back down it did not gimbal in any direction. Only on landing did it finally fall forward.

Nobody spoke. Nobody moved. The only sound was a soft splat as a piece of Sandoval dropped to the floor from where it had stuck to the ceiling.

"I demand a regular bath. No way will I be grooming myself of this mess."

Lawrence turned to Lady with a raised eyebrow. "Is she saying something?" Stephanie asked him. Her voice was high, almost cracking. Lawrence relayed Lady's comment, his first words since rising. Stephanie began to laugh. "Sure. Bathroom's right there!" She laughed wildly before collapsing to the ground in sobs of endured terror, exhaustion, pain, and relief.

* * *

Lawrence was very nearly overwhelmed. Where to start? Stephanie needed comfort; Lady was lying directly on her broken legs; Mac, still unconscious, was pinned to the wall. And there was a familiar cop passed out in the hall. Stephanie got a kiss and a promise. Lawrence also draped his mildly slashed suit coat around her to help preserve her modesty, covering her bare torso. Lady's legs were reorganized to the greatest amount of comfort possible under the circumstances. Gently, the blade was removed and Mac was laid down next to Lady. A quick check confirmed Jamon had a steady, firm pulse and was breathing normally. As he was reclining the detective into a more dignified position, Lawrence saw Sara pop back up the stairs.

She looked suspiciously at Lawrence. "What's wrong with Jamon?"

Lawrence explained that Jamon had simply passed out as she confirmed his state of health for herself.

The detective woke up about five minutes later. In the trashed bedroom, the four vampires were huddled together in a corner, though Mac had still not reawoken. They were silent, taking comfort from the mere presence and survival of each other, basking in the love shared after the deadly ordeal they had all completed together.

In the hall, Sara held Jamon's hand. "Let's go home. Lawrence said it was okay, and asked us to come back tomorrow."

Shaking his head at the mess in the room, Jamon put his arm around Sara and walked out of the house.

CHAPTER TWENTY SEVEN
(EPILOGUE)

Detective Schroeder didn't return the next evening. Lawrence had called and set the appointment back a week.

Instead of meeting with the detective, they recuperated and discussed the events of the last two weeks.

Mac had woken up some hours after the attack, but neither he nor Lady were in condition to hunt for the next couple of days. Between the numerous silver-inflicted cuts and sheer quantity of damage done to them in general, they didn't move much on their own for the first two days, though they both got the bath Lady had asked for. Lawrence and Stephanie caught a few cats each night for them to feed on. They also carried the convalescing animals to the new apartment Stephanie wound up renting, as hers had no vacancies. They decided to sell both houses. They had no way of knowing if other assassins, or the Council, had been informed of their locations by Sandoval. "I'd been planning to sell both places anyway," Stephanie claimed. Lawrence didn't know if she spoke the truth, or gave him a white lie to ease his feelings of guilt over causing her so much trouble.

She had no other vacant properties, so she selected a moderately-priced apartment to serve until more solid plans were made.

Lawrence was pleased and impressed the first time he heard Mac communicate with Stephanie. "That may well prove to be a useful ability."

"You don't seem all that surprised, Lawrence. This is my Calling, right? It's a unique ability, isn't it?" Mac asked him.

"Well, Mac, truth is, I rather expected at least one of you to acquire your

Calling sooner or later. I have found over the years that about half my animals wound up getting a Calling within their first six months."

"And you didn't mention this *why?*" Lady asked.

"Well, I didn't want to build up false hope, or watch you two make... ill-advised attempts to force your Calling to manifest. After all, it's evident you're already jealous of Mac's, and almost overly eager to find yours."

"You are quite mistaken, sir," she sniffed.

"Oh. Well, my apologies then, Lady." He hid his smile behind his hand as he coughed lightly.

"Accepted," she granted regally, failing to notice his obvious subterfuge. "Lawrence, what's with your eyes? I swear they were silver when you...uh, woke up yesterday."

"Yes, Lady. You are correct. Of course, I haven't seen it myself, but Stephanie mentioned it to me. It seems as though they change back to silver when I'm hunting. My fangs grow and my eyes turn silver."

"Your fangs?"

"Didn't you notice, Lady?" Mac asked. "His fangs are gone." Lawrence smiled to show her. Mac addressed Lawrence. "You say they grow when you're hunting? I figured that'd have to be the case. Can you show us?"

"I really don't have that degree of control over it. It's kind of automatic, almost a reflex."

"Why do your eyes silver over?" Mac asked.

"No idea. But, I think I'm feeling better, even more powerful, than I did before I got sick."

"Can you still fly?" Lady asked.

"Stephanie asked the same thing. She says I levitated?" Stephanie and Lady both nodded. "I don't remember it at all. I certainly can't do it now - I tried when Stephanie suggested it earlier tonight."

"I think it's obvious we were wrong," Stephanie said, marginally altering the topic. "Premetamorphic refers not to a changing virus, but a change you were to experience yourself."

"My thoughts exactly," Mac barked. "Which would also confirm that Jamon didn't catch anything from him; his odd traits are due to his three bites."

"What was that?" Lawrence asked.

"Oh. Yeah. That one kinda slipped our mind. Been so much going on," Lady noted. She proceeded to fill him in on how he'd apparently bit Jamon three times, and the resultant symptoms he'd been exhibiting.

"Hm. I guess that could have been him. I certainly remember that night. It's the first time I started to notice my weakening. The two gunshot wounds pressed the evening pretty firmly into my memory, as well. Yeah, that must have been him."

"Bit of a coincidence, isn't it? Just happening to bite him three times?" Stephanie asked.

"Well, I've often said coincidence walks in the very footprints of the undead. Most of it is to be expected, though. After all, even with significant odds against any given event occurring, after several hundred years, it's quite possible, even likely, that off chance will come up. Consider the old adage of a million monkeys on a million typewriters churning out Shakespeare after a million years. In our long lives, we are likely to encounter odd circumstances."

He pressed his fingers together. "Besides which, who's to say it's coincidence?"

"What do you mean by that?" Stephanie asked.

"Well, have you never wondered who put those Dreams in your head? Who it is that knows what will happen and gives you a peek at it? Have you ever given thought that perhaps there is a divine power behind it all?"

Lady snorted inelegantly. "You're not going all religious on us now, are you, Lawrence? Please tell me your metamorphosis was not just an elaborate way for you to be 'born-again'! Show me God, and I'll show you a divinely vain sadist!"

Lawrence turned the full power of his gaze on Lady. "One should, on occasion, exhibit restraint in what one mocks. Anyone could be listening, including the potentially divine subject of derision." His features softened. "But no, I am not 'born-again'. I'm not going to go on some religious crusade. I can't even step foot in a place of worship - I'm sure that much hasn't changed with my 'metamorphosis'. That is not to say, however, that I don't believe in at least the possibility of a higher power."

"How could you not believe. Lady? Look at what affect divine implements have on us!" Mac argued. "Crosses, holy water, all that. And you told me about Sandoval's reaction to the blessed wine."

"It's all based on the will of the human," Lady countered. "After all, there can only be one 'true' religion - only one whose beliefs are actually correct - if any are. Look at the Jewish faith as opposed to the Christians. Totally different, but a cross wielded by a Christian works just as well as a Star of David wielded by a Jew. They can't both be right. Obviously, the stuff works because people believe they'll work, so they *will* them to. That's why the cross didn't work for Jamon. He didn't really believe in its holiness, so it didn't have the power of his will behind it. Here's another example. You told me people used to believe that seeds scattered on the ground would slow or stop a following vampire. Perhaps it did work, but no longer does for the simple reason that people don't *believe* it will."

"Your theory has holes in it, Lady," Mac began.

"Actually, Mac, any theory, pro or con, has holes right now. We just don't know." Lawrence said.

"Take the sacramental wine. The blood of Christ brought Lawrence back, but punished Sandoval. It had to have divine thought behind it to know who was good and who was evil."

"Enough, Mac. Let it rest. Besides which, if I were to drink the Catholic's blessed sacramental wine now, I'm rather sure I would end up just like Sandoval."

"Do you have any other abilities we don't know about? Any new ones coming?" Stephanie asked, changing the subject.

"This is as new to me as to you guys. I have no idea if anything more will happen, but it is possible, I guess." He thought for a moment. "Flying would be rather handy. You're sure I levitated?"

"Yes, you did. Lawrence, what are we going to do about the Council? I don't think they're going to stop until you're dead," Lady returned to practical issues.

"Well, I was thinking of simply telling them in a letter or e-mail or something that I simply don't *want* to overthrow them. That I have neither the intent nor the desire to do so, much less the ability."

"Yeah, that'll work," Mac said dryly.

"Lawrence, I'm not so sure about that, either. Over the years, I've had several Dreams..."

"Oh, god, not you too? You've Dreamed of me taking it over?" Lawrence asked.

Stephanie held her hands out from her sides and shrugged.

"Well, I'm going to try it anyway. Honestly, I don't think it will work, either. Plus, I've got Phil to warn me if they're planning something."

Lady sneezed, somehow sending an image of derision or scorn at Lawrence's last statement.

"Yes, Lady? I take it you have something negative to say?"

"You act like I'm the resident pessimist or something. What I was thinking," she continued, oblivious to her three friends nodding, "is that Phil may not be entirely trustworthy. Hear me out," she said, overriding Mac's objections. Mac was also translating for Stephanie. "How did Sandoval find us in the first place? Lawrence had been hiding successfully for years. Freakface came into town rather shortly after Phil left. Suspiciously soon after, I'd say. And Sandoval found us at Stephanie's pretty soon after we gave Phil the house-phone number. With a phone number, it's not hard to find an address.

Right, Mac?"

"Yes," Mac reluctantly agreed.

"And there's no need to mention a rather solid and significant history of betrayal. But I will anyway. He's a traitorous, two-faced, sniveling, conniving, greedy, back-stabbing, rat-loving bastard, and undeserving of our trust."

"Maybe it would be best to be cautious in our dealings with Phil," Stephanie decided.

* * *

"He's dead."

Cold stone walls. Ancient stone table. Flickering, lonely candle-flame. Grim, eternally cold men.

"How do we know?" the junior member, Candiano, asked.

A single sheet of paper spun towards the center of the large, round table with a practiced flick of the wrist. "Lawrence Hermanson himself had the audacity to throw it in our face. At the same time, he claimed he has no interest in acquiring the power of the Council," Berengol sneered.

"He can't be serious," Candiano protested.

"Of course he's not serious, you simpleton!"

The dark figure, still aloof from the rest, quietly cleared his throat. Berengol lowered his head in acknowledgement of his faux pas, his display of emotion.

Lord Rabus, at the other end of the table, spoke. "It is evident we need to step this project up. Call in the Seekers."

* * *

Four days later, Jamon stopped by, as promised.

"I didn't need the address, you know," he said accusingly to Lawrence. Jamon had taken the farthest seat from him in the new apartment's living room. It was evident he would have preferred one of the more spacious rooms of the prior two houses, affording him even more space between Lawrence and himself.

"How's Sara?" Stephanie asked, seeking to ease the tension.

"Much better, especially since Sandoval's death. I must apologize, by the way. It appears as though I inadvertently led him to you that last time. He must have been following me, which is how he got to Sara." His face reddened in anger as he mentioned Sara's straits of that evening. "He must have planted a tracking device on my car. Sara says he was using some sort of tracker-locator to find me after he snatched her."

"How did he get her?" Stephanie asked. "Didn't she have her crucifix on her?"

"Yeah. He snuck up on her and yanked the chain off before she could do anything."

No one spoke for several minutes. "I've decided to bury your case, Lawrence. I've removed some of the information I'd not yet entered into the computer. Officially, you're dead, anyway."

"Thank you," Stephanie said.

"Don't be too hasty," Jamon countered. "I can reopen it at any time. In fact, if anything happens to me or Sara, certain documents will be found..." he let the threat trail off.

"Oh, how cliché," Lawrence noted.

"Don't knock the clichés, Lawrence," Lady countered. "Like I told Mac, some things are clichéd for a reason: they work."

Mac obligingly kept Stephanie and Jamon in the conversation, relaying Lady's thoughts to them.

"That said, Lawrence, am I finally going to be able to continue living my own life and not have to worry about you popping in to disrupt it again? You're not going to be killing or robbing anyone, right? No one will know that you..." He shuddered, remembering the feeling. "Fed on them?"

"No. I think that you can forget about vampires entirely. We are the only vampires in the area, so far as I know. It should be pretty tame here now."

"What do you mean he can just forget about it all?" Stephanie protested. "He's your...I don't know, whatever it's called, your thrice bitten. You can't just *abandon* him!"

"I'm not abandoning him. It's not like he's a stray puppy. He is an adult man. He was simply unlucky enough to have been my prey." He grimaced. "Repeatedly. I can only hope that the few benefits can eventually outweigh the inconvenience I've caused him. Of course, if he *wishes* to associate with us, it would be different. What say you, detective?"

"I am in complete agreement with Lawrence this one time, Stephanie. I definitely just want to be done with this supernatural hocus-pocus and return to my police work."

Lawrence stood and walked over to Jamon, his hand extended. "Very well, then. I expect our business is done. I wish you the best of luck, detective."

Jamon stood and hesitantly clasped Lawrence's hand. "And you, Mr. Watts. Or Hermanson. I do wish you well, too, and hope that we don't cross paths again. Goodbye to you as well, Ms. Roberson, and good luck." He left.

"Hmph. He didn't say goodbye to *us*," Lady complained. "Not that it mattered. I didn't really like him anyway. I think he's more of a... a *dog person.*

Pathetic."

The author would love to hear from you - good or bad!

Please drop me a line at: frank@frankbarvitch.com and let me know
your thoughts on Fangs. Or anything, really: I'm lonely. Lady's not
talking to me, and Mac just comes around when he's hungry.